THE MEADOWS

THE
MEADOWS

STEPHANIE OAKES

DIAL BOOKS

DIAL BOOKS

An imprint of Penguin Random House LLC, New York

First published in the United States of America by Dial Books,
an imprint of Penguin Random House LLC, 2023

Copyright © 2023 by Stephanie Oakes

Dial & colophon are registered trademarks of Penguin Random House LLC.
The Penguin colophon is a registered trademark of Penguin Books Limited.
Visit us online at PenguinRandomHouse.com.

Library of Congress Cataloging-in-Publication Data is available.
Printed in the United States of America

ISBN 9780593111482

1 3 5 7 9 10 8 6 4 2

BVG

ISBN 9780593619636 (INTERNATIONAL EDITION)

1 3 5 7 9 10 8 6 4 2

Design by Jennifer Kelly
Text set in Janson Text LT Pro

FOR JERILYNN, JUST AS YOU ARE

THE
MEADOWS

CHAPTER 1

I glance up at the eye, a shining black bead atop an old telephone pole. I walk briskly through pelting droplets, head bent. A cascade of water skims off my hood.

I show my face again to the bead on the awning of a shopping center, and again to one on the bus shelter where people huddle like cattle.

Each eye, memorized.

Not to see them. For them to see me.

My face.

I've become very familiar with it since I moved to the city. When I arrived a year ago, I found a book about the muscular system, fallen behind the desk bolted to the wall in my room. The apartment block where I live was a girls' college dormitory once. The book must've slipped back there, forgotten by some long-ago student when women could still attend universities.

I hid it beneath my mattress, memorized the meaty striations bisecting my face, the delicate fish fin between eyebrows, the birds' nests encircling each eye. In front of the mirror—hours of practice—working each muscle like a marionette. Now I can make myself look like anything at all.

The face I show the cameras is my most faithful: placid, thoughtless, empty.

I arrive downtown well before my next adjudication. To pass the time, I sit in a café, scan my calendar. Colored squares fill the screen—different adjudications around the city, documents of profiles and background information on each of my reformeds.

My eyes close for a moment, and my ears range the café—plasticore plates sliding against each other, clink of utensils. A soundscape I never could have imagined where I grew up. In the Cove, only the shush of the ocean, carts on a rocky roadway, the scrape of a tiny knife slipping into the tight mouths of oysters, occasionally slipping into the pad of my thumb, a silent gush of red falling through my hands.

Seated nearby, a man some years older than me scrolls through the endless, bright feed on his screen. I watch his fingers fling past pictures. Palm trees forking the sky. A baby held in a man's arms like a loaf of bread. A woman sitting on artificially green grass in the high-necked, bulbous dress popular with young wives.

And then, an image unlike the others. A white building, rounded and hut-shaped, fashioned from opaque material. Against a backdrop of marshy jungle, the building glows. It makes a light all its own.

I stand from my chair. Water that had collected in the folds of my raincoat unfurls to the ground. I barely notice. My eyes, transfixed. That photo. A facility building. Not from the Meadows, but another, shrouded in overgrown foliage. Above the screen, the man suspends his fingers, engrossed in the image too.

Can't believe it's been well over a decade since I last saw the Glades, the photo is captioned.

"The Glades," I speak, and the man with the screen whips his head around, eyes wide. He doesn't know me, doesn't know if he's been caught.

"The Meadows," I say, placing a hand on my chest.

His shoulders dip, relaxing.

"I haven't met many of us," I tell him, though of course it's not true. By now I've met dozens. Hundreds.

The man scans the café for anyone who might overhear. "Not that you'd know," he mutters.

He's right. If we've made it here, we're reformed. What happened in the facilities, what they did to us, are closely guarded secrets.

A gold band encircles his finger. For a moment, his eyes trail to my own wedding finger, bare. "They haven't matched you yet?" he asks.

I shake my head. "They made me an adjudicator. My time's up in a year, though." An adjudicator's term is two years and already I'm half-done. Then a ring will be my fate too.

"You can't have been out long," he says.

I pull my shoulders back, trying to appear my full eighteen years. "About a year."

"I've got almost fifteen," he says. "Mine was one of the first cohorts." The muscles beneath his face are controlled but too tight. Hiding something. "I don't understand reminiscing," he says, gazing again at the screen. "I'd never go back."

"I would," I say, surprising myself.

He frowns. "You would?"

And I nod, an unexpected knot forming in my throat.

For them. For her.

Rose.

The night I first saw Rose, the air was dim, blushing with dusty violet, as close as it got to night in the Meadows. Just past dinnertime. The girls would be filing from the glowing walls of the dining room, having eaten their carefully portioned meals. From where I sat inside the yew tree, I could see for miles, a sea of purple flowers, hazy in the evening, stretching for what I knew was farther than a person could ever walk.

The shuttle was a slim black knife, cutting first with its glint, then with

3

its sound. The rumble up the dirt road meant only one thing: another girl. Her hair, cut short at the sides. Her body, muscular. Stocky. She wore a shiny black raincoat, thick metal zipper laddering up the front— an alarming contrast to the thin white dresses we wore. Most of us were twelve, thirteen, fourteen when we arrived, but she was older. A dart of grief passed through me. The Meadows would strip all of it away. Her body, forced to be still, would lose its muscle, and her hair forced to grow, and that coat thrown out with the trash.

That coat. I didn't know how it was possible but her coat, I could see, was stippled with rain. No rain in the Meadows. No snow. No weather of any kind.

This girl carried rain with her.

Two matrons met her at the door, bulky white figures with a hand hovering over her shoulders. The girl took a few paces, and paused. She turned, so even from the yew tree, I could see her face. For the first time, I had an awareness of how many muscles must live inside a human face. I could see them all, the anatomy of her.

Every girl who'd entered the Meadows wore the same face: wondrous, bright-eyed. Hands clutching acceptance letters. Minds daring to imagine a future of easy breath in these bright halls and purple fields.

Rose's face—nothing like that. Looking like it could grip the sky and rip it in half. Looking like she wanted to.

CHAPTER 2

Neon sprays of weeds and scabby rust-colored scrub covered the rockside. I picked over the basalt and peeked over the edge of our cliff where, far below, the ocean had peeled back to reveal a circus of tide pools, the violet blush of urchins, pink sea stars holding the rock like grasping hands. The ocean could sneak up on a person there, surging unexpectedly through blowholes in the pocked surface. You had to listen. You had to be always on guard.

This is the place I grew from, this dirt, this sea wind, this salted air. I didn't look at the ocean much in those days. It felt mean, uncontrollable. Now I know about the tides that pull at it, the moon—forces the sea couldn't possibly understand. I imagine it might've wanted to do something different, to stretch long and thin, to muscle inside the hidden pockets of caves and the every-color cavities of tide pools. To feel itself unfold across the midnight depths that nobody else got to touch. Perhaps it threw itself against the rocks for a reason.

The only cause strong enough to pull my eyes toward the sea was the hope of spotting June's boat. I'd known her since we were little, back when I recognized her only by sight, the fishergirl tying ropes, smelling of ocean and guts. She sailed with her father, pulling creatures from the depths, some grown grotesque from radiation. June saved them for me. "A three-headed crab," she'd whisper as we passed each other on market day. Or, "An eel with one huge glowing eye. Come by later and I'll show you. But you have to play for me." And I'd spend the evening at her house, scratching a song from my shabby violin.

That day, it was nearly dusk before June's boat bounced through the white-tipped froth, returning to harbor.

"Get back to work, Eleanor," my mother called.

I tore my eyes from the wooden shape of the *Musketeer* and pointed them toward the ground. I harvested crab squash, and a blushing bouquet of sea radish. I reached over to pull up an apple-shaped kohlrabi, spidering green limbs reaching toward the sky. My mother had fashioned this plot years ago from a piece of land that nobody wanted. She'd hauled dirt, forced the ground here to mean something.

I looked at my mother and longed to ask her the question. The only one that mattered. Now and again I would slide it to her across a silent morning or afternoon.

"Where did I come from?"

She'd avert her dark eyes, continue assembling a candle from old drippings or rewiring a toaster there wasn't enough electricity to use. "Somewhere else," she'd say, gruff.

This was all she'd ever tell me. The people in town whispered, though. They said that I was left in a linen blanket on the doorstep of my mother's cliffside cottage, that I'd simply shown up one day, a squalling pink bundle so incongruous in this windswept place. They said that I didn't really belong to my mother.

This, the earliest knowing I had, reinforced every trip to market where people would stare and then not, and my mother's face was still square-shaped and mine still soft and round. Even before I had words, I already knew I was not meant to be in that place.

Nearby, there was a tree, just outside the cottage. My tree—a craggy maple, clawing at the cliff, always threatening to send a root into rock and crumble us into the sea far below. "Shouldn't even be here," my mother complained, kicking at its leaf-fall each autumn.

The tree was not native to the area—leaves with points like daggers that flushed crimson in autumn—suited to a different climate, perhaps even from across the sea. How it came to grow in that spot, no way to know.

I'd imagine, though. A green seedpod blowing in on a strange, wayward wind from northern parts. Or clinging to the wagon wheel of a traveling man trading radishes and copper trinkets, unsticking when it arrived in the Cove. Or carried in the pocket of a girl fleeing her town as it receded under water, like so many towns had in the decades before I was born.

The tree and I were both transplants, growing in dirt not our own. We were both meant for other things.

On the cliff nearby stood our cottage, abandoned for years before my mother made it a home. "How'd you do it?" I would ask her.

"No choice," she'd say. "Nowhere else to go. Nothing to do but make the most of it."

"Look at you now," I'd said once, smiling.

"Look at me now," she'd grumbled. "I've got a shack, a deviant maple tree, and a plot of rock the size of a football field that really, *really* doesn't want to grow carrots."

I didn't reply, didn't put voice to the flare of pain that filled my chest, didn't say *But you've got me*. Instead, I asked, "What's a football field?"

She waved me off, in that way of adults when they didn't have the energy to explain about Life Before.

I placed the vegetables I'd gathered in my mother's knit sack. There was an oval of dirt printed just above her cheekbone, placed there by one of her thumbs, those tiny squared trowels. I lifted my own thumb, already calloused and careworn at twelve, and, without thinking, placed it on the dirt-shape on her cheek.

She swatted my hand away.

"I just—I wanted to see if my thumb would fit. If our thumbs were the same size."

"You can see plainly that they're not," she said. And with that she bent at the waist and meshed her fingers into the winding petals of lamb's tongue.

People lived like this now, like ancient pictures I'd seen of feudal times, women bent over, plucking bits of wheat from a field, their task stretching for acres. I wonder if they ever recovered from a life facing the ground.

At sundown, too dark to work, we walked the short distance to our cottage, folded our limbs onto the threadbare couch, and turned toward our state-provided screen to watch dispatches from the city. The screen flickered to life, the picture ebbing and flowing with the unreliable current of electricity. The announcers were never named, but we knew they were important—messengers for the state. The women especially resembled each other, like dolls pressed from the same mold, merely in different colors, with glossy hair, thin limbs, delicate features. Not like in the Cove where people had the option of growing wild—fishermen with beards to their sternums, women whose faces were cracked by weather and time. A very few wore makeup and tamed their hair, but most didn't bother.

This night, two announcers spoke in front of a blurred white background. A man with a waxen face, as though carved from soap, and a woman whose brown skin was buffed with makeup. The dispatches had told us that, during Life Before, all people hadn't been treated equally. But, by the time I was a baby, the state had officially eradicated discrimination based on race. Their words, the certainty of them, reassured me, even as they snagged in my mind.

On our screen, the announcers said what they always said. *We're working hard to fix this. We care about each of you, so much.* The tone was of a parent consoling a sick child. What was wrong in our country was a malady that needed to run its course. *We are so sorry for your hunger, for your aches and pains. If we could take them, we would. If we could put them into our own bodies, we would. We are trying our best.* My mother made a gruff sound with her throat, but she didn't speak her true feelings, though there were no ears in our cottage. Illegal, to speak ill of the state.

I knew what she thought already. My mother didn't approve of the state, though I always wondered why. They'd saved us after the Turn, when nature rebelled, swallowing whole cities beneath oceans, the sun burning so hot, it turned much of the country to wastelands. The Turn happened slowly. People could ignore it, put it out of their minds. And then, fast. The country collapsed within a few years, and for a long time, all anybody did was survive. Until the Quorum took over.

My favorite part of the dispatches was any mention of the facilities, the schools where the most remarkable children in the country were sent. I watched hungrily for the occasional video of a child tearing open their letter of admission. "Congratulations! You have been accepted to the Estuary, a place where the best and brightest of our country learn to burn even brighter."

I'd never been in a car—had never traveled beyond the Cove—so the dispatches were my only means of seeing how others lived. Sometimes, enormous houses out of my dreams—screens that took up whole walls, slick self-driving cars shaped like bullets, bowls mounded with fruit in colors brighter than anything we got at the market. Other times, dim huts, worse off than any place I'd seen in the Cove. And it was those that gave me the greatest thrill. Because *any* child could be chosen for a facility. The state knew each of our names, could track us on satellites and cameras affixed to roofs and defunct telephone poles. The algorithm conducted intelligence tests just by watching us handle everyday problems, Mrs. Arkwright told us, always compiling and weighing results.

It didn't matter where the child was going—the Estuary, the Pines, the

Archipelago. Their faces beamed when they opened their letters. Parents wrapped them up, crying proud tears.

That is how I grew up, dreaming of a place beyond the Cove. Each night, lying beneath my woven blanket, wishing alternately for June, imagining the soft places of her, imagining her touching the soft places of me, and for one of those letters. Wishing with every muscle of me, every cell.

There was no camera crew like in the dispatches, but otherwise it happened remarkably the same. Thick envelope, an unbelievable white. Same words: *The Meadows, a place where the best and brightest of our country learn to burn even brighter.* Same gasp from my mouth. Same eyes searching for my mother's. There, the comparison ended. No joy in her gaze. No feeling at all but a sullen mouth, drooping in a familiar frown. I swallowed disappointment. No matter, I told myself. In days, I'd be gone.

The Meadows. I tasted the word.

Next morning, I ran down the hill, through fields of waist-high thistle that scratched my fingertips, toward the market square, ignoring the threat of gopher holes that could snap an ankle in a heartbeat. Had to reach the dock before the boats went out.

I pulled up in the market square, huffing. There—her father's boat, still rocking against the dock. June would be here soon, in her leather overalls, waxed and thick-smelling from seal fat, but beautiful. Perfect.

The square felt strangely hollow, market stalls covered with tarps, the only sound the wind faintly flapping a canvas poster hanging above the marketplace. The poster was secured to the wall of an old brick cannery. Stenciled across the top, in enormous red letters, *Strong Families Build a Strong Nation*, and beneath that a giant-sized illustration of a family. A man, smile cutting his meaty pink cheeks. Beneath him, two white children, plump and healthy-looking, one boyish and one girlish in the obvious ways, blue gingham and pink gingham, as though masculine and feminine were perfect inverses. And beside them, a woman.

For as long as I could remember, my eyes had drawn to her. Her gaze was positioned permanently sideways, peering adoringly at the man and children, her mouth red-glossed and smiling toothlessly. Something in her carefully arranged face felt like a riddle I could solve, if only I looked long enough. One of these days, she'd break character and show me who she really was.

"You're leaving."

June's raspy voice. It sent a shiver through me. She stood in the doorway of an alley, backlit by sun. Her hair made a fraying halo around her head.

"Not till tomorrow," I said.

June's face was downcast, a wrinkle between her brows that had deepened in the last year since her mother had died. June's mother, smile eternally dimpling her amber cheeks, voice slightly accented from the island where she'd been born, had come here after that same island was erased by the sea. She fell for June's father, with his scrub of red beard and fair skin permanently flushed from the wind. After June's mother died, he remarried within the legally permitted six-month grieving period. It was customary.

June's face was already becoming copper like it did every summer, a scattering of freckles across her nose. The color she got from her mother, the freckles from her father. I thought about this often, the particular blending of features, and how much more sense June made, knowing what she was made of.

And me. Who did the brown of my eyes resemble? Who the lobe of my ear? Who the squirming in my chest, longing to be free?

"When did you get your letter?" June asked.

"Last night," I told her. "News travels fast."

"Stella the spinster's daughter chosen for a facility—bound to be the thing on everyone's lips." She cocked her hip to the side. "What's it called? Oh, yes, the *Meadows*. Sounds lovely."

"You could be happy for me," I suggested.

The intensity on her face melted a little. "It's just that I'll miss you."

"You'll miss me?" Most of our lives, we never went more than a day without seeing each other, in the market or at the schoolmarm's. Still, I felt a punch in my heart from surprise.

"Of course I'll miss you," she said.

Sometimes, on community devotion day, my mother would have us trudge to the rough-hewn sanctuary building for a service. The state had eradicated every shred of religion, but this was allowed, this sitting together in silent thought. It was always hair-pullingly dull until my favorite part, the Wanting Hat. Down every bench, the brown felt hat passed between hands—gnarled hands and salt-chapped hands and young hands not yet thick with calluses. The hat filled with whispered wishes, hushed desires. When it was my turn, I'd lower my mouth to the hat's empty hollow, and wish for June. To do what with, I hardly knew. To be close to her, was all. Facing her in the market that day, I wondered, had she ever wished for me?

"What will I do without you? Nobody else cares about my daily catch," she said. "Who else will I show the fish with no eyes?"

I smiled. "Who else will play music for you? Who else will draw you crass pictures of Mrs. Arkwright on their chalkboard? Or pick you a flower from the field and put it behind your ear before you even notice?"

Her face brightened as I spoke, then clouded, like the sky does. "No one."

The buoyant feeling in my chest dissipated. I had always thought of June as permanent. Imagined our childhoods stretching out before us—walks among the junipers and cliff-diving and one day being brave enough to reach out and touch her skin.

"We could've had all our lives," she said. "We could've had a million years."

I took a step closer. "I'll see you again—" I started, but bit off the rest. I didn't know if it was true. Instead, I looked around, and walked backward into the alley, unobserved by any villagers. "Come closer."

Her face rearranged, a smile breaking through her dubious expression.

When she moved close, I leaned near to her ear, cheek brushing hers. "June."

I felt her shiver beneath my breath. Slowly, I moved my mouth from her ear, and she moved her mouth to mine. Our lips touched, softly. She moved closer, the movements like an unwritten language that we never needed to be taught. I cupped her bottom lip in my mouth, held it like something precious.

Five years have passed, and it occurs to me, the most miraculous thing about that moment: not June's breath in my mouth. Not the current that arced through my body. Not the way she looked at me when our lips pulled away, her eyes wide and wondrous and reinventing the world.

Just this: Not once, not even for a second, did I think I was doing anything wrong.

CHAPTER 3

Light. This—what I noticed first about the Meadows.

Light in hanging lamps, and beaded along hallways, and inside the walls, glowing translucently from someplace within. Later, alone in my room, I'd run my hand over the wall. Plastic, the texture of fine-grained sandpaper.

At home, electric light was precious, and my mother doled it out frugally, more often using candles reassembled from wax drippings and thumbed into a metal mold that, when lit, made the air a waxy, smoky stew.

I huddled together with a few dozen girls in the Meadows' bright foyer. The white walls were smooth and rounded, a rabbit warren of tunnels and chambers stretching in unknowable directions. A giddy nervousness seemed to bounce off the gleaming floor. I studied the girls' faces openly, too excited to be self-conscious, drew my eyes across their noses and mouths and skin, some pale like me, some with skin shades of olive or brown, hair flat or wavy or curly, tightly coiled or ironed straight. Many with a bottom lip pinned nervously under her teeth, a wrist clamped inside fingers.

I'd seen several of these girls on the shuttle here, but we hadn't spoken. Now I wondered where each had come from, if any were from a place like the Cove. I couldn't tell by looking. We'd shifted into our new white dresses, tiny pearl buttons cupping the light. Here we were. Best. Brightest. The hope for the future of our country.

My heart yearned behind my fresh new dress—to run, to carve through these abalone hallways. Anything was possible here. We were made blank.

"My dears." A voice echoed through the room.

We swiveled to face the woman striding into the foyer, followed by a procession of others in thick white dresses that belled at their waists. A tall girl nearby flashed a smile at me. The air inflated with anticipation.

"I am Matron Sybil," the woman said. Her voice was gentle as wind in heather, and I found myself smiling just looking at her. Two blue eyes sat brightly inside her fair, lined face, and her hair was tucked in a silver bun. "We are delighted to welcome you to the Meadows. This will be your home for the next four years. Here, you will grow into the young women that our country needs."

I turned again to the girl next to me, looked up to her face, deep brown and inviting. She stood taller than me by a head, her hair in tight twists.

I darted my hand into hers, and grasped.

"Want to be friends?" I whispered.

The girl breathed a surprised laugh. I hadn't made a friend in years, had known June and the other children in the Cove since I was born. Maybe this wasn't how it was done.

A smile spread across her face. "Friends," she said, squeezing my hand.

Matron Sybil introduced the matrons behind her. It was hard to distinguish them, so similarly dressed. Some looked stern, and others like kindly, weathered grandmothers. My eyes rested on the face of a middle-aged matron, who Matron Sybil introduced as Matron Calliope. She wore pearl earrings that shone against her dark skin.

"This place feels magical," I whispered to the girl beside me. "Doesn't it?"

"Exactly." She nodded. "I'm Sheila."

"Eleanor," I said, smiling.

I noticed, then, a different matron, watching us. She was younger than the others—closer in age to the girls gathered around me—with a shock of reddish hair falling past her shoulders. Her eyes alighted on our clasped hands, and her mouth formed a gentle curve. She pulled a screen from the pocket of her dress and tapped on it, as though taking notes. A prickle walked up my spine.

"And lastly, Matron Maureen," Matron Sybil said, indicating the young red-haired woman. Matron Maureen did a little comical curtsey. A ripple of laughter filled the foyer.

"I suppose you're all very curious as to what this building holds," Matron Sybil continued. "Shall we explore?"

We followed behind the matrons, a white-clad school of fish, and it struck me that I had never been among so many other girls. Smart and capable girls destined for great things. I let out a breathy laugh.

Sheila looked down at me, a grin lighting her face.

The matrons led us through rounded white corridors toward classrooms. "So bright." Sheila's whisper found my ear. The other girls' awed mutterings surrounded us, a tight-fitting sleeve of voices.

They showed us the dining room. *So wide. So gleaming.*

They showed us the meadow fields. *So far. So free.*

We lingered on the edge of the fields, where the lawn erupted in hip-height stalks tipped in purple petals. We were surrounded, a white boat in a great, undulating sea of purple. The only variation was a single yew tree, sprawling and ancient, growing a few paces inside the fields.

A girl asked if we were allowed to walk there. "Of course," Matron Sybil said.

"How far does it go?" another asked.

The matron paused. "Forever," she said. And somehow, I thought she spoke the truth.

While the other girls filed back inside, I stayed at the edge of the meadow fields. I remembered fishermen describing the call of the ocean and I thought, *Yes, it's like that.* I rolled a single stalk between my thumb and forefinger, texture downy as lambswool. Along the stem were bundles of blooms, each petal a miniature purple trowel. Their scent filled the air, gentle but insistent, like the sweet green of new growth in spring.

Sheila waited for me in the hallway while the others funneled into an auditorium. The room's velvet seats were clean and crimson, and the domed ceiling shone opalescent. On the polished wooden stage stood Matron Sybil.

"I'd like to formally welcome you to the Meadows," Matron Sybil said. As she strode down the stage, I took in the gently creased white of her face. And her eyes, piercingly blue.

"You are all here because you're special," she said. "We've been watching you since you were very young, and we discovered something bright glowing inside each of you. Places like the Meadows were created to nurture that which you possess already. To grow it. To help it burn even more brightly, so that one day you might give it to the nation."

The audience of girls seemed to inflate with held breath. Matron Sybil strolled the stage, each girl's eyes carefully tracking her movements. The stiff fabric of her dress hardly moved with her, pleats encircling her waist. If the others looked like bells, Matron Sybil resembled a tall white column.

"Of course, in every cohort, there are some who may struggle to unlock what's inside of them," she went on. "Do not be afraid of that. Struggle is a vital part of this process. Those who give every effort will leave here and step into beautiful lives."

A hunger opened up inside of me. I felt I'd do anything to prove to her that I was as good as she thought.

I felt Sheila lean close. "My parents didn't want me to come."

I glanced at her. "Did they say why?" I whispered.

"Just, 'There's things about you that we don't want to see taken away.' " She shrugged. "Overprotective, probably."

"They thought this place would do that?" I shook my head, wondering at the idea of a parent standing in the way of this.

"The Meadows will teach you to become women, as women are meant to be," Matron Sybil was saying. "Some of you perhaps have not had ideal examples of women in your lives. Some whose mothers discarded feminine traits inherent to womanhood—grace and composure and sacrifice. Some whose fathers foisted their duties on their wives. Some raised *without* a mother, or without a true mother." For a flicker of a moment, Matron Sybil's eyes rested on me. A flush crept up my cheeks.

"Regardless of your upbringing, we will help you blossom into remarkable women."

An image flashed into my mind, the poster hanging above the market square back home. The husband and children gazing out at the world, and the woman only ever looking at them, absorbed by these people.

My hand shot into the air. Just as quickly, I regretted it, but Matron Sybil's eyes had already clapped onto mine.

"Yes?" she asked, surprised. Clearly, this was not the kind of speech meant to be interrupted.

"W—when you say we'll have beautiful lives," I asked, tentative, "what do you mean?"

She smiled good-naturedly. "You will become useful, dutiful members of society. Brilliant wives. Adept mothers."

"You mean, we'll—get married?"

Her head tilted slightly. "What else would an accomplished young woman do?" I thought her smile was something other than a smile now. Something like a tool. "Not right away, of course. But eventually, you will find a husband, or the state will help match you to one."

Husband. A squirming loosed in my stomach.

Matron Sybil's eyes seemed to pin me to my seat. "Don't you want to find an adoring husband to provide for you? To endow you with loving children to speed the regrowth of our country?"

"Oh yes," I said. The lie came smoothly, without hesitation.

Matron Sybil smiled again, but the squirming in my gut didn't ease. "Then study well, and listen to your matrons. And your future can be anything that you can dream."

CHAPTER 4

"What's that cloud make you think of?" Sheila asked, pointing to one rimmed with sun.

The excitement of the first day had shifted into a deflated kind of exhaustion, and Sheila and I reclined on the grass, watching the clouds make their way across the sky, a blue so bright, it seemed unreal. Other girls clustered in groups nearby, and the matrons walked the perimeter of the lawn, white-clad sentinels. I'd assumed some of the girls would venture into the meadow fields, but none had, and as much as I wanted to, it seemed unwise to be the first.

"A crown," I said, following the line of Sheila's finger. "Or . . . a bridle maybe."

Sheila laughed. "A what?"

"You know—what you put on a horse's head. You've never heard of it?"

"The only animals I've ever seen were in the ecological center, and all they had was a cow, a hawk that could shell peanuts with its beak, and a really old turtle. When I was little, my parents showed me flashcards of animals, though, even the extinct ones."

I turned over in the grass, wondering at her. I couldn't fathom a childhood spent outside of nature. The other girls seemed unknowable to me, and Sheila should have, how she'd grown up in a suburb, how I had no better reference for the artifacts of her life than she had for mine, the words that tripped off her tongue—ice cream, magneboarding, basketball court. But, something happened in the first hour of our arrival. Sheila's hand in mine. Friendship is really just a decision, one you make over and over again.

My eyes traced the fields. They stood strangely, knuckle-sized clusters of blooms perfectly still. Something shifted uncomfortably in my chest. I'd sensed it all day, but out here in the expanse of open air, it became oppressive. My mind had searched, unconsciously, for the buzz of an insect, the trill of a bird. I listened closely now. But there was nothing, not even the hush of a breeze.

Silence.

A loud noise can take up space inside the body, vibrating muscles and tendons and the tiny bones deep within ears. Silence, I realized, had a physical presence too. A heaviness.

The train station had been loud. My mother and I had had only a moment before I boarded the train to the Meadows. She had stood out in the bustling station—the busiest place I'd been in my life. Her eyes darted around as people swept past, and every so often a young girl boarded the train. She'd asked a porter where this train was bound, and he'd replied, "The algorithm's programmed the route. Not even I know."

My mother's eyes had flared. "Learn where you are, first thing you do," she muttered to me. Then she'd hugged me quickly, unexpectedly. "Be good," she'd called, her voice a whisper smothered by the churning noise of the train, and I was gone.

Only now, a day later, the question pulsed in all this silence. *Where are we?* I'd heard some of the girls whispering that we must be in the Annex, a huge expanse of land in the middle of the country that the government had cordoned off because the climate had grown too harsh for human habitation. Perhaps the state had found a way to reestablish an ecosystem, calm the effects of the oppressive sun. Grow flowers farther than the horizon.

"My dad would tell me about growing up in a small town," Sheila said, "but it's gone now. The whole thing wiped out by a mudslide."

I nodded. Everyone's parents and grandparents had stories like that. Their entire worlds shattered when the climate broke, whole swaths of population just gone, buried beneath land collapses, devoured by fires, starved. It had taken years for the world to settle, and when it did, the Quorum was who everyone thanked.

"My mother doesn't talk about Life Before," I said.

"What about your dad?"

"Don't have one. I'm—not really my mother's," I said, clumsy. I'd never had to explain it before. Everyone in the Cove simply knew.

Sheila's forehead folded as I recounted the story: a wrapped-up bundle on a doorstep, under the shadow of a maple tree, ocean swirling darkly below. "And nobody knows where you came from?"

"There were rumors. None of them made my mother look very good."

Sheila squinted. "Because she didn't have a husband?"

I nodded. "I think I made life hard for her. I try to imagine, sometimes, what her life would've been like if she'd never taken me in. Easier, I think."

"You shouldn't think that way about yourself," she said. "I made life harder for my parents too, but that's what children do."

But I should have been different, I thought. *More like what my mother needed.*

I looked up at Sheila again, shoving my thoughts away. "What are your parents like?"

"My dad works at the university," she said, smiling. "Teaching architecture. He could make a skyscraper out of plasticore, and it would stand for a thousand years."

"And your mom?"

"She's just as smart as my dad. He brings her books and they read together and debate. They can go for hours." Sheila's smile shone through

22

a veil of sadness. "When I started school, she was allowed to apply for work. She was assigned to a job on a printing row. The harvested material comes out in perfect white sheets, and she works a machine to shape it into objects. Cups. Plates. It's tedious, and she has to hide her natural hair under an ugly kerchief, but she says it's worth it, to be in the world."

I felt my forehead frown, imagining the options available for most women.

"Do you ever want to find yours?" Sheila asked. "Your real parents?"

She threw the question out lightly, as though it held no weight. Heat prickled my neck. I rarely thought about them. "No hope of that. If there was an answer, somebody in the Cove would've told me by now."

"But if there *was* hope?" she asked. "The algorithm must know."

"Then . . ." I trailed off. My birth parents were behind a door in my mind, heavily bolted. Impossible, so not worth worrying about. But sometimes, the lock slipped and I let myself half wonder: If they left, could they come back? Maybe they'd intended our separation to be temporary. My mind would trail its fingers through the possibilities . . . family around a dinner table, stories and laughter. Someone to love me the way my mother couldn't. I looked up at Sheila, her expectant face. "Then maybe I'd wonder."

A hairbrush made of opaque white plasticore. A tiny hand mirror. A sewing kit in a woven basket, its latch a knob of mother-of-pearl.

"What fine things," I whispered, fingertips resting on each.

"Only the best for us," Sheila said, laughing. But wasn't she right? We were the cream that had risen to the top of the country. And this was our reward.

"I wonder why they didn't allow us to bring anything," I said, thinking of my violin.

"The same reason we can't call home, I guess," Sheila said, frowning. "A 'fresh start.'"

From a small dresser, I pulled out clothing, let the silken fabric fall through my fingers like milk—white dresses, undergarments edged in lace, socks soft as calf hide. A whisper in my mind, my mother's voice, scoffing. *What kind of fools make socks from something so flimsy? You'll be freezing when winter comes.*

For the first time, I allowed myself to really think of home. Of June, the wide delight of her smile, the memory of her like the jolt of jumping into cold water. Of town, and the bustle of market days, the clatter of carts on the prairie road, the lowing of cattle carried on the sea wind. And my mother. There was a wringing in my chest, my feelings never quite complete—never angry enough to be truly angry, never loving enough to feel like I loved her. I remembered her startlingly long hug, the bones of her chest pressing into me when she left me at the train station the day before. Her final words, *Be good.*

"Can't sleep?" Sheila asked later, curled beneath the covers of her bed. The lights had automatically dimmed, though the walls still glowed faintly. Our room, doorless, faced an inner common room, and spoking out from it, other bedrooms, and other girls nestled in their new beds. I could make out the shushing of whispers.

I shook my head. My body felt wrung out, but I couldn't imagine sleeping.

"I thought for so long about coming here," I whispered. "And now that I *am* here, I wonder, *What now?*" A knot formed in my throat. Stupid, to cry in this bright, perfect place. "I feel sort of . . . under water." Warm tears slipped from my eyes.

"Hold my hand." Sheila reached across the distance between our beds. "I know how to swim." And though she smiled, I thought she was right. If we held on, we could keep each other afloat.

Crisp bedsheets held my body like an envelope, but Sheila's hand was soft. Most everything my body had ever touched had been soft—clothes patched and fraying, and sheets boiled soft as corn silk. And if there was the rare moment I stepped on a nail while picking for supplies in the junkyard, or felt the curved black claws of Captain, June's dog, great shaggy white hair always dried in saltwater curls, there'd been many more soft things.

Sheila's hand grew limp, her eyes drifting closed. I was nearly asleep too, when I heard it.

Banjo strings on the air.

The backward pull of memory, years before. I'd stood on the cliff beside my cottage. We had no neighbors, and there was rarely anything to overhear, so my ears perked at the music. I'd darted to the village, following the sound.

They'd set up in an alley—a kind of megaphone, the music funneled and shot out to the surrounding hills. And soon a small collection of us swayed at the ends of the street, and on rooftops, and heads hung out of windows up and down the buildings.

The band was shabby-looking. The trumpet player had an arm in a dingy sling, so she played one-handed. The cellist's cheeks were hollow and hungry, but she sawed away like a lumberjack. It took moments of watching before I realized each one appeared to be a woman. None wore metal bands on their fingers, though they were old enough. They should've been inside, shrouded by a home, smelling of milk and children and their husbands' skin. But they were not homed at all, I would later learn through town whispers. No money for food, but enough for a dented van to convey them across the country.

What for?

To play their song. To let it live.

There was something very right about each of them, about their faces, their movements, the smiling glances they passed to each other like prayers whispered into the Wanting Hat.

Watching them, I felt an itch to play my fiddle. Mrs. Arkwright had taught me until I outgrew her skill, and after that I'd scratched out my own music, practicing into the night. My favorite, the Longing Song, was filled with everything I dreamed about. Ginger cake, and June's mouth, an anorak like the fishermen wore, a letter from a facility. My wishes collected and lined up inside the song. I wanted to play it for them, to show everyone that I was like them. And they were like me.

I see you, I wanted to tell them. *Do you see me?*

The alley grew crowded with villagers. I spotted Mrs. Arkwright, the schoolmarm. And June and her mother, still alive. Even Mrs. Johns, the local busybody, who looked more like the woman on the poster above the market than anyone else in the Cove.

The alley—a kind of megaphone. So when the shout rang out, the big meaty voice of a peacekeeper, it forced its way violently into our ears. And the screams of the crowd were magnified, and so too the painful silence of the music ceasing, instruments clattering to the ground. They dragged them by their ankles and elbows, those officers, threw them as though those bodies hadn't just created something wondrous and rare.

I huddled for a long time in a doorway, twisting away from what I'd seen. Why had they been dragged away? As though they'd committed some awful crime. I didn't know.

And I did.

On some level deeper than thought, I was piecing it together.

CHAPTER 5

On the sidewalk, breath rises in front of the pedestrians beside me, shrouded in wool, pre-married women in neat, dark work suits, and mothers with babies stuffed inside buggies, and men in slacks and jackets and hard shoes walking importantly. I twine between skyscrapers, white and silver, that grab at the sky like reaching arms.

For days after, the image of the white building has rested at the corner of my mind, even after leaving the café, even after performing my daily adjudications, listening to a half dozen girls answer my questions—*How is your job? Your boyfriend? How much or how little are you pleased with your life?* Even now, I see the words on the man's screen: *Can't believe it's been well over a decade since I last saw the Glades.*

How had someone even managed a photo? Could a person go back? I'll save that thought for later. Because today will be a good day. I'm nearly to Sheila's apartment.

When Sheila opens the door, her face brightens. "Did you have eggs for breakfast?"

I squint at her. "How'd you know?"

"Egg, with a runny yolk," she says, pointing at my shirt where a yellow blot of yolk has dried into the navy blue of my blouse. "Always was your favorite."

I smile, stepping into her kitchen. "Some things don't change."

"You mean the eggs, or the spilling things on yourself?"

"Both," I say, laughing, taking her in. These days, Sheila hardly resembles the girl I first met in the Meadows, her hair now falling in a straight golden drape around her shoulders, her deep brown skin polished with makeup. But when she smiles, I can see her still. The Sheila I once knew.

"Ed's out," she says, leaning into her kitchen counter and regarding the spacious apartment she shares with her boyfriend. My job allows me to meet with her every month. Our visits can extend no longer than thirty minutes or I get reprimanded for being too social. It's necessary to keep up the impression of impartiality or they'll replace me with someone who truly is.

Sheila asked, on our first adjudication, why I'd been assigned the position. "You weren't like me, or Rose." A shadow had crossed her face. "But I still can't understand it."

I squirmed a little. "They must trust me," I'd said. Sheila only nodded and didn't ask again.

Sheila fixes me a cup of tea now, squeezing lemon juice from a metallic pump on her counter while I scrub my shirt with a tea towel. She wears a tangerine-colored dress, cinched at the waist. She seems diminished, smaller each time I see her.

When we're seated on the balcony, I ask, "How are you?" out of genuine curiosity, not only because I'm required to demand answers and she's required to give them.

Sheila's apartment overlooks the river. The waters lap the concrete foundation beneath her balcony like a searching tongue, and of course I think of Rose, and her tongue slipping across my teeth, and I have to swallow a shiver that wants to ripple across my body.

"They finally found me a job," Sheila replies, blowing on her tea, her breath white in the late autumn air. "A deli, cutting big pieces of meat into smaller pieces of meat." The corners of her mouth downturn deeply.

I think back to our first year in the Meadows, back to a time when I never could've imagined Sheila's face like this. I don't write anything while we talk, but later, on the train, I'll need to record each detail. My reports could then be checked against the ears around us, small mesh coins set into the walls—one above the clock in her kitchen, one set into the balcony wall. When you start to notice, they're everywhere, always listening.

"And how's Ed?" I ask.

"Ed's . . . good. He's made great progress at his internship."

I nod, picturing Ed in his office, working busily in his starched work shirts like an over-eager schoolboy. Shirts that Sheila, I think reluctantly, must iron for him.

"Do you feel like they made a good match?" I ask. A year ago, when we arrived in the city, Sheila opted to be randomly assigned a mate rather than search for one on her own.

Her mouth shrugs. "Better than the Registrar's Office," she says. "Flicking through profiles, knowing boys are doing the same to mine. I heard they have some kind of ..ew tech that lets you talk to a digital version of your potential mate. The idea felt . . . violating. It just seemed more"—she searched for the word—"honest this way."

Better to be randomly assigned than to accept the sham of a false choice. "And how are *you* . . . and Ed?" I'm supposed to ask all kinds of questions. About compatibility, about the amount of affection the couple has achieved. Premarital togetherness is allowed but not required. The state tracks menstrual cycles, so if a girl finds herself in a family way, a wedding is scheduled for the next day. This is considered a grand success—a marriage and a new citizen in one fell swoop. The option of choosing not to be a mother is, of course, strictly forbidden.

At once, Sheila's eyes begin to blur. She turns toward the brown strand of river beyond the balcony. This, the kind of thing I should be reporting, any glimmer of discontent with her state-appointed boyfriend. Any sign that she's not entirely reformed. But I never do. Not for Sheila, or anyone.

Sheila coughs into her fist, and when she turns to face me again, her eyes are clear. "Things are great with Ed," she says, voice bright. "He's very . . . considerate. He brings me flowers every Friday. He brought me a prototype of something they're working on. Here, I'll show you."

Sheila goes back inside. By myself, as always, my mind tugs back to Rose. It's like that now, my mind like a boat, and Rose an anchor. The last time I saw her was in the common room. *"Coming?"* Her whispered voice. The surface of my skin dimpling with gooseflesh. And what came next. A long walk down a corridor. My hand on a doorknob.

When Sheila sits again, my muscles twitch, startled back to reality. She places an object on the table between us, a small square of plastic, like an empty picture frame. I've seen gadgets like it in shop windows.

"A periscope," I say, turning it over in my hand. Most periscopes like this are chintzy and can only materialize a few preset items before they run out of medium and stop working. I've used something like it once, in the Meadows. The memory chills me, mouth filling with the acidity of orange.

I run the pad of my thumb against the words etched into the surface of the periscope: *A Taste of Paris*. "Ed's office is working on a series of travel periscopes," Sheila tells me. Due to the fact, I assume, that actual international travel isn't allowed. To the general population, it's unknown how much of the rest of the world even remains. "Try it," she says.

I study a row of tiny buttons along one edge of the frame. A croissant. A steaming mug of something—coffee or hot chocolate. A crème brûlée. "That one."

Sheila holds down the button and, as though imagined out of thin air, a perfectly made crème brûlée in a round white dish appears, perched inside a background of endless black.

I slide my hand through the square, and my stomach lurches at the sight of my arm disappearing up to the elbow. My brain barely comprehends when my fingers brush cold ceramic.

"I still don't know how these work," I say, clinking a spoon against the caramelized sugar of the crème brûlée. My stomach is still nervous eating something assembled from a string of lactose and sugar molecules, though most food in the city is engineered. When I spoon a dollop into my mouth, extraordinary flavor blooms on my tongue. But before long it grows ashen—like color that's faded over time.

Sheila shrugs. "Even before the Turn, they knew how to print objects. Food too. Even human organs." Her face lights up as she goes on. "The big change came after state scientists discovered how to create space. With infinite space, infinite possibilities. That's what Ed says." Her mouth turns downward then, and I wonder how she stands it, Ed doing the work she dreamed of. "Something about printing molecules in another plane. A space between spaces. And the frame is a kind of a doorway there?" Her forehead furrows in a familiar way, frustration at all she doesn't know.

"They didn't get around to teaching us much science in the Meadows," I say.

"Or much else."

A few weeks ago during a bad windstorm, I watched from my apartment balcony as an electrical cord pulled away from a building. It flailed on the street, naked wire sparking, shooting white filaments of light before a gray-clad maintenance crew contained it.

And here's Sheila. Sparking with ideas. Desires. All that energy with nowhere to go.

She holds the periscope out to me. "Why don't you keep it?"

I startle, then sit back. "It's yours. What would Ed think?"

"Please, take it," she insists quietly. "I'll tell him I lost it."

I squint at her, watching her mouth form a slow frown. "Sheila, what's the matter?"

She stares out at the water. "They used to have car alarms," Sheila says, so softly I can barely hear. "My parents told me. They'd go off in the middle of the night, waking everyone in the neighborhood. It'd blare until someone clicked a button to turn it off." She sighs. "I've got alarms going"—she gestures at her head—"all the time. Have since the Meadows. Before, even. You get tired. You'd do anything to make it stop."

I lean toward her and reach out, but I don't touch her. "What do you mean?"

Sheila's eyes grow unfocused as she looks out over the river. "I've asked Ed to talk to his boss," she says. "About letting me take the aptitude test. If I pass, I'd start in a low-level position in the department, but I could climb."

"Ed's really going to do that?"

She nods. "He says he just needs some time. To earn some clout in the department."

"Well," I say. "I hope his boss says yes."

"If he doesn't, I don't know what I'll do. My mind is starving, Eleanor," she whispers, quiet enough to be drowned inside the steady rush of the river. "Ed never puts his things away. His screen's always on the counter. When he's sleeping, I type in his passcode. I find papers and articles. And I just—I read." Tears perch on the ridge of her lower eyelid. "But, even if I learn everything there is to know, what good will it do? Someone needs to do something. Someone needs to fight."

I lean closer, voice hushed. "I'm fighting."

Sheila fixes on my gaze, and I know she recognizes the truth of my job. Changing reports. Collecting stories and rewriting them in safe words. "It's not enough," she says.

I blink. "What do you mean?"

"Keeping them safe until they're reformed," she says. "And then what?"

They get married. They start having children. Their future narrows to a small set of tasks, repeated daily. But what can I do to change that? What can anyone? I do what I can: listen, and see them, and hold on to their stories.

"It's the best I can do." My voice sounds weak.

And now I'm thinking of Rose, and how she railed against the courses in the Meadows. "Needlework, Eleanor," she'd say. "And Homemaking, and goddamn Comportment—what kind of life do you think they're preparing you for?"

"Rose," Sheila says. "When you wear that face, I imagine you must be thinking about her."

My heart seems to cram into my throat, and my pulse flickers nervously. This conversation—a tightrope. Can't step too far, one way or the other.

"She was a good . . ." I clear my throat. "A good friend."

Sheila nods. "You haven't heard anything of her, have you?"

A cold fork of lightning strikes my chest. Each meeting, I've held out hope that Sheila might have heard something about Rose, a scrap of news that could mean she didn't really die that night.

"No," I tell Sheila. "She's long gone."

I recall what my supervisor, Mrs. Collier, told me the day I was placed as an adjudicator, assigned an apartment in the city, the scent of the Meadows still clinging to me. She pulled up the report of Rose's death and read me the pertinent details. The night Rose tried to escape, a scuffle with peacekeepers. They'd had guns. My mind conjured an image then—a rain of blood falling from Rose's temple into the stalks of purple flowers, soaking into the earth.

"I heard something—" Sheila says, and shakes her head.

"What?"

She glances sideways. "Something Ed mentioned," she says. "That, no matter how harsh the facilities were, at least everyone made it out alive. No reformed has ever died inside."

"But—Rose."

"Her death might have been classified," she says quickly, "and the average intern like Ed wouldn't hear the full truth. But maybe—Eleanor, maybe she didn't die."

I picture it then, the unkilling of Rose, as though watching a backward video. The bullet pulling free from her mind like a silver cork, blood siphoned from the earth and returned behind the walls of her body. Rose, *alive*. Could it be?

I take a breath and fold the muscles of my face back into place. "No," I say, with practiced calm. "I'm sure Ed was mistaken. Everyone knows what happened to Rose. Everyone knows she's dead."

CHAPTER 6

A cheek. A mouth. An eye made of paint.

We sat in a ring, drawing paintbrush across canvas with precise strokes, glancing occasionally into a small mirror clipped to the side of each easel. The air was full with the chalky smell of paint, the clink of paintbrushes dipped in water, the shuffle of Matron Sybil's footsteps as she paced the perimeter, her silver hair swept back in a precise bun.

I could hardly tear my eyes from the circle of girls. It had already been a month, but my heart still felt full at the sight of them, arranged before me like spoils from a treasure chest. Sheila. Johanna. Alice. Margot. Penelope. Betty. And so many others.

"I always assign a self-portrait in your first month, and another in your final." Matron Sybil's voice fell over us like cool water. "Not only will it demonstrate how your painting skills improve, it will illustrate your growth, from who you are today, to the lovely young ladies you will be when you depart here."

"I think that's her way of saying we're not quite lovely yet," Sheila whispered beside me, turning her head and squinting at her portrait. In the painting, her face looked a little funny, the proportions off, as though flattened.

"Yours looks great," I said.

"Don't lie to me," Sheila said.

I stifled a grin. "It's . . . unique," I said. "You have a fresh eye."

She let out a cackle. "Is that what you call it?"

Sheila glanced at mine, and her smile fell away. I'd painted my shoulders in my new white dress, buttons following the line of my sternum. All but my face. There, only a white hollow.

"I've never painted before," I explained. "I don't know how to—to make myself."

Sheila only nodded.

The truth was, I didn't like the mirror. When I first saw it attached to my easel, my impulse was to wrench my eyes away, a thunderclap of shock to see myself inside that metal circle. I'd never owned a mirror, had only glimpsed myself in June's palm-sized one, so tiny, I could see just one piece of me at a time—small mouth, brown eye, slightly snubbed nose.

I heard laughter from a few seats away. My eyes fell on Margot, her blond hair in a close crop. Next to her, Penelope, who had the kind of face you can't look away from, resembling an old-fashioned doll's—high round cheeks, face tapering toward a small, pointed chin. Her dark brown skin was stippled with white paint flicked from Margot's brush.

Penelope gasped. "How . . . *dare* you," she said, a smile pushing through her shock. She held up her brush and flung a constellation of paint onto Margot's face, laughing.

"Decorum, girls," Matron Sybil said, wafting toward them.

Margot's smile didn't slip. "I don't have much decorum, matron," she said. "We didn't learn that in the sticks."

"Then we shall have to teach you," Matron Sybil said, smiling. "Lesson one: We do not throw paint at other young ladies."

"Yes, matron," the two of them replied obediently, but as soon as Matron Sybil turned, Margot ran her finger over the brush and shot Penelope with new freckles of paint. The two suppressed their laughter.

A point in my chest tightened. I thought of June. In the month since arriving, we'd been thrown into classes, my fingers dotted with pinpricks from clumsy efforts at needlepoint, sinuses burned from charring sugar while attempting a caramel in Homemaking. I'd been happily distracted, but now—now, the missing crept in like a poison. I slid out the memory of the alley—June and me, our lips touching. Thumbed it like a rare coin.

"Well done, Eleanor," Matron Maureen said, walking past. Other matrons sometimes dipped into classes to observe us. Matron Maureen was a welcome presence compared with the hawk-eyed glare of Matron Gloria or the unimpressed *tsk*s of elderly Matron Mary. "You've got good painterly instincts," Matron Maureen said, smiling the same smile she'd worn that first day, when she saw Sheila and me holding hands, like we were in on a joke together.

"But," I said, glancing at my painting, "I don't have a head."

"I noticed," Matron Maureen said, laughing. "But what you do have is excellent."

"Thank you," I said, a little astonished.

And then she whispered, low enough that not even Sheila could hear, "I believe in you, Eleanor. I can tell already that you'll do great things one day."

"Me?" I asked. A place behind my sternum glowed like an ember.

"Just wait," she said, eyes glimmering. "See if you don't prove me right."

"Chins high, girls!" Matron Maureen called later that day. "Glide, like you're walking on air."

Around the room, a swarm of us in billowing dresses conveyed our bodies silently through space, stockinged feet slipping across the white floor.

"I don't think our bodies are capable of gliding," Sheila said, tracking us in the enormous mirror that spanned one wall.

I laughed. "I'm not sure what you mean," I said, moving like a baby deer, with uncertain knees. "I'm the most graceful one here."

On cue, I glided away, and collided full-force into Betty, a pale girl with thick white-framed glasses and a plume of orange hair.

"Watch yourself!" Betty cried.

"Just an accident," I said. Betty cradled her arm, twisted against the parachute of her dress. Her face, a white expanse bisected by two thin brushstrokes of orange eyebrows, quivered, as though she might cry. "Oh, my goodness, you're really hurt. Let me help—"

"No." Just before Betty hid her arm behind her back, I saw it. Through the gauzy white material of her sleeve, a bloom of red. Blood.

I could only stare. Surely I hadn't crashed into her with enough force to draw blood. "I'm fine," she snapped. "But you ought to look where you're going."

"Betty," I said. "I'm sure—I'm sure there are bandages. You're my friend. Let me help you."

She leveled her eyes at me. "Friend?"

The single word sliced like a small knife. "We're here, aren't we?" I asked. "We might as well be friends."

Betty frowned. "I'm not in the habit of befriending girls from the Outskirts," she declared, "who walk like lumberjacks and stink like dead fish." She walked away.

I blinked, the air ripped from my lungs. I had the impulse to lift the back of my hand to my nose, to smell myself, though I knew I had none of the Cove left on me.

"Don't listen to her," Sheila said, gliding up beside me. "She's a stuck-up cow you wouldn't want to be friends with anyway."

"Thanks," I said.

"And you only smell a little like dead fish."

I smiled at her.

"Gliding is all in the toes, girls!" Matron Maureen said, flitting about the room like a slip of paper caught in the wind. "Imagine your bones are made of feathers."

She winked as she moved past us. Every so often, I noticed her watching me. It felt warm, her gaze resting on my cheek.

"Why are we doing this in socks, matron?" Penelope asked.

"For a very important reason," Matron Maureen said, twirling around in a pirouette. "Because gliding in socks is more fun."

"Wouldn't shoes be more sensible?" a light voice called from the open doorway. We came to an abrupt stop to face Matron Sybil. "After all, there aren't many society events that will admit them without shoes."

"Don't worry," Matron Maureen said. "I won't send them out into the world barefoot."

"I hope not," Matron Sybil said, moving through the room. She paused before each girl, lightly pushing shoulders back or instructing one to adjust her duck-footed stance.

When Matron Sybil stopped in front of me, she smiled slightly. I felt my heart beating inside my fingertips. She lifted my chin lightly with a finger. "Eleanor," she said. "Eleanor from the Cove. You've never had a class in comportment."

I shook my head.

"Well, we've had many girls from the Outskirts leave the Meadows as lovely as anyone," Matron Sybil said. "You'll be one of them, I'd wager."

I smiled. "Thank you, matron."

Matron Sybil turned to Sheila. "All the makings of an elegant young woman, Sheila," she said, "but your movement needs refinement."

"I'm trying, matron," she said.

Matron Sybil's eyes swept across Sheila's face. "You didn't grow up with comportment either," she said. "Or needlework. Or fine arts. But not for lack of access, as with Eleanor," Matron Sybil said without question, as though she already knew. "Why is that?"

"Well," Sheila said, hesitating. "I have aspirations. To work for the state. The Department of Engineering."

"Do you?" Matron Sybil asked, fine eyebrows rising.

Sheila nodded. "My dad gave me machines to take apart, and I could always put them back together better than him."

Some sort of emotion grew inside Matron Sybil's blue eyes. Sadness, perhaps. "Well, I hope you get all that you want from life, Sheila."

"But she'll never become an engineer." Across the room, Betty had elbowed forward, frizzy orange head emerging from the wall of girls like a marigold in bloom. She held her injured arm behind her back. "Women can't work for the state. Everyone knows that."

Sheila's face grew sour. "I've heard there are special positions for women. For—for the best ones."

I watched Sheila lift her chin, weathering the dubious glances around the room. "I've heard that too," I lied.

Betty screwed up her pale face. "It sounds like a fairy tale."

"Whether it's a tale or truth isn't for us to say," Matron Sybil offered. "Bickering isn't a ladylike trait, Betty." Betty frowned, letting her gaze fall to the ground. "And Sheila, I hope you'll give Comportment a chance. Everything we do here is for a reason."

Matron Sybil moved away, her momentum already shifting toward another girl, when Sheila spoke. "But, Matron Sybil, if I already know I'm not going to be a painter, or—or seamstress, or whatever Comportment is for, why do I need to learn these things?" She asked it frankly, but the room stiffened. We weren't afraid of Matron Sybil, exactly. Only, it seemed a bad idea to cross her, as if, in doing so, the careful serenity of the Meadows might shatter.

Betty's hand went into the air. "Matron, should she really be asking things like that?"

"There's nothing wrong with asking questions," Matron Sybil said. "That goes for all of you. Better to speak them out loud than to hold them inside where we can't see."

"Perhaps you should answer her question, then, matron," Matron Maureen said, a flash of mischief in her eyes.

Matron Sybil scanned the room and sighed. "I can see you're done with Comportment for today. Go on, take a seat."

Each girl pulled up a chair and Matron Sybil gathered herself in the middle, her posture perfectly erect. Something about her made me lean in to listen.

"Before the Turn, people went against nature's laws," she said. "Sometimes, I try to imagine what those people were thinking, before things went wrong. Before nature fought back. They must have believed that they could act however they liked, without consequence. But, of course, nature saw."

I cast a glance at Sheila. What did this have to do with our classes?

"I want you to imagine all the way back to the moment things began to go wrong," Matron Sybil said. "What do you see?"

From around the room, voices called. We knew, from the dispatches. The reasons for the collapse of humanity. Why the Quorum had to take over.

"Divorce," one girl said.

"Children raised without fathers, or mothers," another added.

"Debauchery and freedom run amok." Betty's high voice rang out. "Wickedness and—and *whoredom*."

I heard Sheila giggle beside me, and I had to bite the inside of my cheek to stifle a laugh.

And then, from behind us, Matron Maureen's clear voice: "Women with women, and men with men," she said. "In the ways only a husband and wife ought to be together."

A chord of shock struck inside me, my body ringing. For a moment, my vision went blank. My ears pulsed with the ocean sound of my own blood.

Women with women, the reason for the Turn? My mind flitted, testing the information. I'd never seen two women together, so it must be uncommon—uncommon enough to be wrong?

Suddenly, I felt like a child, small and stupid. Hadn't I always sensed, on some level deeper than knowledge, that I should keep it hidden? That, when I kissed June, we should have ducked inside the shelter of an alley instead of staying out in the bright sunlight?

I dared a glance at Matron Maureen. Her mouth was a straight line, but her eyes sparkled as they always did, with some secret meaning.

My mind again picked up that precious coin, the memory of June, kissing her. Thumbed it like I had, but this time, I winced as though it were hot.

"Nature created men and women," Matron Sybil continued, "and it expects us to perform as such. And to some, it may yet feel like a performance. This dress, a costume if you've been used to pants. To comport ourselves with elegance, like putting on a character." She rested her bright eyes briefly on Sheila. "But, after a time, it stops being pretend. It becomes who you are. This is the first stage of your time in the Meadows."

I set my eyes to my hands, the creases of my knuckles still showing dried paint. I concentrated on this image until it filled my brain.

"Here, you are learning to become fine young women. So that you can have fine families, and raise fine children. Vital to this is learning the role nature intended for you. Perfecting feminine arts." Matron Sybil looked at Sheila again. "Painting, and needlework, and comportment."

My gut wrestled. I glanced at Sheila. A deep crease had formed between her brows. "But, who decided those are only for women?" she asked.

"Nature did," Matron Sybil said gently. "Learning these subjects isn't frivolous. Just the contrary. It's guarding our entire country from nature's wrath."

At that, Sheila said nothing.

"Praise family," Matron Sybil said, eyes still on Sheila.

"Praise family," Sheila muttered, her words drowned out by the voices of the others.

CHAPTER 7

"Maybe she's barren." Betty's voice carried down the table.

I looked up from the array of dishes laid out before us, salmon mousse on cucumber, scones with apricot jam, pink curls of shrimp on packed ice that I could tell had been engineered because they tasted nothing like the sea. The other girls seemed accustomed to invented food, but if my thoughts rested on the idea too long, my stomach grew tight. The flavor, bold for a moment, bled out like ink.

When the matrons told us it was already the dawning of autumn, I could hardly believe them. The air hadn't chilled, mild as ever. And shouldn't the sun have started spending less time in the sky? We gathered for the harvest feast at a long, white-covered table set on the lawn a few paces from the meadow fields. Here we were meant to "practice cordial conversation," as Matron Sybil had instructed. Instead, the conversation had turned to Matron Maureen.

"Yes, I bet she's barren, and she's here doing the next best thing to having children of her own," Betty continued. "Why else would someone so young choose to be a matron?"

"Bold of you, Betty, gossiping about the matrons," Sheila said.

"Hardly gossip," Betty said. "We have a right to wonder who's educating us." Betty glanced toward the main building, eyes focused on something, and smiled. I turned behind me to look, but there was no one there. "Why?" she asked. "Going to snitch to the matrons?"

Sheila shrugged. "Don't you think they can hear everything we say?"

"There are no ears in the Meadows," Betty declared. "We've searched."

It was true. Eyes were mounted in various places, shining black bulbs the size of my fist set into the ceiling of the common room and the cafeteria, and over the curved overhang above the front entrance, but no ears that anyone had found.

We'd been here two months, and already Betty stood out vividly in the pale serenity of the Meadows, with her plume of orange hair and voice that never shut off. Absently, she fidgeted with a tiny pendant hanging from a string bracelet: a wafer of plasticore shaped like a cloud. I'd seen those on a few wrists in the Cove. Religion had been killed years ago, around the Turn, when the faces of churches were stripped bare, and people lined up to silently pass metal tokens shaped like crosses and stars beneath vestibule windows in local offices of the Department of Unity. There were some who prayed to the algorithm, though they couldn't call it prayer. They spoke aloud their wishes and dreams, hoping the algorithm was capable of hearing. Some said miracles occurred (though, of course, the word *miracle* was itself forbidden)—like electric lights switching on the moment an intruder entered a home; emergency services alerted to a drowning child, though no people were around to report it. Some replaced the old religious tokens with new ones—computer chips or pendants shaped like clouds.

"Alice, sit up," Betty snapped, eyes boring through her white-framed eyeglasses. "You're slouching. My goodness, what are you training to be, a potato farmer?"

Beside Betty, Alice straightened quickly, pulling on a lock of smooth black hair. She had very faint eyebrows that almost disappeared against her russet brown skin.

"Betty, I didn't realize you'd been made a matron," Sheila called across the table. "Congratulations."

Betty carefully repositioned her glasses, her features settling into something pious. "I only believe in helping those I can."

Something inside me hollowed watching Alice, who, though her spine was now rod-straight, seemed to crumple. "My mother always told me you should help yourself first, before looking around for someone else to change," I said.

Sheila nodded seriously. "Good point, Eleanor. By the way, Betty, your collar's inside out."

Betty's hands fluttered to fix her collar, pink erupting on her cheeks.

Sheila wore a satisfied expression. "I knew girls like her back home," she whispered, turning so her voice funneled into my ear. "The ladylike police. Always running off to tattle if you burped or swore."

"Did a lot of swearing and burping, did you?"

"Oh, no," Sheila said. "I did far worse than that."

I laughed and sipped my tea, hot and floral, from a blue-painted ceramic cup, nervous touching something so fragile. And even more so beneath the flinty gaze of several matrons from across the lawn.

The matrons were, for the most part, older women. It was believed that they were widowed and had already raised their children, so could afford to take years away from normal life. But Betty was right—Matron Maureen was too young for that. Why she was here, when she could've been leading a real life, had become a topic of conversation before lights out, when we gathered in the common room in our high-necked night-gowns. Matron Maureen acted in ways the other matrons never would, like kicking a ball around during free time with a few other girls, rather ridiculous in her dress, like a magnificent white bird running across the grass. To the girls, she seemed like someone you could talk to, and her class, Comportment, was everyone's favorite.

"*Drat.*" Across the table, Johanna, a mousey, pale girl who'd hardly spoken a word so far, clattered her teacup clumsily. Since the first day, her hand had been heavily wrapped in white bandages. Johanna was one of only a few raised in a setting more remote than the Cove. Shakily now, she carried the cup to her mouth and breathed a sigh when she returned it to her saucer without incident.

"Do you ever get the sense that the matrons are watching us?" Sheila leaned over to ask.

My eyes found Matron Sybil, conversing with stern-faced Matron Gloria and Matron Calliope, who always seemed to be half smiling, her face a pleasant, practiced mask. "They're teachers," I reasoned. "That's their job, isn't it?"

"They're not like any teachers I've ever had," Sheila said. "What do you think they're looking for?"

My mouth opened, but no sound emerged. My mind had tripped, remembering what Matron Maureen had said during Comportment. Women with women and men with men, the reason for the Turn. What would happen if they found out about me? Would they decide they'd made a mistake bringing me here?

Matron Sybil swept her blue-eyed gaze at us, and I recalled a device June's father had saved up for, a palm-sized screen that, if held over the side of his boat, could detect the cool bodies of fish in lemon-bright clusters beneath the ocean's surface. I had the sense that Matron Sybil's pale eyes had the same power. To slice beneath the surface, to search out what I'd rather keep hidden.

"Surprising they don't have this place covered with ears," Sheila said.

"Why would they?"

She shrugged. "The algorithm likes to know everything," she said. "Ears are standard."

I turned to her. "You had ears in your house?"

"You didn't?"

I shook my head. In a place as remote and inconsequential as the Cove, where peacekeepers made rounds only every few months, all we had were a handful of eyes above the market and docks, and the ever-presence of satellites, shining above like pale stars.

What must it be like, I wondered, to never be completely alone. "Really, every house?" I asked.

Sheila nodded. "In the cities and suburbs. Except for people with privileges. Quorum members and the like."

"Well, that explains it," I said. "We're the best and brightest. They trust us."

"Maybe." Sheila glanced toward Matron Sybil again. "It's like they're waiting for us to do something. I wish they'd just come out and say it."

If I had the same sense, I brushed it aside, my chest still swollen with wonder at this place—the stiffness of my new dress, the pristine white of the round buildings studding the lawn like pearly teeth. The smell of the flowers, nectar-like and faint. And yes, even the matrons, with their watchful gazes, their eyes grasping at my face, my skirt, my hands. Something in me delighted in being seen. My mother's eyes only ever skimmed off me.

I cleared my throat. "I'm sure the matrons do everything for a reason."

"You think the best of everyone, don't you?" Sheila asked. "Even Betty. You probably still think you can make her your friend."

"I don't know about that," I said, watching Betty across the table, loudly demonstrating the proper way of grasping a fork.

"That's sad, if Matron Maureen's barren." Penelope spoke, and a row of heads turned to look at her. She'd come from a wealthy family in the city, and moved with an elegance that didn't need to be manufactured. Margot sat next to her, the two hardly ever apart. "I mean—she could at least get married."

48

Betty scoffed. "Nobody wants to marry a woman who can't have children. That's the whole point."

"That's awful," I said, without thinking. "A woman is for more than that."

A strange silence followed, broken only by a scattering of tinks as several girls set down their teacups.

"What do you mean?" Betty asked, face crumpled with confusion.

"That's just—something my mother would say." A deep heat crept into my cheeks. My mother muttered such things when I'd come home with another story about a girl who'd left school early to get married. *They think a woman is for one thing only. We are so much more than they know.*

"There are rules for a reason," Betty declared, and again her eyes twitched toward the main building, a faint smile on her lips. I glanced behind me, but there was nobody there. What did she keep looking at? "If women didn't get married and have children, we'd die out." Betty had come from a traditional family, with ten siblings and a mother who'd barely survived her last pregnancy.

Beside me, Sheila bristled. "Maybe Matron Maureen doesn't *want* to be married."

"By the time you're Matron Maureen's age, you have to be married," Betty said. "Or else become a dried-up old shoe."

"Well, I'm not," Sheila said lightly. "It's not like they can make me."

Betty laughed derisively. "Are you dim? Of course they can make you."

Just then, a clattering of dishes. Johanna's bandaged hand had wobbled her teacup and now watercolor splotches of red erupted over her arms. Sheila and I stood, helping to mop up the tea spilled spectacularly down the front of her white dress.

"I'm no good at this fancy stuff," Johanna choked out, her accent lifting each word.

"I spilled egg on my dress this morning," I told her. "Yellow yolk right down the front. We'll get the hang of it." I glanced at the heavy bandage, itching with curiosity at how she'd hurt herself. "And it'll be easier when your hand's healed up."

"I wonder if they made a mistake with you, Johanna," Betty called. "Some of us aren't the best and brightest, clearly."

A rivulet of laughter ran down the table. I felt my body light up, struck by Betty's words. They could have made a mistake with me too.

Sheila straightened. "Oh would you shut up, Betty?" she said. "That's how you treat someone who needs help?"

"She certainly *does* need help," Betty said. "Probably more than this place can provide."

I gaped at Betty, sitting back in her chair, her mouth in a satisfied twist. Sheila was right. I had plenty of practice searching for good in people, panning for it as though for gold. But this I couldn't make sense of. "Betty, how can you be so cruel?"

Betty's face slackened, and the pain she'd so successfully put away that day in Comportment flashed again on her face.

"All going well, girls?" Matron Sybil strode across the lawn, followed by Matron Calliope, who helped Johanna to her feet, speaking something low and comforting.

The table grew silent.

"Yes, Matron Sybil," Betty said. "Only, I wonder if some of us could benefit from additional lessons. I've already attended finishing school, but others could use some pointers." She looked beyond me again, with that faint, simpering smile, and then I saw it: She'd been glancing at the black bauble shining over the front entrance—an eye. Smiling at it, as though at a friend.

"Matron Sybil," Sheila pronounced, a fire lighting in her eyes. "Betty could use reminding that everyone is here for the same reason. And nobody, not even someone who attended *finishing school*, is better than anyone else."

Matron Sybil's face was quiet, though I sensed her mind turning. "A vital lesson each of you must learn," she spoke at last. "No matter the vehemence of your feeling, it's far from ladylike to tell someone they're wrong." Her gentle scrutiny passed between Sheila and Betty.

Sheila frowned. "But what if they *are* wrong?"

Matron Sybil paused, her pale face in profile against the blue sky. "Then simply be satisfied that you know the truth."

CHAPTER 8

The shower room was white tile, a single stall and a mirror perpetually shrouded in mist. We were to never undress in front of others. "Modesty, girls," Matron Sybil intoned, "is the highest virtue of all." So we went one at a time, stuffed our damp limbs back into stiff cotton, and emerged with dripping hair finger-painting wetly down the backs of our dresses.

The others were on the lawn, taking in the fresh air after a day of classes—the perfect time to find the shower room unoccupied. When I'd taken a shower for the first time—hot stream of water punching my back—I'd doubled over, breathless, as though someone had ripped a sweater roughly over my head. But months had elapsed, and I'd grown to enjoy this time, the dormitory empty, when I could sit inside the steam and imagine myself washed clean.

I pushed open the shower room door.

Anything other than white stood out vividly in the Meadows, so my eyes found it immediately. Blood. Drops of it, ribboning over white tile.

I traced the line of red. Where it had fallen across her pale leg. Where it began, inside a jagged wound along her forearm.

Betty stood in blousy underpants and bra, struggling to bandage her arm. The wound looked old, fringed by puckered pink scar tissue, healed and reopened many times.

My breath pulled in sharply. At the noise, Betty looked up, eyes flaring. Her whole face seemed to tremble, a gush of rage pouring from her mouth: "Get out!"

My mouth fell open. "Betty, I—"

"Leave!"

She screamed it, but I found myself unable to move. This was something I couldn't make meaning of, this wound, this slash of blood across the pristine floor. But the desperation in her eyes felt like that fleck of gold I'd been panning for. "Let me help you," I whispered. "Please. Let me help."

Betty was silent, wavering a little back and forth, as though seasick. Her glasses rested on the edge of the sink. Without them, she looked wide-faced, pale.

"Just . . . keep the door shut," she said. Her eyes gestured toward the common room, its ceiling, where I knew an eye was mounted. She didn't want to be seen.

I lifted the bandage from her hand. Slowly, she offered me her arm. As I wound the bandage, Betty didn't make a sound. She had the look of a doe I'd seen once, its hoof stuck between old metal fence posts, where a house must have been once but was now a grassed-over field. Her expression, a mingling of gratitude and fear. My sense that she was only accepting help because, without it, she would die.

"How did it happen?" I asked, tying off the bandage.

Betty's eyes screwed up in confusion. "Are you really that stupid?"

I shrugged. I guess I must have been. To not put the pieces together.

When I finished, Betty took several steps backward. A doe springing free.

"Don't tell anyone about this," she said. "Ever."

"I won't," I said, not knowing what I'd even tell. I didn't understand. Only that she needed help, and I was able to offer it.

Betty clamped her lips together. "We're not friends."

"I know," I said. We were now something very different from that. I wasn't sure what exactly.

I found Sheila a few paces inside the meadow fields, staring up into the tangled limbs of the enormous yew tree. This was the only tree in the Meadows, and it must've been ancient, its gnarled branches opening like a loose hand.

"I thought you were taking a shower," Sheila said.

I reached to touch my hair, still dry. "I—decided not to."

Sheila hoisted herself to sit on a low branch, her shoes swinging. "I just heard the wildest thing," she said. "Penelope wants to be a messenger on the dispatches when she's older. All made-up and talking for the state."

The messengers were beautiful and mild, with reassuring voices. It made sense for Penelope. "I can picture it."

"At least she wants something," Sheila said, sighing. "The way the matrons talk, it's like they expect us to get married and have kids and that's it."

"Isn't that what most women have to do?" I asked.

She shrugged. "I want more."

"The Department of Engineering," I said.

She nodded. "My dad told me that's where the state's real power is. They're just people. I keep thinking, if someone started it, someone can end it."

"But how? What would you do?" I asked.

She said in a hushed voice, "There's an aptitude test for the Department of Engineering, and anyone who scores in the top percentile automatically gets a placement. My dad's going to sneak me in with his students."

"Are women allowed?"

She shrugged the question away. "When the algorithm sees my score, it'll have to place me where I can be most useful. That's how I change things. From the inside."

My eyes traced the serious line of Sheila's mouth, the daring in her deep brown eyes. I wondered why I had never dreamed something so big for myself. I remembered the Longing Song. My only wishes: a coin to buy a handful of cherries on market day, my mouth warm with June's breath, to enter a facility, to leave the Cove, but to do what?

"I think you will change the world, Sheila," I told her. "I think if anybody will, it's you."

She smiled. "I applied for the aptitude scheme at my old school. Each year, they passed me over. No one who looked like me was ever accepted. One teacher even told me maybe I'd have better luck if I changed my hair and tried to look more like the women on the dispatches."

"What?" I exclaimed.

Sheila nodded. "In the cities, it's fine to be Black, but only if everything else about us is white."

I felt a sharp prickling at my neck. "That's so unfair."

She nodded again, stepping onto a higher branch and peering toward the lawn, where the girls sat in clusters on the grass. Betty was seated among them now, laughing, as though the moment in the shower room had never happened.

"Couldn't even point it out," Sheila went on, "without hearing 'We don't see differences, and neither should you.' When I got my letter here, I thought, *Finally, another way.*"

On the dispatches, the messengers sometimes spoke of the barbaric days of the past, when a person could be killed for the color of their skin. *Now, what once caused division—all color, creed, religion—is wiped away. In the eyes of the state, we are all one race.* I could tell that the words were meant to pass over us easily, like a breeze, but something in them always created an uncomfortable itch in my mind. Because, I thought now, if everyone was expected to be the same, anyone different had the burden of conforming, of cutting away the parts of themselves that didn't fit.

"I just don't want to be anything but what I am," Sheila said.

"You won't have to be," I told her, hoping it was true, even as my eyes looked back to the lawn, tracing the image of each girl dressed identically, cloud-white. "Did your parents tell you anything about why they didn't want you to come here?"

She shook her head. "They said people sometimes come back from these facilities changed. And I told them, isn't that the point? It's a good change," she said. "Before I left, they said, 'There's nothing wrong with you. You are good just as you are.' Over and over, they told me."

I swallowed an unexpected bloom of sorrow. I couldn't imagine my mother saying those words to me. "Why didn't they make you stay home?" I asked.

"My dad tried, but there's a penalty if you don't come."

Sheila hoisted herself onto a higher branch, holding the trailing end of her dress in her hand and revealing strong legs. "Bet you can't climb as high as me."

She negotiated the branches, up and up and up, kicking down her hard black shoes with a shout of "Heads!" Even with her draping skirts, she'd climbed so high, I could barely make out the slip of her dark skin against the sky, her dress a white flag.

Back in the Cove, I'd occasionally play with the village boys, run races, wrestle each other to the ground. When June joined in, I was uncertain, at first, of her wonderful face, her mermaid hair, until she placed a knee in the soft tissue of an organ and I wrestled her just as hard. Girlish grappling. Too young to mean anything except that we both had the instinct that *strong* meant *good*.

Sheila did too—the way she carried herself, her body spring-loaded. But the Meadows was a different place. In our classes, we were learning to hold ourselves as though made of glass. I told myself, there must be a good reason.

School in the Cove had been basic, what Mrs. Arkwright deemed important—her patchwork knowledge of history and science. And while we worked, she usually prattled on about Life Before: Sunday nights watching films around the glow of a television, and grocery stores stuffed with vegetables shiny with wax, and trips to cities that rest now under the sea. It felt like being read to from an old storybook—dusty and thread-bare and full of words we don't use anymore. I wouldn't learn until I got to the city that some people in our country still lived like this.

In our three months at the Meadows, the matrons had only spoken about Life Before to orient us to a new future. "The way we were then," Matron Sybil told us, "people running wild. We saw what came of that. The Turn. The earth ravaged. Millions dead. Wildfires charring whole swaths of the country, oceans stealing back the land. You see what can happen again, if we don't take measures."

I had watched her, rapt as ever, to hear how the world had looked not long ago. Before the Quorum came and righted the ship. What would have happened if they hadn't?

"Every one of you contains something special," Matron Sybil had said. "Something our country needs. If you use what you already have, what will happen?"

"We will be rewarded," we chorused.

She nodded. "You will marry men in the highest offices. You will live in the most beautiful homes." She took a breath. "Praise family."

"Praise family," we had chanted back.

"That's a new record," Sheila said now, hopping from a low branch of the yew tree and dusting off her palms.

57

"Not for much longer." I threw off my shoes and hauled myself into the gnarled branches, that familiar rush of blood in my veins, to be wild, free. When I finally stopped and looked down through the pick-up sticks of limbs, Sheila was tiny below.

"That's too high, Eleanor!" she called. "It's not safe."

"You're only saying that so I don't win," I called, placing my foot on the next branch, a thin one, I realized, just as it cracked beneath my stockinged foot, and the world fell out from under me.

I found myself on the ground, my right foot pinned beneath me. Pain gushed, hot and liquid, from my foot through every sinew and nerve. I cupped the air around my already inflating ankle and stifled a scream.

Matron Maureen was the first there, her knee grinding into the dirt, staining her impeccable white dress. "Oh," she said, tutting over me. The ginger curves of her eyebrows thrust together. "This doesn't look good, does it?"

"Will she be okay?" Sheila called. I looked for her, but the other girls had crowded around me, a ring of bent heads. A small bright feeling flickered in my chest, even as I bit the inside of my cheek to avoid groaning.

"Of course she is," Matron Maureen said lightly. "Girls, why don't you run along to dinner? I'll help Eleanor to the infirmary."

The girls wandered off, all except Sheila, who wore an expression that said she wouldn't be going anywhere, not even if ordered.

An arm slung around Matron Maureen's shoulders and Sheila's waist, they steered me across the grass. My eyes traced the sky, and there it was again, in precisely the same spot it had been that first day, the cloud shaped like a crown. I craned to look, but they steered me inside, to the infirmary.

On a cold metal table, Matron Maureen pressed her thumbs lightly into my ankle, already bulbous and shining crimson.

"A sprain, I think." Tenderly, she wound a bandage around the weird orb of my foot, and I had to bite back a new rush of tears. From the hurt, or the feeling of being tended to in this motherly, strangely painful way, I wasn't sure.

"I—I can do that, Matron Maureen," I said.

Matron Maureen shook her head. "Nonsense. You need help, Eleanor."

I nodded, breathing labored. Sweat had gathered on my forehead. "I suppose."

Matron Maureen cocked her head, considering. "Didn't your mother take care of you? Didn't she tend to your wounds?"

I searched Matron Maureen's eyes. Surely she knew—surely all the matrons knew—about my mother. My mother who, when I flayed the skin off my knee falling in a tide pool, would merely point to the trunk that held our meager medical supplies. From a young age, she taught me to disinfect my own cuts with the evil-smelling liquid from a copper-colored bottle, to not bother her with less than a shattered bone.

Matron Maureen met my silence with a soft smile. "Well, you're not alone now. Not here."

CHAPTER 9

Penelope ducked inside our room. "The others are in a tizzy about something Winnie found," she said. "From the old cohort. Want to see?"

The cohort before us had graduated a few months before we'd arrived. Only one group came to the Meadows at a time, as twelve- or thirteen- or fourteen-year-olds, and they graduated four years later. Afterward, the facility was reset, some new matrons hired and old ones retired, and it all started again.

In our first year, the girls became very occupied with the previous cohort. Adults now, accomplished and fully formed, but they'd started here. We pictured them, and we pictured ourselves. Our futures.

"I found a thimble," Winnie said in the common room that day, cupping it, reverent, in her pale brown palm. Sheila shot me a look as though to say, *That's it?*

It became the thing to do, looking over our rooms, searching for some scrap of the person who once slept in our bed, any sign of who she was.

Weeks later, Alice showed us before Latin, our heads bent over her desk: a bird feather. Somber blue. Discovered sandwiched in the crack between wall and floor. The room hushed. There were no birds in the Meadows. No animals of any kind. Not a field mouse bobbing on the stalk of a flower, not a deer dipping its head to tear a tuft of grass to grind it between square molars. The Meadows hummed with its own breath, but no one else's.

We took turns holding the feather, fingertips running over its edge, skimming it against each cheek. Whoever this belonged to had brought it from outside.

"She must have loved birds," one girl said.

"Maybe her family gave this to her."

"To remember them."

"Maybe it was her name."

"Wren."

"Dove."

"Heron."

When Sheila and I searched our own room, pulled out each dresser drawer, wrenched the side table from the wall, we found nothing. Finally, I wriggled beneath my bed, careful of my injured foot. I lay under there awhile, inside the tight coolness. Let my eyes rove around the space.

"Find anything?" Sheila called.

"No," I said, reluctantly. The girls who had stayed in our room had left no signs of their existence. My heart twisted slightly. When I left this place, I'd be erased from it too.

I started to slide out from beneath the bed when I saw it. On a wooden slat, something was carved. Words. Clumsy, from a sewing needle, perhaps. I touched them with a fingertip, breath tight in my lungs.

She lied.

"Sheila," I said. "Look at this."

Sheila slid in beside me, our shoulders touching.

But when I looked at the underside of the bed again, the words were gone. I ran my fingers over the wooden slats, now completely smooth. "I thought—I saw words," I said. "It's like they've been erased."

Sheila's face turned serious. "You sure? What did they say?"

I cleared my throat. "'She lied.'"

Sheila's eyes grew wide. "Who lied?"

That was the question. We lay beneath the bed for a long moment, Sheila running a thumb over the unblemished wood.

After I hurt my ankle, Matron Maureen offered me small white tablets that would take the pain away, but I declined. The dull ache pinned my mind, filling the corners. Without it, thoughts might swim in. Questions about the strange logic of this place, the absence of weather, that cloud that repeated in the sky. I'd seen it twice more, always in the same spot. And Matron Maureen's words. *Women with women and men with men.* The fear of them finding out about me. Memories too: the cold air off the ocean, the gust of heat from the fire when I'd arrive back at the cottage. The smell of herbs, and sound of my mother tinkering with an old appliance, an eggbeater or alarm clock she found in the junkyard, that she might sell if she could only unlock the mystery of those slippery cogs.

It was worse at night, the only time the Meadows quieted. During the day, the schedule absorbed every moment, the air constant with the sounds of girls talking, breathing, moving. But at night, silence.

"Can't sleep?" Sheila's voice whispered from her bed.

I tore my eyes from the alien light of the ceiling to glance at her. "What gave it away?"

"All the sighing," she said.

I smiled. "You're awake too," I observed.

"Just trying to figure something out," she said.

"What is it?"

"I'll tell you when I do." She turned onto her side, her eyes twin spots of shine in the dark. Then she said, "Do you think we're allowed to go outside at night?"

We tiptoed into the dimmed corridors, through the foyer and onto the lawn, my gait slightly hobbled, though I'd graduated from crutches.

I heard Sheila's breath catch.

A dense sheet of fog obscured the fields. Where the lawn ended, a milk-white wall had erupted, encircling the oblong of grass and buildings. The fog—if that's what it was—extended into the sky, meeting overhead in a milky lid.

Sheila passed me a wide-eyed look. Our feet sunk into the cool grass and we approached the gently rolling mass. It was *like* fog, but too opaque. Too perfectly encircling. I held a hand to its surface, semi-transparent rivulets falling across my palm, winding through my fingers. It felt insubstantial as any fog, but somehow also like a barrier.

"What the hell?" Sheila finally asked.

My mouth opened, but no explanation came to mind.

Sheila turned to me, her mouth hitching into a smile. "Dare you to go inside."

My eyes widened. "But—what if it's a poison gas?"

"Surrounding a school?"

I sighed, but I was too curious to just stand there. "Fine."

I held my breath and took a marching step into the fog, worried that, inside this blankness, I'd no longer exist. When I opened my eyes, it was almost true. Nothing but dull white pressing against my eyeballs. I didn't exist. And I found I didn't mind. My fingertips grazed the tops of flowers, eerie in this opposite of darkness.

After, Sheila ventured in, striding inside and then slowly emerging, first her fingertips, then the brown plane of her nose, then the dark points of her eyelashes, surfacing from the fog as though she were bathing in milk.

"Nobody would get very far out there," she said. "If they were running."

I nodded, struck silent. As isolated as I'd been in the Cove, here, in this flower-colored ocean, we were truly marooned. But, really, what did it matter? Surely nobody would ever run from this place. Especially not me. Still . . .

"It's not natural," I said, staring out at the fog.

Sheila looked at me, her eyes ablaze. "I'm not sure how much of this place is."

Sheila and I revisited the fog the next night, and the next. It always washed in around midnight, beginning as a slim white shadow on the horizon, coming to rest where the lawn met the fields, obscuring even the massive yew tree. Every morning, just before the girls woke, it slid away as though pulled through an enormous drain.

We made a game of it, one of us hiding inside while the other fumbled to find them. Once, Sheila got turned around, and the three paces it should've taken for her to return to the lawn turned into ten, twenty.

"Eleanor!" she called, a muffled, strangled sound. I plunged into the fog. A moment later, I felt the warmth of her forearm. My fingers encircled her wrist, tugging her back toward existence.

Tears soaked her face. "I was afraid I'd be stuck in there all night," she said, shuddering.

"I'd never leave you," I told her.

"Same," she said. I felt something in my chest tug, a cord running between us. And my eyes again found the fog, our silent observer.

"They're keeping something from us," Sheila said.

I'd sensed, for a long time, that something was strange here. Sensed too that Sheila was working toward what it was. I rarely allowed my mind to rest there—on the fog, on the absence of animals. On the fact that, by now, winter should've blown through, yet the air felt as mild as it had on our first day. On how, since we'd arrived, my mind was drawn constantly to the woman in the marketplace poster, as though she held the secret to everything.

We stood, gazing out at the fog. If the meadow fields went on forever, I wondered if the fog did too. Did it cover the world, far enough to touch the doorstep of my mother's cottage?

"Where are we?" I asked.

The question bloomed in the air, larger by the moment.

CHAPTER 10

There's never been a death in a facility.

I leave Sheila's apartment, muscles shaking, the words burrowing into my mind like weevils. It cannot be. Mrs. Collier was clear. Rose died that night. Still, a part of me writhes with hope, a point of pain, just behind my sternum. I do the slow work of making myself numb, swallowing the pain like honey.

My next adjudication is with a girl from the Tides. I force myself to listen to her describe her work. How she begins each day tying her hair back in a gray kerchief before approaching the enormous metal machinery she's been assigned to operate. She will work this machine until she's married or pregnant. Till that day, she wrestles and sweats and bleeds for the machine. The machine collapses on itself, punching holes in thick steel sheets, and opens itself up again. The sound is murderous. Her heart has never grown used to it. Her job: to push the next metal sheet into place, careful to whisk her hand away in time. *Punch, open, hand, whisk.* There is barely enough time to save her hand. There seems to be less and less every time.

"And are you happy with your work?" I ask, numb.

The girl only stares.

On the street, I keep myself together. Zipped up. For blocks and blocks. To any passing observer, I'm calm, my face stoic, a young professional, going about her day. But inside my chest, there is only a crumple of lungs and bone.

There's never been a death in a facility.

And then, passing near a bridge on a pedestrian pathway, a sharp pain stabs my side, doubling me over. I duck under the bridge and empty my stomach onto the ground. Yellowed poison and fizz.

I lean against the cool stone of the bridge. Nobody ever suspects that the inside of me is eating itself alive. I look down at this evidence, striated with blood, like marble. Almost beautiful. Every feeling, I feel in my stomach. I picture it, that muscular balloon, and sealed inside it, every ache, every morsel of shame, all the fear I've felt about Rose. I've learned to live with the looping video, a single metal oblong meeting the soft place below her ear. But this—*never been a death in a facility.* Hope. Worse than pain.

Then, a new feeling. The panic. Cresting above my head. I can make out the waves and whitecaps of it, the blades of it that in a moment will sink into my back.

The first time, it came without warning. I could only duck behind a dumpster and quietly die, because that's what it felt like. Now I watch it happen. My knees buckle and I fall to the ground. Soon, my muscles will jerk, and I will grow scared. My breath will come in spurts, gasping in my throat, and telling myself to *breathe* will only make it harder to *breathe*, and soon, the building blocks of me that I try so hard to keep together will tumble apart, and I will be a mess of organs and vertebrae and blue veins unspooled across the pavement like wire.

But, for now: I observe. Far away. Not in my body. My forehead puckered. Muscles tight. Single strand of saliva stretching from upper lip to bottom tooth. In my eye, one tiny vessel filling with blood, fruit punch sucked through a straw.

A door opens, a black-painted door set inside the stone wall of the bridge that I'd assumed led to a service room for a groundskeeper. But the room beyond isn't a closet with rakes and shovels. Within, there's a large space, a bustling restaurant. And the people who emerge don't look like anyone I've seen in the city. A young man steps out, his long brown limbs clad in leather, black heels, and stockings spiderwebbing up his legs. He looks like someone my mind fabricated, a fascinating dream.

"We'd better not be seen," he says. "It would serve us right too, risking being spotted, just for a gulp of fresh air."

"It's so good, though, this air," a softer, lilting voice says. His companion breathes, taking in a huge lungful of cold, crackling with almost-winter. Even in the state I'm in, this person makes me stare. Neither male nor female, or both at the same time. Wearing pants, with blond hair cut short, skin fair and slightly flushed. "Nobody comes down here, Ezekiel. And anyway, it's a blackout zone. No cameras."

"I hope so," the man, Ezekiel, says. "I've been dead for three years. Would be quite a shock for the algorithm to see me again."

The man's eyes sweep around, and fall on me. His boots skitter backward. "Shit!" he says. "Nobody comes down here, do they?"

He squints at where I kneel on the ground, my cheek pressed against the wall, relaxing as he registers that I'm not a threat. "What's wrong with her? She on something?"

"She's just having a hard time, aren't you?" His companion has blue eyes that sharpen as they regard me. A light bulb goes off on their face. "Eleanor?"

My breath is still clutched tightly in my chest, my thoughts a hurricane. My eyes flit between the two. "H—how do you know my name? Who are you?"

"Your fairy godmothers," Ezekiel says, laughing, then turns to his friend. "But seriously, we need to go back. Not safe out here. Even in a blackout zone."

They ignore him, continuing to stare at me.

"What's going on?" I ask, glancing between the two of them. My breath catches strangely in my throat, shallow sips of air because I can't dig deep enough for a whole breath.

"Just breathe," they tell me. "All you have to do is breathe."

I do as they say, close my eyes and focus on the gradual inflation of my lungs.

When I open my eyes, they're gone.

CHAPTER 11

So a fog appeared and disappeared every night. So the clouds repeated. So there was a complete lack of animals, of insects, of sound, and the days in the Meadows grew no shorter or longer.

Today, the sun made a graceful arc across the sky and came to rest just behind the yew tree—now decorated with strands of silver to mark the winter holiday—and tomorrow it would do the same. And tomorrow. And tomorrow.

So I hadn't felt the sticky sweat of a too-hot day or the chill of cold in nearly half a year, and sometimes I wondered if we were perhaps all dead, and this place was whatever came after.

That first holiday, we each received a small box wrapped in a satiny red ribbon—inside, a pearlescent compact that opened to a tiny mirror. I'd stuffed mine beneath my mattress, but kept the ribbon. Anything other than white stood out vividly in the Meadows. I took to running its redness through my fingers, as I did now, savoring its color.

"It is odd, Eleanor," Sheila agreed. We sat together on the lawn, a little apart from the others, dresses pooled around us like milk. We hadn't discussed the fog in the week that had passed, each quiet with our thoughts. Now we talked around it. "I'm sure it's like we assumed," she said. "We're in the Annex. They've somehow made it habitable."

"Habitable but . . . strange," I said, regarding the sun that didn't hurt my eyes like it had in the Cove.

"It's not like we're *nowhere*," Sheila said at my anxious face.

An idea burbled to the surface of my mind, wondering if Sheila was wrong. I couldn't shake it, the sense that we were out of time here. Like a clock had stopped when we'd entered.

"We must be near the equator," Betty declared, scratching the orange poof of her hair. Most of the girls only had a rudimentary education in things like science and geography.

"It's not hot enough," I said. "And that wouldn't explain the clouds, always in the same pattern over the sky, or the lack of birds or insects."

Betty huffed. "Know-it-all," she snapped.

"Everyone looks like a know-it-all next to you, Betty," Sheila replied.

Several of the girls snorted with laughter. An incensed sound escaped from Betty's throat. "Didn't anyone tell you it's vulgar to rely on insults?"

"Must've missed that lesson," Shelia said, smiling pleasantly. "You too, apparently."

Betty turned away as though she hadn't heard. The conversation moved on, and I turned to Sheila, voice low. "What you said the other night—they're hiding something from us."

Sheila looked at me as if relieved, something expectant in her face.

"We should do something," I said. "Try to find out. How?"

"We ask," she replied, ready. "Matron Sybil said there's nothing wrong with asking questions."

I nodded. "So we ask her about the fog."

Sheila shook her head. "I always have the strangest feeling, listening to Matron Sybil. Like she's delivering a spoonful of sugar to hide the taste of poison."

I nodded again, silently agreeing. "Matron Maureen, then?"

Sheila turned to face me. "I think it should be you."

"Me?" I exclaimed.

"You'd have the best chance of getting a real answer," she whispered. "She likes you."

I felt my shoulders rise. "I can try."

I saw Alice look up from where she'd been picking blades of grass and twirling them between her fingers. "I know! Maybe we're . . . underneath a dome," she ventured.

"A dome?" Betty sneered.

"It would explain it," Alice said, seeming to shrink a little.

"It's far too big to be a dome," Betty said. "A dome that stretches miles? Whoever heard of such a thing?"

"Well, what, then?" Alice asked.

No one could answer. And, like that, it was dropped. It wasn't a productive conversation. Or ladylike. "Always avoid making someone feel awkward," Matron Sybil had told us. "A lady's job is to smooth the wrinkles in conversation, not to create them."

But I didn't forget.

I thought about the fog. I thought about the cloud. And I retraced my journey here, on a train for days. The windows had been black plasticore, totally opaque. Seeing that, my chest had tightened, a nervous claw in my throat. They must've had to shield us from whatever was outside. June and I used to wait at the docks and ask the fishermen what lay beyond our village. Wastelands, they said in a tone we weren't ever sure was serious, state prison complexes, festering places. Marauders, and packs of wild dogs descended from the house pets of Before.

I'd been instructed to leave my compartment only for the bathroom. I did, finally, that night. Traversed the train's rumbling darkness down a hallway lined with identical black doors, each with a sleeping girl behind it.

Outside the bathroom door, another girl waited. She was the kind of beautiful that makes your heart stutter-step. Dark hair, shining and straight, and a miraculous row of mother-of-pearl buttons spanning her emerald dress. I wondered what kind of place had girls in dresses like that.

"I like your necklace," I said. At the hollow of her neck, a thumbprint of green rock hung from a chain. She pinned it between her fingers.

"Thank you," she said stiffly. "It's been in my family forever."

"What does the symbol mean?" The stone was carved with an etching that looked like a letter *I* slashed through in the middle.

"King, my last name," she said, before adding, "Actually, Wang, but my dad had to change it."

My mother had told me how, after the Turn, the state initiated naming protocols. New parents pulled names from approved lists, and last names that hinted at cultural differences were replaced. In that way, everyone was equal, the state said. "You can't erase who people are," my mother had told me. "The sun is still the sun even if you call it the moon."

I'd studied my mother's face then. "How did I get my name?" She'd stiffened, sensing the undercurrent of my question: *Who named me—you or my real parents?*

But she'd just rubbed her nose with the back of her hand and said, "I don't remember."

Frustration had risen in my chest. My real parents, then.

"Where are you headed?" I asked the girl.

"The bathroom," she said, voice droll.

"I mean, on this train?" I clarified. "I'm going to the Meadows."

"The Bay," she said. "I've been hoping for my letter all my life. My older sister didn't get one, and she was supposed to be the family's great hope. Not now." She glowed with pride.

"I don't know anyone who's been selected either," I said. "A boy from my village, five years ago maybe, but hardly anyone before or since."

"A village?" She let out a little laugh. "Never thought I'd meet someone from a village."

The bite of embarrassment inched up my throat, sharp as bile. "And you're from?"

"A development," she said. "Walled on all sides. Everyone's father has an important job. Mine's a city warden." She turned her head, appraising me. "I have to say, you hardly look like the best and brightest to me. Not to offend."

She thrust this claim toward me, as though it was now my responsibility to refute it. I peered down at myself. Homespun trousers cuffed above my leather work boots. Patched shirt I'd used to wipe my mouth, unthinking. Shame burned inside of me, a hole in the exact center of my stomach.

I couldn't meet her gaze, eyes falling to the side of her neck. Where a mark rested. I squinted at it. A bundle of capillaries, broken, just above the lip of her collar. Obvious it had come from a mouth. Maybe from the mouth of someone she loved. Or at least, someone she liked enough to let them that close.

"Who gave you that?"

Her hand went to cover it, a blush filling her cheeks. "Nobody."

And then, a sort of realization. A recognition in the deep color of her cheeks. My mouth fell open, a feeling of mischief rising up inside me. "What's her name?"

The girl's forehead pleated, her entire face really—folded and desperate. "How could you tell?" And before I answered, she darted back to her compartment.

I stood there a long time, startled by this moment, by my ability to recognize a piece of myself in her. And by her reaction. Kissing a girl was not usual—I'd never seen it in the Cove. But then, there were many things that hadn't reached the Cove. Why had she run away? As though ashamed. As though I'd revealed some terrible secret.

CHAPTER 12

"May I borrow Eleanor, matron?"

Matron Maureen had ducked into the Homemaking classroom. Matron Gloria narrowed her dark eyebrows. "We're doing important work here," she snapped. "Eleanor will never learn to make hollandaise sauce if she misses this."

"Be that as it may . . ." said Matron Maureen, smiling good-naturedly.

Matron Gloria huffed and waved her hand. I followed Matron Maureen from the room. As I left, Sheila caught my eye. I gave a quick nod.

"I've always thought that Matron Gloria looks like she put a lemon in her mouth, but has to pretend she didn't," Matron Maureen said, in the corridor. She imitated Matron Gloria's stern face.

I laughed. It felt like a miracle, striding the halls with Matron Maureen while the others were in class. "How's your ankle?" she asked.

"Better," I said. After the first weeks, I'd watched it slowly deflate, bleed of ache, and now months later, I could walk on it without remembering pain.

"I'd like to check on it," she said. "Is that all right?"

"Yes. And I was hoping—could I ask you something?" *About the fog*, I thought. But more too, about the repeating cloud, and the strange lack of seasons, and all the questions I had.

"Of course," she said. "But first, I'm starving."

The hallway terminated in metal doors that opened to a kitchen. The matrons took shifts preparing meals for us, and next year, we'd start cooking as part of our Homemaking curriculum.

The kitchen was larger than my cottage in the Cove, shining pots and pans hanging from the ceiling, an enormous steel table spanning the room. A large refrigerator stood near us, but Matron Maureen bypassed it, striding instead toward the tiled wall.

Hanging there was an empty picture frame made of white plasticore, the size of a large painting. Only the white tile wall was visible behind it.

Matron Maureen pulled a screen from her pocket and tapped. As she did, the frame seemed to hum to life and, inside, the tile wall was replaced at once by black. But a black like I'd never seen, depthless and infinite. I gaped, trying to make sense of it.

"Hungry?" Matron Maureen asked.

I only shook my head, confused.

She selected something on the screen in her palm and, when I looked up, an orange had appeared within the frame, perfectly round and goose-fleshed. It rested in midair, suspended inside the black.

I gasped. The orange was round, and dimensional, and very clearly *real*. My brain fuzzed in astonishment. If I'd been able to slow time, I could have observed the milliseconds that it had taken for each molecule, each chain of fructose and sucrose to etch itself in the air, as though by an invisible painter. As it was, to my unaccustomed eyes, it looked like magic.

When Matron Maureen reached into the frame and wrapped her fingers around the orange, it appeared as though she was reaching inside the wall.

"How'd you do that?" I asked.

Matron Maureen laughed. "I forgot they don't get much tech in the Outskirts."

I was still blinking at the orange, miraculous, like a miniature sun in

Matron Maureen's hand. "It's the most amazing thing I've ever seen."

"Wait till you get to the city," she said. "An orange isn't the half of it."

She peeled the orange and handed me a semicircle of slices. It tasted like a distant memory, less bright than the oranges I'd had, but I savored every piece, needling out each purse of juice with my tongue.

Matron Maureen tossed the peel inside the frame and tapped her screen. This time, the opposite occurred. The peel was unmade, as though suctioned by some invisible force, and slowly it disappeared, its structure first bleeding of color until what was left behind resembled a white geometric skeleton. After a blink, even that had dematerialized.

"That's where any refuse goes," she said. "It'll recycle back into medium, to be used to make something new."

My face must've shown confusion, because she clarified. "Medium. The elements required to print something. This one is designed for food-stuffs, but the bigger ones can print anything. You always need carbon, and hydrogen. Calcium helps, and obviously oxygen. That's how we get specialty items that don't come on the monthly shuttle."

I nodded, though this still baffled me—making objects from empty air.

Matron Maureen threw an orange slice into her mouth and sat on the large metal counter, her red hair splashing against the precise white shoulders of her dress. She slapped the place beside her, and I hauled myself up.

"I never knew there were places like this," I said. "So beautiful."

"All the facilities are," Matron Maureen said. "It's on purpose."

"It makes me wonder—where are we, exactly?"

"Why?" she asked, eyes twinkling. "Thinking about escape?"

Escape. The word made a wrinkle in the air. "Why would anyone want to escape?"

"Oh, there's always someone. Trust is very important—your ability to trust the matrons, to trust the Meadows, and all it will teach you. But not everybody has the natural ability to trust." She gestured as if to take in the whole of the Meadows. "There's more beauty in the world than you even know, Eleanor. I grew up in the city, in a beautiful neighborhood called Teagarden. My mother still lives there, and she has the most wonderful garden. A greenhouse roof stretches over top, and it's dewy and warm all year. Even in January, her orange tree makes fruit."

It seemed right that Matron Maureen had come from a place like that. "Sounds lovely."

"You ought to see it one day, Eleanor, when you live in the city."

"Me?" I asked. I'd hardly registered that, after the Meadows, I'd move to the city.

"Most girls have apartments, but a few get assigned a homestay. You'd make a good candidate." Matron Maureen glanced to the side, as though gauging whether to say more. "What would you think about—perhaps, after you graduate—doing a homestay with me? Well, *us*. At my mother's house."

I studied her. "Live—with you?"

Her mouth seemed to shrug. "It's hardly a Quorum member's mansion, but it does nicely. We have dinner each evening under the greenhouse roof, and my mother insists we celebrate all the holidays in really far too much splendor, and our housekeeper is an excellent cook. And—I think you would like it there, Eleanor."

"But, you're a matron," I said. "Won't you be reassigned when I leave here?"

"I'm thinking, after this cohort, of retiring from matron duties."

I could only stare at her, blank with astonishment. "But . . . why?"

"Why what?"

"Why me?"

Matron Maureen chuckled, a warm ripple of sound. "A better question might be 'Why not you?' You're remarkable, Eleanor. And I just have a feeling . . . a feeling that the precise thing you need is the precise thing my mother and I can provide, a sense of . . ." She looked at me then, and the gentle weight of it felt like sun on my face. "A sense of belonging."

I felt myself blanch, being so closely seen. But like a coin, on its flip-side, a different part of me glowed. What a marvelous new feeling—being noticed.

"Of course, nothing can undo what you've gone through—with your mother, in the Outskirts, alone. But maybe I could help, just a little, to make up for that." She smiled. "You'll always be welcome in Teagarden."

Color rose to my cheeks. Into my mind came the image of me as a child, years trying to chip away at my mother's hard exterior like a miner chiseling out the tiniest fleck of gold from a hillside of rock. And here Matron Maureen was offering it on an open palm.

I felt my heart wrap around the idea like a fist. "I would like that very much."

Matron Maureen beamed. "Though, perhaps you'll be tired of me by the end."

"I doubt that," I said, smiling.

She jostled me with her shoulder. "So, to the more immediate point, that ankle doesn't seem to be giving you trouble. And how are you liking it here?"

"I like it," I said simply. "The girls are—lovely. Everything—everything is lovely."

She cocked her head to the side. "I know these places. Not everything is lovely. Some of the girls are twits. The classes might be boring your brain to dust. Surely there's something at least a little bit . . . unlovely."

I fumbled for words, realizing that, prior to this moment, I hadn't spent much time considering how I felt about being here. "It's . . . an adjustment. Where I grew up, I got used to—to freedom."

She nodded. "Not much freedom in a place like this."

I thought of the fog, the feeling it gave me, of being totally cut off from the world. I cleared my throat. "Matron, I wanted to ask—Sheila and I found something." I looked up to find her pale green eyes peering at me curiously. "This . . . *mist* rolls in each night, at exactly the same time."

She nodded. "First in your cohort to discover that. Been exploring after dark?"

I looked away, a nervous wrench in my stomach.

"No need to look panicked," she said. "The fog is . . . well, it's just fog."

My brow hunched. "It doesn't seem strange to you?"

She turned her head to the side. "Not particularly."

I stared at her. "But, what is it really?"

Matron Maureen set down her orange slices, her eyebrows tweaked, as though annoyed. "Eleanor, I've told you all that I know. It's a natural phenomenon. You grew up near the ocean. Tides are predictable. It's like that."

My eyes fell to the remaining orange slice cradled in my palm. Its structure perfect, each pocket of juice identical. Designed. I considered mentioning the cloud that appeared in the same place every day. But I had seen the irritated quirk of Matron Maureen's eyebrows, recalled what she'd said about trust, about her mother and Teagarden. So I kept quiet about the repeating cloud, and the grass that seemed never to grow, and the lack of animals, and the unbearable silence. Kept quiet about my question of where we were. Quiet about the woman in the marketplace poster who lurked always at the corner of my mind, always at the edge of her picture, her red smile that showed no teeth.

CHAPTER 13

"A *natural phenomenon?*" Sheila asked.

"That's what she said."

Sheila picked up a painting, thick with dried paint. "But, what does that even mean? It didn't act like normal fog."

In preparation for Matron Sybil's speech the next day, the two of us had been tasked with arranging artwork on the walls of the foyer, evidence of what we'd accomplished in our first half year in the Meadows.

"Natural—like the tides," I said, my voice containing more confidence than I felt. I hung a pained-looking needlepoint that Johanna had made, a child's scribble of flowers in thread.

"You think she was telling the truth?" Sheila asked, fixing my newest self-portrait to the wall. I looked away, grimacing. I'd painted two more, each with an attempt at a face, paying meticulous attention to every feature, but they both came out looking wrong.

I shrugged. "She didn't seem very interested in talking about it."

"Did you press her?" Sheila asked.

"No," I admitted. "She looked—" I shook my head. "I didn't want to irritate her."

"Matron Sybil said we should always be asking questions."

A shameful fist sunk into my gut. I read frustration and disappointment in Sheila's expression. Still, I closed my mouth against the truth resting on my tongue like a pepper seed.

I couldn't tell her that pressing Matron Maureen that day in the kitchen would have been impossible. Not when sitting inside the bright aura of her kindness. Not when being around her felt like the moments I'd half dared imagine of my real parents, like being wrapped in a blanket warmed by a fire. Not when she'd offered to let me stay with her after leaving the Meadows, in her mother's home where oranges grew all year long.

"I can always try again," I said, knowing, even then, that I wouldn't.

Sheila nodded, exhaling. "There," she said, stepping back. She'd finished attaching the last painting to the wall. Betty's self-portrait, hanging upside down. "Perfect."

Around the common room, the girls were a churning flurry of white dresses, elbowing to use the bathroom, asking a friend to tie a ribbon around their waist, even though the event wasn't for hours. Matron Sybil's speech marked the start of spring, and afterward, we'd have a feast on the lawn to celebrate. We'd arrived exactly six months before.

"Did you learn to braid from your mom, Sheila?" Penelope asked from where she sat on the ground.

"Every Sunday," Sheila said, pulling a hank of Penelope's dark hair into a precise braid close to her scalp. Penelope had asked Sheila to braid her straightened hair. Every week or two, Sheila posted herself on the common room couch, weaving cornrows or twists for some of the other Black girls, hair oil turning the air sweet. Some, like Penelope, used chemical straighteners or heated wands, fancier than the kind I'd helped June use to straighten her hair once, pressing her loose, dark curls beneath a clothes iron heated on the stove. Her hair had sizzled, a slightly noxious, burning scent lingering in the air. June had never tried it again.

"They won't let you on the dispatches with this hair," Sheila said, deft fingers working at a braid.

"Then I'll change it before I get on the dispatches," Penelope replied, smiling.

When Sheila finished, Penelope examined herself in a hand mirror, cornrows tight across her crown, curling into a bun at the base of her neck. The edges of her hair swirled against her temples. She looked like artwork.

"Thanks, Sheila," Penelope said, smiling. She turned to Margot, who didn't have much in the way of preparation to do, her fair hair still not grown out since we'd arrived. I suspected this was connected to the small, blunt brass scissors in each of our needlework cases. "How do I look?" Penelope asked.

"Decent," Margot said, eyebrows jutting sarcastically.

Penelope's face broke into a grin. "I wish I'd learned to do this. My mom wouldn't teach me. She thinks straight hair will give me opportunities."

"My mom made me learn," Sheila said. "Her friends would come over and she'd recruit me to help until my fingers ached." She smiled sadly. "Never thought I'd miss it."

"Me too." Johanna had been sitting so quietly on a nearby couch, I hadn't noticed her. She clamped her pale fingers over her mouth, as though she hadn't meant to speak.

"Braiding?" Sheila asked coaxingly.

"I have four sisters," Johanna said, voice feather light. "Lots of long hair." She seemed to pull each word out with difficulty, her shyness actually painful.

Several others had stopped their preparations to watch her. Johanna had, prior to that moment, hardly spoken a word to anyone, in class only whispering answers tentatively, to the consternation of the matrons.

"Would you braid my hair?" I asked her.

A smile crept onto Johanna's face. She gave a quick nod.

Johanna's fingers sliced through my hair. The bandage she'd worn when we first arrived was gone; in its place, deep, pink gouges scarred her knuckles. Had someone done this to her? Instead I asked, "Will you tell me about your sisters?"

Johanna hesitated. "After baths, we'd sit in a circle in front of the fire," she said. "I braided my mother's hair, and my younger sister Bridget braided mine, and on and on until my littlest sister. I always wanted to cut mine off, but they wouldn't have it. If I did, Bridget would have nobody to braid."

"Where did you grow up?" I asked.

"Doesn't have a name. Deep in the woods. Just me and my mother and sisters."

"No father?"

"He died." She dropped the words like a heavy stone.

We didn't talk much after that. I regarded myself in the bathroom mirror when she'd finished—two braids encircling my head. I thought again of the cloud I'd seen, repeating in the sky—a crown.

"Johanna," Alice said, touching her own waist-length black hair. "Do you think you could do that to mine?" Johanna, nodded, glowing. By the end, she'd braided four other girls' hair and spoken more words than she had since we'd arrived.

The matrons rarely ventured into the common room, but today Matron Sybil inspected us, reminding us about proper posture and ensuring we hadn't skipped a button.

"Lovely," she said to Lizzy, a tall girl with her chestnut hair in a long, straight braid. Her fair skin flushed from the praise.

"Very nice," Matron Sybil said, smiling at me.

"Beautiful, Alice," she said. Alice had woven purple blooms from the meadow fields into her braided crown.

When Matron Sybil's eyes fell on Penelope, her expression shifted, smile tightening. "Penelope," she said. "Your hair was so beautiful."

Penelope's face fell, eyes flicking to Sheila. "Well—I just felt like something different, for the special occasion."

Sheila stepped forward. "Matron Sybil, you complimented the other girls' braids," she said evenly. "What's wrong with Penelope's?"

Matron Sybil rotated in an easy motion, fingers steepling before her. "Nothing at all," she said. "You're still young girls. No need to rush the future." Her light voice gave the impression of a broom, sweeping away discomfort.

"Meaning, one day, you'll force us to change." Sheila, in contrast, had a voice made of metal now, solid and immovable.

Matron Sybil turned her head to the side, as though surprised. Around the room, eyes bounced between the two, our breath synchronized.

"My dear, there is never force. Only guidance," Matron Sybil said. "If you change your hair, Sheila, it will be by your own decision. I wouldn't be surprised if, one day, you will. In the outside world, a woman's hair is her glory. Smooth, straight hair is known to be nature's preference."

"Nature's preference," Sheila repeated.

"The Quorum listened to the wishes of nature," Matron Sybil said. "Differences only drive us apart. Distinct cultures were erased long ago. We are all one people now. One race. We are all equal."

I felt my cheeks burn. These were the words of the dispatches, designed to pass through our minds without resistance. I recalled what Sheila had said about Matron Sybil's way—a spoonful of sugar to disguise the taste of poison.

"I thought nature wanted us to be what we are naturally," I said.

"Yes," Sheila said. "Why would nature give me this hair but want me to change it?"

Matron Sybil smiled broadly. "You ask such good questions, Sheila.

Some things don't make much sense, even to me. But I promise, I wouldn't steer you wrong."

Sheila frowned. "I'll wear my hair how I like," she pronounced. "And cover it with a kerchief in public, like my mother."

"That's a fine plan," Matron Sybil said. "Only . . . your mother doesn't work for the Department of Engineering. An attendant on a printing row might have more freedom, but we want something better for you. For all of you."

Sheila's face contorted. In her gaze, I could see every one of her ambitions line up. Everything she stood to lose.

"Matron, why don't you simply make her?" Betty broke in, her own hair bound in two thin, orange braids, fraying like twine. She flashed a quick smile at the eye in the center of the ceiling. I had the impulse to slap her.

"We're here to counsel you in the ways of proper young women," Matron Sybil said. "That process takes longer with some. And it can't be forced."

"In other words," I heard myself saying, "Sheila can do what she likes with her hair."

The eyebrow that Matron Sybil arced at me was enough to turn my eyes to the floor, fear blooming inside my gut.

"Of course she can," Matron Sybil said. "All of you may, at any moment, choose to take our counsel or not. Only, remember why you're here, girls. To become something you could only dream of. What a shame it would be, for dreams to falter"—she looked at Sheila—"because of something as silly as hair."

There was something working in Sheila's face. She chewed on her lip. A dial seemed to turn inside her jaw. "Okay, matron," she said at last. "I'll change it."

I blinked back surprise. Matron Sybil, though, smiled as though she'd known all along that Sheila would yield. "I'm proud of your choice,

Sheila." She turned to the group. "See you in a few hours, girls. Remember—a lady is never tardy."

In our room, Sheila worked her fingers into her hair, doing the slow work of unwinding her twists, separating the strands until each popped free. Then with a comb, she fluffed her hair until it radiated from her head. A beautiful cloud of curls.

As we entered the auditorium, Sheila beamed at Matron Sybil. "Is this more of what you had in mind, matron?"

For a fraction of a second, Matron Sybil's eyes widened. "As I said, Sheila, no need to rush the future."

We walked to our seats, and Sheila turned to me. "Do you think she liked it?"

I laughed. It felt important, this small victory. "I thought for a second you—"

She shook her head. "I won't let them change me."

"You don't like your hair straight?"

"I don't mind it at all," she said. "As long as I get to choose."

A hush fell as Matron Sybil stepped onstage, haloed in golden light falling from a spotlight. Something in the planes of her face grabbed my focus. Illuminated, she reminded me of someone. My mind reached for the answer, but I couldn't quite grasp it. Behind her, lined up onstage with the other matrons, Matron Maureen shot me a quick wink. I smiled.

"My," Matron Sybil exclaimed. "How lovely you all look today. It's six months since you arrived. I hope you've learned much in your time here so far."

We all nodded, but as I did, a knot of objection formed in my throat. I scanned the faces of the matrons seated behind Matron Sybil. Though Matron Calliope had taught me to puncture a piece of muslin with a faultless blanket stitch, and Matron Mary had taught me Latin conjugates, and Matron Gloria had even cajoled me into producing a passable hollandaise sauce, it wasn't the kind of education I'd expected. How had our virtues added up to this?

"Now that you have been set on the path to becoming proper young women, there are additional matters you must address in order to progress," Matron Sybil said. "Not one of you will leave the same person who entered. That transformation is why you are here, and why you were selected over many other girls."

Sheila and I passed each other a look. In her stare, I could read the questions brewing: *What are these additional matters? How will they change us?*

Matron Sybil beamed at us. "And like other schools, there will be exams. Not necessarily the kind you may be familiar with. Your progress is noted each day, nothing too small to escape your matrons' notice. And, at some point in your final year, there will come a final test."

Whispers broke out across the room. *A final test.* A slick feeling crept up my throat. Acid-tasting.

"This final test will determine what becomes of you after you leave. Those who exit with top marks will receive the greatest opportunities on the outside. Those who fail will have . . . other options."

I shared a concerned glance with Sheila, my stomach suddenly thrashing.

"The girl who performs most impressively will be named Best Girl, and have her choice of opportunities." I noticed Betty turn her head excitedly between Alice and Winnie. "The final test," Matron Sybil continued, "will be the single most important factor in determining your future. Our world is waiting for you. We want to send them the best."

Matron Sybil stood, radiating with light, letting her words fall over us. My stomach twisted, something in there flailing as though alive. I held my middle.

"You okay?" Sheila whispered.

"I must've eaten something bad," I said, though everyone consumed the same food.

I walked quickly toward the dormitory. I needed to lie down, or else evacuate whatever bright, burning liquid was inside me.

I stopped short. In the common room, against the far wall, a figure moved. No, two, pressed so tightly together, they'd resembled a single person. I watched for a beat, my mind working to make sense of them.

"Margot, Penelope," a crisp voice called from behind me. The two girls broke apart. Only then did I realize what they'd been doing. Kissing. Bodies gripped together. A row of buttons undone. My throat hitched at the sight. Behind me, Matron Maureen stood, her expression carefully neutral. "Girls, Matron Sybil's speech wasn't quite finished. Why don't you run along? The matrons are expecting you."

Penelope's eyes widened in terror, but Margot looked a little self-satisfied, her cheeks tinged pink. They hurried from the room.

"I had a feeling those two were up to something," Matron Maureen said, turning to me. "Pretend you didn't see that, Eleanor."

I opened my mouth. "Will—will they be in trouble?"

She stared down the now empty hallway. "I don't think so."

"Isn't something like that against the rules?" I asked, deliberately avoiding touching any memory of June. A tiny part of me feared the image would project out of my eyes into Matron Maureen's mind.

"Against the rules of society," she replied. "But this is a school. If I want a flower to bloom, I don't punish it. I care for it. Girls aren't so very different."

Something inside me leaned toward her. Like a flower, I thought, toward the sun. "So, Margot and Penelope—they'll—"

"Find another path, with our help."

"But—" I said, searching her face. "If they don't listen?"

"Like all good teachers, we have many methods," Matron Maureen said. And then she smiled, the kind of smile that forces you to smile back. "But, don't worry yourself, Eleanor. I have a feeling you won't be that kind of girl."

All the rest of that day, through the feast, and over the following months, through the ushering in of springtime, the girls spoke often of the final test. The feeling of dread lingered, knocking around my rib cage like a bee against a window, but I swatted it away. I was becoming skilled at this—pushing aside thoughts I didn't want to think. I only had to look at the sky, where the sun was a glowing yellow orb, and the meadow fields in constant, gorgeous bloom, and know that I was good because I was here.

"What do you think will be on it?" I asked Sheila. "The test?"

She sat on the lawn after the feast that day, facing the fields, our white dresses hiked above our knees. The soft socks that I'd run over my cheek that first day had torn beneath my calluses. I'd flung off my hard shoes, smudging the bottom of my socks with grass.

Sheila sighed, the downy plume of her hair bobbing. "She said it was a *final* test. Maybe some kind of summary of everything we're going to learn?"

"I already don't remember stupid Latin roots," I said. "And we just had that class."

"I'll help you," she said. "At least Latin feels like a real subject. I'm tired of learning the proper way to fold laundry." Sheila's brow knit. Sometimes, my muscles and bones ached to run free, as they had in the Cove. There was a similar ache in Sheila, I knew, to exercise her mind.

Just then, Margot and Penelope ran past, chasing each other across the lawn. Their laughter scattered through the air.

A fist clenched in my gut. "Can I tell you a secret?"

Sheila turned, eyes wide. "Always."

"It's not my secret," I said. "You have to promise to keep it."

When Sheila nodded seriously, I cleared my throat, darting a glance around, and told her about discovering Margot and Penelope, kissing.

Sheila's mouth fell open. "Right out in the open?"

I nodded. "They didn't even get in trouble."

Sheila reclined on the grass, stretching her arms and legs out as far as they'd go, a windmill made of girl. "But they must take points off on the final test for kissing girls," she said, her deep brown skin shining against the green. "Do you think it's one of those 'We're always watching' kind of tests? 'Grass stains on your socks in your first year, minus ten points'"— she nudged my grass-stained sock with her foot—"'tripped over your laces in Comportment, minus fifty.'"

I shivered, glancing into the faultless blue sky, picturing satellites up there. "I hope it's not that kind of test." It sunk in, though, the possibility. It's how we ended up here. Watched, measured. Noticing our brightness. Satellites could do the opposite. Take in the things we'd rather keep hidden.

My mind flashed on June, in the market square. Suddenly, that moment felt dangerously bold. Only here, in the Meadows, had the pieces begun assembling: the poster of the smiling couple and their children, that traveling band hauled away. The couples I saw growing up, always a man and a woman. The almost complete absence of anybody like me.

I considered telling Sheila—how I was like Margot and Penelope. How the memory of June's mouth delivered a sharp pang deep in my gut. My mind touched the idea—confiding in someone, speaking it aloud. And then I recalled Matron Maureen's words. *I have a feeling you won't be that kind of girl.* I felt desperate to be what she thought I was. Maybe I'd feel that way about a boy one day. Maybe it would be different when I grew up.

I sat and shoved my feet into the hard shoes I'd discarded on the grass.

"What are you doing?" Sheila asked.

"Just—being safe."

CHAPTER 14

In the kitchen, I watch Clark, his lithe brown fingers cracking engineered eggs—easy-break shells and yolks so bright, I think they managed to capture the sun. Graceful—the word I think of for Clark. Long, tawny limbs working in the way of music. Clark moves differently outside—footsteps heavier, joints filled with sand. In our place, I wonder if he's the closest to his true self. No cameras here, only the small mesh circles of ears dotting the walls.

My apartment hangs high above the city, in a building once used as a dormitory for university students. Clark and I are the only ones assigned to this wing. Our rooms share a common space and kitchen, and we have our own bathrooms, ten shower stalls long.

After I got home yesterday, I let my body drop like a chopped tree into my bed, and slept until morning. The panic, when it comes, bursts through the doors of my mind like peacekeepers. Like the ones who took those musicians in the Cove, and I fight the panic like they fought, because if I don't, I know what happens—what probably happened to them. I'll die. In the past year, I've become convinced that what's inside my mind can kill me.

What I saw yesterday—was it even real? Or just a figment of the panic? Those two people beneath the bridge, who looked like nobody I'd ever seen. Except, one seemed to recognize me. A vague familiarity itched at the edge of my mind.

"Damn," Clark says, gazing into a cupboard. "Out of coffee."

I sit up straighter. "I might have something for that," I say, returning a moment later with the periscope from Sheila, the one that had printed me a crème brûlée.

"Fancy," Clark says, and presses a button with a line drawing of a steaming cup. When he reaches into the frame, his hand disappears briefly, and my breath catches at the sight of his arm tapering to a stump in midair. His hand emerges holding a saucer, a dainty cup balanced on top.

"*Merci*," he says, lifting his cup to me, "*pour le café*."

I feel my forehead wrinkle. "What?" I ask, smiling.

"*Thank you*," he says. "My grandmother taught me French and Creole when I was little. She died when I was in the Gulf, so she can't get in trouble for it now."

Over the last year, Clark has told me a little about his time in the Gulf: the heavy humid sky, buildings on crisscrossed steel risers, suspended above water. Shore just visible miles away, the promise of land, the torment of it. Boys would jump in and swim and swim but arrive nowhere. Hours later, still no farther. They'd come out exhausted but somehow dry, say the water felt like warm static, vaguely electric, the feeling of standing near the vent of a hot computer. "It was enough to drive you mad," Clark told me. "It did, some of them."

"Not you?" I'd asked him.

"I never tried to get out," he'd said, voice low and measured. "I knew I was supposed to be there. I wanted it to teach me its lessons."

I paused before asking, "And, did it?"

He regarded me with small bright eyes that gave nothing away. "Yes."

What was contained in his answer could have been pride or pain or shame or rage. Clark was as skilled as me at concealing what was behind his face.

This is how I've gotten to know him, weaving around each other, concealing more than we share. Never quite comfortable. Never quite knowing how reformed he is, or whether he'd inform on me if he knew the sorts of things I do, the things I keep from Mrs. Collier.

I knew, from my first meeting with her, that I wouldn't do the job the way Mrs. Collier wanted. I'd been fresh from the Meadows then. We met and she'd quickly determined that I would be a good fit for the position. "You've been recommended by your matrons, and your record is impeccable. You have your pick of positions, but you'd do well as an adjudicator."

She'd smiled, decided, but I wasn't as confident. I didn't know how I'd survive. My head still reeled from the sudden vacant space left by Rose, by Sheila, by all of the Meadows. And perhaps most shocking of all, being named Best Girl. I was in the city, with my choice of jobs, given a food voucher and a screen that I didn't comprehend.

"What would I be expected to do?" I'd asked.

"The state knows who shows up for work," Mrs. Collier had explained, her olive-toned face impassive. "And who commits obvious crimes. Your job is to see what the state cannot. Their expressions. Their enthusiasm. In short, their devotion to their new lives."

Mrs. Collier had explained that the public perception of adjudicators is that we monitor people, ensuring that the state's expectations are complied with. Rules exist for everything: proper comportment, mental fitness, wifely duties. "There are all kinds of adjudicators," Mrs. Collier said. "In your case, you'll be monitoring a caseload of reformed girls."

"What happens to them?" I asked. "The ones who aren't devoted?"

Mrs. Collier looked askance, an uncomfortable ripple in the air. In her silence, I could imagine the truth. Violent, forced re-education. Prison. Places you don't come back from. I felt myself squirming. I didn't want this job. I didn't want to inform on girls just like me.

"The matrons," I said. "They told us—we'd be rewarded." I searched Mrs. Collier's face for any foothold, for any sign that the matrons hadn't lied about that. Everything else, perhaps, but not that.

Mrs. Collier smiled curtly. "And you have been," she said. "Simply being in the city and not some shanty town in the Outskirts—many would consider that a reward."

My mind rested on Rose. She would've taken a shanty town over this place. "There was a girl I attended the Meadows with," I said. "There was a—an incident, at the end. I wondered—do you know what happened to her?"

The briefest shuffle of emotion crossed Mrs. Collier's face, something pushing through her steely professionalism. "I was reading the report just before you arrived," she said. "I'm sorry—Rose Walters appears to have died the night you left the Meadows."

My vision throbbed black. I heard my voice say, "And—the others? Johanna?"

"Rehabilitated, all of them. All except Rose," she said. "These things happen. Not every girl is meant to reform."

All at once, my blood seemed to fall through my body. I don't know how I stayed upright. Rose hadn't just been taken. She was gone.

"So, what do you think?" Mrs. Collier had asked, her voice coming as if from a distance. "About the job?"

I blinked rapidly. "What—what exactly is *your* job?"

"To ensure you're doing yours," she'd said, smiling. "I can't possibly check every interaction you have, but I audit your work from time to time, checking against audio recordings. And the algorithm is constantly processing footage from outside the home, of course."

"But if I did miss something," I'd asked, "I'd be fired?" There was a wobble in my voice.

Mrs. Collier shuffled some papers on her desk. It seemed she was already preparing for her next meeting. "Not everyone is suited. If I notice a lot of misses, I'll bring them to your attention. You'll have some time to improve before facing disciplinary action."

I wrapped my arms around my middle. A small crackle of an idea had ignited inside my chest. Mrs. Collier would be listening, but she couldn't catch everything. It wouldn't be difficult to fabricate reports. The idea unwound in my mind. I'd failed Rose. But maybe—maybe I could protect these girls.

After breakfast, Clark and I sit in front of the large screen in the common area, filled with thready-textured couches and coffee tables made of waxed wood, to watch the dispatches. Today, the messengers—two men—speak in calming, serious voices about crop development in the Lower Marsh region and instructing young mothers in proper child handling. Their words feel glossy and incomplete, but I enjoy this feeling of being tethered to everyone in the country, also sitting before their screens at this exact moment. My mother. Sheila. June. I haven't seen her in years, but my mind meets her often, the feeling like pressing a bruise to see if it still hurts. I wonder, does she ever think of me?

"And finally, you may have heard rumors of terrorist groups, particularly in the cities," a messenger says. "We want to assure you that there is absolutely no threat to our country. The algorithm guarantees complete security. But, as always, should you witness any suspicious activity, simply speak into your home listening device. We'll get the message. We promise."

The screen winks to black as the dispatch ends. "Do you think that's true?" I ask, turning to Clark. "Terrorists?"

Clark gives me an appraising look. "It's true."

"How do you know?"

"I see peacekeepers looking for them. Opening doors in alleys and under bridges. They're searching for some secret haven for people resistant to reform."

As Clark speaks, his eyes search mine, as though gauging how much of this I already know. Shock breaks over me: Those people I saw under the pedestrian bridge. Terrorists? "But if they wouldn't reform, they—they'd be rehabilitated. Wouldn't they?"

Clark shrugs. "Maybe some people are beyond rehabilitation."

Or maybe it's that rehabilitation doesn't work, I want to reply. I scan the room, my eyes hopscotching between ears imbedded in the walls, and hope my thoughts aren't loud enough to hear.

"A reformed mentioned something to me the other day," I tell Clark. "She heard there's never been a death in any facility."

Clark's face is placid as ever. "I'm not surprised," he says. "Dr. Collier told me that, when the Quorum was deciding what to do with us, they made a vow to save as many as possible. They keep us safe, at least inside the facilities."

My head tips to the side. "*Dr.* Collier?" I ask. "Is that Mrs. Collier's husband?"

It's the first time I've ever seen Clark flustered. For just a moment, his eyes widen. "Right," he says. "Dr. Collier, he—oversees adjudicators too."

I study Clark's face. Why does it seem like he's lying? "Well, Mrs. Collier told me something," I say. "That, in the Meadows, a girl died."

His eyebrows flick upward. "She told you that?"

I nod. "I wonder—I wonder which is the truth."

Clark remains silent for a long moment. I see something shift beneath his face, like movement behind a drawn curtain. "Maybe . . ." he says, trailing off. "Maybe don't mention that to anyone else."

I blink at him. Was that a warning?

Clark stands. "Well, back at it," he says, turning toward his end of the wing.

"Clark?" I ask. "What did you do to get this job?"

"Do?" he asks, stopping in his tracks. "I . . . didn't *do* anything." He looks confused. "No grand gesture, if that's what you mean."

"But you must've done something in the Gulf that proved to them they could trust you."

He considers this for a long moment, his lean body held in suspension. "I learned that I could hurt myself better than they could hurt me."

A pinprick in my heart, at his honesty. Because this is the real secret. With their words and lessons, they gave us the weapons. But it's only some of us who picked the weapons up and used them against ourselves.

"Did *you* do something?" Clark inquires. "To have them trust you?"

"Nothing in particular," I say, swallowing the lie. "Nothing more than you."

*

I find it after I leave the apartment, stepping onto the train toward my first adjudication of the day. I reach into the pocket of my coat. And my fingers graze paper. The sinews in my chest pull taut. I press the paper between my fingers, a tiny miracle. Nobody uses paper anymore, too hard to find, and no need. I pull it from my pocket, shelter it with my fingers. The paper is green, folded into a square.

I scan the train car, searching for who might have dropped the note into my pocket. It could've been anybody. Every day I pass a thousand people on the street before lunchtime. Quickly, I unfold it, shielding the precise block writing with my hand.

The Registrar's Office. Go, if you want to learn the truth.

Beneath, a drawing of a rose.

CHAPTER 15

The first time a new girl arrived at the Meadows, at the start of our second year, Matron Sybil walked unexpectedly into a needlework session. Matron Calliope had been teaching us a slipstitch, her brown hands carefully working thread into crisp white fabric.

"Pardon the interruption," Matron Sybil said, her arms clamped around the shoulders of a girl, her hair a black curtain framing her face. It had been some time since we'd seen a pupil without braids.

"Girls," Matron Sybil declared, "please meet your new classmate, Marina."

My breath caught. It had been a year, but I recognized her. The girl from the train. The row of buttons. The mouth of whoever she'd been kissing printed on her skin.

A girl, she'd been kissing. A girl.

We all stared at Marina for a long moment, the air swelling like skin around a splinter. This girl, something that didn't belong. Marina's cheeks flared with red, but she kept her eyes pointed forward, chin high, like in a royal portrait from a thousand years ago. Her last name, I remembered, was King.

When she discovered me, her expression grew focused. A filament of danger burned at the center of each eye. I looked away.

"If I may interrupt your needlework for just a moment longer to say a few words," Matron Sybil said. "A new year means new experiences. New uniforms"—she indicated our dresses, longer and without the girlish ribbon around the waist—"and recommitment to our mission here."

I steered my eyes away from Marina with effort, focusing instead on the back of my embroidery hoop, a thicket of loose threads.

Sheila held her hand in the air. The last several months had been one jubilant experiment in hairstyling after another. Today, she wore her hair in twin puffs on either side of her head. In all that time, she hadn't said more about the fog. Neither had I. And we hadn't returned in the night. What was the point?

"Where's Margot?" Sheila asked now.

The others looked around the circle. I hadn't noticed Margot's absence, but now it was obvious. One of us gone, like missing a limb.

"Margot has been transferred to another facility," Matron Sybil replied.

A gasp circled the room. Sheila's gaze connected to mine as though magnetized. Several girls began to cry shuffling, astonished sobs. Impossible to imagine one of us disappearing. I darted a glance at Penelope. Her eyes were fixed to the floor, fingers nervously pulling at the end of her single smooth braid.

"Why?" Sheila asked.

"We received a new pupil, and so we must let a pupil go," Matron Sybil said. "It's always sad, but it is how it happens."

"But why Margot?" I asked, glancing at Penelope again.

"Trust that we have our reasons," Matron Sybil said.

"What reasons?" Sheila demanded.

"It became clear that Margot would be better served at a different facility," Matron Sybil said. "Now, back to your lesson." The air still rang with shock. When none of us moved to pick up our needlework, Matron Sybil sighed. "Matron Calliope, a story comes to mind," she said. "Of a girl who strayed."

Matron Calliope nodded. "I know that story. Perhaps you should share it with the girls."

Matron Sybil smiled and pulled a stool to the middle of the circle, sitting.

"Once, there was a girl who lived in a village," Matron Sybil began. Immediately, a warm glow seeped into my middle. To be told a story again, like a child, in front of the fire when, if I begged, my mother would extract a contraband storybook and read to me in her halting, gruff voice.

"A small village, beside a river," Matron Sybil continued, leaning forward. "The girl was headstrong, and she challenged her parents whenever she could. Her father and mother loved her very much, and so did her siblings, but that wasn't enough for the girl. She sought affection from elsewhere. Every day after school, she met another girl beside the river. Together, they took part in acts that I dare not speak out loud."

Around the sewing circle, held breath. I searched their faces. A spot of blush on Alice's cheek. Johanna's gaze firmly affixed to the ground. Sheila's eyes wide and fascinated. And Marina, her face set hard as ice. I followed Marina's mouth with my eyes. She had the kind of face I wanted to stare at. She glanced up, eyes meeting mine, and I quickly looked away.

"The girl didn't know," Matron Sybil said, "but the one she met beside the river carried a terrible illness. Each night, when the girl placed a kiss on the cheek of her mother and father and siblings"—Matron Sybil tapped her cheek lightly with a fingertip—"she was placing on them a curse."

Betty gasped, and some of the other girls giggled. I leaned forward, not wanting to miss a word. This story seemed important. Like it could contain an answer.

"One day, after gallivanting for hours, the girl returned home. Her house was eerily quiet. She found her family in their beds, swaddled and crumpled and broken from the inside. They had shivered and writhed.

All of them, dead. The girl knew she had done this. Killed her own family with her wickedness."

Matron Sybil fell silent.

I watched the words settle on the group. Alice, gnawing on her bottom lip. Johanna, deflated, empty as a grain sack. Sheila, the hint of a scowl between her eyebrows. And me, looking everywhere but at myself.

"I started at the Bay," Marina said. Absently, she touched her hair, hanging in two long sections across her chest, thick as horse tails. "It was far more beautiful than this place. The bay curved around like a crescent moon, with water to the horizon."

During free time after dinner, the girls clustered around her, still disturbed by the loss of Margot, but nonetheless entranced by the newness of Marina. Penelope sat on the edge of the group, staring at the floor, eyes unfocused.

"Why did you leave?" Betty asked. And in her voice, the rest of her question—*if it was so great?*

"Overcrowding," Marina said. "Several of us had to transfer. Random draw. Just, unlucky." Her hands twisted in her lap. Unconsciously, she flicked her eyes at me.

"Did they let you see your families in the Bay?" Sheila asked from the couch beside me, her legs bent beneath her.

"Not yet," Marina said, "but they spoke of it as a reward for good behavior."

Around the room, the girls held themselves tighter, nursing a shared ache. Johanna's face turned stricken, and Lizzy's eyes were suddenly rimmed with red. We generally didn't talk about our families. After the beginning, most realized that the missing would never lessen. A tender scar tissue had grown over the topic, and a silent agreement to leave it be.

"How is the Bay different from here?" Alice asked.

Marina tossed her hair over her shoulder. "It's all the same idea—same buildings and classes, and the matrons could've been twins with these ones. But, I can't help wonder what they've been teaching you. Your posture is really very poor, all of you."

The other girls instinctively straightened, but Sheila let out a snort.

"Do you have something to say?" Marina asked.

Sheila looked at her, head tilted. "Our posture?" she asked. "Really?"

"Well," said Marina, throwing her own shoulders back, "what reason are we here but to improve ourselves? I'm just pointing out that you have room to grow."

Sheila nodded. "As do you."

"What does that mean?"

"Lies aren't a very ladylike trait," Sheila said. "Overcrowding? You can't expect us to believe that."

Marina took a quick breath. "Believe what you'd like. It's no bother to me," she said lightly, even as her entire body lit with a kind of trapped kinetic energy that could've rattled windowpanes.

The girls might have shunned her, their bonds already so tightly formed, but the next day, she was invited to eat with Betty, Alice, and Penelope, each borrowing a little of her regal grace. As I watched her, all I could think about was the fact of her mouth, how it had been so near the mouth of a girl. No matter how different we were, among the millions of building blocks that made us, Marina and I shared one in common.

CHAPTER 16

It happened two months later in the Comportment classroom.

"Eleanor, I need to speak to you." Matron Maureen looked up from her desk as the others filed out. "Only a moment," she added.

Marina cast me a curious glance as she left.

Something in Matron Maureen's energy felt different from when she'd snuck me out of Homemaking to eat an orange in the kitchen so many months ago. As I walked over, the mirror spanning the length of the Comportment classroom reflected only the two of us.

"Recognize it?" Matron Maureen asked as I sat beside her desk.

A gray-toned image had appeared on her screen. A surveillance video shot from above showing a few slanting buildings and a cobblestone road.

"I don't think—" I began, but as I spoke, the image settled into my mind—the market square in the Cove. My mouth drew into an unconscious smile, and I leaned toward the screen, hopeful that I might see someone I knew, women shopping, fishermen hauling in their catch. My mother, even, running errands. But the square was empty.

"My home." I turned, investigating Matron Maureen's face.

"I was perusing your file when I discovered it," she said. "Watch."

On the screen, a figure appeared, halting from a run in the middle of the square. I squinted, something about her familiar—her squared-off gait, the ruff of hair that poked from beneath a knit cap.

My breath made a sharp sound in my throat. The figure was me. I watched myself traverse the market square, realizing that the video was not from today but over a year ago, after I'd received my letter. Just as I understood what was about to happen, June walked into the frame.

The video had no sound. I didn't need it, the conversation imprinted on my memory. We began standing feet apart but, as we spoke, the space between us closed, one footstep at a time, until there was almost no separation.

I watched myself pull June into the alley, lean in to kiss her. So bold. So unafraid. I recognized a piece of myself that I'd put away when I entered the Meadows. Like meeting an old friend who I'd stopped writing letters to without knowing why.

"I hardly know who that was," I said, as the video cut to black.

"You know who it was," Matron Maureen replied, and the seriousness in her voice made me look up. Her hard stare left me breathless.

My hand spread over my abdomen, suddenly turbulent with fear. "Well, yes," I said. "It was me."

"What were you doing, Eleanor?"

A hot itch crept up my skin. "That girl—June—we were saying goodbye. Just being friendly. It was . . ." *Innocent.* The word stuck in my throat.

"Eleanor, I'm not showing you this to hurt or embarrass you," Matron Maureen said, pressing her lips into a firm line. "Rather because I care about you. It was a crime, what you did. Did you know that?"

Dread, like a heavy stone, dropped inside my stomach. "I didn't."

"Given how you were brought up, I shouldn't be surprised," she said, as though chastising herself. "Stella, the woman who raised you—I've been learning more about her too. Pants wearing. Wood chopping. If I didn't know, I might assume she wasn't a woman at all."

Woman isn't any one thing. My mother's voice flooded me. And following, a searing anger. At her. She taught me nothing about the world. Not that kissing June was wrong. Not that so much of me needed changing. She didn't teach me anything I was learning here, anything I was meant to already know.

"Eleanor, can you possibly know how disappointed I am?" Matron Maureen said.

My hands shook. I grasped them together in a way that would've hurt had I been inside my body at all. Frantic tears pricked my eyes. "Are you going to throw me out?"

Matron Maureen's eyebrows bridged together. "Nobody gets thrown out for the missteps of their past. Not one girl here is perfect. I just didn't expect this of you, Eleanor."

In my veins, shame coursed, hot as tar. I glanced at the mirror and scanned myself, sitting in the chair, surprised on some level to see my dress still in place. I felt unclothed, a pale and private part of me revealed, and I could never again cover it up.

"Oh, Eleanor," Matron Maureen said, gentleness in her voice. "I can see how regretful you are." Her face softened, and I felt myself grasping toward that expression like a drowning person toward a rope. Maybe there was a way to save this.

"What can I do?" I asked. "I'll do anything you want."

Matron Maureen regarded me with gentleness. "It's not about what we want," she said. "It's about what *you* want for yourself."

I stared at her, tears hot on my cheeks.

She smiled. "The choice can only ever be yours."

I walked into the hallway. The hallway I'd walked down hundreds of times. The hallway that now seemed fuzzy at the edges, as if dug from slowly melting snow. "Eleanor—?" Sheila tugged on my arm, her face folded with concern. "What happened in there?"

I dragged the back of my hand across my cheeks, wiping away tears. "Nothing."

"Hardly," Sheila said. "What did she say to you?"

My pulse felt loud in my ears. "She—she told me I need to try harder."

Sheila came to a halt. "Try harder?"

"She's not wrong. I should listen more in Homemaking. And I hardly even study my Latin." And, I thought, I had to learn to become a different kind of person. To pour lye on the Eleanor in that video, watch her distort and erode until she disappeared.

"Eleanor," Sheila said, dipping her head so I'd look in her eyes. "You put enough pressure on yourself to be perfect. You don't need Matron Maureen telling you too."

I was struck then by how clearly Sheila saw me. It was not an entirely comfortable feeling. "I want to learn to be better," I said. "That's why I'm here."

Her brows knit. "Their version of good isn't the only one," she said. "You're good just as you are. You don't have to change a thing."

These were the words Sheila's parents had told her. They hit my system like a pebble thrown into moving cogs. It wasn't true. If it were, Matron Maureen would never have looked at me with such scorn. If it were, wouldn't my mother have told me, even once? If it were, wouldn't my real parents have kept me in the first place? Would they have ever let me go?

"Keep up, girls!" Matron Gloria stalked through the flowers with sharp, meaningful strides, back straight as a flagpole. "So much to explore."

Our group left the sanctuary of the lawn and crashed into the flowers like we knew what we were doing. In our second year, we were afforded recreation time, soft sporting activities on the lawn—the clack of croquet mallets, the smooth patter of tennis balls. Sheila had opted for handball, Matron Maureen's activity. I'd chosen the walking club. Finally, a chance to explore the meadow fields properly. On that first day, I'd assumed we'd make frequent excursions out here, but nobody had ever ventured farther than the yew tree. And now it loomed like a great ocean, untouched.

I watched the others meander through purple flowers, girls in white dresses, short-cuffed sleeves cutting into plump arms, hair braided in crowns, frayed flyaways forming a kind of halo around their heads against the bright sky. Several had woven a crisp white ribbon into their hair, a gift from the matrons during winter holiday time, just passed.

Matron Gloria led us in a tight turn, and soon I realized we were making the same circle, still in view of the school buildings. When we'd walked the same loop four, five times, I grew impatient, my eyes roving the wild expanse beyond. To run. To plow ahead.

"We're not going farther into the fields?" I called.

Matron Gloria glanced back at me. "No need. It's all the same, believe me."

None of the others seemed to mind. They laughed, enjoying the freedom of the afternoon. I should've played handball with Sheila. Alone, I couldn't distract myself. I slowed, watching the girls cut a path through the flowers. I did the work of reminding myself where I was, this beautiful, wondrous place. Something in my chest stumbled. A slow, creeping dread. A knowing, impossible to ignore.

I am not really one of them.

When I was little, my favorite thing at Mrs. Arkwright's was her paper dolls. The thick cardboard dolls were all the same girl, and I'd imagine she was me—narrow body, brown hair, wide-set eyes. I could hold a stack in my hand and slide them apart like playing cards. Bride girl. Horse-riding girl. Doctor girl, which is how we knew these were made Before.

There was a stack of girls inside of me. On top, the one shown to the world. Meadows girl. Proper and perfect, posture just so. White dress, and brown braid taking a straight path down my spine.

Beneath, the Eleanor I showed Sheila. Adventure girl, tree-climbing, sneaking out at night and laughing till it hurt.

And at the bottom of the stack, an unshowable Eleanor. Shadow girl. The one with desires she couldn't explain. Whose hands would not stop twisting each other, whose stomach had already begun tearing tiny red holes in itself. Who kissed June, and followed the line of Marina's mouth a little too closely. Who had a doubt, that perhaps she wasn't good at all. Because she liked girls. Because, a voice whispered, nobody has ever loved you. Because, the voice said, nobody ever will.

The group was far ahead now, a white ribbon threading through violet. I was truly apart from them. Alone. Unobserved, I felt lighter.

I let my gaze rove across the fields, and spotted the road. Chalk-colored. The only way in or out. I wondered how far it went. I wondered, if I walked and walked, would it take me somewhere new?

I broke into a run, white flecks of gravel spraying from where my feet struck the ground, striding deeper into the Meadows than I ever had. I felt what I'd been longing to feel, a warm ache in my muscles, my lungs inflating all the way.

It was twenty minutes before I spotted anything but flowers.

I squinted, trying to make sense of it where it sprang up from the horizon. An archway of crumbling brick straddled the road, just large enough for a car to fit through.

I approached, ran a hand over the rough brick, over the insistent green fingers of vines that pushed into cracks. It seemed like the whole thing could come down with one swift push. It must be the remains of a bridge. Or a doorway. A—a portico. That was the word, rummaged from one of Mrs. Arkwright's books. There must have been a house here once. I imagined it, outlined like a ghost—a huge brick mansion, full of people and dreams, now fallen away, only this archway remaining.

Gooseflesh raced up my arms. I took a sudden step backward and glanced around the empty fields. There was a feeling here. Not of being watched. The algorithm meant I always felt watched. More like being . . . cornered. My heart beat low and thudding. Whose house had this been? And why did its remains now straddle a dusty road leading to a facility in the middle of nowhere?

I debated heading back. Recreation time would've ended, and I'd arrive late to Comportment, and all the girls would look up from their slow walking, Matron Maureen's eyes stamping me with disappointment again.

I'd head back later, I decided, slide in after classes with a good excuse.

I rested inside the archway, legs splayed before me, and after a while I dozed. It was then that something strange happened. A humming sound, like a distant beehive. A sudden bolt of green. A shock of shine.

I sat upright, neck cranked to attention. A frog. *A frog*, where it had not been before. Leapt out of blank air between the brick legs of the archway.

"What?" I breathed, blinking at the frog where it landed on the dry, chalky road.

Before it could hop away, I scooped it up into my hands. I swiveled around. Nobody here to witness this. This cracking open of reality. This perfect little purse of organs and breath and soft bones, arrived from nowhere.

"Where did you come from?" I asked it, breath barreling through my chest. I held the frog up, peered at its strange oval pupils, the tiny flicker beneath the ivory of its chest.

It was late. The sun had made its way across the horizon, and my stomach kicked with hunger. The whole walk back, excitement thrummed

inside me. I held the frog against my chest and felt its heart beating, *blub,*
blub, just beneath the membrane of its skin. The girls would all want to
hold it. Together, we'd name it. It would live with us until graduation. On
the last day, perhaps someone would fashion it a gown, and it'd receive
a certificate of completion too, tiny enough to place in its odd, wet paw.
And everyone would say, *What a good thing Eleanor found it, our little dear*
creature, our pet. What a comfort it's been, these years.

I pushed open the front door and stood inside the foyer. Empty and
pulsing with its usual strange light. I stood for a moment, waiting for a
matron to descend, but none came.

The common room was full, the girls already in their white night-
gowns. A hush fell.

"Eleanor!" Sheila said, standing. "Where have you been? Someone
said you ran away."

"Were you taken somewhere for punishment?" Betty asked.

"No," I said, feeling suddenly hot, crowded.

Marina stood, squinting. She pushed through the other girls. "What
are you holding?"

I opened the shelter of my hands so they could see inside. "It's the
most amazing—"

"Ew!" a few girls chorused, and hopped backward. "Eleanor's brought
a toad!"

"A frog," I corrected.

"It's disgusting," Betty said, nostrils flared.

"It's the most amazing thing," I said, ignoring her. "It appeared out of
nowhere. It wasn't there one second, and the next it was."

"You're making that up," Marina said, whipping her intricate braid
over her shoulder.

"I-I'm not," I stuttered. "There are no animals in the Meadows. It
must've come from—from somewhere else."

"You don't know that for sure," Betty said. "Have you searched every corner? It goes on for miles."

"Yes," Marina agreed. "You probably stole it from its home."

My mouth fell open. "I—I caught frogs growing up," I explained. "I had them as pets."

"You think your *pet* leaped across the country just to find you?" Betty asked.

I shook my head. They didn't understand.

"Look at her cling to it," Betty said, flashing a conspiratorial smile at the eye in the ceiling.

"Oh, shut up, Betty," Sheila snapped.

"But just look at her," Betty said. "Like a baby with a stuffed toy."

Marina flung out a laugh, the kind that aims to hurt. It lodged in my sternum like a shard of glass. And I'd thought it meant something, what she and I shared. More girls laughed, and more.

"Marina," I said, voice low. "You—you ought to be nice to me."

Instantaneously, Marina's face changed. Clouded. The hint of threat in my words was audible only to her and me. And I could see right away that I'd miscalculated. "Why is that?" she asked.

My mouth opened, but there was only silence. Marina gathered herself up just like she had that day on the train. Her backbone must've been forged that way, rod-straight. "You're not allowed to have things like that here."

I held the frog closer to my chest. "There's no rule against it."

"I wonder if the matrons will agree," she said, and marched off.

Marina returned a moment later with Matron Maureen, forehead deeply furrowed. "Eleanor, what have you got there?" Her eyes fell on my cupped hands, and I sensed, in that moment, I had lost.

Marina stood behind Matron Maureen, a satisfied gleam in her eyes. "What is wrong with you?" I demanded, tears brewing.

Marina only let out a laugh.

I ran into my bedroom, though there was no door to close them out. I pushed myself into the corner of my bed. I could still feel the frog's heart beating against my fingertips.

"Eleanor," Matron Maureen said, approaching the doorway. "You have something you shouldn't, I think?"

"It won't harm anyone," I said. "I'll take care of it. Nobody will even know it's here."

"I understand," Matron Maureen said. "But, Eleanor, I'm afraid that's not possible."

"Why?"

"We must consider hygiene. And appropriateness. Do you think we're working so hard turning you into upright young women so you can carry around a frog, a pet of little boys?"

Her meaning rang through the room, clear as any bell. The bodies we'd arrived in had morphed from stick-straight or lumpily genderless to something called *young woman*. Something that needed to be beaten back like wild foliage. Hair on limbs erased, new blood hidden. Fingernails made clean with a tiny, special knife the matrons had demonstrated on us, shoved so sharp under the nail that my eyes watered. The truth of our bodies obscured. Suddenly, I felt encased in a plaster cast, their expectations of *girl* tightening around me.

"This is the kind of girl I am," I told her. *This is how I feel like* girl.

"Eleanor," Matron Maureen said. "You'll do the right thing. I know you will." I sensed the shades of her meaning. Not only, *You'll give up the frog.* But also, *You'll choose the right path.*

I forced my heels into the mattress, pushing myself harder into the corner. Tears crashed down my face. "Please," I begged. "Please don't take it."

Nearby, Sheila sat on her bed, her own tears coursing silently.

"Eleanor, consider compassion," Matron Maureen implored. "This is no place for a pet. Picture its life here, away from nature. Away from water. This isn't where it belongs. I'm so glad you found it. We can offer it release."

I looked down at the frog. Marble eyes. Strange, long fingers. Its wobbly green body and network of bones and the knowledge of life coursing wild and resilient within it.

"Release?"

Matron Maureen nodded. "And what a relief that will be for him."

I felt in a daze as I followed Matron Maureen to the kitchen. The others instinctively hung back, but I could make out Sheila's quiet footsteps behind us.

Matron Maureen clicked on the white plastic frame inside the kitchen wall. It flickered to life, the depthless black, the infinite place where anything could be made. Or unmade.

"Why can't we put it back where it came from?" I asked.

Matron Maureen's mouth pursed. "I'm afraid there's no way to put it back."

Chin wobbling, I held the frog out to her. But she shook her head. "You must do it, Eleanor."

I backed away, horrorstruck. "Like the orange peel?" Departicalized. The carbon and calcium and oxygen of him absorbed by the machine.

"A merciful death," Matron Maureen said. "A painless death." Her green eyes latched onto mine, watching.

Sheila approached from the doorway. "Matron Maureen, you can't make her do that."

Matron Maureen held up a hand. "Please do not stand in the way of your friend's progress, Sheila."

"This is progress?" Sheila demanded. She closed the distance between us and took my hand. "Eleanor, you don't have to do this."

I lifted the frog, gazing into its dark pupils. She was wrong. There was no choice. There was only what the matrons wanted. And wasn't Matron

114

Maureen right? What could I do for it here? What kind of life could it have? Perhaps this was kinder.

Sheila leaned in close, voice a breath from my ear. "Sometimes, I think my parents were right," she whispered. "About this place changing us. Maybe—maybe it's not like I thought. Maybe it's not a good kind of change."

"Oh, Sheila," I whispered back. "I think you're right."

I pulled my gaze from hers and placed the frog inside the blackness of the frame.

Matron Maureen pressed her screen into my hand and pointed to a glowing red button. I lowered my fingertip.

We are all made of specks. I understood this right away. Immediately, the color drained from its body, skin cells evaporating, miniscule green dots flying off like backward rain, revealing muscle, and the scaffolding of bones. The bubble-gum wad of its heart beat once before pulling apart. The unmaking of it. In a moment, it was gone.

I stood perfectly still, afraid that if I moved at all, I might fly apart too, ripped in pieces by sudden pain. Sheila was near, grasping my hand. I pulled a scream from the core of me. The air trembled with the sound.

I pressed my tear-soaked face into her neck and heard her whisper, "I miss home too."

Sheila wasn't exactly right. If there was a Meadows Eleanor, and a shadow Eleanor, there had once been a Cove Eleanor, the one in tattered trousers with scabbed knees, who ran and made music and didn't yet understand how wrong she was.

The pain wasn't missing home. It was missing me.

CHAPTER 17

My eyes trace the outlines of layers of paint visible beneath black. I should be in my apartment typing adjudication reports, but I stole a fork from my kitchen drawer and started walking and now I'm here, under the pedestrian bridge, in front of that door. What lay beyond, I can't put from my mind. A room bursting with sound and light. Those people. The promise of others.

Hardly anyone in the Cove locked their doors, but June and I taught ourselves to pick locks one summer. My hands have gone tight and pink from cold, and I strain to fold back every finger of the fork but one. Kneeling, I fidget the tine into the lock, raking it over and over against the metal teeth within.

The handle doesn't move. I lean my head against the cold door. June was always better at this than me. The missing her is always there, a low throb, but now it pounds through me like a drum.

I glance up at the small black box containing the retina scanner, standard on most doors in the city. *Why not?* I stand and let the red light slide across my eye. But, of course, it doesn't work. Only someone with access would be able to unlock it that way.

My screen buzzes, the sound an insistent drone that will stop only when my eye views the message. A note from Mrs. Collier: *Meet today at the mosaic garden.*

Behind my ribs, a thunderclap of fear. It hits me, the danger of being here. For all I know, that retina scanner is actually an eye. Peacekeepers are looking for a secret haven of unreformeds. *Opening doors in alleys and under bridges*, Clark had told me. What I saw here—I should have reported it to Mrs. Collier. Even blurred by panic, I made out the man's words: *I've been dead for three years. Would be quite a shock for the algorithm to see me again.*

Who was he? And the other one, who seemed to know me?

And who slipped that green note into my pocket the other week? Why?

If only I could ask Clark. Like I peppered Sheila with all my impossible questions in the Meadows—why the clouds repeated, why we never saw animals. Curiosity never did sit easy inside of me. My muscles itch. To do something. To find out.

I'm struck by a feeling I had as a child, holding a fingertip over a candle flame. Slowly, I'd inch the pad of my finger closer and closer. Thinking perhaps this time, I won't be burned.

I take the train north to meet with Mrs. Collier, a queasy swishing in my stomach. I decide I won't tell her what I saw under the bridge. It's mine, secreted away inside of me. But if she discovers I withheld it from her, what will happen then? My mind turns away from the question.

I step onto the train and let my thoughts fuzz.

A year ago, the city was still new to me. The air felt caustic—the electric whirr of self-driving cars, the smell of ozone on days of a sun flare. I didn't know how I'd survive here.

Early on, when I still had to squeeze my eyes shut on the train, my body unaccustomed to hurtling through space, a girl took the seat next to me. She had a black bun and a serious mouth. She pulled out her screen, efficiently tapped, and opened a file. A reformed file, I recognized. Another adjudicator.

She made a sweep with her eyes at my wardrobe, my briefcase, and nodded. "I'm about to retire. Just about run out my two years."

I frowned, wordless. She was now eligible for marriage. She'd come from a facility, so it was hard to know if I should offer congratulations or condolences.

"Goodness, you look new," she said, leaning back. "Where'd you go?"

I shifted in my seat. "There are all kinds of adjudicators," I said, echoing Mrs. Collier.

"I'm aware," the girl said dryly. "But the ones who work with the mentally unsound look stressed and wear a lot of black. And I've known a few of the wifely duties adjudicators. Bunch of fuddy-duddies, no fun at parties. But *you*—you work with reformed girls. So, where'd you go?"

I swallowed. "The Meadows."

She nodded. "Should've known. Meadows girls all come out soft. Sit up," she commanded. "Look sharpish. Your eyes are your best weapon. Use them well."

I sat up as ordered, flustered that she'd declared me so obviously unfit, but grateful to have someone telling me what to do. I still felt as though I didn't know the first thing about being an adjudicator. Though I'd left the Meadows, I suspected I was still being tested.

The girl's eyes roved across the train car. She pointed with her chin. "What's your read on them? Reformed or naturals?"

Across the row, a young couple sat. I studied them, taking in the coil of her hair, the sharp, formal crease down the front of his pants. They spoke too openly, about his day of work, about the dinner party they had to jet home to prepare for. Their eyes free of shadows.

"Not reformeds," I ventured, glancing back at the adjudicator. "Unless they're very good at performing."

She smiled, nodding. "And he's too high-ranking."

"How can you tell?"

"That little gold bead on his lapel. There're rumors it's a tiny camera—an eye. Marks him as a senior official. I'd say . . . Department of Engineering. Or Surveillance."

I squinted at the miniscule dot of gold on his suit jacket. I leaned back, impressed. She knew so much, just by looking.

"Not often a reformed girl would be paired with the likes of him," she said, her eyes raking over the woman. "No, she's the real deal. The type that's never known hunger, or pain."

My mind touched on Marina. Her father had connections. She might already be married to some son of a low-level Quorum member, set into her life as a silent, agreeable wife.

The girl carried on. "Most reformeds are working meat-packing, or chemical plants, or sorting parts for satellites. You'll see. The worst is when you're assigned one you knew. They do it on purpose, I think. To keep us on our toes."

"That's why?" I exclaimed.

"Hey!" the girl barked, darting me a swift look. "Control your face. You're telling the whole world how you feel."

"So?"

"You really are new." She sighed. "The algorithm flags any facial expression that reads too emotional. Once you're flagged, they start listening to you. And don't even think of whispering. That'll get you pegged faster than shouting."

"I thought they listened to everything anyway."

She shook her head. "Not possible. The algorithm looks for cues. So, if you don't enjoy the feeling of being watched, never do anything that makes them start watching. If you do, they'll *keep* watching. And avoid trigger words. It listens for those." She mouths a few words. *Protest. Revolution. Circle.*

"Circle?" I repeated.

"What did I just say?" she snapped. She radiated annoyance, but she'd molded her face to reveal nothing, her flesh disconnected from the person beneath. "You really haven't heard of them? They're . . ." She mouthed *subversive*. "You know, up to no good. Must've chosen a common word for their name so every time someone says it, the algorithm gets gummed up."

I frowned. "I thought all of—*that* kind of activity was shut down years ago."

"Not entirely," she said. "That's part of what you're doing here, you know. Unreformed girls and"—she mouthed *subversives*—"often go hand in hand. It's my stop next, by the way. Any last questions?"

I turned toward the girl, her hawkish eyes still fixed on the young couple, her irises flitting microscopically as though scanning for every detail. "The matrons told us if we worked hard, we'd be matched with elite mates," I said, quietly. "They told us we'd be rewarded." Even then, a small part of me held out hope that their untruths were all part of some master plan, a grand and noble truth only sugared with lies.

The girl pulled her eyes from the couple. "Some last advice," she said. "Let go of the Meadows. Bad things happen to girls who stay stuck there."

"You didn't answer my question."

She let out a short sigh. "The girls with family connections, or the ones with matrons' recommendations—sure, they'll get matched pretty well. And the rest? Well, they're alive, aren't they? Not in prison, or worse. What more could they want?"

The train doors hissed open, followed by a gush of cold air.

"Happy trails," the girl said, and turned toward the door.

"Wait," I called, and the girl pivoted. "H—have you ever been the reason a girl was sent away?" I asked. To prison, or worse. This, the terrible undercurrent of all this observation.

She cocked her head. "Of course. And so will you. That's the job."

I step off the train in a quiet city square strewn with rust-colored seedpods, wind making cyclones of them on the flagstones. I make my way toward a walled, mosaic garden, where Mrs. Collier occasionally likes to meet. I've explored nearly every neighborhood by now, and the speed of trains no longer makes me feel seasick and trembling. The air has turned, the snap and crunch of autumn becoming winter. Time for snow to fall in stacks on the streets, for men and women to swaddle themselves until we're nothing but dark shapes in the snow, and I can pretend that we aren't so different underneath. I can pretend we're living in a time long ago, when it wasn't against the law to say men and women were created equal.

My mind rests on the note I found the week before. *The Registrar's Office. Go, if you want to learn the truth.* Green paper, conspicuous as a bomb. Nobody I know has access to paper. It feels wrong, recalling the barbarian days of cutting down trees when screens work just the same.

Not quite the same, though. A screen is within the algorithm's line of sight. Paper is not.

The drawing was unmistakable—a rose. Someone has information on Rose, an idea too tantalizing to ignore. Still, it could just as easily be a clever and convenient trap. It hardly matters, in the end. Unlike going to the pedestrian bridge, there's no way of going to the Registrar's Office without drawing suspicion. Adjudicators can't be matched.

The buildings here are shorter than the metallic spires of downtown, made of brick and marble—the materials of Before. I enter the walled garden lined with mosaic pathways and find Mrs. Collier beside the pond. Gold and black fish the size of feet huddle on the bottom.

"Eleanor," Mrs. Collier says when I sit beside her. I still have to steel myself in these meetings. There is something powerful in her serene face. She's lanky, without makeup, and her hair is long and fraying. Strange, to see a woman in the city shirking beauty expectations. "Thank you for meeting me here. I like the change of scenery from the office."

I nod, and for a moment we sit in silence, observing the garden. People wander soundlessly, the metallic smell of cold verging on the air. My heart perks up: Somewhere within the overgrown vegetation, the sound of a violin. An old piece that I recognize, the notes always reaching for something but never quite arriving. The state came down hard on music in the beginning. "Encouraged wicked acts," they said. "Encouraged free thought," my mother muttered, and that's why they also burned books, and shuttered the universities, until only a few remained, solely for male scholars. But even my mother only whispered it. Illegal to speak ill of the state. Mrs. Arkwright showed us pictures from old newspapers, bonfires of cellos and violins and, deep within, the wheeled carcasses of pianos. "It was horrible," she said, eyes wet. "Their strings grew so hot, they burst. Their dying notes."

Then Mrs. Arkwright would have me play something on my violin. My mother found it before I was born. "Saved it from a scrap heap," she said. "Figured I could use it as firewood if I got desperate." I never knew if she was joking. It was my most prized possession, somehow surviving the Turn, scarred and scuffed, but playable. Some past owner had scratched their initials—CSJ—near the neck. Sometimes, June and I speculated who CSJ was, inventing names—Charles Smith Johnson. Charlotte Serena Jones. Catherine Seraphina Jameson. It always made me a little sad. Whoever they were, they were surely long dead.

"It's pretty," Mrs. Collier says of the music. "Though I could stand to hear something a little less mournful." Since the Turn, the rules around music have relaxed, though nobody would dream of playing music that might cause a body to move in wicked ways. It's allowed now but controlled. Like careful paintings. Neat needlework.

"I—I used to play," I tell her.

She perks up, a look on her face like she's socking away that piece of information to use against me later. "Do you still?"

I shake my head. "I had to leave my violin at home before the Meadows."

I watch Mrs. Collier, her hawkish nose, the confident set of her mouth. She's good at her job. Meticulous and watchful. And sometimes, I wonder if she was truthful about the process of warnings and transfers. I wonder, if she ever discovered what I was doing, whether she'd skip ahead to the part where I quietly disappear.

The idea slips into my daydreams—men in white tactical suits dragging me by my armpits in my nightgown, their handprints visible on my skin days later. The rotting cell they'll throw me into, wails of despair rising like smoke. Sometimes, I let myself feast on these possibilities. They hurt, but pain has taken on a different quality now, inside my mind. A kind of control I never had in the Meadows. I can make it feel like anything. I can make it taste like something delicious, pour a cupful, drink it like honey. Only recently has that control begun to slip.

"Eleanor."

I jerk to attention. Mrs. Collier is looking at me.

"You had the most interesting expression on your face. Like you were gone completely."

A flush creeps up my neck. *Stupid*, I berate myself, to lose control in front of her. If I'm good at noticing, Mrs. Collier must be even better. "I—was just remembering when I started as an adjudicator. I think I must have been very . . . tentative."

"I remember," she says, smiling. "Something like a field mouse trapped under a jar."

I smile, but my stomach writhes. "I'd like to think I've progressed since then."

She pulls a screen from her bag, flicking through files. "You take your interviews very seriously. Your reports are always thorough. And your charges have some of the best success rates of any adjudicator. Why is that?"

I consider before answering. "I only notice. I think I must be very good at noticing."

"It's *what* you notice that interests me," she says. "I oversee many adjudicators, not just those from facilities like the Meadows."

I quirk an eyebrow. "Oh?"

She nods. "There are myriad ways to violate nature, so the state is vigilant. Some adjudicators monitor charges with criminal tendencies, mental irregularities, those who've committed violations against the family. All to say—I've read many reports. Your notice spreads farther than most. You notice when their eyes light up around their boyfriend, or how fondly they remember their facility."

I pause. "It's possible I've been assigned charges who are determined to use this opportunity to its best advantage."

"Charges are assigned at random," she says.

Something cold and slick moves in my stomach. A moment like this teaches me that, though I can't stop imagining it, I don't want to be ripped from sleep by uniformed officers. I want to keep going. Though handed a skirt and a briefcase and told to act like a grown-up, I am only a girl from the Meadows, still trying to impress the matrons. But Mrs. Collier isn't a matron. Her job isn't to teach me. It's to destroy me.

I blink and do what you're supposed to do when you're pretending to be good.

I pretend to be good.

"Mrs. Collier, I take pride in my work. It's all I have. And if my charges have better success than others, perhaps it's because I provide them something they wouldn't get otherwise. Understanding. Acknowledgment that this perhaps isn't the life they would've chosen. Maybe this is all they need to accept a life that was handed to them."

My chest grows tight as Mrs. Collier considers me, and I wonder if I've gone too far.

She lets her screen rest in her lap. "You're right. If they feel a normal, an *acceptable* degree of displeasure, they should have someone to listen to them."

My heartbeat pounds through me. Relief.

Mrs. Collier shifts in her seat. "But, something you said concerns me. *My work is all I have.* Eleanor, you're not being punished. On the contrary, in this position, the state is celebrating you. Don't you deserve to live?"

The violin music has stopped, the only sound the occasional blip of a bubble breaking the surface of the pond. The silence feels encasing. "I suppose so."

She leans in. "There's value in attending the young people's mixers," she says. "And have you thought of going to the Registrar's Office, just to see?"

My stomach jerks, recalling the note. Though I destroyed it that same day, ran sink water over it until it degraded to a green pulp, I fear Mrs. Collier can somehow smell the paper on my skin. "Adjudicators can't engage in romantic relationships," I say.

"You won't be an adjudicator forever. It wouldn't hurt to look through some profiles. There are some fine young men there. It's how I met my Harvey." I glance at the gold band around her finger. *Harvey*, her husband.

"Your husband oversees adjudicators too, doesn't he?" I ask.

She glances at me in confusion. "Harvey's an overseer in the Department of Industry."

I bite my lip. I knew it. Clark was lying to me about Mrs. Collier's husband. But—*why?*

Seeming to read my mind, Mrs. Collier asks, "What about the boy you live near—Clark?"

Adjudicators often find matches with those they room with. Likely why they have young men and women living so closely together. I shift in my seat. "Mrs. Collier, isn't it true that most women have to give up their jobs when they marry?"

Mrs. Collier tilts her head. "And you're wondering why I was permitted to keep mine?" she asks. "Harvey and I couldn't have children. We were monitored for a time, but when it becomes clear someone isn't biologically suited, they're given other ways to support our state's mission. Now," she says, sitting up straighter. "I'm recommending you go to the Registrar's Office. Avoid being like your reformeds, handed a life you don't have control over. Take a friend if you like. You were close with Sheila Evans in your facility, weren't you?"

I swallow. I'd never told Mrs. Collier that. "We're not supposed to socialize with our reformeds."

She smiles. "I hardly think anything untoward can happen at the Registrar's Office."

Another kind of test then.

The Registrar's Office. Go, if you want the truth. Rose elbows to the front of my mind, the persistent tweak of smile at the corners of her mouth. Whispering in my ear, "If we ran away, we wouldn't have to marry anyone."

I didn't know Rose well enough then to tell if she was joking. "We'd be caught in a minute," I'd whispered.

"We'd outrun them."

"They're too powerful," I'd said, grappling for the right words. "They're dangerous."

I was still learning Rose, but I'd already grown acquainted with the swell of heat that filled my body when she was near. Rose ran her mouth down my neck. "Eleanor, haven't you figured any of this out yet? *We're* the dangerous ones."

In the mosaic garden, a flush rises to my cheeks. "Mrs. Collier," I say, before I know what I'm doing. "Something else I've been pondering, from when I started as an adjudicator. A year ago, you told me a girl in the Meadows died."

"I recall. Rose Walters."

"It's just—I heard recently that there have never been any deaths in a facility. I was wondering how to explain that."

"Well, that's easy. You don't need to explain it. Many things are unknown, even to me."

"But . . . is Rose alive?"

She frowns. "I'm not sure why it matters, Eleanor. You won't see Rose again, even if she were."

My face is placid, but inside, I burn. If I'm a field mouse, Mrs. Collier is the one holding the jar.

CHAPTER 18

There was pain. And there was acceptance.

This was the tide of the Meadows. The frog hurt, until the hurt grew too great and I had to swallow it. Accept it. Clams, I remembered, don't fight the grit that enters their body, cutting their soft flesh. They coat it with iridescence until a pearl forms.

After the frog, I surrendered. It was surprisingly easy. In every moment, there was a clear yes and a clear no. Every time, I surrendered to yes. I surrendered over and over, until doing so seemed natural. Seemed almost like my true nature. Until I forgot my true nature altogether. There was no fight. Only swallowing the pain, covering it, until it looked like something beautiful.

I didn't speak to Marina for weeks. And weeks became months. It was well into the spring of our second year before we spoke again.

"Will you pass me those brushes, Eleanor?" she asked, during Fine Arts, her hands in the sink and the air thick with the turpentine oil she was using to clean brushes. I turned away.

"The brushes?" Marina repeated, indignant, and again I ignored her. She barked a mocking laugh. "You're still really not going to respond to anything I say?"

I darted her a look, and her eyes did a kind of astonished flutter. It felt like a tiny victory.

I turned back to my painting. "Eleanor, lovely work," Matron Sybil said, walking by. I'd painted a brown vase overflowing with daisies. "Any plans to do another portrait?"

I bit my lip. "I think I'll focus on still life for now."

"Well, whatever you paint, it's sure to be splendid."

"Thank you, Matron Sybil," I said, glowing. I felt myself straighten on my stool, as though her praise had gifted me a few extra vertebrae.

"Why do you do that?" Sheila hissed.

My smile fell away. "Do what?"

"Light up when they compliment you," she said. "Act like you need their approval."

Sheila had always resisted parts of the Meadows: the curriculum, the decorum, the feminine pursuits. But her feelings had soured more since the frog. "Matron Maureen has lost her mind," she'd muttered the day after. "Getting rid of the frog is one thing. But making you do it?" I couldn't tell her the truth, that Matron Maureen knew what I really was. This, just one more unspoken truth that swelled between us. I had never told Sheila about Matron Maureen's offer of a homestay, about the oranges, about how my heart had wrapped around it with a fist-tight grip.

"Why do you act like accepting their approval is a dangerous thing?" I asked now.

"*Accept* it," Sheila said, voice low. "But don't need it. Needing it *is* dangerous."

I was silent. I didn't know how to not need the matrons' praise. It smothered my thoughts. Touched by it, I could forget for a single moment who I really was.

"Hey," Marina whispered, leaning away from the sink. "You know why they make us lock up the turpentine?" Her eyes darted to the cabinet where it was stored, unlocked only with a tiny silver key that hung from Matron Sybil's belt. "Because too many girls drank it."

My mouth fell open. I glanced at the glass bottle. Inside, clear liquid that could've been water. "Why are you telling me that?"

"Because, if you're not careful, you might end up like them," she said. "Drinking poison to make the pain go away. That's what your friend's trying to help you see."

I scoffed, glancing at Sheila. "I'm not in pain," I said. "I'm happy here."

"Keep telling yourself that," Marina said, winking.

Matron Maureen sat perched on the edge of her desk when we arrived in Comportment that day. She still came up with games for us, holding spoons in our mouths and balancing eggs, or relays with different objects on our heads. When she had to teach proper etiquette, she'd pretend to be a stuffy old lady, at times strongly resembling Matron Sybil.

"Ladies," she pronounced in her exaggerated accent. "When dining with a gentleman, cross your ankle behind your leg like so, with an upright carriage and eyes softly focused. He'll believe you're daydreaming about him, but you can think of whatever you want. Shoes! Or, cake! Or doorknobs. It doesn't matter."

The girls giggled.

"And no slouching!" she said. "Remember: *Sensible girls seldom secure suitors with slouching shoulders!*"

"I'll keep slouching then," Sheila muttered to me, and I fought to hide a grin.

In the beginning, even in our new white dresses, we were each different. Still with hair cut by our parents' scissors. Still with the drawls and mannerisms particular to our towns.

Over time, it seemed we had silently vowed to forget each other's beginnings. We'd been transformed into quiet, indoor creatures. It was the dresses and the cleanness and the braids that had done it. But more, I suspected, it was comportment and painting and needlework, the precise placement of stitches and brushstrokes, holding our bodies still and silent, until, without realizing, we were something close to domesticated.

It felt like a natural evolution, a growing up. No wondering about fog. No crying over frogs. We all went along. All but Sheila. She watched the assimilation with a steely gaze, a remark of "Are they becoming robots?" at Betty and Marina, sipping their tea identically. I grew familiar with the way Sheila bristled when the matrons said something that didn't sit right with her. She wore the dress and painted and sewed, but inside, Sheila was immovable. I suspected she would remain exactly who she was forever.

Nearing the end of year two, we'd circle together on the floor at the end of every Comportment class while Matron Maureen allowed us to ask any question we wanted.

"What exactly will we *do* with our husbands after we get married?" Alice asked, chewing on her bottom lip. "Only, I've . . . heard things."

"As an unmarried woman, I surely don't know," Matron Maureen said, a hand on her chest. "But you'll have courses on wifely duties when you're pre-married. They don't send you in with no ammunition, don't you worry."

"Matron Maureen," Betty asked. "Why are you here instead of having a family? The other matrons have already lived their lives, but you haven't even begun yours yet."

Several girls let out little gasps of shock at the nerve of Betty's question, but Matron Maureen only smiled. "I believe I will one day. First, I had a debt to pay to our country. Did you know I attended a facility too, not many years ago?"

A pall of surprise fell. The information lined up in my mind, making a perfect kind of sense. Of course Matron Maureen had been one of the best and brightest.

"My matrons saw something in me that I didn't at first," Matron Maureen said, her eyes still fixed on Betty, though it felt as though she were speaking to all of us. "By the end, I'd earned my way to Best Girl. Part of winning that title is having a whole choice of options for what I did next. And I wanted to give back."

"Is that why you are the way you are?" Penelope asked.

"You mean not an old fuddy-duddy too focused on proper stitching?" Matron Maureen asked. Several girls laughed. "The matrons mean well. They just don't remember what it was like to be a young girl. I've tried to persuade them to relax some of the expectations. I think I've convinced Matron Sybil to invite some young men from a neighboring facility for a garden party. Who knows? Perhaps you'll make a match and find your future husband."

"That's going too far," Sheila muttered.

When I quietly chuckled, Matron Maureen's eyes found mine, inside them the quietest reproach. I felt the smile slide from my mouth.

"Matron Maureen, I have another question." Betty's voice came tentatively. "What you said, in our first year, in Comportment . . ." She bit down on her bottom lip.

"Yes, Betty?" Matron Maureen asked.

Betty opened her mouth. "What you said, about women being with women." Her cheeks bloomed a sudden, startling pink. "I heard a story once—Just something I overheard in the town square—years ago—probably not even true—"

Sheila snapped, "Just get it out, Betty."

"I heard that once, it wasn't just women and men who were married. A woman could marry a woman," her voice trailed off, quieter and quieter. "And a man, a man."

The air vibrated. Girls who had been giggling a moment before froze. Held breath. Eyes clapped on Matron Maureen.

Matron Maureen settled her face. "This was true, once."

Around the room, our eyes connected with one another, and in the air, a cloud of questions.

"This might come as a surprise to you," Matron Maureen said, all signs of her joking tone gone. "I'd be in some trouble if the matrons heard I was telling you. But it's an important lesson. What such hubris wrought."

I whispered to Sheila, "Did you know that?"

She shook her head, forehead pinched.

Matron Maureen spoke, her voice the faintest imitation of Matron Sybil's serious timbre. "You're already aware that, before the Turn, people lived beyond nature's means. Somewhere in time, the idea of family grew distorted. Family could be just a mother and children. Or two women or two men. Or divorced people in new marriages, with children from different marriages living under the same roof. Or an unmarried woman raising a child on her own. Some of you grew up in situations like this. But none of those are *family*."

Sheila stiffened beside me. Inside my abdomen, a place the size of a coin began to burn.

I looked down at my hands, clasped in the white of my lap. I traced a finger across my wrist, a network of veins sprawling bluely, and drew pictures there with my index finger. A cat face. A smiling face. Focused my entire mind on this small action, again and again. A holiday tree. A rainbow.

"Every moment the perversion of the natural order was allowed to persist, the laws of nature were thrown off. Why should they have expected nature to treat them kindly?"

I kept my breath low and even. Cat face. Smile face. Holiday tree. Rainbow.

"Those who went against nature's laws contributed to the destruction of our world."

Cat face. Smile face. Holiday tree. Rainbow.

"But the Quorum came along, wrapped us all up, and led us to a new, beautiful future. Thank goodness for them," she said. "Wouldn't you say so, Eleanor?"

My head snapped up. I glanced around the circle, every face angled toward me.

"Y—yes," I said dumbly.

"But you have some doubt?"

My eyes drew down to my lap, stomach seizing like a closed fist. "I just wondered . . . why wouldn't they tell us? That this was how it used to be?"

I heard the fabric of Matron Maureen's dress shift. "Does anyone have a guess?"

Sheila's hand went into the air. "My father said the state doesn't want people to know certain things because if they find out how it once was, they'll want to do it again."

Matron Maureen nodded. "The state has a saying. 'You can't be what you can't see.' To guide someone in a moral direction, we erase anything immoral. That way, we've saved them the awful choice between right and wrong. They'll choose right because they don't know that wrong is a possibility."

I found myself speaking. "But what if someone . . ."

Matron Maureen nodded. "Go on, Eleanor."

"What if someone wants a choice?"

Matron Maureen's green-eyed gaze was mild, but it also felt unbearable, the knowledge of me that she held behind those eyes. "When you're raising your own child one day, Eleanor, and you come upon the edge of a cliff, should you give them a choice between the cliff edge or life?" Her head tilted slightly. "The laws of marriage were once relaxed. In the wrong mind, that knowledge might be empowering. As Sheila's father said, it might feel like, if they did it once, they can do it again."

I looked into Matron Maureen's eyes. A reply rested on the edge of my mouth.

"What is it, Eleanor?" she asked. "You have ideas, I can see them, ready to spill out of you. What are you thinking?"

"I'm thinking," I said, "that we're not going to be children forever."

The circle of girls watched, the air brittle with tension. My gut churned, sharp elbows of fear throwing themselves against my stomach's walls.

"You're right," Matron Maureen said lightly. "All we can do is place you on the right path. And when you're no longer a child, you *will* get a choice. I sincerely hope you choose the right one. Girls, what do you say?" she asked, her voice almost a singsong. "Which path will you choose?"

"The right," they all chanted back. Sheila, alone, was silent beside me.

"So what do you think, Eleanor?" Matron Maureen looked at me again. "Wasn't it good of the Quorum, to set us on the right path?"

Every molecule in me strained away from the question. I didn't want the path she described, but I knew what Matron Maureen wanted to hear. I nodded. "I'm grateful for their decisions. And—and I hope I can give back one day."

Her face split into a smile, and a starburst of relief lit up my insides. I avoided looking at Sheila.

"I'm so glad to hear you say that," Matron Maureen said, and turned to the rest of the girls. "Our country is on the path to healing, and it's all because of you. Soon, we will return to the strong families of yesterday, with the help of this new generation. Praise family."

"Praise family," we chanted back.

"Can't sleep?"

I chuckled softly into the dark. "Want to do something?" I whispered back.

Sheila sat up. Her hair had grown in two years, woven now into thick cornrows that touched her collarbone, covered at night with a silk scarf. "Like what?"

We hadn't visited the fog in over a year. It wouldn't roll in for another hour, so we walked just past the yew tree and made a clearing in the flowers.

At night, the sun dipped low, but the sky persisted bluely, never fully darkening. There was something inebriating about the blushing night air—the stars made of our secrets, waiting to be plucked out and handed to each other.

"I can't stop thinking," I whispered. "About what Matron Maureen said. The planet destroyed because women married women and men married men."

When Sheila spoke, there was a carefulness in her voice. "Do you believe it?"

"I don't know," I said, turning to her. "If a matron says it, it must be true."

She arched an eyebrow at me. "You don't honestly believe that."

"Well," I said, considering. "Matron Gloria *did* suggest that if I didn't learn to make hollandaise sauce, I'd never lead a happy life."

Sheila grinned, turning over onto her stomach and propping her jaw on a hand. "Why did you agree with Matron Maureen?"

I glanced away. "So she'd nod and move on to someone else."

"I'll never lie to make the matrons happy."

I sighed. "It's just easier, going along."

"Easier," Sheila repeated. In her voice, a question. *Is that all you can dream of life being, Eleanor?* "Just promise you won't ever become like Betty," she said. "Did you hear her in Latin? Trying so hard to impress Matron Mary. '*Sus me ad macellum.*'"

I grinned. "*My pig went to the grocery store.*"

Our laughter rang out around the fields, and the sound seemed to usher us into a new place, where we could still be friends though we disagreed. For now, at least.

She turned to me. "What do you think will happen to us when we leave here?"

I looked at the sky, glowing palely. "Is it strange that I can hardly imagine it? I know logically. Job, husband, children." I turned to her. "And then what?"

"You die," Sheila said, laughing, though it wasn't funny, not really, this very real future that awaited us. In this flower-printed place, in this night air that tasted of sweetgrass, it seemed too far-fetched. There existed a dim reasoning in the back of my mind that by the time we were grown, the world would right itself and we'd get to live as we pleased.

"Sometimes, I think I'd like just a little of the old world," I said. "Even if it did almost bring about the fall of civilization."

"*Wickedness and whoredom!*" Sheila whispered.

I doubled over, laughing. Though Betty grated on me, with her simpering to the matrons and constant winks at the cameras, at least she supplied an endless variety of things to laugh at.

"If you were back home, right now, what do you think you'd be doing?" Sheila asked.

My eyes traced the pinpricks of stars. I thought of my violin, nestled inside the threadbare crimson velvet of its case, the initials etched into it, CSJ. And the traveling band, the daydream of playing with them, through the Outskirts and wastelands. I imagined June, the missing never fading entirely, even after all this time, and wondered how it was possible that the warm wriggling feeling in my chest when I was near her could really destroy the world. I closed my eyes, breathing deeply. "Same as I was doing before, probably," I said. "Playing my fiddle, getting scolded by my mother for daydreaming, meeting June after the catch."

"June," Sheila said.

I turned to face her. "A friend."

Something in the downturn of Sheila's smile made me wonder if she suspected more. She fell backward, hands behind her head. "If I was at home, I'd be kissing Katie McGee."

"You what?" I asked, the breath socked out of me.

"Katie was beautiful," Sheila said. "Her dad taught at the university too. In the summer, we'd run around campus together. Once, she showed me this storage closet in the chemistry building, full of weird old scientific instruments. It was dark, so I didn't even see her mouth until it was pressed against mine. It surprised me, so I pulled away. She must've thought I was saying I didn't want it, because she moved toward the door, so I grabbed her hand and pulled her around, and I—and I—I kissed her." Sheila's eyes were far-off with memory. Her chest seesawed with breath.

My body was a live wire, sparking dumbly with electricity. "Are you sure the matrons don't have ears out here?" I asked.

"Where? In the flowers?" Sheila laughed.

We'd never found ears anywhere in the Meadows, but I leaned in close anyway, whispering. "I kissed someone too."

"June?" she asked.

My lips pressed together. I couldn't form the word. Even when I opened my mouth, it stayed lodged, fishhooked somewhere beneath my lungs.

Sheila peered at me for a long moment. "You're not *bad*, you know. Neither am I."

"But, it's wrong, isn't it?" I asked. "The matrons said so."

"No." Sheila stamped the word in the air. "*They're* wrong. And I'm not changing. I could marry like they want, but even then I'd still be what I am."

I was shaking my head. There were Sheila's words and the matrons', equally certain. "But, kissing a girl—that's exactly the kind of thing that they want us to change."

And as I said it, the lightest shiver trilled down my spine. The reverberation of a jammed lock finally sliding open.

Margot and Penelope, pressed together in the common room. Marina, her tender blood vessels broken by the force of another girl's mouth. Sheila in the supply closet. My mouth on June's in the market square.

"I think . . ." I whispered. For a moment, the only sound I could make. "I think . . ." Sheila watched me, my mind a slow machine. "I think that's why we're here."

When I looked into Sheila's face, her expression was unastonished. "You think?" she said.

"When did you know?"

"Weeks ago," she said. "Months. But on some level, almost from the very beginning."

Yes. Hadn't the truth shadowed the corners of my mind since the moment I pulled on that white dress? Since Matron Sybil had addressed us from the stage that first day?

"What my parents said before I left—" Sheila spoke. "I think they were telling me without telling me."

" 'People come back from those places changed,' " I quoted back to her. *There's nothing wrong with you. You are good just as you are.*

Sheila nodded. "That's what they want—to change us."

"Yes."

"All of us."

All of us, I thought. And the longer I thought, the more it I knew it was true.

"All of us," I said.

CHAPTER 19

I could still remember how it felt, the envelope—thick and smooth and cream-colored. So clean, and paper so unusual, I imagined it had been delivered by the algorithm itself. For a moment, I didn't open it. Didn't even touch it. Only looked at it where it lay on the cottage step, just as my mother must have looked at me a dozen years prior, bundled in linen. A knowledge passed through me, from my toes to the roots of my teeth: Once opened, the future would become much more than I ever could've imagined.

"They lied to us," I whispered to Sheila in the dark. We'd walked silently back to the dormitory and lay now in our beds, unsleeping. "How do we ever believe a thing they say again?"

"We don't," Sheila said.

"Should we tell the others?"

"If they don't figure it out. If they haven't already."

I opened my mouth, grasping for words. "I—dreamed about coming here."

For a long moment, only silence. At last, she said, "Maybe they have a good explanation."

I looked at her, dubious. "You don't believe that."

She shook her head. "But I think you do. Or maybe you need to."

Her words stung like the brush of a jellyfish. The sting of truth. My letter arriving—permission at last to believe I was good for something. But now, the knowledge that had lurked always on the edge of my mind— *not good enough, even for your birth parents, even for your mother*—crept in from the dark.

Sheila shifted her eyes around, though there hadn't been a whisper from the other rooms for an hour. "They have the whole world fooled," she whispered. "The Quorum, the messengers on the dispatches. People must suspect—my parents did, I'm certain of it now. If we could only tell everyone that they've been lied to, I think—I really think we can change things."

As she spoke, I followed the path of her eyes sweeping the dark room, moving in and out of focus. Awed by her certainty. My own heart felt like a rock teetering from a very high place.

Sheila investigated my face. "You don't believe them," she said. Almost pleading. "You don't believe they're right about us."

"Of course not," I said. "At least, I don't believe there's anything wrong with *you*."

"But you and I are the same."

I shook my head. When I looked at Sheila, I saw someone made of gold. And inside me, a growing suspicion that I was made of nothing at all.

"There is nothing wrong with you," Sheila said. "Nothing at all wrong with you."

I winced, her words like something molten.

"Eleanor," she said. "When you kissed June, did you feel it was wrong?"

Hearing the words out loud, I flinched, my stomach writhing. "I knew other people would think so."

"But did you?"

"I'd never seen two girls together. I knew it wasn't done."

"But, deep down," she pressed, "in your gut, when you kissed her, did you think it was wrong?"

It felt strangely painful to meet her gaze. "No."

It hadn't felt wrong, that kiss. But knowing this changed nothing here, in the Meadows. Because, at night, I lay awake inside the insomniac glow of the walls, and imagined them making me pure. Imagined this place could be like the periscope in the kitchen. Disassembling me, taking only what I wanted. Black specks suctioned through layers of me. Falling to the floor like ash.

A shiver of nervousness in the air. The lawn strung with hanging light bulbs the size of apples, and a large white tent erected over tables and chairs. We stood in neat lines before the main building, waiting to greet the boys.

The garden party had been presented to us as a special treat, but it felt like a test. Matron Maureen stood with the other matrons. Could she know that Sheila and I had learned the truth? She'd been watching me, unconsciously, her face slack and her eyes intense, as though searching. The moment she registered my gaze, her face changed, smile pushing through her features. I turned away.

The boys stepped out of shuttles, as we had two years before, dressed identically in white shirts and dark navy suits, gawky limbs, Adam's apples bobbing.

"These boys," I whispered to Sheila. "Do you suppose they're like us?"

Sheila passed her eyes over them. "I expect so."

I thought of what she'd told me a few days before. In the still air of the market, in the pale early morning, I hadn't felt there was anything wrong with kissing June, had I? I knew to kiss her only in the shelter of an alley, but my worry was for prying eyes. Not that it was wrong. Not that *I* was wrong. A wedge felt driven into my mind.

"If you had to, which one would you choose?" Sheila whispered in the practiced way we had, funneling words directly into each other's ears so we couldn't be overheard.

I glared at her. "I'd rather be with Marina."

She snickered. "I half wondered. When Marina first got here . . ."

I turned to her. "What?"

"It's just," she said cagily, "you spent a lot of time looking at her mouth."

I let out a snort of a laugh. "Well," I said, glancing at Marina where she stood with Betty. "Not anymore."

"I hope they don't ask us to dance," Sheila muttered. She smelled warm and sweet from the hair oil she put on most mornings, her hair arranged in a dozen coiled knots all over her head. Each girl had had a haircut the day prior, a once-monthly ritual when Matron Calliope would set up a large mirror in the common room, the sound of shears audible for hours. When it was Sheila's turn, Matron Calliope always asked the same question: "How about a taming treatment, Sheila?" Matron Calliope's own hair was pulled back in a sleek, formal bun. She navigated the world in the same way her needle did, precise and somewhat stiff, as though bracing against something.

"You mean straightening?" Sheila had replied. "No thank you."

"It's your decision," Matron Calliope said briskly.

Sheila had looked at Matron Calliope for a long moment. "Why did you change your hair, matron?"

Matron Calliope frowned, pausing before speaking. "I prefer my appearance this way."

"And that's fine for you," Sheila said. "You got the choice. Shouldn't I?"

Matron Calliope surveyed Sheila in the mirror, sadness engulfing the matron's face, a deep bitter sadness that seemed to unsettle the air. "Even I didn't get a choice, Sheila," she said, voice low. "All women must change, us more than most, if we want a chance at happiness."

Matron Calliope cut her eyes to me, and I looked away. Then she did as Sheila wished, clipping only the frayed edges of her hair. Finger-length bundles of black curls drifted to the floor. I gazed at Sheila, a sliver of worry between her brows as she watched Matron Calliope sweep her hair across the immaculate white floor into a pile of blond and ginger and brown.

"Good evening, ladies." A boy approached, a flush creeping through light brown skin on his neck. He coughed into his fist. "My name's Edward. Would either of you do me the honor of taking a turn about the lawn?"

I bit the inside of my cheek, making a concerted effort not to laugh. It seemed he'd practiced this speech many times.

"She'd love to," Sheila said, pushing me forward.

I turned back to her, scowling. She smiled, cocking her head to the side.

"This is a lovely place," Edward said, leading us to two chairs in the shade of the tent. "The grounds are so pretty." He cringed and rubbed his forehead. "I mean, so . . . *pleasant*."

My eyes flitted around the lawn, spotting Betty leading a terrified-looking blond boy to the refreshment table, the pale skin above her upper lip already stained with fruit punch.

I turned back to Edward. "What are the Pines like?"

"Like you'd imagine, I expect," he said. "We live in buildings much like yours. All around are fields of pine trees. The smell is incredible."

"Are there animals?"

He shook his head. "It's strange. Never seen an animal of any kind. I've wondered where we could be, where no animals come, even in such a dense forest. Must be somewhere in the middle of the country. Where else would there be room?"

"That's what we've figured too," I said. "The Annex."

A heavy-browed man with salted gray hair strolled past. "All going well, Edward?"

Edward swallowed heavily. "Y-yes, Patron Gilbert. Allow me to introduce my companion . . ." Edward's voice evaporated, a twinge of panic in his eyes.

The patron shook his head. "Neglected to request your companion's name?" he asked. "Not very gentlemanly, Edward."

A deep, blotchy flush crept across Edward's cheeks. "I—I was—" he stammered.

"He did ask," I interjected. The patron's cold eyes fell on me. "I can assure you that Edward has been the perfect gentleman."

The patron made a gruff sound and strode away. Edward's shoulders relaxed.

"Thank you," he mouthed silently.

"It's Eleanor, by the way," I told him, smiling.

"I really ought to have remembered to ask," he said. "For weeks the patrons have been drilling us in how to properly approach a young woman."

I watched as Edward wiped his brow with the back of his hand. "Is that the sort of thing you learn in the Pines?"

He nodded. "Mostly how to be upstanding men," he said. "Plus science, and athletics, and masculine body awareness."

"No needlework then, I take it?"

He shook his head, smiling. "But if you want me to teach you how to light a fire, you only need to ask. They teach us survivalism too. Seems strange, since most of us will be assigned jobs in a city. I wonder who it was who decided what men need to learn."

"And women."

He nodded, something somber in his eyes. "It's not all bad. In our fourth year, we'll start work training in a department. I'm hoping for Engineering."

"Why so?" I wondered if it was for the same reason as Sheila. Because that's where the country's power lay.

"In the cities, they can engineer anything," he said, eyes bright. "Inventions, and food like you've never seen. Lavender-colored apples. And—and cherry-flavored celery. Whatever you want, printed out of thin air."

"What use are lavender apples to anybody?"

"It's only a diversion," he said. "But I like the idea of inventing something completely new. I've got my sights set on Best Boy at the end, so I can pick my assignment. Which reminds me—I'm grateful for the save earlier. Patron Gilbert remembers *everything*."

I examined Edward's smooth brown face, his deep eyes. Was he already reformed, or were there still parts inside of him that wrestled? From the corner of my eye, I caught sight of Matron Maureen. The matrons always watched us, but she was doing more than watching. Her eyes stared, taking in my every movement.

I angled toward Edward. "Tell me more about the Pines."

"We do archery, and mathematics—"

"Not what you do there. *Why* you're there," I said, keeping the movements of my mouth small. Matron Maureen's gaze was a hot stamp on my face. I flicked my eyes to the other boys sprinkled across the lawn. "Why any of you are there."

His forehead furrowed deeper. "Everybody knows that. To help the country."

"Yes. But it's not for another reason too?" I asked.

Edward blinked rapidly, his flush returning.

"Forget it," I said. Maybe they hadn't figured it out.

And then Edward leaned forward and spoke. "There was a boy—"

he began, checking to see no patrons were nearby. "A boy named—named Danny. The more time passed, the more certain Danny grew that something wasn't . . . right about the Pines. He was convinced there was something ugly hidden under the surface of the place. He wouldn't tell me what he suspected until he had proof. He needed to break into the patrons' quarters."

I leaned forward. "How? It must be locked."

"I don't know how Danny did it, but he said it was easy," Edward whispered. "He said, 'We have the key.'"

We have the key. What could that mean?

"Danny was always bothered by how strangely easy the patrons made it to break the rules," he said. "'Give us the rope to hang ourselves,' he'd say."

My mind stuttered with confusion. Apart from Margot, nobody had ever been punished in the Meadows. "What happened?" I asked.

Edward glanced around again before settling his eyes on me. "He begged me to come with him to the patrons' quarters, but I—I was scared." A pinch formed between Edward's eyes, a grief he was not yet expert at concealing. "Danny must've found something, because the next day, he was gone. The patrons said he was transferred." Edward's mouth twitched, the faintest sketch of a frown.

"You never saw him again?"

Edward shook his head. "So, word of advice. Be careful. Whatever's going on, we're not supposed to know. Even if they might let us."

My heart thundered. What had the boy—Danny—found? And if it was such a secret, why had the patrons made it so easy to find? An image came to mind. A worm wriggling on a hook. A fish opening its mouth. Inside the pale noodle of its brain, no awareness of the concept *bait*.

CHAPTER 20

I waited for the others to figure it out. Waited and waited. In classes: the managing of our bodies, the continued clipping away of anything unfeminine, the sound of our voices lowered as though by a dial, more each day. But like the question of where we were, I watched the others' eyes skip off the evidence like stones off water.

Between Sheila and me, the air seemed heavy—in our shared glances, in the growing weight of what we knew—until I almost couldn't stand it any longer. "When are they going to figure it out?" I whispered to her during an assembly, Matron Sybil's voice a pleasant drone in the background.

"If they don't soon, I might burst," she said. "They can't be that stupid."

"Maybe not stupid." No, it wasn't stupidity to turn eyes away from something too terrible to consider. For weeks, the truth had stuck in my mind like a burr. From the stage, Matron Maureen's gaze rested on my face. She was the sharpest point of all. Had her promises been lies too? Was any of it—*any of it*—true?

From the beginning, the Meadows had contained a kind of magic. It seemed on purpose, the eternal light inside walls, the air still and open the way it is in stories before something wonderful happens—a spell cast, a girl transformed. The matrons, like kindly grandmothers. And Matron

Maureen. The mothers in storybooks always die, but if they lived, they'd be something like her, with her patient smile and promise of oranges even in winter, the feeling like a warming drink filling the entire cavity of my abdomen.

Now I felt cold. What magic there'd once been had burnt off like morning fog.

We all sat together in the common room that night, around the time of the midsummer festival in our second year. Marina set down a tea service before Betty, Alice, Penelope, and a few others the matrons favored, who formed the straightest stitches, made the lightest soufflés. From these, we had tacitly agreed, the Best Girl would come.

It was my job to make a garland for the midsummer festival. I observed my fingers as though from afar, twining together white flowers and bright green leaves with wire in their veins. At once, it felt absurd, this action, when the Meadows was never washed with the warmth of summer, when time seemed not to matter. When truth didn't either.

"I heard something from a boy at the Pines," I said.

I don't know why I said it—only, with my fingers in fake flowers, it felt important, bringing one piece of truth into the light. I could see a moment later that it was a mistake. Every eye in the room looked at me, even Sheila, who already knew the story.

Marina quirked an eyebrow, steam from her teacup veiling her face. "That was weeks ago. Kept us in suspense long enough?"

I cleared my throat. "One of his friends broke into the patrons' quarters," I said. "He found something. Some sort of secret about the facilities."

"What secret?" Marina asked.

"He didn't say. But I wonder if—if there are things the matrons aren't saying."

I watched these words cross their faces, watched the loops and pulleys of their minds work. Surely one of them would say it. One would have figured it out.

"The only mystery I see," Betty said, lifting a teacup to her mouth, "is how Johanna's dress is always so wrinkled."

Several girls laughed. Johanna, hunched over her needlework, pretended not to hear.

Sheila muttered into my ear, "They're all such idiots, I can hardly take it."

"Maybe they just need more time," I said. Though even I questioned that. We'd waited and waited.

"Alice, why don't you tell them what happened with *your* Pines boy?" Marina prodded.

Beside her, Alice buried her face in her hands. "No," came her muffled reply.

"Alice tried to kiss her boy," Betty said, relishing. "When Matron Gloria saw, she pulled her by her ear and sent her inside. Said the Meadows isn't a place for *fast girls*."

Alice lifted her head from her hands. "Matron Maureen said maybe we'd find our future husbands. How am I to know if I want to marry someone unless I kiss them?"

"You're not getting married *tomorrow*," Marina said. "You'll have to live with a boy for a year before you get married."

Alice looked down. "I didn't know that."

"She's not Best Girl material anymore," Betty declared.

"My money's on you, Betty," Winnie said.

"Betty tripped in Comportment last week," Penelope pointed out.

A flash of anger crossed Betty's face. "I seem to recall you burning through a shirt yesterday. Matron Gloria told you she'd never seen a second year muck up basic ironing."

"That's hardly on the same scale as what Alice did," Marina replied, chuckling.

When I looked at Sheila, she held her face still, somehow resembling a storm cloud, not yet unloosing its hail and rain and fury.

I cleared my throat. "I don't understand why any of that matters," I said. "Mistakes happen to all of us."

Betty scoffed, jamming her glasses farther up the slant of her nose. "Not to be indelicate, Eleanor, but you're hardly in the running for Best Girl, so pardon me if I don't take your opinion to heart."

"Maybe she is," Marina said, smirking. "Maybe Eleanor will surprise us all."

"Or maybe it'll be Johanna," Betty said with a snort. From across the room, Johanna's needle hovered above her embroidery hoop, frozen.

Sheila stood then, the breadth of her dress unfurling like a sail. The eyes of everyone in the room found her. At last, the storm, breaking. "Are you all so brainless?" she said, voice low. "Caring so much about—ironing and dresses and stupid Best Girl."

Marina rolled her eyes. "Not like we have anything else to care about in this place."

"It's just harmless fun, Sheila," Betty said. "I don't know why you act like you're singlehandedly responsible for ensuring the earth still spins."

Sheila set her jaw. "Here you are—*inventing* things to be bothered about, when there's something bigger happening under your noses that you won't even look at."

At once, the room grew quiet. Girls who'd been in their bedrooms stood in their doorways now, watching. The place between Marina's eyebrows pleated. "What are you talking about?"

Sheila took a breath. "The reason we're here."

The air in the common room shifted. Below the surface of each white dress, I sensed muscles clenching, hearts thudding.

"We already know why we're here," Betty said.

"Yes, the algorithm," Alice said.

Sheila nodded. "The algorithm saw *some*thing in us."

The others blinked, watching her. The entire room oriented to Sheila.

"Do you really need me to say it?" she asked.

Nobody spoke, but their need hung there, the truth suspended in air.

"How many of you have kissed a girl?" Sheila asked.

My vision went gauzy white.

"How many of you have thought about it?"

Out in the open, her words fell like a fist. A public exposure felt different than one whispered in twilight. I blinked and saw only snippets of the other girls: a neck prickled with red, a pair of wide eyes, a face grown ghostly pale.

My own veined wrist. *Cat face. Smile face. Holiday tree—*

"That doesn't mean anything," Marina declared. I found her face, a shine of panic in each eye. "You can't know that's why we're here." She blinked rapidly, realizing too late that she'd more or less affirmed the truth.

"What are the odds that we'd all be the same?" Sheila asked. "*All* of us."

"I wondered too," Alice said, her voice small.

Johanna nodded slightly.

Hearing the words cracked something open in the group. A spell cast. Truth now more important than our social alliances. The whole of us, together. It had never happened, and it wouldn't again, not in all our time to come in the Meadows.

"I kissed my best friend," Winnie said, twisting her hands.

"Me too," said another girl.

And another: "She kissed me."

And soon, a chorus, their voices like bells ringing with identical notes.

"I knew it was wrong but I did it anyway."

"To me it felt good. Better than good."

"It felt like nothing. It felt . . . harmless."

"I've kissed no one, but I know I don't want to kiss a boy."

"Me too."

"But I'm going to have to, aren't I?"

Alice bit her lip. "What Matron Sybil said on that first day," she said. "About getting married. I thought right then they'd made a mistake with me."

I followed Marina's eyes, drifting, stunned, across the circle of girls. A moment ago, she would have done anything to protect this secret, nestled behind muscles and ribs, a piece of her she must have imagined would stay buried there for life. Perhaps we all did. And here it was, spread out before us. Twin tears escaped Marina's eyes. "I imagined I was the only one," she said. "The only one in the world."

"You're not the only one," I told her. She looked at me, her expression kaleidoscoping—sadness and shame and relief, sliding from one to the next each second.

Penelope shifted in her seat, touching the end of her braid. "Well, I like boys *and* girls."

"I think I do too," Johanna said, voice hushed. Around the room, several others nodded.

"You've got it easier than the rest of us, then," Marina said, thoughtful. "The idea of being with a boy"—she seemed to stifle a shudder—"it feels wrong, deep in my bones. But you— Isn't that good? You could be happy with a boy."

"They'd still be giving up a part of themselves," I said. "No different from any of us." Sheila's words echoed in my head: *I don't mind it at all, as long as I get to choose.*

"I want to know why the matrons would hide it from us," Alice said.

"They've been lying," Johanna said, her voice wilting. "All this time."

"Matron Maureen—do you think she knows?" Winnie asked.

Concerned glances were passed around the circle. It seemed worse to consider that Matron Maureen might've been behind it too. The betrayal sat like a peach pit in my throat.

"She knows," Sheila pronounced.

Marina nodded in agreement. "She's a matron. She attended a facility."

Penelope stood. "We're here so they can change us. That's it?"

"Maybe—" I said. "Maybe there's more to it. The whole country knows the facilities are for the best and brightest. It can't all be a lie. We'll still get rewarded if we do well here."

Sheila cast me a dubious glance.

Alice chewed her lip. "Maybe this whole thing—maybe they're doing us a kind of favor."

"A favor?" Sheila asked.

"It's not as though we can marry whoever we want," Alice said. "The matrons are doing exactly what they've always promised—preparing us for the real world."

"By making us cut out parts of ourselves," Sheila said sharply.

"Please." Marina shook her head. "Tell me you're not that naïve, Sheila. Do you know what they did to people like us when the Quorum first took power?"

Sheila grimaced. "So we should be grateful they're not shooting us?"

"There's no fighting reality," Marina said. "You can hate me for saying it, but it's the truth. Alice is right. The matrons didn't make the laws. If they're changing us, it's because we *have* to change. Most of us probably figured that out a long time ago."

Sheila sat down, an unfamiliar slackness to her face.

Johanna leaned forward. "The matrons said this sort of thing caused the Turn."

"It's not true," Sheila said. "It was cars and airplanes and—and companies filling the air with ash that almost destroyed the planet. Not us."

"Where'd you hear that?" Marina asked.

Sheila bit back her reply, and I felt certain it was from her father. If true, it must be prohibited information. "I just don't think nature cares about girls kissing girls, or boys kissing boys," Sheila said.

A laugh bounced from Alice's mouth. She held a delicate hand to her lips. "Sorry. It's just—it does seem silly, when you put it that way."

A smile pulled at the corners of Marina's mouth. "Can you imagine?" she asked. "Nature tears the whole world apart because I kissed a girl behind the gym?"

Marina laughed, and Sheila followed, and so did I, laughter passed around the circle, each joining until the room rang with it. Because wasn't it absurd, this suggestion that anybody cared whose mouth mine touched? Who filled my heart? I laughed, and so did the others, until the muscles around my stomach ached and the common room burbled over with the sound of ourselves.

A shout cut the air, loud and ragged.

The laughter silenced at once, like something physical ripped from our lungs. In its place, an eerie quiet. All eyes found Betty. I hadn't noticed her, sitting unusually silent, but now her whole pale face was wrenched as though wrung like a cloth, her wide cheeks stamped with pink flush. That sound—it had come from her.

"There's been a horrible mistake," she rasped, looking around at us.

Marina broke the quiet. "What do you mean, Betty?"

Betty opened her mouth, gulping in air. "I've never even thought of kissing a girl," she said. "It's—it's disgusting. It's *wrong*."

Several girls winced. The air rang with silence.

"I want to get married and—and have children." Betty sounded frantic. Her eyes kept flying up to the eye in the center of the ceiling. "I want to run a home, like my mother. That's all I've ever wanted. Listen to me! There's been a *mistake*."

The room inflated with breath, full of the sweat and energy of thirty teenage girls.

"I suppose it's possible that the algorithm got it wrong," Alice offered.

"It just watches," Marina said, a crook of confusion between her brows. "I don't think it can make mistakes."

"It made one with me," Betty said, cradling her arms in her lap. I'd never told anybody about what I'd seen in my first year—Betty's tortured arm, her reluctant surrender in allowing me to bandage it. I'd held on to the knowledge like a book in another language, to learn one day.

"Betty," I said, soft. "If there's anyone in the world you don't need to hide from, it's us."

Betty's face twisted into a sneer. "Is that so?"

I blinked. "Well, yes."

Betty focused the full intensity of her eyes on me. "What do you suppose will be on your life footage after you die?"

Life footage? Around the circle, the others looked just as confused as I felt. "What do you mean?"

"Didn't your parents tell you what happens when you die?" Betty asked. "The algorithm records our whole lives, and what do you think happens to all that footage? They show it to your family after you die, clips of all the bad things you've done in your life."

Marina snorted. "That sounds made up."

Sheila nodded. "The kind of story they tell children to make them behave."

"It's *not* made up," Betty said, eyes ranging across the girls. "Your life footage is probably already full of horrors. Swearing and fighting. Talking back and—wearing pants and touching yourselves. And—and kissing girls," she said, gulping. "But mine will only show goodness. Mine will be perfect. *That's* how I know I'm not supposed to be here. I'm—better than this."

Sheila had her eyes fixed on Betty. The room seemed to shift toward her, waiting.

"Betty," Sheila said finally. "Do you even know what you want?"

Betty blinked at her. "I think I'd know better than anyone."

"Maybe. Or—or is it that you saw nothing but men and women your whole life? Is it just that your life's purpose is to please? Please the matrons, please your mother and father, please the algorithm even. Do what's expected of you, so much that you never even get a glimpse of what *you* want?" Sheila was quiet a moment. "Betty, do you know who you are?"

Sheila's words, true and hard, sunk into Betty, whose breath left her in a wheeze. Her face filled with heat, the triangles of skin beneath each eye becoming dappled pink.

"I know I am *not*," Betty pronounced, voice shaking, "like you."

CHAPTER 21

Nobody slept that night. The air was full of the rustling of sheets, fitful creaking of beds, the quiet shuffling of tears. I found myself standing and leaving the dormitory, not even pausing to tell Sheila where I was headed because I hardly knew, until I was on the lawn in front of the matrons' quarters. It was smaller than the main building, and off limits to us. My fingertips glided over the smooth surface of the opaque glass door. The red glowing dot of a retina scanner studded the doorframe. *We have the key.* That's what that boy Danny had said. They made it easy to break the rules. Could it really be *this* easy? I held a finger out, and the light made a red circle on my fingertip.

At the sight, a chord of terror struck me. What was I thinking? That boy was sent away for breaking into the patrons' quarters. Even if I managed to get inside, what would I look for? I turned around, shaking myself, and strode across the grass.

"Eleanor?" Matron Maureen's voice was soft. "What are you doing out of bed?" She stood in the doorway of the matrons' quarters, still in her pleated matron dress.

When I spoke, the sound came soft, hardly more than the idea of words. "You lied," I said.

Matron Maureen blinked, stepping forward. "Eleanor?"

"You lied to all of us."

Matron Maureen held her lips together, drawing a slow breath through her nose. My stomach clenched. What happened to girls who disrespected matrons? A simple reprimand? Or would she pull me by the ear to Matron Sybil's office? Would I disappear like Margot?

Matron Maureen came toward me across the lawn and said, "Take a walk with me," her white shape like a lonely boat setting off to sea. I no longer knew how to feel about Matron Maureen, but I still felt pulled to follow her. "I'll never get tired of this view," she said at the lawn's edge, blooms stretching to the horizon. "I think this must be the prettiest facility of them all."

I barely heard her. My ears were rushing with ocean-sound. "What was yours called?"

"The Redwoods," she said, smiling. "Matrons practically identical to these, same white buildings, and the tallest trees you've ever seen. Like being inside some ancient cathedral, with giant pillars and a ceiling of green boughs."

I felt myself frown. "And—they taught you to change yourself?"

She considered this. "They did. I suppose you must have questions about that."

All along, Matron Maureen had known what the Meadows was. It was as though someone had turned the lights on inside all my memories from the past two years, making visible what wasn't. Our conversation about June, her expression of shock and distress. Was it a performance—with no other goal than to hurt me?

I'd never had much use for anger. With my mother, anger changed nothing, only made her harden more, sealed shut like an oyster. But now, it hung on the edge of my mind, waiting like a coat that I could slide on if I wanted.

"When you showed me that video—of me and June," I said, voice trembling. "You seemed so . . . disappointed. And surprised. But you hadn't discovered some awful secret. You knew—before we even met. You *knew*."

Matron Maureen's brows drew together, a delicate hand moving to her breastbone. "I *was* surprised. And I was disappointed."

"Why?" I demanded, my voice filling with heat.

Matron Maureen's eyes flitted around the darkened field. "The algorithm often only observes potential. We catch most of you before you act on anything. But you—well, I had an idea of who you were, and that video threw it all into doubt. I wouldn't have guessed you'd been quite so . . . so unashamed."

My body trembled with a cold energy. Before the Meadows, I would've thought being without shame a good thing.

"Eleanor, I should ask—have you told the others?"

I watched her, noticed now the nervous set of her jaw. And a new feeling rose in me. Was this what power felt like—having knowledge someone else didn't? Even if the matrons had watched us through the eye in the common room, they only saw the group of us talking, hardly different from a normal night.

"No," I lied. "Nobody else knows except Sheila and me."

Matron Maureen's eyes latched onto mine. "Then, Eleanor, for everyone's benefit, I hope you'll allow them to come to the truth on their own."

"Why?"

"Everyone is on a journey here," she said. "Some more precarious than others. You wouldn't want to be responsible for someone . . ." She sighed. "Slipping from their path, would you?"

I squinted. "Why wouldn't you just tell us the truth from the beginning?"

"Imagine how that would've gone," Matron Maureen said, smiling. "You sweet girls in your white dresses. With all your hope and wonder. The truth would've been overwhelming. No, it was decided long ago that the nature of the mission should be meted out slowly, so you could digest it better, come to it on your own."

"But why not tell *me*? That day with the video."

"I wanted to, Eleanor. But we're under strict orders to allow you to acclimatize to the truth on your own," she said. "Telling would've derailed your progress. You might've been transferred elsewhere."

I looked up at her. I hadn't considered this. "Really?"

She nodded, putting a hand on my shoulder. "Eleanor, I don't judge you. Anything you did in that video, I did worse at your age. My own mother went to great lengths to set me on the right path. It's how I know anyone can change. It's why I want so badly to help you."

My own mother, she'd said. A space in my chest fluttered, a space I could see now was the exact shape of a mother, a shape that Matron Maureen fit inside of easily. A glance from my own mother could drop the temperature in the room. And here was Matron Maureen with her warmth, her compassion that seemed to fill the air until it was all there was left to breathe.

She ducked her head, looking me in the eye. "This—this *part* of you isn't *all* of you. You are good, Eleanor. I saw that the moment you stepped through those doors."

"You did?"

She nodded, smiling.

I studied the dim sky, threaded with the frayed black lines of clouds. My forehead still creased, my mouth still hunched in a frown, but at some point, the anger had fallen off my shoulders and crumpled to the ground. "Then why do you want me to become—someone I'm not?"

"Oh, Eleanor," she said. "I only want you to become better. If you have a disease and we gave you medicine, are we trying to change you?" She shook her head. "We're trying to *heal* you. Because we care about you. Because we love you. Because you are worth saving."

There was a choking in my throat, a hot gush of tears. My thoughts felt wrenched in opposite directions. They didn't want to change me—

only to heal me? But also, in my mind, Sheila's voice responded: *There is nothing to heal. You are good just as you are.*

The next morning, Matron Sybil stood beneath the white vaulted ceiling of the auditorium, hands clasped. Golden light doused her from a window above.

"What clever girls you are. It seems you have puzzled it out."

I looked around, confused. Within each velvet seat, a girl sat, bracing. We'd woken to Matron Gloria announcing that classes had been canceled for today. The discussion in the common room the night before burned like an ember in my stomach. It now felt horribly brazen—we'd dislodged their secret and held it out to everyone, like the feather we'd found in our first year.

"You've learned the truth, and ahead of schedule," Matron Sybil said, beaming. "Just this morning, I was chatting with the head matron of the Grove, and her girls still hadn't caught on. You are a credit to us, my dears, and to your country."

Sheila passed me a disturbed look. Around the auditorium, girls exchanged confused glances. My thoughts tumbled together. This was how Matron Sybil responded to the discovery of their secret? The calm—like Matron Maureen's reaction the previous night—was somehow worse than punishment. Behind her, the other matrons sat in a row on the stage, smiling blandly.

And how—*how* had the matrons learned what we'd discussed? There were no ears in the common room, or anywhere in the Meadows. I searched the rows of girls before me. Had one of them told?

"*Betty*," Sheila whispered into my ear. I nodded. Of course it was Betty. And Matron Maureen would know I'd lied.

"You must have so many questions," Matron Sybil said. "Normally, this subject is one we don't speak of in polite society. The unspeakable crime against nature."

My vision tunneled. I'd never had a word for us, only these vague descriptors. The charged silence around who I was—I was a fact too horrible to name.

"The algorithm searched for specific parameters," she continued. "Inversions of gender. Unnatural attractions. You were so young when selected, perhaps you weren't even aware of this defect, though it may have been visible to those closest to you. And it was decidedly clear to the algorithm."

Betty made a sound—not quite words. The tips of her ears had reddened. Her wide eyes desperate and defiant.

Matron Sybil peered down at her with gentle understanding. And in that look—I knew. She had done this before. So many times.

"I can appreciate that this must be jarring for you," she said, "if you haven't yet accepted the truth about yourself. But, my dears, accepting it is the first step toward fixing it."

Betty's hand flailed in the air. "But isn't it possible the algorithm got it wrong?" she asked, voice thin. Her eyes bounced from Matron Sybil to the eye nestled like a black jewel in the arch above the stage.

"The algorithm knows all," Matron Sybil spoke. "It notices what causes the capillaries in your cheeks to warm. What makes your heart race. It notices where your eyes rest when you think nobody is looking. *It* knows you, even if *you* may not have the full understanding of yourself yet. It's amazing, the ways we can lie to ourselves."

Matron Sybil spoke to Betty, but her words sunk into me like slow bullets. There was no hiding, not even in your own mind. My sight flickered over the room. Matron Maureen caught my eye, smiling her mischievous smile. The truth of the Meadows—it had been nestled inside that smile, all this time. I'd lied to her last night, but she'd lied all along.

I leaned into Sheila. "Do you think the algorithm was wrong—about Betty?"

"No," Sheila muttered, decisive. "I doubt Betty's ever listened to her own thoughts for longer than a second."

I sat with this. If held too long, some thoughts burned like hot coals. Better to drop them, to kick them away. Better to ignore them entirely. "They must be scary."

"What are?" Sheila asked.

"Her thoughts," I whispered, assembling the idea as I spoke it. "If she can't stand to hear them, I wonder what they say. I wonder what's inside her mind that makes her so afraid."

A wrinkle formed between Sheila's eyes, her mouth rounded.

"But do not despair," Matron Sybil was saying. "What's gone wrong can be rectified."

"So, we're not the best and brightest," Marina called out.

"Of course you are," said Matron Sybil, surprised. "You can still go on to have wonderful lives. Why, my own daughter attended a facility and is living a very productive life."

These words, something like a balm, soothing me, warming my blood. Could it really be like Matron Maureen said? There was one thing wrong with us—just one—and it could be healed?

"That is why we have invited you here," Matron Sybil continued. "Obviously, this unmentionable vice is a threat to the stability of our nation. After the Turn, the Quorum grappled with the right course for those like you. Throughout history, societies placed boundaries around people who were a threat. Lepers. Heretics. Witches. Drive out the evil to keep the whole community safe. And that's effective—to a point. The difference is that the Quorum doesn't see *you* as the evil. The evil is *within* you, and we believe it can be cured." Matron Sybil gestured behind her. "Your matrons are working from a specialized curriculum, and already, it's effective. These are very different young women before me from those who entered just two years ago."

Though Matron Sybil delivered this speech breezily, my stomach tightened—tight, tighter—lungs and ribs and heart held in the grip of a giant hand.

Sheila raised her arm into the air. "Why did you need to lie?"

Matron Sybil smiled warmly. "*Lie*—such an ugly word. We merely . . . elided the truth. I assure you, it's entirely for your protection. The majority of the outside world only knows about the facilities what we say on the dispatches: They are finishing schools for the best and the brightest. If we advertised their true purpose, integrating into society would be impossible. The population of our great nation being what it is, we need each of you to have the best chance at a productive life."

Sheila's mouth formed a frown, momentarily silenced.

"I see you are not convinced," Matron Sybil said. "Let us borrow a lesson from nature. Not all of you would have seen a butterfly before. They're rare now, but once they flew in every garden in the country. Butterflies have the most remarkable nature. When it's time to become something new, they build a chrysalis and allow their bodies to dissolve. They erase themselves in the pursuit of transformation."

Matron Sybil regarded us seriously. "That process requires complete trust. Trust that by submitting to the undoing of your past selves, you will emerge the most beautiful creatures our nation has yet seen."

I scanned the room. Everyone watched, absorbed by Matron Sybil's words.

"My dears, this is my favorite speech to make," Matron Sybil said, opening her arms. "You're about to embark on a thrilling new chapter in your time here. If you commit to reforming, when you leave, you'll begin life anew, as though reborn. So keep looking, my dears. Keep asking questions. Keep digging deep into all that the Meadows has to offer. And as a reward for clearing this important hurdle, you'll be awarded a special opportunity—a screen conversation with your families."

Gasps broke out across the room, white-toothed smiles switched on like light bulbs. We hadn't been allowed to speak to our families since we left home. I looked over at Sheila. She appeared suddenly younger, her eyes round and filled with longing.

"First," Matron Sybil said, "a simple formality. You must declare that you are willing to take on what we are teaching you here. You are willing to reform." She turned toward Betty, sitting in the front row. "Betty, are you willing to continue on the path to reform?"

"Yes," Betty declared, nodding so seriously, her glasses slipped down her nose.

And in that *yes*, and in Matron Sybil's smile, the tide began to shift. Perhaps last night it would've been different, but now, in the sunlight, under the gaze of the matrons, in the real world where rules mattered— Last night, one question had remained unspoken: What now? Confront the matrons, demand to leave, to go home? They'd never agree. Stage a mutiny and overpower the matrons? They'd only call in peacekeepers.

I should've anticipated it. What most girls would choose: To forget.

The magic was gone. But whatever magic held the Meadows together wasn't in the air, or the light, or the matrons. It was in us, carried from our towns and villages, carried inside our hearts that questioned whether we could truly be good. That magic was diminished now. But we could choose to breathe it back to life. To believe in it still.

"Marina, are you willing to continue on the path to reform?"

Marina took a bracing breath. "Yes."

Matron Sybil smiled so the whole white fleshiness of her face gathered at her cheeks. Gradually, she touched her blue gaze on every girl, and each replied, "Yes."

"What will you say?" Sheila whispered, a tinge of panic in her voice. Matron Sybil was speaking to girls only a few seats away.

My mouth had gone dry. I hadn't told Sheila about meeting Matron

Maureen the night before. I'd never told her about the promise of a homestay—if it was still a promise. And now there was no way to explain to Sheila the wrestling in my mind, the desperation to do the right thing, but no idea what that was. I stared at my wrist again. *Cat face. Smile face. Holiday tree. Rainbow.*

"Eleanor?" Matron Sybil asked. "Are you willing to reform?" My eyes clenched closed. I couldn't fathom what I'd even talk to my mother about. But saying no—what good would it do? We couldn't fight this. The matrons were changing us, yes, but only in the way the world demanded.

"Eleanor," Sheila whispered from beside me. I could see the clarity in her eyes.

"Eleanor?" Matron Sybil repeated. My gaze was pulled to the stage, where the matrons sat. Matron Maureen nodded slightly, smiling. And in that smile, the future she offered was confirmed: dinners under the greenhouse roof, the orange tree that made fruit all year long, the chance of belonging somewhere. *You'll always be welcome in Teagarden.*

"Yes," I whispered. And then, louder. "Yes."

Sheila made no sound, but beside me, her presence seemed to radiate.

"Sheila?" Matron Sybil asked. "Are you willing to reform?"

Every face in the auditorium oriented to her. Sheila's gaze found mine. A shine of tears, but there was more than sadness. She was brimming with fury. My stomach clenched, every muscle in me wanting to tear my eyes away.

"No," she pronounced, eyes still on mine.

In my periphery, Matron Sybil only nodded. "Everyone proceeds at their own pace. The rest of you, I'm proud of your choice to march into the next phase of your life."

Sheila finally released my gaze, but I felt no relief. I'd been let go to float inside my own ocean, and I wasn't sure I could swim.

CHAPTER 22

Downtown. The noisy, teeming heart of the city.

The first time I ventured here, I felt like a seedpod blown in on the wind, buffeted by the rush of traffic, men in shining shoes, their sharp steps ricocheting around a canyon of the tallest buildings I'd ever seen. But I've grown to appreciate downtown, the way buildings reveal who they were before the Turn. A large glass-fronted former shopping center now houses the Department of Prisons, its sign a neon scrawl high on the side. A steepled brick building that must have been a church transformed into a center for commerce, consumers emerging with white plasticore shopping boxes pulled behind them on light metal trolleys. A feeling grows in me today, a longing to have seen them as they were, their original purpose intact.

I've nearly arrived at the Registrar's Office, when I hear a noise—a man's voice, shouting. Several pedestrians stop, tracing the noise to the top of the city wall, a white concrete structure just visible through buildings. There, a man stands, unfurling a sheet painted with a red circle. When he shouts, I strain to catch the words—almost grasping them—before a white-clad peacekeeper wrestles the man away from the edge. The sheet drops, flailing through the air.

We have always been here. Those, the words the man shouted.

This sort of tiny rebellion pops up from time to time, quashed just as

quickly. Foot traffic resumes, and wherever the sheet landed, a maintenance worker will already be disposing of it. Still, the words thrum alongside my heartbeat as I walk.

We have always been here.

What do they hope to accomplish, these subversives? But then, what
do I? Changing reports. Delaying the inevitable. I'm doing my best for
them. Aren't I? My mind tries to sidestep to my adjudications from yesterday. A girl who sits all day at a computer, one typist inside rows and
rows of other typists. There, she hums a song that her mother sang, that
her ancestors sang long ago, in fields where they were brought without
consent, hands made raw by the spines of tobacco. She shouldn't be humming at work. She shouldn't be recalling this time Before, this history
that makes the country look bad. She hums anyway.

And another girl, who lies in bed with her boyfriend every night.
When he places a hand on her belly, begins stroking her skin, every
muscle clenches. She has made the most of him, his stories, his terrible
jokes. In many ways, she has grown to enjoy him. But she hates this part.
She hates it.

And a girl who is not a girl, but nobody would believe him. In the
early morning hours, he reports to work at a bakery, and in that flour-
strewn air answers to the name given at birth, though it's harder and
harder each time. On the walk home, he dares to imagine another
name, another life.

And another, fresh from the Arches, who has been assigned as a cleaner
in the house of an important Quorum member and his wife. She's obser-
vant. They didn't consider this when they hired her. The man helped
author the policy on family purity, created places like the Meadows. The
pictures she dusts on the bureau seem factory-made, a perfect family. But
the girl knows a secret. Knows the man meets another man in the pot-
ting shed. Knows the man exits the shed with cheeks the color of ripe

apples. "After I left the Arches, I thought I'd used up my lifetime's worth of anger," she said, eyes blazing.

I stayed up late writing their reports, smoke-screening the truth of them. Keeping them alive. *It's not enough*, Sheila had told me. *It's not enough.*

Sheila stares up at the rounded glass side of the Registrar's Office. "What are we really doing here?" she asks. "I got your note about looking for matches. I'd assumed you'd had a brain injury." She turns to me. "How many fingers am I holding up?"

I push her hand aside, laughing. "I'm fine," I say. I can't tell her I'm following a command written on a green piece of paper. She'd have too many questions, especially for a crowded sidewalk.

Anyway, I didn't have the answer to the most important one: Who left it in my pocket? I've cycled through the possibilities endlessly. Perhaps someone who knows me but is unable to speak out in the open. There's Clark, skillful at obscuring what's inside him. And—there's Sheila. She knew Rose. Maybe she discovered something—information she found when reading Ed's screen at night. I search her face, a serious expression on it now. She catches me and turns on a bright smile.

But wouldn't it make far more sense for this to be some kind of loyalty exercise? For Mrs. Collier herself to have sent the note, to catch me out? To see what I would do once here? Haven't I been tested most of my life, after all?

"You look nice," I tell Sheila. And she does. Her hair is in a neat bun, and her lips are painted in a vibrant shade of red.

Sheila frowns. "Ed asked me to put in a bit more effort when I leave the house," she says. "In case I run into one of his bosses' wives."

I know better than to reveal my real feelings, so I just grit my teeth and say, "Hm."

"Didn't have much of a choice," Sheila adds, and I know she's right. If Ed wanted to, he could report her for not following his guidance. "So, what are we really doing?" she asks again.

I glance around. "I wonder," I say, looking directly at her now, "I wonder if I might learn something here." The street noise would surely drown out any ears, but my blood pumps dangerously, even thinking Rose's name. "What Ed said—no deaths in a facility. I wondered if—"

Sheila brings a hand to her mouth. She lets my intent gather, and then looses a long breath. "That's why?" She tilts her head toward the glass building. "What a rebel you are."

"Learned from the best," I say, smiling,

But Sheila doesn't return the smile. Her face shifts, a line creasing her brow. I notice she's got her hands clamped together, twisting. "Eleanor," she asks. "Is that safe?"

"I'm allowed to look at profiles. My supervisor even encouraged it."

I know I may be walking into a trap. But it's that or walk away. And I can't walk away, not when there's the smallest chance of finding Rose.

"If you say so," Sheila says, glancing around the street, almost as though she's debating whether she should've come. I swallow a swell of confusion.

"You don't have to," I say. Of course I could be endangering her too.

She only shakes her head and moves toward the doors.

"You never know," I say, jostling her lightly with my shoulder as I catch up. "Maybe I'll match with a boy and fall madly in love."

Sheila laughs dryly. "I hope I get a wedding invite."

"Don't be silly," I say, relieved to be joking with her again. "You'll be the maid of honor."

We push through the doors of an enormous glass sphere several stories high, once used as a leisure space for office workers. It now houses the Registrar's Office and the Department of the Family. In addition to helping couples with fertility treatments and counseling pre-married girls in wifely duties, here the government also makes matches.

The din of the city quiets. I arch my neck, taking in the fish-bowl view. Light filters in through the triangular panes of glass high above, and buttoned-up office workers move about importantly inside half-walled offices. From behind a welcome desk, an older woman rises to greet us. "Welcome," she says, her voice warm and creaking. "I'm Mrs. Turner. How may I direct you young ladies?"

I hold out my identification badge, hand shaking slightly. "We're here to look through some profiles."

"Wonderful idea, dear," Mrs. Turner says. "Wise to get a head start on these things."

We hang up our coats behind Mrs. Turner's desk, and she leads us deeper inside the sphere, away from the bustle of offices, toward a row of tall cubicles that resemble dressing rooms, except they're doorless and walled in opaque glass. Only the first cubicle is occupied, by a girl about my age, wearing the blue-striped, sharply ironed garments of a shopgirl. She sits before an oversized screen, a boy's profile visible. My breath catches at the sight of a large, freestanding white doorway beside the screen.

My eyes find Sheila's, her expression wary.

"What's that for?" I ask.

"Never seen a periscope before?" Mrs. Turner replies.

"Never one this . . . large." At the apartment, I still have Sheila's chintzy periscope. Out of something similar, Matron Maureen had once pulled a perfect orange, seemingly from air.

"This model's state-issued," Mrs. Turner says. "Not available for commercial sale. Capable of much more than your typical periscope."

"But they all work the same way, don't they?" Sheila asks, running her eyes across the periscope. "Instead of printing food or clothes, this one conjures a . . . person?"

"That's right." Mrs. Turner nods approvingly.

The shopgirl presses a button, and the boy from her screen materializes inside the white doorway. Not simply his image. An actual boy, life-sized, standing inside a seaside café. The boy and his surroundings look incredibly, astonishingly . . . *real.* "We are pleased to introduce Tucker Cairn," a smooth automated voice declares.

The girl steps through the doorway, and I stifle a gasp, but it's as though she merely entered another room. The boy's about a foot taller than her, and she has to crane her neck to take him in. "Nice to meet you," she says.

"Nice to meet you too," the boy says. "My name's Tucker. What's yours?"

Mrs. Turner places a hand on my arm. "Let's leave them," she whispers. "Best to give privacy for moments like this."

I pull my gaze away and glance, big-eyed, at Sheila. "It's possible to re-create a person?" I ask, looking to Mrs. Turner.

"Oh, no," Mrs. Turner says, leading us past a row of empty cubicles. "That wasn't a person, not like you and me. You can replicate objects, but that was just a stand-in. Might as well be made from plasticore. Enough to give you the general idea, though. I think she'll see that the boy is much too tall for her, but that's only my opinion."

"But—he spoke to her," I say.

Mrs. Turner nods, smiling. "The algorithm re-creates a semblance of a personality. Nothing like the real thing, of course. But when you've been watched and recorded your whole life, it's not difficult to predict answers to basic questions."

I recall the faded taste of crème brûlée. A shiver winds up my spine.

Mrs. Turner points to a cubicle at the end of the row, shielded on three sides by tall, frosted glass. "I'll leave you to it," she says. "These nooks are designed for privacy, but do find me if you need advice. Matchmaking is a skill of mine."

When Mrs. Turner leaves us, Sheila moves to the periscope, running her hands over the slick white frame, almost like she can't help herself. I can see her mind turning, taking it apart.

The screen propped on the smooth surface of a desk asks if I'm interested in male or female matches. I sigh and click *Male*. If someone *is* watching, best to be seen doing what's expected. At least to start.

I let my fingertips flit through the pages of profiles. For a moment, I see Clark's serene face flick by. Beneath his picture, there is a glowing green button with the words *Meet Me*. His term as an adjudicator is nearly done. He must already be eligible for matches.

I navigate back to the main page. Through the transparent dome above, skyscrapers loom, seeming almost to lean in, looking. I exhale a tense breath. "Any sign of Mrs. Turner?"

Sheila ducks her head into the hallway. "All clear." My skin prickles with nervous heat. On the screen, I touch the word *Female*.

Sheila gasps. "Sorry—it's just . . . you're really doing it."

I let out a confused laugh. "That's why I'm here."

Sheila's eyes are wide. I can't read their meaning. Impressed or disapproving.

A new desperation unspools in me like smoke. "Sheila—you don't have to stay." I choke back a rise of emotion. "I just thought—"

Sheila's face twists, a dozen thoughts shifting over her features. "Come on," she says. "Let's find her and get out of here."

I turn back to the screen and scroll through dozens and dozens of pictures. Some I recognize, reformeds I've adjudicated for. They are not marked in any way. A fresh start. At least here.

"No sign of her," Sheila mutters after we've scanned the faces of hundreds of girls. I can sense her getting fidgety. A dull panic thuds through me. Mrs. Turner could check back at any moment. What would she think of me looking at girls?

Rose, where are you?

An alert chirps from my briefcase. "Of course," I say, stifling a groan.

"Adjudication?" Sheila asks.

I pull out my screen, and nod. I've just been assigned a new reformed girl, scheduled for thirty minutes from now. I look back at the screen, but it's no use. I wonder if I'd even recognize Rose. People change in a year. And I might scroll for hours before reaching the end.

I'm standing when Sheila says, "Wait."

She points to the screen, to the tiny symbol of a magnifying glass in an upper corner. Possible, then, to search for a specific person. My muscles are already oriented toward the door, my mind on the street, mapping my way to my new adjudication. But I set my briefcase down and touch the magnifying glass. "Here goes," I say. I don't type Rose's family name, Rosario Gutiérrez. Instead I tap out the letters of her state name.

Rose Walters.

When her picture appears, my breath catches. She looks the same, smiling broadly even in her state identification photo, but the image is grayed.

"'Not eligible for placement,'" Sheila reads, passing me a serious look. This could mean Rose has already been assigned a partner, or, like me, she's in an occupation that postpones her eligibility. Or she's dead. I touch her picture, but the screen beyond shows no relevant details. No height, or occupation. No family information. Nothing. But—there is the pulsing green button saying *Meet Me*.

The doorway stands about a foot taller than my head, obscured by the frosted glass walls, but if anyone rounded the corner, we'd be seen. I glance behind me again, around the side of the wall of my cubicle, and down the hallway. Nobody in sight. Even the shopgirl from earlier seems to have left.

"This is a bad idea," I whisper, looking at Sheila.

For a moment, she seems to mull this over. "I'll keep watch," she says. My fingers hover over the screen. After a breath, I touch the button.

"We are pleased to introduce Rose Walters," the smooth voice declares.

I cringe at the sound, hoping it wasn't audible at the desk where Mrs. Turner sits. The hollow frame of the periscope flickers to life with a momentary buzzing, like someone's shaken a hive of bees. Inside the doorway, Rose appears, her short curls ruffled by an invisible breeze. She stands inside an environment of rolling green hills and sparkling sky. Sheila's face stretches in surprise. Rose is here, and she looks *real*.

I hesitate. I'm all but certainly being recorded. Prior to this point, I could explain away any of my behavior, could claim that searching for Rose's name was merely idle curiosity. But stepping into that doorway, I'd be stepping onto a dangerous path.

I take a breath, and walk through.

My hair is lifted by the soft wind of the plains. The long green grass stretches to the horizon, rolling in undulating waves, and the air smells vibrant and clean. I imagine I could have customized this environment like that shopgirl had. A dance hall or a moonlit river. This must be the default.

Rose squints a little from the brightness. "Nice to meet you," she says, leveling her dark eyes at me. My mouth falls open. The air siphons from my lungs. *Rose.*

"You'll catch flies that way," Rose says, eyebrow arching.

I take a tentative step toward her. "Rose?"

"That's me." I examine her closely, the slight frown at the corners of her mouth, long eyelashes beneath heavy brows. The careful arrangement of features, both soft and hard. The algorithm has even captured her delivery, always skirting the edge of a laugh.

"Are—are you alive?"

"Alive and kicking," she says. "What else would I be?"

Tears fall from my eyes, missing my cheeks and hitting the ground. I reach for her hand, and she fits hers inside mine, as though to shake it, but I don't let go. Her fingers feel smooth but tepid, like touching something not alive. In this moment, I don't care that she's not real. "Rose, I—I have so much to tell you."

"Speak away, darling," she says. "I'm all ears."

"I'm sorry," I say, words tumbling from my mouth. "Sorry for—for everything."

"Consider it forgiven," she says. "Now, who is it that I have the pleasure of meeting?"

I blink rapidly and glance behind me. The periscope protrudes from the earth like a freestanding door frame and inside, a view into the cubicle where Sheila stands, chewing her lip, a crease of nervousness between her eyes. "I—I'm Eleanor," I tell Rose. Surely she knows me. "From the Meadows."

"Well, Eleanor from the Meadows, you've got the prettiest eyes I've ever seen."

I take a slow breath. "Do you—do you not know me?"

"Not yet," she says. "But I'd like to."

My heart seizes. "They told me—told me you died."

"Don't believe everything you hear."

I scan her face. Each of Rose's replies sounds a little disjointed. Canned. And there's a detached quality in her eyes. It's just as Mrs. Turner said—like talking to someone made of plasticore.

I let go of her hand. "Where are you now, Rose?"

"Why do you wanna know that?" she asks, teasing, her eyebrows lifting upward.

"I need to see you," I say, urgent. "Where are you?"

"I'm right here, with you."

"But where is the *real* Rose?"

"Why do you wanna know that?" she asks again, in the same teasing cadence she used the first time. Rose's face is frozen in a smirk.

Heat creeps through me, my breath growing frantic. "Where is Rose?" I demand.

"Can't tell you that." She leans in close. "Top secret," she says in a stage whisper.

My hands curl into fists, frustrated tears springing to my eyes. "I am an adjudicator of the state," I say. "Under the jurisdiction of the Quorum. You are required to answer my questions. Now, what is your place of residence?"

"Place of residence: 341.43.980." She speaks efficiently, robotically, her voice a dull monotone.

I stumble backward. Have I broken something inside her? "What did you say?"

"Place of residence: 341.43.980."

I try to commit the numbers to memory. "But what does it mean?"

She cocks her head to the side again, eyes sparkling. "Why do you wanna know that?"

CHAPTER 23

They followed us down corridors, twining in our hair, pulling on the tails of our skirts. The *yes*es. For three days, they'd trailed behind us, since Matron Sybil asked, "Are you willing to continue on the path to reform?" and the air had filled with *yes*. And a single, insistent *no*. The loudest of all.

"I hope it was worth it." Sheila stood at the center of the packed common room. The others fixed their gazes to the floor. Soon, we'd each be taken into a classroom with a screen to speak to our families.

"What about everything they did?" Sheila demanded. "I suppose you were all swayed by the idea of becoming beautiful butterflies."

Penelope stood, looking plaintive. "Sheila, you couldn't expect us to say no."

Sheila made an impatient sound. "Don't you think I want to see my family too?" she asked.

Betty scoffed. "Then you should've said yes."

Sheila's face turned to stone. "Haven't you done enough, Betty?"

"Done what?" Betty demanded.

Sheila turned to the group. "Did any of you pause to wonder how the matrons found out what we said last night?" she asked. "Somebody must have told."

"And you think it was me?" Betty asked, outraged.

"You, or someone else," Sheila said. "There are no ears in the Meadows."

"*Or*," Marina spoke up, "they don't need ears to hear us, genius."

The possibility rang in the air. If true, there would be no secrets from the matrons, not inside these walls.

"If they heard," Sheila said. "If they're listening right now, it makes no difference. I'd say it to Matron Sybil herself." She set her jaw. "They lied to us."

When Sheila looked at me, the shame in my chest grew branches, spoking through arteries and veins. "Why did you do it?" she whispered. "Not to call home—I know that's not why."

I shook my head, grasping for an explanation. Not the truth, the many truths I'd kept from her, and the others I'd secreted even from myself—how I longed to be just one thing, for the Meadows girl on the top of the stack to be the only Eleanor, the other versions burned to cinders.

"We need to be strategic, that's all," I muttered at last, tensing under the combined gaze of everyone in the common room. "I—did it to go along."

Sheila studied me. "Then you're worse than any of them. You're—you're—" She cut herself off, shaking her head, but I sensed what word she'd snagged on.

"What am I?"

"Forget it," she said.

I looked at her again, the ticking of my blood slowing, filled only with a deep and deadly desire to hear Sheila say it. "What am I?"

"A coward, Eleanor," she said. "You knew it was wrong."

I closed my eyes, the word sinking into my chest like a slow-moving knife. I heard Sheila stride from the room. In her wake, an itchy quiet fell.

"Sheila has no ground to stand on," Betty said, sniffing. "I think I speak for everybody when I say the cowardly thing was saying no."

I glanced up at her. "Oh, shut up, Betty," I said, and hurried from the room, black shoes clopping on the floor. I ran down the corridor and into the foyer.

"Sheila!" I called. "Wait."

Sheila paused in the open curve of the main entrance, framed by a glowing arc of white wall, the meadow fields behind her. The anger on her face had peeled back to reveal a pulsing sorrow.

"I—still want to be your friend," I said in a rush.

Her eyes pinched. "You think everyone's your friend."

The words hit like a slap. "I want to be *your* friend."

"How can we?" she asked. "When you still do what they say, and all they've done is lie."

"Not about everything," I said, a bulb of panic rising in my throat. "You heard Matron Sybil. We're still the best and brightest."

Sheila's expression filled with pity. "Eleanor, we're just the ones they thought they could change. Why do you think they bring us here so young? They watch to see who will obey. And what do you think they do with the ones who won't?"

My mind touched on Margot, and for the first time questioned if she really had been transferred to a different facility. I'd heard rumors: state prison complexes, forced labor camps. Fear bored through me. But not for myself.

"How many times do I have to tell you before you believe it?" she demanded. "They're lying to you. Whatever defect they imagine is within you is a lie. There's nothing wrong with you. You are kind to everyone. You are good just as you—"

I turned away, wincing.

Sheila's face grew hard. "You don't believe me?"

There was a wrenching inside me, a tearing. "I don't know."

"Would you rather I tell you you're horrible? Is that what you want to hear? That the matrons are right and we have evil inside of us?" Her eyes shone with disbelief.

I shook my head, desperate.

"This is the problem, Eleanor," Sheila gasped. "This has been the problem all along. As much as you say you agree with me, I think a tiny part of you wants to believe that you're some unspeakable evil even the matrons can't name."

I stumbled backward. Did I want it, that part of me that I believed was so bad? Had I coated it with so much pearl I now guarded it like a dragon around its hoard?

"It doesn't make sense to me," Sheila went on. "Why you'd try so hard to see something wrong in you. There's nothing there!"

I rounded on her. "Of course it doesn't make sense to you. Your perfect family. You've got proof that you're good. But I—" I broke off.

"Your own parents didn't love you, so how could you be lovable?" she demanded.

"And?"

"You are my best friend, Eleanor," she said, quiet. "But I can't do the work of convincing you you're worth something. You have to do that for yourself."

"You don't understand—" I started.

"I understand a lot," she said. "I understand that I'm completely alone here."

The hurt in her face pierced me, a quick clean jerk through ventricle and muscle. "You came here because you had dreams," I said. "The only way is to play their game."

"I don't want to play games." Her voice was tired.

"*No,*" I cried, stamping the words in the air. "You're smarter than that, Sheila. They'll send you away. Don't you see? Don't let them. *Please.*"

Sheila's eyes gleamed with tears. "What do you want me to do, Elea-

nor?" she asked. "Change myself? Flip over all my cells until I'm someone I'm not?"

"If it keeps you alive—" I said, swiping at my wet face. "If it keeps you
here with me—"

"I exist for more than being your friend," she said. "I won't become
my parents' worst fear. I won't let this place change me."

"Then don't change. Just . . ." I lowered my voice. "Stand down. Have
your doubts, but—but keep them quiet. For now. Till we get out."

Sheila shook her head. "I won't," she said. "I *can't*. And you shouldn't
ask me to."

I glanced around the foyer. This room—the beginning of Sheila
and me, a hand slipped inside a hand. "They sent Margot away," I said.
"Whatever you believe about the matrons, doesn't that make you even a
little bit afraid of them? Of what they can do?"

"Let them," she said, voice airy but with an edge of despair.

"Sheila, please—" I started, but she was already striding from the
foyer, through the entrance, stark in her dress against the sea of purple.

I looked down at my fingers. They were trembling. I hadn't realized.
Hadn't realized I even had a body. Now that I had, I didn't know how I
would tolerate it. I stood, gaping at my limbs, these white-clad things I
was tethered to, this body full of pain.

"Eleanor?" a tentative voice called from behind me. Matron Maureen.
"I'm afraid I have some bad news."

I hurriedly scrubbed the tears from my cheeks. "Yes, matron?"

"We contacted your mother about speaking with you."

"Oh?" I asked.

"We had a difficult time getting in touch," she said. "We sent a
direct line to her screen, but it seemed the cable had been disconnected. We had to contact the local peacekeepers about reestablishing
her connection."

My heart fumbled in my chest. Peacekeepers at my mother's doorstep, because of me.

"We finally got in touch," Matron Maureen said. "And, I'm sorry to say, she declined."

"Declined?" A slow fist sunk into my diaphragm. "She—she didn't want to speak to me?"

Matron Maureen's eyes turned down, concern printed across her face. "Matron Sybil was going to tell you, but I thought it might be better coming from me."

I nodded, my vision pulling in and out of focus. I hadn't looked forward to the call. Between the two of us, there'd rarely been anything to say. But now I understood that a part of me had wanted to see her. For her to see me. "She was stuck with me for years," I said. "It makes sense that she . . ." A black feeling pooled in my gut. *Of course she wouldn't want to see you. Of course. Just look at yourself. Look at who you are.* I conjured the thoughts and like honey, devoured them. My mind, searching now for pain, touched on Sheila. What a waste, she'd think. To say yes and not even get the reward.

"Are you feeling okay, Eleanor?" Matron Maureen asked.

My hands were gripping my middle, dress caught in my fists. "My stomach hurts sometimes."

"We have medication for that."

"I have a feeling it wouldn't help."

"Why not?"

I jammed my eyes shut. "Sometimes," I whispered. "Sometimes, I feel like an apple that's gone bad. Like if you cut me open, inside I'd be black from rot."

I expected the warmth of Matron Maureen's hand on my shoulder, consoling, reassuring. But when I opened my eyes, I saw that her mouth was tweaked in a strange smile. Sympathetic or satisfied, impossible to tell.

Just then, the gravel crunch and plume of dust that meant a shuttle approaching. "Here already!" Matron Maureen said. "I'm sorry, Eleanor. I must get ready to go."

I looked up at her, a strange punch in my chest at the idea. I felt confused by it. "You're leaving?"

She waved at the shuttle driver, who pulled up beside the main building. "Just a quick trip to the city. Meadows business." And then her eyes focused on me closely. "Something is bothering you, Eleanor. You know you can tell me anything."

I looked out at the violet fields. "Sheila," I said. "I let her down."

Matron Maureen smiled. "Our friends are important. But only you can know what's right for you, Eleanor."

And what is that? I wanted to ask.

"I'm afraid of what will happen to her." I swallowed the bile taste of fear. "I worry that, if she doesn't change, she'll be sent away."

Matron Maureen shrugged. "You're not wrong."

I searched her face, her smile so mild, it said nothing. "She'll be transferred?"

"Perhaps," she said. "But don't fret. That would only happen if we're sent a new girl. And we haven't given up on Sheila. The matrons have a plan for each one of you."

I found that I was pressing my teeth together so tightly, I feared they'd splinter. "Do you have a plan for me?"

Matron Maureen grinned. "Of course."

I wanted to ask more, but I had a sense, far in the back of my mind, that this conversation was part of that plan. And that every interaction with Matron Maureen had been, all along.

CHAPTER 24

The truth of the Meadows settled around us like snow.

"Everything should feel different," Johanna said one morning, about a week after Matron Sybil's speech. I sat beside her on the grass, comfortable near her gentle quiet. "But it's like any other day." Several groups were scattered around the lawn. Matron Maureen had challenged some girls to a game of charades, all of them laughing uproariously.

"I thought something would change too," I agreed.

There had been a moment, the night we spoke the truth, when we were almost unified. But the matrons, throwing light on the secret, had removed its power, and the girls had moved on, accepting it as just another part of the Meadows. Like you accept fog that doesn't make sense. Like you accept a crown-shaped cloud in the same place every day. Like you accept a lot of things.

Some things had changed, though. Sleep had never been easy in the Meadows, but now it became a fleeting thing, a wild hare slipping my grasp, caught only in the early morning. During the day, time passed like sleepwalking. At night, while the others slept, I roamed. Around the grounds, though classrooms. Nobody ever found me. I always went alone. Asking Sheila to walk the lawn like we had in the beginning felt impossible.

The bonds of our friendship had stretched to nearly breaking, and

I sensed one swift tug would snap them altogether. We still loved each other, still needed each other, still rolled our eyes at Betty. But Sheila and I moved around each other tentatively.

One thing I noticed on my nighttime excursions—Matron Maureen left more and more often. Trips to the city. *Meadows business*, she'd called it. I stood in the flowers and wondered, every time I saw her shuttle disappear over the horizon, what pulled her away.

One night, early in year three, I stepped past darkened classrooms, snatches of windows, violet ovals the color of sky. Past the dormitory where, branching from the common room, more than a dozen bedrooms held the girls I'd grown up with, their quiet murmurings, their breath in sleep.

In the foyer, the memory of footsteps shuffling. New dresses sweeping the floor. Little girls filing inside. Little Eleanor, so small. Small, all of us. The chatter of our tiny voices. The peeping of our tiny dreams. *Best. Brightest*. And ahead of us, years learning to make a perfect stitch, learning to unstitch myself from my body.

All leading to the final lesson: a knowledge that something large and integral had to die in order to go on living.

It wasn't this that made me run away. Or Sheila—the bruise I'd left on her heart, the bruise she'd left on mine.

It wasn't what Matron Maureen had said—a plan for all of us.

It wasn't even the possibility that the matrons were listening, that they had been all along, and that I'd never—not since I first walked in here—had the upper hand.

It was that the fragile equilibrium of the Meadows felt broken. I couldn't decide how I felt. About Sheila, about Matron Maureen, about the Meadows. I could ignore it before. Take only what I needed from this place and leave the rest. But the Meadows would no longer allow us to buy in partway.

That night, I found myself outside. I started walking. And walking. And walking. Down the white dusty road where the shuttles had driven that first day. Where Matron Maureen's shuttle had roared out of sight earlier this evening. Under the strange brick archway where I'd found my frog. I walked till my calves ached. Hours and hours. Through pale twilight that marked the entire night. I walked farther than I'd ever gone.

Until, suddenly, the road ended. Cut off cleanly, like a ribbon between scissors. Where the road should've been, a thatch of purple flowers jutted up. I searched them, parted them, imagining maybe the road had simply been overgrown. I drew my eyes over more flowers, and more, all the way to the horizon.

My heart knocked against my ribs, cold dread filling me. There was no road. How had we arrived here? This, the only way in or out. How had Matron Maureen's shuttle left this place? The questions, too strange, too heavy, stacked up around me. I sat on the ground, my dress splayed in a circle.

On the horizon, the fog rolled in. Slow-moving, it unfurled its pearly carpet. I thought about outrunning it back to the Meadows, but I couldn't move. The closer it got, the greater my horror at the way it propelled itself, a great white ocean. I closed my eyes, waiting for it to swallow me.

But I felt nothing. I opened my eyes and found myself inside a cloud. Depthless. I was alone in it. Completely alone. My breath hitched. Every muscle shivered. At once, I was gripped by a feeling of wanting my mother. Stella, or my birth mother, I didn't know.

How could I want Stella? Always conflicted about loving me, as though eternally standing before the linen bundle on her doorstep, still making up her mind about whether to pick me up or leave me to the cold.

And how could I want my birth mother? Who chose to place my

squirming body on the doorstep of a stranger in earshot of the scream-ing sea?

They were not good. I wanted them. Both could be true.

A tight, hot knot burned in my gut.

I stayed in the fog all night, head cradled in the crook of my arm. I dreamed that this would be the way someone might hold me one day, in our warm bed, grown up. A man, it would have to be. A boyfriend, a husband. A dull dread shook me awake. Why did I always forget that my future would never be what I wanted?

Pale sun hit my face, the fog gone. I rose from the flowers, knuck-led the sleep from my eyes. I felt my cheeks, printed with flower-shaped marks. Dusted myself off. Marched back to the school.

On the edge of the grounds, I paused. I couldn't go in. Not ready to be contained within those eggshell buildings again.

I climbed into the yew tree and watched as the day unfolded. Mid-morning, the girls came outside to lounge on the grass. Propped their jaws up on the meat of their hands, the chatter of their voices just out of range. I would never see them again, I realized, when we left this place in less than two years. Would I miss them? Certainly Sheila, and Johanna. The rest I thought, with a twist in my heart, were already preparing for bridedom, for lace dresses, for lives of easy acquiescence, passing away their power.

Would I miss this place? I didn't know what awaited me outside, but I knew the Meadows. I had mapped the precise ways it could hurt me. There was safety in that knowledge.

The Meadows was not good. I wanted it. Both could be true.

It was past dinnertime again. I should have been inside, pulling on my nightdress. I debated with myself—Stay? Return?—when a plume of dust erupted over the horizon.

A shuttle, black and shining, appeared on the road, coming to a stop before the main building. The noise of the doors opening sliced the night air. Matron Sybil and Matron Gloria emerged by the main entrance.

And, suddenly, a girl. Her face, an angry fist. Her black coat wet, zippered. Her hair, cut short. The matrons ushered her inside.

She couldn't have seen me. The yew tree at night was backlit by the odd sky, only a black skeleton on the horizon. But I could swear, while she tried to wrench her arms away, when she looked back, her eyes found me, saw me, and smiled.

CHAPTER 25

Something flickers alive in my body and I burst out the glass doors of the Registrar's Office, back into the torrent of the city. There's shaking in my limbs. Uncontrollable like the panic, but not like that at all. *Joy*. A bolt of lightning through every nerve.

Rose is alive. *Alive*. She has a place of residence. Which means I can find her. See her. Speak to her. Touch her. Means I can peel off the shame for how things ended between us.

The air is cold but I hardly feel it, my body alive and hot as a motor.

You find her, Eleanor, I think. *Find her.*

I stuff my hands into my pockets, and abruptly my focus funnels to my fingertips. A slip of crisp paper. It will be green, I know before looking, penned with precise block letters. Guarding it inside my hand, I read the note.

You'll find her behind a door.

My heart thuds low and foreboding. *A door*. I cast my eyes around, but pedestrians simply pass by, fish fixed on their course downstream.

Sheila grabs my arm. "Is that paper?" she hisses.

I throw the note into a sewer drain. "Follow me."

Sheila sweeps her eyes over the underbelly of the stone bridge, the black-painted door. The one place I know where we can speak without being overheard, where we can simply be Sheila and Eleanor again. Where I can ask her for something that, even last week, even a half hour ago, I wouldn't have dared.

"Don't you have an adjudication to be at?" Sheila asks.

"It can wait a few minutes," I tell her. "We won't be overheard here."

"What is this place?" she asks.

"A dead zone," I say, reminded of the sanctuary building in the Cove, that close, cool stone chamber swirling with whispers from the Wanting Hat. Behind us, it's the river that whispers, its tiny whitecaps punching the air.

"Do you bring all your reformeds here?" she asks. It sounds like a joke, but I know it's not.

"Just the ones I'm friends with."

"You think everyone's your friend," Sheila says, smiling a little sadly.

Sheila's warm brown eyes meet mine. And for a moment, we're back there. In that sweet-smelling place. With the people we left behind.

"How is it that sometimes I miss it?" I ask.

Sheila releases a slow breath. "We had each other."

A nervous fizzle erupts in my gut, because in the next moment, Sheila's smile slides off her face, and she looks at the ground, and—why does it feel like Sheila's in another place, far away?

"What are you going to do with that residence number?" she asks. "Tracing it to an actual location—you'd need access to a state device, and clearance."

"I might have an idea about that," I say.

She smiles incredulously. "Did they start giving adjudicators security clearance?"

I weigh my words. "I don't have clearance," I say. "But Ed does."

Though the nearest people are strolling the pedestrian bridge far above us, out of earshot, Sheila flinches and glances around. "You want Ed to look it up?"

I shake my head. "I know you have access to his screen."

Sheila takes a breath. "Even if I could, Eleanor, even if I *would*, how do you imagine finding Rose would fix anything? Would it really make up for what happened?"

Shame blooms hot on my cheeks. "Well . . . yes."

Sheila's voice lowers to barely above a whisper. "Eleanor, think. They're holding Rose somewhere. Some prison, or under house arrest, or inside a state agency. Say you find the address. What next? You think you're going to barge in there and—what? Rescue her?"

"And?"

"Have you considered that this might not even lead to an address? It could be a cemetery vault for all you know."

I step backward. "That's— No, that's not possible."

"Your vision is obscured by your hopes, Eleanor," she says. "I've been there. It never worked out well for me."

I squint at Sheila, a spark of irritation lighting in my chest. "You're not yourself," I say. "What happened in the last two weeks? You're the one who told me I need to do *more*. With Rose, maybe I could. Now you're talking me out of it?"

Sheila's face slowly rearranges until I almost don't recognize her, like how a familiar street can feel unknown as darkness falls. "I shouldn't have told you that."

I shake my head, confounded. "Sheila, I have a chance to help Rose."

"Even if it means breaking the law?" Sheila asks. "When peacekeepers catch you, you'll not only put yourself at risk, but me and Ed too!"

"I—I wouldn't do anything dangerous."

"This entire *idea* is dangerous," Sheila says. "I admire you. This new—

effort. Parts of me wish I could join you. But, don't you think it's time to—to grow up? Would you really throw your life away for someone you knew for a few months?" She sighs. "I know you feel guilty, but Eleanor, it's illogical. You'll end up locked up. Or—or killed."

I feel my resolution flagging. What if she's right? And I'm putting a dangerous spotlight not only on me, but on her? And what if—what if after all of this, Rose isn't even alive?

But if there's a chance she could be . . .

I clear my throat. "Some things are worth the risk."

Sheila shakes her head, eyes full of disbelief. "Who *are* you?"

"Who are *you*?" I demand, a desperate anger filling me. "In the Meadows, you would've been helping me. You would've been leading this."

She closes her eyes. The silence underneath the bridge seems to encircle us, a cold quiet larger than the sea. "You're right, Eleanor," Sheila says at last. "I'm not myself. But where did that ever get me?"

I gape at her. Sheila is turned slightly away, as if to seal me out. But that can't happen. I can't let it happen. Sheila is the strong one. The determined one. But the moment she leaves, we'll both be alone.

I look at her for a long time. My adjudication must be starting soon. But I look, and I see what I've been too distracted to notice. A shadow on her features, a shadow that's been lurking quietly on the edge of this conversation. "Did Ed talk to his boss yet about you taking the aptitude test?"

A line scribbles between her eyes. "No," she says. "And he's not going to."

I take a surprised breath. "That lying—"

"Eleanor, stop," Sheila says. "Last week, Ed told me—" She swallows, setting her jaw. "He told me there are no women in the Department of Engineering, not above coffee girls and secretaries. There never have been."

"Oh, Sheila."

"He didn't tell me before because he didn't want to hurt my feelings.

Seems they learned all about women and our delicate constitutions in the Pines."

"Sheila, I'm so sorry. I—"

"It's fine," she says, snapping on a smile. "Really, I'm perfectly happy."

Someone who doesn't know Sheila might believe her. But briefly, the artifice peels from her face, and I see all the muscles there braced against an incandescent anger, helplessness, hurt.

"Sheila," I say softly, "you're not happy."

"I *want* to be happy," she says, blinking away the beginning of tears. "Ed isn't so bad. Maybe I'll end up with a baby. I could find joy in that, couldn't I?"

I grimace. "Have you been talking with Betty?"

She levels her eyes at me. "Maybe you should update your opinion of Betty. She's not like she was in the Meadows."

"You didn't answer my question," I say.

"I'd better go," she says, turning away. "Can't be late for the Young Wives Club."

"They make you go to those?"

"Every week," she says cheerlessly, adjusting the waist of her dress and pressing her collar with the flat of her hand. Her face changes too, as though she's thrown water on the fire behind her eyes.

It's what we all must do. Watching Sheila put herself away, though—

It's not enough. Her words. Like a chant, now, in my mind.

No amount of careful disguising of the truth by her adjudicator has helped Sheila.

"Rose's number—" I say, because I can't let her leave without actually asking. "Will you look?"

Sheila sighs. "I don't know, Eleanor. I'm not saying no, I just—don't know." As she turns to leave, she pauses. "What was that paper in your pocket? I almost forgot."

My eyes twitch to the black-painted door. I'd planned to tell Sheila everything. About the notes and the door and the people beyond it. But she's suddenly like someone I don't recognize, and it scares me. A small, suspicious part of me wonders anew if maybe it *is* her leaving me the notes. But not for the reason I'd assumed—not to help me. If the state suspects me, it would be like them to use a reformed to draw me out—to trap me.

I clear my throat. "Just—something I found. An old scrap. I tossed it."

Her forehead crooks in confusion, but she nods, and turns, and mounts the small embankment to the street.

My screen alerts me, a tinny insistent trilling from my briefcase. The meeting with my new reformed starts in ten minutes. She lives in an apartment building in the south Wall District, not far from the towering white barricade that encircles the city. If I hustle, I can make it. As I walk, I scan the file for her name.

I stop in the street, fingers half curled over my screen.

June Forster.

My heart is a punching fist. Somehow I've made it to the other side of the road. *June?* It can't be. Not her. Not *here*.

I search the street, shadowed by high-rises and the warning white bulk of the wall, but no one glances at me. Only a round black camera, perched on a store awning. My cheeks fill with heat. I want to scream at whoever's behind that black glass eye.

June's building slouches on the horizon, a wide white expanse that takes up an entire city block, one of these quick-built housing units meant to hold thousands. June, in a place like this? June, with eyes like a squall. June, her fingers enmeshed in a fishing net, casting it out in a perfect sheet. June, who breathed in the air of the sea with her eyes closed. I teased her about that. *What are you thinking, June? What's so lovely it makes your face do that?*

It's just—endless, she said.

She said.

She said she would miss me.

I've wondered about that too.

Up twenty floors, I press the doorbell. A palm-sized screen embedded in the door flickers to life. A face appears, and a long moment passes before recognition washes over her.

"You," she breathes.

CHAPTER 26

"June." The muscles in my cheeks torque painfully, and I hardly know if I'm smiling or grimacing, hardly know what to feel, because it's her, with her bright brown eyes that verge on green, and her tawny face still thick with freckles, and though her loose, dangling curls have been straightened, and on her center part a handprint of oil, and her face looks dry and unaccustomed to joy—it's June.

"Eleanor," she says, grinning.

I don't know who moves first, but the next moment, our arms are wrapped around each other. My throat holds in a gasp, to feel her warmth. "Is it really you?" she asks into my ear. Her voice has the same husky rasp she's had since childhood, and I want to stay this way, wrapped up in each other, for the next ten minutes, the next ten years.

"It's me," I say.

She pulls away, eyebrows coming together in a frown. "But what are you—doing here?" She closes the door tightly behind her, but not before I see into the apartment beyond. A careful chaos, dishes and trash and clothes scattered. "I was expecting someone. I thought you were them, just now."

I feel my smile slipping. I try to tug it back into place, but it falls. "I think I am."

June's forehead crumples. "You?" Her eyes draw down the length of me, the briefcase, the sharp coat, the white buttons running up my torso. She tilts her head back. A tactic, to keep tears pooled. "Well, won't you come inside," she says, dead-voiced, and swings open the door to her apartment.

I want to pull her back to the landing, back in time a few seconds, to linger longer inside the warmth of each other. But the moment is gone.

Her apartment looks as though a giant has lifted the place and shaken it, the rumpled contents of every cupboard and closet flung across the floor, dishes decomposing in the sink. The view beyond her window is overwhelmed by the enormous white presence of the city wall, so close it seems possible to open a window and touch it. At this height, I can make out the shining silver zippers running down the white jumpsuits of the peacekeepers patrolling the top.

I perch carefully on the edge of a chair. Dishes covered in desiccated food clatter as June lowers herself to the sofa. The air stretches between us, and all the time that's passed. This is not the Cove, and we are not the girls we were.

"Your file says this is your exit interview," I say. After today, June will be a real citizen, able to move forward with her life. To get married. "Last month, your adjudicator wrote that you were in good health. She noted that you kept a clean house."

June glances around. "Don't you like what I've done with the place?"

"It's not my job to judge," I say, a common refrain. "It's my job to notice."

"I know all about your job," June says, in a way that brings to mind a snake spitting venom. Her whole body, tightly coiled. "They offered it to me, you know. I was Best Girl. I got to choose."

I pause. "You didn't want it?"

"I'd rather do some good in the world."

I ignore the barb, concentrate on my questions, try not to become distracted by the bruised pits beneath her eyes, by the way June holds her elbows, protectively, it seems. "And you enjoy your work in—" I glance at the file. "Medical?"

Since she realized why I'm here, June hasn't looked at me, eyes fixed on the dull, wood-look flooring. "Better than I would informing on innocent people."

Beneath my face, a struggle. To stay neutral. To not gasp with pain. To keep the truth of what I do from tumbling out. "Were you close with your last adjudicator?"

"No." June stamps the word in the air. "She wasn't very good at *noticing*."

In our first meeting, Mrs. Collier told me what happens to those who refuse to reform. *There are all kinds of facilities.* June must be aware, so what reason could she have for speaking this way? Might as well say *I am unhappy*. Might as well say *I don't want to live this life*.

I clear my throat, glancing at my screen. "When your last adjudicator visited, you were about to attend a company party with your fiancé. What's new in your life since then?"

The muscles in her face pull taut. "Nothing."

"And how is your fiancé . . . Charlie, is it?" In my chest, the tiniest squirming, the idea of June having a fiancé. Even a state-appointed one who, by the look on her face, she doesn't like, let alone love.

"I have nothing to say about him."

I lower my screen. All these years, I've pictured what it would be like, meeting again. Never did I consider that the June I once knew might be gone. Or, not gone—hollowed out like an oyster, until only a shell remains. "You're about to be exited from the program."

"And?"

From my throat comes a noise halfway between desperation and annoyance. I feel tempted to take her by the shoulders and shake her. "If you don't at least try to respond to my questions, I'll have no choice but to document that in my report."

"And I should care because?"

"Because—" I falter. "Because you know what they do—You know what the consequences may be."

At last, June lifts her eyes to mine, a gaze so deadened, I feel something inside me scramble backward. "I have a message for whoever *they* are. Tell them, do your worst."

I grew up hearing how dangerous it can be to help someone who's drowning. They can drag you under, and you both end up dead. I've only encountered a few girls who refused to even pretend to reform. Throwing punches, trying to run. Even one who cut off her hair in the night, tossing strands of blond down the trash chute to be incinerated before anyone could wrench the scissors from her fist. No fabricated report could save those ones.

But.

But June. Even in this stark, disordered shoebox. Even in this city so far from the ocean. Even with her mouth shoving words into the air that could see her burn, she's still June.

On the street far below, a father walks with his children, a holiday tree on his back, flexible plastic branches bobbing in the air. I can tell it smells nothing like the real thing, like the trees June's father cut down and strung with pencil-sized candles.

"I remember the holiday nights at your house," I say.

June glances out the window and then at me, wary.

"The grown-ups sipping little glasses of brandy by the fire," I continue, "and I'd play my fiddle, and your parents would start dancing." Not long after that holiday, June's mother called mine to her house, complaining of a deep and radiating pain. My mother kneaded her stomach like bread dough, but whatever was in there had already braided deep into every fiber of her, no way to pull it out. Inside a month, she was dead, and before long, June's father matched with a new wife.

But June isn't thinking of that, it seems, because a smile—the barest brushstroke of a smile—pulls at the corner of her mouth. "And soon enough even Captain was shuffling around," she says, "wanting to join in, bouncing on the floor with his giant paws."

I laugh, a place in my chest glowing as though I'd drunk a capful of brandy too, warmed from within.

June seems to make a decision then. She stands and rummages in a kitchen drawer, and comes away with something small in her hand. She approaches one of the mesh coins in the wall and plies a white sort of putty over it. She holds up a finger, as though to say *Wait*, and moves on to the next.

When she covers the final circle of mesh, she turns to me. "Blocks out the ears."

"I thought they could tell if someone obstructs them," I say.

"They only do routine scans every twenty minutes. Anything more would slow the algorithm down to a crawl."

"Who taught you that?" I ask.

"Charlie," she says, and the look on her face makes me not ask any questions.

June sets a timer on her kitchen counter and turns to me.

"Well," I say. "Let's use our minutes wisely." I feel my neck prickle. I haven't been inside somewhere I couldn't be overheard in years. It feels strangely . . . exposed. The freedom to say anything. Do anything. I can make out the individual ticks of the clock in her kitchen, the kind of oddly vintage choice popular with young people in the city. June pulls her bottom lip into her mouth. The silence flexes between us. There seems too much to say.

Finally, June speaks. "What was that song you played all the time?"

My eyes lift to her face. "The Longing Song." Pulling the name up feels like reaching into the back of an old, unused closet. The Longing Song—filled with everything I wanted.

"I always wondered," June says, "whether I had a place in that song."

I stand and face her, words insufficient, trying to communicate in a look how often I've thought of her. How she never left my mind, not for a day. "Do you even have to ask?"

June's mouth barely moves, but there's the smallest suggestion of a smile.

"Something happened to you where you went," I say.

She turns, runs a finger over the smooth white countertop. "You could say that to everyone who leaves a place like the Canyonlands." She nods at me. "Like the Meadows."

"June," I say. "What happened?"

She sighs. "I'm sure you can read all about it in my file."

"Here." I pull my screen from inside my briefcase and extend it to her. Her eyes narrow. "Is this allowed?"

"No," I say, pushing the screen into her hands.

She takes it and sets it on the counter near me, so close our shoulders nearly touch and the space between us soon fills with warm breath. I study her face as she scans the screen, a year-by-year summary of her time in the Canyonlands, all my sinews and muscles cranking tight. Her face is bottom-lit by the screen's glow, and my heart squeezes at the sight of her. *June.*

"'Near the beginning of her final year, June Forster engaged in illegal relations with another Canyonlands pupil, Tasha Briggs,'" she reads. "'Matrons became aware of the relationship after the two began meeting regularly in the kitchen pantry, believing their actions to be clandestine.'"

June throws a flat-eyed glance out the window. "They knew. And they let it go on."

I nod, thinking of Margot and Penelope. Of Rose. "Our secrets weren't secret from them."

June frowns. "We weaved each other rings, Tasha and I, out of thread. When we met that night, five matrons pulled open the door. Shined lights in, yanked us out. They took the rings." June's chin begins to quake.

"I'm sorry, June." A spot inside my chest aches, a knitting needle pressed precisely into my sternum. The Meadows. The Canyonlands. And who knows how many others. What did they do to us? What have they done?

June sets the screen on the counter. *Briggs resisted attempts to reform and was eliminated from the program. Forster completed the program after a probationary period and showed no signs of relapse.*

"Relapse," June says darkly. "Like a disease."

I imagine it. Dark seeds burrowed inside the lining of my heart. Cells blooming and splitting their membranes, forming new ones. "That's what they think of us, yes."

Rage gathers on her face like a thunderhead. "Well, they're fucking wrong."

"They're fucking wrong," I say.

June's mouth opens, surprise relaxing her features. "But you work for them."

I only shake my head.

June examines me for a long moment. She frowns. "You lost someone too."

I nod. "They—they told me she died."

"Killed?" she asks, her voice a whisper.

I hesitate for only a moment before I tell her everything, everything I wanted to tell Sheila but couldn't: about what Mrs. Collier said—that Rose had died on the night of the escape. About what Sheila told me—*As bad as it was, nobody ever died.* About the notes and the Registrar's Office. About finding the place of residence number.

"And you think she's out there somewhere," June says, searching my face for something. Pain, or anger, but I know my expression is as neutral as a mannequin in the expensive shops downtown. "Where are you, Eleanor?"

I stutter a laugh. "Right here?"

"It's like you're here, but . . . not," she says, squinting at my face. "It's—it's how I feel most of the time." She swallows. "The girls we were got lost somewhere."

"I think I lost her on purpose," I say.

June frowns. "Then I hope you find her, Eleanor."

"How?"

At once, an idea lights up her face, eyebrows lifting, and she darts from the room, returning a moment later with a photograph. "I snuck it into the Canyonlands," she says. "Hid it inside my dress."

June passes me the photo. Mrs. Arkwright had a camera that she brought out on special occasions, using up precious squares of film sparingly. The photograph shows the dim, brown-tinged interior of Mrs. Arkwright's house. We'd just performed a class skit about weather, and June was dressed as a wildfire, red and orange maple leaves stuck into her hair. And beside her, a dozen tin-can sun rays fanning from my head, violin clamped under one arm—me. Smiling in a way I can barely recollect.

"There you are," June says, pointing at the image. "You could make anyone laugh. You were Mrs. Arkwright's favorite, even when you drew rude pictures of her. She found one and cackled along with you, remember?"

On my face, a slow smile; I can feel it, the memory illuminating some dark space in me.

"And you loved books," she goes on. "Magic stories, the ones Mrs. Arkwright read to us."

"I made my own magic wand," I say. "And you'd pretend to be a mermaid."

"A *siren*," she says. "Able to lure men to my island, smash them apart on the rocks, and steal away with all their treasure."

I laugh, and the muscles around my belly ache, unaccustomed. "You were brutal."

Her bright eyes meet mine, the full brunt of them socking me in the gut. Maybe this is why she couldn't look at me before, because this is what happens when you find someone again. You look and you can't stop looking. My heart thuds so I can feel it in my fingertips. A fork of electricity between us, stretching tight. June's laugh falters. She puts her eyes away again.

"What I said earlier," June says, "about them offering me the adjudicator job—the truth is—after they caught me with Tasha, I worked to convince the matrons I was the best reformed. I took the spot in medical because I—I wanted to keep impressing them."

I glance around her apartment. The disarray of her life. "So, what happened?"

Her gaze hardens. "Charlie happened."

June considers me for a long moment, her eyes containing a grief I saw only once before, after her mother died. With her fingertips, she needles the blue buttons of her dress, unfastening several. She pulls the gap apart.

My breath clutches at the sight of her stomach, so long since I've seen the skin of a girl, goosefleshed and curled over the coral-colored waistband of her underwear. My eyes walk up the ladder of her ribs. To a dark purple smudge, emblazoned, fist-printed.

"I like when it leaves a mark," June says, fingers skimming the large bruise. "Like I have something to show for this."

"I'll report him."

"You think I haven't already tried?" she asks, buttoning her dress.

"He'll never face a consequence, not until he does it to someone else. My apartment looks this way for a reason. You'll report everything you saw. My domestic duties have fallen off. I'm not reformed. I think—I think I'd rather go wherever they send me. I'd rather die, Eleanor."

I keep my voice low. "I lie on reports, June. To save girls. Nothing obvious. Just . . . enough. I don't have to say anything about your house."

"Don't lie," she says. "Charlie's reported it by now anyway." She sighs, resigned.

I brace a hand against the window frame, feeling suddenly like I'm falling. No—not falling. Becoming dislodged. Like a large hand has shucked me from my shell and now who knows where I'm headed. *It's not enough.* I've been comfortable here, doing this job, performing my own quiet, unnoticed brand of rebellion. But now—now Sheila is locked inside a life that's slowly killing her. But now June, and the purple unfolding across her ribs. But now Rose, who might still be alive, or who might be dead. Now there's the knowledge that what I've been doing isn't enough.

An hour ago, I felt if I lost Sheila, we'd be alone completely. But here I've found June. And maybe I'd find Rose. Maybe Sheila would be all right if I could find a way. And still—it breaks over me, a heavy wave—we all have been alone for so long. This world has made sure of it.

June glances at me sideways. "Eleanor, will we ever be okay again?"

And in the look she gives me, I break the surface, and I remember it all with her—home, the Cove, the freedom of feeling buoyant on water, the knowledge that tomorrow would be just the same. And if there was boredom in that, there was also peace. Just the normal scratching of our hopes at the walls inside us, the pulling toward our dreams. For the future. For what we could be.

CHAPTER 27

On the street, my face trembles as I walk from June's apartment, passing through the shadow of the city wall into sunlight. I grip the muscles in a practiced way, but my face won't obey. Beneath is a war—the joy of seeing June, this person I know inside my bones, and her bruises, the unfolding of ancient memories, my mind creaking open like an old trunk.

The center cannot hold. Whole pieces of me fling apart now, and in a moment, they might fly off into the street, nose, eyes, mouth scattering on the pavement. I duck into an alley, heave a cupful of acid onto the ground. My forehead rests against the cold brick wall. How long can this go on? This unraveling.

I spit out gobs of the evil-flavored stuff, straighten up, do not allow the word *panic* to step into my mind. Into my mouth, an efficient mint. Now I go back out into the world. Now I pretend that there's nothing inside my body that wants to pull me apart. Even better: that I don't have a body at all.

You find her, Eleanor.

This year in the city, I've considered the possibility that I was born in the Meadows, fully formed, layers of muscle and fat and bone printed inside a periscope like that orange.

June, though. If June's here, it's true that I existed before, that once my fingers were calloused from violin strings, my knees patched with scabs, my hair salt-thick and wild.

I almost wish I could forget. It would be easier.

I hurry home, remembering. The smell of lavender drying in bushels from the ceiling. The maple tree. The bustle of market on a spring day the year before I left. The muttered words that followed us. The villagers were kind to me, but Stella was what happened when you broke the rules. Punished for every possibility. Maybe I really was hers, the result of an ill-planned evening. But she didn't treat me like her own, and I looked nothing like her. I came from elsewhere. From an unwed mother, or a woman whose husband had been out at sea too long for a baby to make sense. My mother took me. Took the shame, strapped it to herself. I still couldn't fathom why.

We stopped, that spring day, at the market. Despite the dark cloud that followed my mother, despite the glances we both drew, I suppose June was right—I was liked by the villagers, chatted with fishermen and cattlefolk who came down from the plains. Sometimes, I accompanied my mother at the market to help facilitate trades, more tactful than she could be.

Our last stop was a market stall operated by Margaret Johns, who traded in produce and town gossip. She had several daughters, and the youngest, Tilly, kicked a ball in the alley behind. Mrs. Johns, body like a reed though she'd had many children, fair skin protected beneath a wide straw hat. I felt my eyes draw to her like they would to a bright star, so different from my own mother.

"Stella," Mrs. Johns said as my mother plopped down a bag of vegetables we'd picked. "I'm sorry, but we've decided not to buy from you anymore."

Somewhere in my mother's jaw, a wire was drawn taut. Tilly stopped playing to watch the exchange. "And why would that be?" my mother asked.

Mrs. Johns started intently arranging her produce. "I'm sure you heard. The Millers' stall was removed by peacekeepers, broken up right in front of everyone. Last market day."

The Millers had been spotted giving food to unhoused men by the waterfront. Aiding vagrancy. I stepped forward. "Mrs. Johns, won't you reconsider—"

"Those men weren't hurting anyone," my mother cut across my words.

Mrs. Johns's mouth puckered. "Those men could be contributing. Instead, they choose a life of *freedom*." She said the word as though it were frivolous. "Living like vagabonds. I have a duty to uphold the values of our nation. Of our village. It's why I called the peacekeepers on those musical women. Making a mockery of everything we stand for."

A rage so sudden and complete filled me that, later, I'd feel scared of it. "*You* called them?" I said.

Mrs. Johns looked taken aback. "Stella, mind your ward. She's practically feral."

"I don't think I have to do anything you say," my mother said. "As we are no longer in business."

"Oh, Stella, don't take offense. You know accepting food from you is a risk. Who knows where you got it, and if we sell stolen vegetables, what will become of us?"

"I don't steal," my mother growled. "I grow them, as you're well aware."

Mrs. Johns pulled Tilly close to her side. "Well, I have a family to protect. Assuming the best of people is what made the Millers destitute."

I knew my mother would never try to sell her vegetables to Margaret Johns again. Pride was knitted into her bones. And so she threw back her iron shoulders and flattened her eyes. "We're all in the same goddamn place, you know."

Mrs. Johns blinked rapidly. "Excuse me?"

"The men by the waterfront, and the Millers, and me, and yes, even you, Margaret. If you think you're any different from the rest, you're more of a fool than I took you for."

We walked home, the burlap sack still heavy with vegetables. No choice but to feast on them in the coming days. I salivated already, imagining roast turnips warm and heavy in my belly. My mother was silent until we reached the bluff overlooking the ocean.

"I'm tired," she said. "We'll rest here a moment."

She lowered herself to the cliff edge, legs dangling over. Below, water surged in swells of navy and pale blue and milk foam. My mother's face hung loose as a rag. I'd convinced myself that I could see beyond her prickliness. That I recognized love, deep within her, a light burning behind fog. Now I wonder whether it was just that I simply had nobody else. Perhaps I only loved her like a child who has to love in order to survive.

I knew she wouldn't want to talk about what had happened. So I asked her something else. "Why did you never match with someone?"

She didn't look at me but said, "By the time the Quorum took over, I was over the age where matching was required. Women past childbearing years don't have to marry. What would be the point?"

"What about before then?" I asked. "Was it different, when you were young?"

"Many things were different when I was young."

"What did you dream about being back then?"

"Doesn't matter." She shook her head. "The dreams of Before don't fit here."

I made a frustrated sound. "Won't you just tell me?"

She sighed. "I thought I'd write for a newspaper. I went to school for it."

I waited, silent. If I pried, she'd clam up and never speak another word on the subject.

"The towns on the coast, out there." She pointed toward the sea. "All washed away. Growing up here, this place had a different name, and we had to drive miles to see ocean. But it found me." Her eyes raked the blue water. "They closed the universities to women just after I graduated. My degree was worthless. Eventually, there weren't newspapers or websites anymore. Around then, the dispatches began."

I held my breath. My mother had never spoken so much about Life Before.

"The Quorum arrived, speaking softly. *It'll be okay. We are here now. We are so sorry this happened to you.* People really believed it," she said, sounding tired. "Not many stopped to think that there hadn't been a vote. Too preoccupied with surviving. I found this spot"—she pointed at the rock beneath her—"and I decided, no matter what else, I was going to be happy. But then . . ."

"But then I came along."

Her dark eyes found mine. "No," she said. "Not entirely."

"Then what?"

She frowned, slashing her eyes out at the ocean. "What do you think might happen to Margaret Johns if she didn't work so hard to be pretty?"

She was changing the subject, but I went along, imagining Mrs. Johns allowing herself to go wild. Hair unruly. Skin taking in the sun. "I imagine she might look quite strong."

In my mother's throat, a grunt of agreement. "We have always had to hide our strength. It makes people nervous." My mother had strong legs, calves the shape of apples, and her face was scattered with brown fingerprints left by the sun.

"But that's up to Mrs. Johns," I said, "to look that way."

"Is it?" My mother continued to peer out over the water.

"I hope I look like you one day," I told her.

"You won't," she said. Because of course I wouldn't. I hadn't come from her.

"Then I'll make myself," I told her, smiling. "I'll color my hair. I'll stretch my limbs. I'll spend forever in the sun till I have your face. I'll do something good with it."

She was silent, her expression unreadable.

My footsteps make an echo through the large bathroom of my apartment. Ten stalls long, a mirror spanning the length of the tile wall. I imagine the college girls who got ready here each morning, brushing teeth, applying lipstick. They're now my mother's age or older, with degrees worth less than their paper. With minds full of knowledge they will never again use.

I never grew to look like my mother. If anything, less so, my face almost translucent in midwinter. Under the white light straining from tubes in the bathroom ceiling, I'm so pale that every imperfection stands out. Dry lips. Chapped red flare beneath each nostril. I force myself to look, eyes repelled as though beholding something decayed.

June told me to look for the girl I used to be. I'm looking. Standing here is someone I don't even know. As foreign to me as the girl who walked with her mother to the market.

CHAPTER 28

A new girl. Still perched in the yew tree, the knowledge hung in the air, and then, like a starburst, exploded: A new girl comes and one of us leaves.

Sheila.

In the upper boughs, I swayed with vertigo. Were the matrons fetching her now? I pictured them, wrestling Sheila from her bed, throwing her into the back of this waiting shuttle. Matron Maureen had said not yet. Hopefully not ever. Why had they changed their minds? I flung myself down the tree and sprinted across the lawn, mind scrambling. I could catch them, convince them to—to take someone else. My skirts clouded around me, slowing me, and I kicked at them in frustration.

I crashed through the foyer, into the main corridor, and came to a juddering stop. Down the white tube of the hallway, entering the Fine Arts classroom, was Sheila, Matron Sybil's hand around her shoulder. "Just through here, my dear," I heard Matron Sybil say, leading her inside.

I opened my mouth to yell, but something stopped me. The strange gentleness of Matron Sybil's hand. The eerie muteness in the air. A finger of dread drew lightly up my spine. For a long moment, I froze, staring at the slant of golden light that fell across the floor from the classroom.

When I padded to the doorway, I saw, sitting just inside, the new girl, quietly observing. She turned to me and lifted a conspiratorial finger to her lips. *Quiet,* the gesture said. *Don't be seen.* My breath balled up in my throat. Up close, she looked even more like a revelation, in her men's pants, her short hair, a dark curl over her forehead.

In the room's bright center, the circle of easels resembled the stretched sails of ships. Behind her small desk, Matron Sybil stood with that motherly hand on Sheila's shoulder. The Sheila of yesterday—incandescent with fury and pain—was gone. Now she sat, doubled over, not making a sound. I could see the blades of her ribs through the back of her dress, rising and falling like bellows with each slow breath. "There now," Matron Sybil hushed.

Doubt scrabbled at my mind, the strange quiet of this scene. If told she was being sent away, Sheila would put her chin in the air, square her stance, never give Matron Sybil the satisfaction of seeing her collapse. I searched for some kind of injury, for a ribbon of blood, but there was only Matron Sybil and her broad, white hand resting on Sheila's shoulder.

"His heart was weak," a tinny voice scratched the air. "He'd been fading for a while." I peeked further around the door. On the desk in front of Sheila, a screen. A woman's face. I took her in like a puzzle, her hair a cascade of twists, her high forehead and wide, bright eyes—all, remarkably, like Sheila. Tears made shining tracks on the woman's cheeks. "I couldn't even get him to the clinic. It was over too fast."

Almost imperceptibly, Sheila began to vibrate. The strong stillness of her was coming apart.

"I—I'll never see him again," Sheila said. Incredulous, as though the idea had never occurred to her, that people can wink out like a light and never come back.

This almost mute agony—I couldn't fathom it. I thought I'd be fighting for Sheila to stay.

The new girl had turned her gaze to the floor.

"I want to come home, Mama," Sheila said, quiet.

Sheila's mother arranged her face carefully. She had never wished for Sheila to come here. "Remember when we'd sit around the table and talk about your great plans?" She leaned close, as though drawing Sheila back there, to the refuge of her childhood home, where she could talk and learn and hope. "You had so many dreams."

Sheila paused. "They seem far away."

"Then bring them close," her mother whispered. "Your dreams are what keep you alive, Sheila. Don't ever stop fighting for them."

"But, I'm so . . ." Sheila trailed off. "I'm tired."

Sheila's mother pushed a smile onto her face. "Your fight might have to look different from what you imagined," she said. "But you are good, Sheila, just as you are. Never forget. There is not a thing wrong with—"

"I'm so sorry, Mrs. Evans," Matron Sybil interrupted, shattering the delicate quiet. "It's time to say good night. Sheila will be excused from classes tomorrow, but she should get some rest."

Sheila's mother blinked rapidly. "I love you, Sheila."

"I love you, Mama—"

Matron Sybil clicked off the screen. Sheila sat in silence. Her head fell to her hands, fingers clutching the downy cloud of her hair.

I stepped into the room. "Sheila?" My voice came out choked.

She lifted her face to me. I was struck by the absence of tears. And then our arms were around each other. "My dad—" she said.

"Oh." I breathed the words into her neck. "Oh, Sheila. I'm sorry."

"I—" she gasped. She started and stopped, again and again until I said, "I know." And I did. The knowledge—it pulled at the hems of our dresses, insistent. She'd had the chance to talk to her father. And she'd said no.

The matrons have a plan for each one of you, I remembered Matron Maureen saying. When I faced Matron Sybil, something molten poured through me, like that day with Mrs. Johns. "You knew," I said. "You knew he wasn't well. And you wouldn't let her call home."

Matron Sybil's face was carefully neutral. "Sheila had an opportunity to commit to reform. It was her choice." Her sudden coldness struck me. "We all make mistakes, my dears. It's this, more than anything, that makes us part of nature. Now, it's late. I'll expect you two to return to your dormitory." She turned to the new girl. "Come along. Let's get you settled in your room."

Sheila squinted blearily, as though only now aware of the strange girl passing her a sad smile and trailing Matron Sybil from the room.

In the quiet that followed, the quavering in Sheila's body began to build. She held her hands before her, watched them shake as though she couldn't believe they were hers. Slowly, Sheila's fingers drew into fists, and she brought one down on Matron Sybil's desk with a meaty thwack. She did it again, and again, at last flying apart, flinging outward. She pounded on the desk with both arms, until I feared she'd break a bone. "Sheila," I whispered, grabbing her wrists, pulling her close. She leaned into me.

From her mouth, a long, keening scream.

She screamed, and I felt it shake the walls of her.

She screamed, and the matrons didn't come.

She screamed, and I huddled with her, two pearls in a shell.

I sat upright in bed, ears reaching for sound. In my sleep, I'd imagined I could hear something in the corridor. A scuffle. A fight.

Almost immediately after returning to our room, Sheila had collapsed into sleep. I looked at her now in the dim half-light—her face slack, her breath slow. The news of her father's death had eclipsed the pain of our fight, but the bruise of it lingered. In the morning, I sensed, everything would be different.

A faint scream echoed through the warren of white hallways. Electricity zippered up my spine, and I realized: If Sheila wasn't being taken, someone else was.

I moved from my bed and edged down the hall, toward the foyer, fingers brushing the wall. There, in that bright white capsule, stood Matron Sybil, flanked by Matron Gloria and Matron Calliope. Between them, tensed like a cornered animal, Marina.

"Why?" Marina demanded, breath coming in gasps.

"We feel you'd be a better fit at the Mesa." Matron Sybil's voice, pleasant and calm.

Marina balled up the sides of her nightgown, eyes bounding from matron to matron. "That's what they told me when I left the Bay. I'm not going to the Mesa. Am I? Nobody gets so many chances."

"It's good luck that your father is such a generous man," Matron Sybil said. "He has ensured that your education will not be interrupted. Regardless of your transgressions."

I felt my forehead. *Transgressions?*

"Come. Your driver is waiting." Matron Sybil took a hand and placed it around Marina's shoulder. Marina tried to walk backward out of her grip and stumbled against the foyer wall. Marina's eyes slashed around as if to spot a hidden doorway, an escape.

When she saw me, her eyes rounded in surprise.

Matron Sybil froze, rotating as if to follow Marina's gaze. And in that split second, I knew she would see me. Marina said, "Matron Sybil!"

The matron paused and faced her. I stepped back and loosed a silent stream of breath. She hadn't seen me.

"Yes?" the matron said.

Marina opened her mouth. "If—" she said. "If I could tell the other girls something . . . a parting note."

Matron Sybil sighed. "Yes?"

"I'd tell them—" Marina continued, keeping her eyes on Matron

Sybil, though her words seemed meant for me, "I'd tell them to—to watch as I leave."

Matron Sybil regarded her with diminishing patience. "The others are in bed."

Marina swallowed. "I mean—to not forget me."

"I'm sure you are unforgettable, dear," Matron Sybil said, gesturing to the door. "Come along." Marina wavered for a moment, eyes seeming to tug toward where I stood. Then she lowered her head, this time going willingly.

I crept into the foyer and hazarded a glance outside. Backs to me, the matrons and Marina approached the black shuttle idling on the dusty road. I stared, fidgeting. *Watch as she leaves?* Why? Where could I even get a view of the shuttle driving away? High in the branches of the yew tree—but no way to cross the lawn without the risk of being seen. There was only one other place. I took a quick, decisive breath, and darted outside and around the other end of the building.

The main building was made of rough plastic, slightly grippy, and sloped to the ground gently, like a low hill. The faint chatting of the matrons was audible from the other side. I ran my hands over the bowed white wall. No footholds, no way to climb up.

From the other side of the building, a cool metallic whirring could be heard. The shuttle was leaving. Frantically, I ran a clammy hand over the wall. The texture, almost sandy, caught on my skin. Quickly, I peeled off my socks, placed my hands high up, and hiked a bare foot onto the wall's curve. I slipped, the rough surface taking a layer of skin from my ankle, but I tried again, scrabbling up, sinews aching, breath quick.

I stood, and took in the whole sweep of the Meadows, buildings pearlescent on the dark carpet of lawn, the fields hung with the slightest mist, like the bluish smoke of a campfire. The shuttle hummed down the road then, and the matrons, quiet phantoms, filed into their quarters. In the distance, I could even make out that strange archway straddling the road, the remnant of some old brick house.

What had Marina intended for me to see? It occurred to me that this could be one last chance for her to taunt me. Fitting. I almost smiled. Almost. I felt certain I'd never see her again.

The shuttle rode the gravel road, a bullet of shining black reflecting patches of periwinkle sky. I remembered what Matron Sybil had said on that first day. The meadow fields go on forever. From here, it seemed true.

But the road didn't, I recalled with a jolt. The road ended abruptly, far off in the distance, cut off by the meadow flowers. Still the shuttle continued with even greater speed toward the archway standing over the road.

The archway.

An idea began whirring in my mind, a second behind reality. Just before the shuttle glided under the arch, the view within its curve changed. As if someone slid a photograph into a frame, the gravel road disappeared, replaced by a slick black asphalt highway fringed with the rust-colored rock, dry and bright like a desert.

"What—" The air socked out of me.

The driver must not have been surprised by this because the shuttle didn't slow, speeding straight through the archway, out onto the asphalt. The next second, the scene inside the archway reverted. White gravel road. Lingering spray of dust. Meadow fields, still and silent and everywhere. The shuttle, gone.

I stood there, small, peering out, the rolling mounds of the Meadows, dipping and rising around me, and beyond them, the calm sea of silent flowers, no land in sight.

CHAPTER 29

Your presence is expected at the upcoming young people's mixer.

When the message appears on my screen, I look out the kitchen window and quietly groan. The state sets up mixers, and picnics, and game nights for young unmarried people in the city. Though the state can easily make matches using the algorithm, they prefer when they happen organically.

"Attendance is mandatory?" Clark asks, reading over my shoulder.

"I haven't been to one in months," I say. "Clark, you don't have any paper, do you?"

He squints at me. "Who has paper?"

My shoulders fall. "Just wondering."

When I head outside, snow falls frilly and white, absorbed by the sidewalk in a moment. My hands scoop into my pockets, searching for a new scrap of paper. I scan faces in crowds, hoping to grasp a wrist before its owner can dart away. But my fingers brush only the coarse wool inside my coat.

I leave behind the cool air for the dank, winding staircase of a massive pre-Turn apartment building. My first adjudication of the day. Strange, going back to regular life, meeting with reformeds, when beneath the surface of me, there's a teeming swirling thing. A desire to help Sheila. To find Rose. And, I think guiltily, a bone-deep ache to see June again.

In the Meadows, I was pulled by the matrons in one direction and by Sheila in another. And now between Rose, the gravity of her, of my guilt, and June. The way she fits me like before, June a hand, and my heart a glove. June, a way forward that would mean death for us both.

Why do I do this? Want people I can never have.

In the dim, rambling apartment building, I interview a new girl, fresh from the Tides. She spends her days before an easel, assigned the job of state-sanctioned artist. "Like the Renaissance painters," she tells me, like the artists hired by the church to paint what they were ordered to: a mother crying tears the shape of pearls, blood falling from crowns made of thorns. Before she left for the Tides, this girl studied the paintings in a forbidden book, loved the women most, their bodies round and wonderful, falling out of silken dresses.

She shows me her paintings. They look like the poster in the Cove: sturdy men and women, their smiles confident, rigid, sheltered beneath sayings like "Family Is Forever." Her brush hovers over the wet smile of a man. This time, she's been asked to repaint the family with darker skin.

On her pallet, she mixes paint to match the color of her own warm brown forearm. She's permitted to alter nothing else about the painting, not the lips or the texture of hair or the cheekbones that look nothing like her lips, her hair, her cheekbones. "Model Yourself After Good" crosses the painting in livid red. The girl's paintbrush falls to her lap. In her gaze, a wish. That just once, she could paint a plump limb, the beautiful curve of a woman standing on a seashell, lounging on clouds.

Halfheartedly, I pull a pin from my hair and wiggle it inside the lock, but the door stays firmly shut. I've spent my lunch breaks visiting the door beneath the pedestrian bridge over the past week, freezing in the early winter chill and watching a door that will probably never open. Every time, it's locked. Every time, I press my ear to the cold metal, hear only silence, and question my own memory. I turn from the door and let my head fall to my hands.

And then I hear it. Music. Not the staid, careful strings from the mosaic garden. This—something alive. Pumping, all brass and noise. Just as quickly, it vanishes. The air pulses with sudden quiet. I look up, and there is a woman before me. Her fingers splay on the closed door, body poised as though she's just passed through it.

For a moment, we only look at each other, breath held. Her eyes widen. Something about her catches in my mind, familiar.

"H-have—" she gasps. "Have you come from the Village?"

I shake my head, confused. "From the Cove," I say. And when I do, something opens inside my brain. I *have* seen her before. *In* the Cove. The cello player in the traveling band, years ago. I grin. She's in normal clothes this time, flats and a yellow dress, no coat. A deep scar cuts through her eyebrow and she's lost a piece of one ear. Despite the dress, she resembles a stray cat. "You—you're a musician."

My voice is full of marvel, but she stutter-steps away from me, afraid. "How do you know that?"

"I saw you—in the Cove," I say. "Five years ago. I always wondered what happened—"

"I've never been to any cove," she snaps. And then her eyes run down the length of me, taking in my clothes, briefcase, buttoned shirt. "An adjudicator," she says, eyes snapping back to my face.

"I'm not—" I start, holding out my hands. "I only want to know about the door. The music. What is that place?"

She stares. "They'll shut this door down before they let an adjudicator in." Her body, spring-loaded with anxiety, bursts with sudden energy. She turns, dress fanning out, and runs.

"Wait!" I shout. I lunge forward, and my fingers reach, finding a single yellow pleat of her dress. She turns to me, a sheen of panic in her eyes, and wrenches free.

"Please!" I shout. But she's already gone. I hesitate for a breath, bouncing on my toes in indecision. I hear the message on the green note like a whisper. *You'll find her behind a door.* At once, perfect clarity: What if Rose is behind *this* door?

I dash after the woman. On the crowded sidewalk I slow to a quick walk, several paces behind, vision funneling so all I see is yellow, weaving between pedestrians, as though tracking the sun. She looks back at me, eyes flaring, and darts across the street.

I follow, running ahead, when a hand clamps hard on my shoulder.

I look up into the face of a peacekeeper. Only now do I take in my surroundings. He's caught me halfway into an intersection, the clicking of brakes as several self-driving cars careen to a halt, their passengers peering dazedly up from screens.

"And what," the officer states, "are you doing?"

I glance from his large face to where his pink fingers grip my shoulder. My breath comes rapid and shallow. "She—dropped her handkerchief," I say, pulling mine from my pocket. "I was trying to return it."

"That's a reason to obstruct traffic?"

"N—no," I say, eyes still following the woman in the yellow dress as she disappears into an office building. It's tall and white, like many downtown. But it's not just any building. My eyes track to the top, where Mrs. Collier's office sits. There must be thousands of offices inside, but my lungs squeeze tight at the sight.

"Did you hear me?" The officer snaps his fingers in my face. "Clear the road!"

I jump and stride away, body moving on autopilot while my mind hums. *You'll find her behind a door.* The more I consider it, the more it feels true. Rose must be there. But why had that woman been so afraid of me? And what had she meant—*shut this door down?*

I want to tear at my hair, kick at a wall, but I prod the muscles of my face into a dull mask. My brain rings, the sense that the truth is close, that

I've got all the letters and just need to line them up properly. My mind reaches, but the answer is beyond my grasp.

Clouds part and a slash of sun falls across my face. I glance around me, blinking. I'm surrounded by neat rows of townhomes. Somehow, I've walked all the way to Betty's neighborhood, twenty blocks or more.

I've seen Betty only once in my time in the city, about a month after we'd left the Meadows. I was to be the adjudicator for her exit interview. Normally it took at least a year, but Betty had been fast-tracked based on the matrons' recommendations, and had moved through the reform process quicker than any girl I'd heard of.

"Eleanor! You caught us sitting down for dinner," Betty had said, her red-painted smile bright. "Won't you come in?" Her glasses were gone, and her hair had been tamed into an attractive poof around her shoulders. She wore a blue dress, sleeves to her wrists.

The house was several stories tall and far nicer than the apartments most reformed girls lived in. The table was set with an enormous pot roast garnished with sprigs of rosemary, a terrine of orange-colored fish gelatin, serving bowls mounded with green peas and corn. For dessert, a glistening pineapple upside-down cake. Recipes I recognized from the Meadows. Betty introduced me to her fiancé, Tad.

"Welcome, welcome," Tad said, grinning. He had an oil slick of dark hair, and a dignified voice, like the men on the dispatches. Most reformed girls were matched with boys around their age, but Betty's fiancé was an overseer in the Department of Prisons, at least five years older. "So how did you two meet?" he asked.

A dart of worry flashed over Betty's face. "At school," she said, locking eyes with me. "Remember, dear? I told you about Eleanor—from Jennings Academy."

Reformeds are required to keep their status a secret from natural spouses. For this reason, many choose to be matched with other reformeds, like Sheila and Ed—secrecy unnecessary.

"Of course," Tad said, smiling. "Jennings Academy for Young Women. You ladies are so accomplished. I don't know how I got so lucky, matching with a catch like Betty. She's the best cook I've ever known."

"Betty was always very gifted at culinary arts," I said. "At everything, in fact."

"Not quite as gifted as you," Betty demurred. "Best Girl and all." A little pride plucked at my heart, knowing how it must rankle her. "But it didn't matter in the end," she said. "I got the life I always dreamed of." She cast a smiling look around the room.

As Betty served her husband, then me, I studied her and thought, *Maybe the algorithm really was wrong about her.*

I interviewed Betty on her own, in her private sitting room. She answered each question breezily, without hesitation. I was new to adjudicating, not yet able to distinguish the subtler signals of a girl's unhappiness. But, I suspect, even if I interviewed Betty now, I'd still call her as close to reformed as anyone I'd met.

"What's your impression of Tad so far?" I'd asked.

"Oh, he's the most perfect gentleman. Everything I could've hoped for in a fiancé."

The state encourages cohabitation before marriage. Lasting unions require a period of testing, they say, to ensure compatibility on all fronts. In the girls I'd met so far, there was usually a stiffness within their arranged match that I imagined wouldn't wear off for years, if ever. Betty had none of that. "You've been acquainted less than a month," I said. "Do you know him well enough to feel you'd be content spending your life with him?"

"If I'm perfectly honest," she said, "I think I could be a good wife to any man. I feel lucky, though. Tad has so many admirable qualities. He's climbing the ranks in the Department of Prisons. He tells me the most incredible stories!"

Betty glanced upward, smiling slightly. I followed her gaze to a black glass ball pressed into the plaster ceiling.

"You have eyes in your house?" I asked, surprised. Residences were generally monitored only by listening devices.

"Oh, I requested them. I have nothing to hide." I noticed she still wore the bracelet she'd had in the Meadows, with the wafer-thin charm shaped like a cloud. "Something I've wondered," she said. "Why do you suppose they made you Best Girl?"

I felt my cheeks warm. "I have no idea," I said.

"They never did get around to administering the final test," she said. "I suppose, with the commotion at the end, what happened with Rose, the year being cut short—I suppose it got forgotten about."

I nodded.

"All the hours I spent practicing my needlework and Latin," Betty went on, "imagining getting the highest score. Sometimes I'm tempted to find Matron Sybil and ask her to administer it." She laughed lightly.

"Do you still think the algorithm made a mistake with you?"

"Undoubtedly," she said.

I'd studied her face then, which carried the finest dusting of face powder. If she were to slip, to reveal the truth, it would be now. "You must feel angry, having been sent to the Meadows."

"Not at all," she said. "I feel grateful. It prepared me well."

"What do you think about what Sheila said, all those years ago, about you not knowing yourself?"

Betty didn't even blink. "With hindsight, I've realized that Sheila was, in her own way, looking out for me. And for that I can only be grateful."

For the smallest fraction of a moment, Betty glanced again at the eye in the ceiling, and smiled.

CHAPTER 30

The silence woke me. I sat up in bed, listening. The bright cavern of the dormitory rang with quiet. Somehow, I'd slept through the sounds of girls rising from sleep, through Sheila neatening the covers on her bed and leaving for breakfast. She hadn't woken me.

I pulled on my dress, my movements slow and mechanical, mind sketching the events of the previous night. Sheila's father, dead. A new girl arrived. And Marina. Her shuttle sliding through the brick archway and disappearing with a wink.

I found the dining room empty. The mild, yellow smell of artificial eggs lingered. Our first class of the day was needlework, but I found Matron Calliope's classroom empty too.

A dull sense of dread broke over me. I had the feeling that I was alone here, in this place but also in the world. Had the Meadows emptied in the night? If something had happened, how would I call for help?

"Hello?" The hallway absorbed my voice.

And then, rather than hear it, I felt it. The solid undertones of Matron Sybil's voice. I followed it to the auditorium.

Matron Sybil stood on the stage beside a pale, neatly dressed woman with an avalanche of white hair stacked on her head. Behind them, racks and racks of clothing. Not the white dresses we were used to, but an explosion of colors and fabrics I hadn't seen in years. Matron Sybil was describing our last year in the Meadows, fast approaching, and the final test that would soon be administered. The girls clustered before her, Sheila near the front, listening attentively.

I skirted down a side aisle, fitting in at the back of the group. "To celebrate your progress, we have prepared a special activity for you today," Matron Sybil said. Silence gathered like clouds, the others standing stiffly. Matron Sybil let her arms fall, sighing. "I can see we're still adjusting to the news of our friend Marina. We ought to be happy for her! Happy knowing that when anything ends, something wonderful may be around the corner."

I wanted to shout out the truth, to shatter the illusion, to tell them all that Marina hadn't just moved, that she'd—disappeared inside a—a— How could I explain it in a way that anyone would believe?

"Ah—there you are, Matron Maureen." Matron Sybil turned toward the door. "Girls, allow me to introduce our newest pupil, Rose."

There came the sound of braids thwacking against several girls' backs as their heads turned toward Matron Maureen, striding up the central aisle with the new girl. My breath came short. *Rose.* So. Her name was Rose. She'd removed the raincoat and wore a white buttoned shirt and white pants that cuffed close to her ankles.

"It's Rosario, actually," the girl said, tongue rolling around her name. "But my good friends call me Rose." The concentrated focus of three dozen pairs of eyes bored into her. I would've wilted beneath it, but Rose smiled, as though basking. "I'm sure we'll all be good friends before the day is over."

Betty snorted a dubious laugh. Sheila, standing near her, smiled. Her face gave away none of what had happened last night.

"Rose, please find a place among the girls." Matron Sybil gestured behind her. Rose's eyes grazed each of us. When they found mine, a shiver forked through me. Rose walked on stage and placed herself beside me. Her body radiated a low heat.

"Now girls, please welcome Mrs. Churchill, a representative from a fine clothier in the city." Matron Sybil gestured to the white-haired woman beside her. Mrs. Churchill looked simultaneously elegant and like the sturdiest sort of worker bee, every part of her carefully encased in tweed.

"For years you've dressed in the uniform of girls," Mrs. Churchill said. "When you venture into the outside, your clothes will tell the world who you are. Will you show society someone elegant, smart, beautiful? Or someone haphazard, sloppy, boyish?" She pronounced that last word with a precise disdain.

"Do you think she's talking about me?" Rose whispered, leaning close.

I raised an eyebrow but looked straight ahead. "You do dress like a boy."

She grasped her chest. "Have you ever considered maybe it's boys who dress like me?"

A smile tugged at the sides of my mouth.

"Clothing is a powerful tool," Mrs. Churchill continued, gesturing to the racks behind her. "What you show people, they will believe. Choose wisely."

Mrs. Churchill explained our assignment: to assemble an outfit we'd want to show the world. The girls fanned out, excitedly sifting through the racks. Dresses with tiers of frills. Puffy jackets with striped cuffs. Shiny shoes that replicated leather. I looked to where Sheila browsed beside Betty. A hot kind of static filled me. What was she doing?

"What'll you choose?" Rose asked.

I turned to her, halfheartedly grazing the clothes with my fingers. "I don't know." I'd worn some version of the white dress for so long, it hadn't really occurred to me that, soon, I never would again.

Rose snatched a bright satin shirt from the rack, decorated with tropical birds. "I might be sick."

I laughed. "I think it suits you."

"Or my abuela."

I looked at her. Dangerous, speaking another language. "What about this?" I held up a floor-length beige gown, heavy as a wet fishing net.

"Yes," she said, placing the crook of her thumb beneath her chin. "Are you planning to become a ghost and haunt an old manor house one day?"

"Definitely."

She smiled. "Then that's your dress."

I felt my cheeks warm, an easy bright feeling opening in my chest. Strange beside the pull of sadness that tugged each time I glimpsed Sheila. I thought of that red ribbon we'd received in our first year. I still took it out from beneath my bed sometimes, to give my eyes the treat of color. Whatever facility Rose had come from clearly hadn't worked on her. She hadn't yet been churned through the mechanism, pressed into the precise shape of *girl*. My mind ran her through its fingers like that ribbon. The shadow of muscle behind her clothes. Her golden skin, wearing the residue of the sun, slightly burned and flakey at her cheeks. Each finger capped with a thimble of callus. Rose glanced at me then, and I turned away, cheeks flushed. I'd been staring.

Johanna stood nearby, thumbing a silk dress, a paralyzed look on her face. "How do we do this, Eleanor?"

I shook my head. "We just get through it," I said. "It's not forever."

A deep sadness punched through Johanna's eyes. *Except, it is*, her expression said. Tears fell over her cheeks, so sudden it was like they'd been waiting there a long time.

"Hey," I whispered. "You okay?"

"It's just—it's all changing. The future's coming like some giant tire on a road, and I feel like the tiniest ant. And I don't know—how I'll survive."

"Then we ants better stick together." I tried to say it with courage. My smile felt uneven.

Johanna nodded. I looked over to find Rose watching, her face a puzzle. And walking past her, arms full of dresses, Sheila.

"Through here," she muttered as she passed me.

I followed Sheila to the back of the stage, behind the muslin curtains that had been hung to serve as a changing area. "Stop staring at the new girl or you'll get yourself in trouble," she said, smiling, but it lacked her usual spark.

I stood before her, unable to speak. The events of the past days felt unbreachable. Her father's death. The hugeness of our fight. Marina. "I—I was worried this morning when I couldn't find anybody. Worried you'd—all disappeared."

"Disappeared?" Her eyebrows rose. "That made more sense to you than us being somewhere on the grounds?"

I ignored this. "How are you?" I asked her.

She shrugged.

An idea had been incubating in my mind, too newborn to speak out loud. "Something's going on here, Sheila," I whispered.

I wasn't supposed to have seen that archway switch on. The matrons likely had no idea I had, not unless they'd thought to check satellite footage from that night, and why would they? They didn't know anyone else was out there. For once, I actually had the upper hand.

"Something bigger than we knew," I added, voice low, nervous about what the matrons could hear. Then I told her about Marina's shuttle disappearing inside the brick archway.

Sheila bit her lip. She said nothing.

I huffed out a breath. "Isn't that—aren't you concerned? We need to figure out what that thing is. Maybe it finally explains the fog."

Sheila pointed her eyes away, frowning. "I can't. Not anymore."

I stared at her. "What?"

"I can't go . . . sneaking off at night, and climbing the yew tree. Asking questions."

I swallowed. "And you can't . . . be my friend?"

Sheila's gaze softened, just for a moment. "I can be your friend, Eleanor. I just can't be *only your* friend," she said. "Did you hear what my mom told me? I have to fight differently. My only chance is to walk the path the matrons have laid for us." She lowered her voice. "Do whatever it takes to look reformed. Fight like hell for Best Girl."

"Best Girl?" I sputtered, nearly a laugh. And then realization hit: Best Girl could choose her position after leaving.

Sheila's eyes lost focus. "My dad was going to sneak me into the aptitude test. For an engineering job."

A desperation began to stir in me. A rope slipping through my fingers. "You can still do it. We'll—find a way."

But something was happening on Sheila's face, as if putting pieces together. "Eleanor, soon we'll leave this place. The rest of our lives stretching ahead"—her fingers fanned out—"like a road, and there's the ones we'll be paired with, and there's the jobs they'll put us in until we get babies in our bellies, and then we'll be *mother* to them and nothing else until we become grandmother, until we die. And even in the ground, all they'll know about us was that we married *him* and we gave birth to *them*. And if I might've wanted that, I don't want *only* that. I don't want to *be* only that."

I watched her, the hollows beneath her eyes, the slackness of her face. "What do we do?"

Sheila paused for a long moment, eyes sharpening. "Nothing."

I blinked. "Nothing?"

"Maybe the Department of Engineering was always impossible. But I'm certain that the only chance I have of getting anywhere close is with a recommendation from the matrons."

I opened my mouth to argue when a hand parted the curtains before us. "Sheila, what's taking so long?" Betty. "I found a gown I think will be perfect on you."

"Be right out," Sheila said brightly.

Betty glanced at me, nose wrinkled suspiciously, then turned, the curtains wafting in her wake.

"Close your mouth, Eleanor," Sheila said. "I talked to Betty at breakfast. She's agreed to help me. With—with reforming."

"You can't be serious."

Sheila's gaze hardened. "I don't like it any more than you do."

"*Betty*," I continued, "who you've hated since the start. Betty, who smiles at the eyes in every room like she's getting extra credit with the algorithm. Betty, who doesn't even believe she *needs* to reform."

"And doesn't that make her the best person to learn from?"

I gaped at her. Sheila, befriending Betty? Trying to impress the matrons? The world had turned inside out. My *body* felt turned inside out by the strangeness of this conversation, the feeling of my heart and organs hanging from me like odd baubles on a holiday tree.

But then, in the space between us, Sheila held out her hands. I took them, grasped them as though they were an anchor. "You were right," she said, eyes shining. "There is no fighting them, at least not the way I was. Going up against them—" She shook her head slightly. "I turned down the chance to see my dad. All for some stupid, stubborn logic. And I'll never know, if I'd seen him, if he'd have—if I could have—"

"Sheila," I said. "Speaking to him wouldn't have made him better."

"Maybe." She cleared her throat. "I need you to know," she whispered, "that whatever you see me doing, it's just a different fight. I need the matrons. Surely you, of everyone, understands this?"

And before I could answer her, Sheila dropped my hands and walked away.

By the time I returned to the racks of clothes, most of the others had chosen their outfits. Rose was looking around, and when she caught my eye, she grinned. "I found this for you," she said, holding up a jacket.

"Oh," I whispered, brushing the fabric with my fingers. Denim, something a laborer might wear, box-shaped and tough. I felt something move in my chest, a kind of recognition. This—the sort of thing those musicians might've worn.

"It looks like you," Rose said.

"More than the ghost dress?" I asked.

"I'm serious," she said. "I think you and that jacket were made for each other."

I frowned. "You've barely met me."

"My mistake," she said, and offered her hand. "Rosario Gutiérrez. Also known as Rose Walters. Seventeen. I love pancakes, rainstorms, and Mrs. Churchill's tweed suit."

Unthinking, I smiled. Meeting Rose was nothing like the garden party, chatting spiritlessly with boys from the Pines. When I shook her hand, its warmth surprised me. "Eleanor Arbuck."

"Eleanor, now that we've met, I can say with authority that you should get this jacket."

I swung the jacket on and glanced at myself in one of the freestanding mirrors set up on the stage. A knot untied in my throat. It seemed right, this picture of me.

In the mirror, I watched Mrs. Churchill approach, her dusty, floral scent engulfing me. "Is this what you wish to present to the world?"

I glanced at Rose. "I thought so."

"What do you suppose a potential suitor might assume?" Mrs. Churchill asked. "If you ask me, this sort of article might suggest you aren't secure in your femininity."

"Then it's a good thing nobody asked you," Rose said mildly.

Mrs. Churchill ignored her, regarding me in the mirror. "Wouldn't you prefer, my dear, something that shows off the fine young lady into which the Meadows has shaped you?"

I felt myself deflate. "I suppose," I said, and pulled off the jacket. Mrs. Churchill, satisfied, strolled away. When I turned to face Rose, she wore a calamitous expression of disappointment. My cheeks burned. "What?"

"You can't live your life changing for others," Rose said.

I nearly laughed. "Do you know where you are?"

"They can't change you if you don't let them," she said, and strode off.

My mouth had fallen open. A quiet kind of rage kicked up inside me. First Sheila. Now this girl. She'd been here less than a day, and she presumed to tell me how to operate in the Meadows?

"Good luck with that," I murmured after her, but she was too far away to hear.

I went back to the racks and found an ivory blouse and a skirt printed with tiny flowers. They gave me a feeling of checking off the correct answer on an exam. They also felt wrong.

Behind a changing curtain, I unbuttoned my white dress, let it fall to the ground like a ghost. *You can't live your life changing for others.* Inside the billowing muslin curtains, inside these borrowed clothes, the threat of tears burned behind my eyes. I swallowed the feeling. Deadened my body. *Cat face. Smile face.* My body was an object that I didn't own. A piece of furniture. It didn't matter what furniture wore.

I parted the curtain and spotted Rose down the stage. She'd attempted to put on a very small pink jacket, shoulder joints swiveled the wrong way so her arms stuck out above her head. Penelope and Alice watched, bent over with laughter.

"Mrs. Churchill, what do you think?" Rose called. "Do you like it?" Mrs. Churchill and Matron Sybil exchanged a glance somewhere between amusement and disbelief.

Dressed, we stood in a line, paper dolls made real. Sheila and Betty had opted for gowns, which Mrs. Churchill cautioned could be perceived as excessive and high-maintenance.

"I don't understand," Betty said, in her teal satin ball gown. "We've learned to look after our appearance, our bodies, our voices. Aren't we *supposed* to be high-maintenance?"

Mrs. Churchill nodded. "Yes, dear," she said. "But we're not supposed to *look* like we are."

"Oh." The syllable dropped from Betty's mouth like a sad pebble.

Rose had opted for a leather jacket, cuffed denim pants, and boots, like a road worker. It was so clearly incorrect, it had crossed over to a joke, and several girls tittered as Mrs. Churchill's heels clicked across the floor to approach her. She shouldn't get used to it, I thought. The Meadows would do its work on her too.

"And what are you hoping to tell the world with this ensemble?" Mrs. Churchill asked.

"You tell me, Mrs. Churchill," Rose said, grinning as though she expected to have a gold ribbon placed on her chest. More giggling filled the room.

"Well," Mrs. Churchill clucked. "Your matrons have their work cut out. I wish them luck."

Rose caught my eye down the line, glanced at my outfit. The smile slid off her face.

"Very nice," Mrs. Churchill said, standing before me, admiring the dull skirt and blouse. "You're telling me you have important work to do one day."

I forced a smile onto my face. When she'd moved on to the next girl, my eyes tugged back to the racks of clothing. Nobody had taken the denim jacket.

CHAPTER 31

"What facility did you come from?" Penelope asked.

"I didn't," Rose said. "I lived in the wastelands."

After dinner, we gathered in the common room, circled around Rose. The others leaned toward her as though magnetized, planets caught in her orbit.

"The wastelands?" Alice exclaimed. "How'd you manage that?"

"Got my letter when I was twelve, but I ran," Rose said, eyes smiling. "Never got caught."

The others passed wide-eyed glances around the common room. Refusing attendance to a facility was a crime. "Why wouldn't you go?" Johanna asked.

Rose shrugged. "Didn't think I'd like the food."

The others laughed. Rose was good at this, slipping out of serious questions. I sat beyond the circle, turned slightly away. I felt just as much fascination as everyone, but I held it, clamped it close like some writhing creature. Let the others admire her. I could still taste her words, bitter: *You can't live your life changing for others.*

"And I suppose the food was delicious in the wastelands?" Betty scoffed.

"If you like cactus," Rose said. "And sandy vegetables, and whatever we could steal from the local towns."

I opened my mouth. "There were others with you?"

Rose turned her eyes on me, dark brown, the color nearly indistinguishable from her pupils. "A hundred, maybe."

Behind her glasses, Betty's nose wrinkled. "Aren't the wastelands filled with bandits and lepers and—and people with faces melted by nuclear waste?"

Rose laughed as though Betty had made a joke. Betty's face sagged.

"A hundred people, just hiding out?" Sheila's voice called, a line between her brows. "With that many, why not—*do* something? You could've joined the state and pulled it down from the inside."

Rose's eyebrows lifted. "Sounds like you've thought about it."

"No," Sheila snapped. "Only saying."

"Well, maybe we should," Rose said, standing. "We outnumber the matrons. I bet we could take control of the Meadows before dawn. Who's with me?" Several girls laughed uncertainly. And inside Sheila's eyes, a single point of light. A spark, burning.

"This is so dull, it hurts." Rose sighed, throwing her paintbrush down. "It actually hurts." In almost every class that first week, Rose sat beside me. As though she sensed I was determined to not be won over. She was determined too.

"Just try. Painting imparts patience," I said in an imitation of Matron Sybil.

"But I don't care about *gourds*," Rose said.

Around the room, girls were circled in white smocks, Matron Maureen and Matron Sybil examining canvases, and at the center, a wooden bowl filled with gourds and corn and other symbols of the upcoming harvest feast.

I peered at Rose's easel and blinked back surprise. The bowl and its contents had been replicated exactly, with perfect, neat brush strokes.

"Where'd you learn to do that?"

The corners of Rose's mouth folded into a smile. "Jail."

"Why do you do that?" I asked. "Avoid answering questions about yourself." In the week I'd known her, she'd had lively conversations with almost everyone, but nobody had learned much about her.

She shrugged. "Not much to tell."

"Sure."

Her eyes were bright. "Everyone's allowed their secrets," she said, cocking her head. "I'm beginning to suspect even the good Eleanor Arbuck might have some."

Rose stood to browse the paint shelf and I turned to my own canvas, biting the inside of my cheek.

A hand entered my field of vision then, offering something.

"I visited my mother's house while I was away," Matron Maureen said, smiling. "I thought you might want to try one of her oranges." She dropped a small bright sphere into my palm.

I looked from her face to the fruit suddenly in my hand. This orange was oblong and blushed with green in patches, and I knew it would taste sweet and bitter and *real*, nothing like the engineered ones here. I also knew that Matron Maureen was again extending her offer—the future she'd promised back in my first year. A knot formed in my throat. *How do I know you're telling the truth?* I wanted to ask her. *How can I ever trust you?* Instead, I spoke my next question.

"Did you know Rose was coming?" I whispered.

"I had no idea," Matron Maureen said.

I examined her face, searching out a lie. But there was only her pleasant smile, her friendly eyes. In my peripheral vision, I saw Rose had returned and was watching. I hid the orange in my pocket.

"Rose, what seems to be the problem?" Matron Sybil strode by, hands clasped.

Rose let out a theatrical sigh. "The problem is, matron, that I don't want to do this."

Matron Sybil smiled. Even she couldn't help but be amused by Rose. "Many young women since time immemorial have secured a handsome suitor with the aid of a well-crafted painting."

"I'm sorry to break this to you, matron," Rose said, "but I don't think that's the right tack to take with me." From around the room, the sound of several small, surprised giggles.

"Rose," Matron Sybil said warningly.

"Maybe Rose is right." Matron Maureen stepped forward. "Perhaps you should allow the girls the freedom to paint what they'd like."

"I happen to like painting gourds," Betty declared.

Matron Maureen turned to the group. "Who here would like a chance to paint something they choose?"

Around the room, hands reached into the air. Matron Sybil gave a small, patient smile.

"There you have it," Matron Maureen said. "Next week, you'll paint whatever you'd like."

Rose turned to me. "She seems nice."

I felt my mouth pull into a frown. "She is."

Rose breathed a laugh. "You say that like it's a bad thing."

Into my mind came an image I must have seen in a book at Mrs. Arkwright's: a soldier wearing a bandolier stuffed with bullets. Nice could be like that. A piece of Matron Maureen's arsenal. A kindness or a bullet, and how to tell which?

"I'm not sure nice is the good thing I once thought," I said.

Rose squinted at me, the corner of her mouth turning upward, as though confused by me but in a way that delighted her. My eyes wanted to take her in. But I was seized by a strange flush of shyness. I pulled my gaze down, to the floor and the hem of her pants.

"Like them?" she asked, extending a leg. "I told Matron Sybil that I'd die—yes, literally die—before wearing one of those dresses, so unless she wanted me running around with no clothes, she'd have to figure something out."

I laughed. "What did she say?"

"Oh, she was great about it," Rose said lightly. "She's nice too."

I met Rose's eyes. She carried herself with muscle and confidence, but her face was softer than I'd first realized, full cheeks and brown eyes fringed in long lashes. She could not have been more different from me when I'd arrived, but all the same, I felt the urge to protect her. "Yes," I warned. "They all are."

Even so, that night, I sat alone in my room, unpeeled the orange, and ate every wedge.

CHAPTER 32

"We're here today to begin the deep work." Matron Sybil spoke from the center of the room in her pleats and furrows of white. The easels and brushes had been stored away. "Imagine life before the Turn," she said, softly, so we had to hold still to catch each word. "See nature bury cities beneath oceans. See her devour swaths of forest with fire. All because mankind lived outside of nature's laws."

On my stool, my foot jangled. I closed my eyes, trying to imagine what Matron Sybil described, but I couldn't get calm. I glanced around at the ring of girls lulled by Matron Sybil's words, staring unfocused at the ground. I was struck by the spontaneous desire to scream. To fracture this stupefied circle. I felt trapped—these mind exercises, playing dress-up. A month before I'd watched Marina collide with another world and disappear. Sheila's father had died and she and I were untethered from each other. Now Rose sat beside me like a freeze-framed explosion.

Matron Sybil glanced my way, drew a disapproving line with her eyes to my jostling foot. I ordered my body to still, clutching my wrist. *Cat face. Smile face.*

"Now, imagine your body is like the Earth," Matron Sybil said. "There are unnatural forces within each of you. In a mind, they look like thoughts."

Betty raised her hand. "What about those of us who don't have unnatural thoughts?"

"Does she shut up?" I muttered to my left, expecting Sheila to laugh, but she had her eyes closed. Instead, I heard a chuckle from my other side. Rose.

Matron Sybil turned to Betty. "Each of you has such thoughts, even those who believe they can hide them." Betty's cheeks pulsed a deep crimson.

"Let's begin." Matron Sybil pulled a screen from the deep pocket of her dress. She pressed a button, and an image projected onto the class-room wall. The footage showed an expanse of forest as observed from above, a flat black river cutting through miles of dry-looking pines. The image had the quick zooming quality of a satellite, trawling for something specific. The video drew in on a clearing, a scattering of wooden shacks.

"I'll get you!" a loud voice rang out.

"No!" a high voice called.

A figure emerged in the clearing. A tall, bearded boy in homemade trousers, pacing strangely before the house. Huddled in front of him were four little girls, each with an intricate braid and a dress that swept the dirt.

"Somebody here stole my gold," the boy barked, striding around the girls. "And I'm fixin' to find out who."

"Please, mister," one of the girls whimpered. "We didn't take your gold."

The boy stroked his beard. I sat up. I recognized those hands. Partially hidden beneath a beat-up cap, a tight braid encircled his head. *Johanna.* My eyes fixed on the real Johanna across the classroom whose face had opened, smiling, as though emerging from darkness.

I made sense of the scene: A make-believe game. These girls—Johanna's sisters. They wore plastered-on looks of terror that, every so often, shattered in a fit of giggles.

"What's so funny, little miss?" Johanna asked, in an exaggerated drawl, pointing a finger at the oldest girl.

"Nothing, mister," the girl said. "Just that your pants seem to be on backward."

Beneath her fake beard, Johanna's face broke into a grin. "I've never heard such insolence in all my life!" Johanna said. "You've left me no choice but to use my greatest weapon." She strode toward the girls, hands held out like claws before her, ready to attack. Then she dropped to the ground, tickling them. They fell into a pile of shrieks and laughter.

I don't know why I had never considered that Johanna was also a stack of paper dolls. Perhaps we all were. I found myself smiling. But when I glanced over, Johanna's smile had vanished, something raw and stricken in its place. Tremblingly, she held curled fingers to her mouth.

"Johanna!" The voice blared from the speakers. An older woman emerged from the house carrying a woven basket. The laughter ceased. "I need you ironing. Not—whatever this is."

The oldest of Johanna's sisters stood. "Please let us have fun, Mama," the girl said. "Jo told us Daddy used to play theater with her when she was little."

"Her name is *Johanna*," their mother said, placing emphasis on the *h* in her name. "And she is not your daddy."

Johanna stepped froward, pulling off the beard. "We were just playing pretend—"

"This isn't pretend for you," her mother said. The rebuke came so gently, it might've floated by without notice. But Johanna reeled as if struck. The four younger girls stood now, their smiles forgotten. "And if you need reminding, Johanna, you have been chosen for the Meadows. If you're to do well, you need to—to at least arrive in a neat dress."

"I'm not going. I told you."

Her mother let go a tense sigh. "This is a great honor. You'll rise above anything you could've been here."

"*I don't want it*," Johanna said, words fierce. "Tell them. I'm not coming."

Her mother's face shifted, her certainty falling away to reveal the pinch and squint of fear. Fear for her daughter, for what would become of her. "You have no choice."

Even viewed from above, I could see Johanna's breath come fast, her eyes darting for an escape. I sensed what she was about to do before she did it—took several steps forward and shoved her mother to the ground, then took off running.

Gasps around the classroom. Betty's hand flew dramatically to her mouth. Johanna shrank into her chair, wracked with silent sobs.

On screen, the camera locked onto Johanna, at times only catching a glimpse through trees before she fell to her knees in a clearing. There were no ears in the woods, but it was clear she was crying the sort of sobs that could crack ribs. She wrapped her hand into a fist and punched the rough trunk of a pine tree. And again, and again. Her hand was bloodied and unrecognizable before she fell to the ground, fist curled beside her, a piece of macerated meat.

I watched Johanna across the room, her hand crosshatched with pink scars. On the video, she had moved with such power. There was something cathartic, watching her. And frightening. Even the most controlled could explode.

Matron Sybil cleared her throat, pausing the video. "It is difficult to see your worst moment played out in front of you. I am conscious of the pain you must be feeling, Johanna."

Johanna hid behind splayed fingers, a whine escaping her mouth like an injured animal.

Matron Sybil approached Johanna like an angel, white-clad and anointing, like I'd seen in a painting in Mrs. Arkwright's house. "Look at me, dear." Johanna could barely lift her eyes. "What did you feel, when you broke your hand?"

"Nothing," Johanna whispered.

"I'd wager you feel it now," Matron Sybil said. "This pain, this shame, is your greatest weapon. It's your body rejecting that which does not belong. No different from the devastation of the Turn. Painful, but also a great cleansing."

Johanna's breath came steadier, pale eyes searching Matron Sybil's. "It is?"

Matron Sybil smiled. "You, like the people before the Turn, were living in ways nature abhors. Shirking your natural role as a female."

Johanna darted her eyes away. The musculature of her face trembled.

Inside me, there was a wrenching, as though a membrane had torn. Across the circle, where Sheila sat, I mouthed the words. *We have to do something.*

A wrinkle rested between Sheila's eyebrows. Her eyes flitted between me and Matron Sybil. *I can't,* she mouthed back.

Dread, thick and acid-tasting, climbed up my throat. Sheila couldn't help. But I didn't have dreams to lose like she did. So, I did the only thing I could think of. I stood and walked to Johanna, swerving to avoid Matron Sybil.

"I'm sorry, Matron Sybil, but I need Johanna for—for something important."

Matron Sybil's eyebrows jerked upward. "And what is that, Eleanor?"

"Like I said." I swallowed. "Something important."

And before the matron could reply, I held out my hand to Johanna. "Let's go."

She blinked up at me blearily. "Where?"

"Anywhere."

In the hall, Johanna shed her sorrow in waves, her steps becoming light, a smile growing on her face. An uneasy awe filled me—that she could shake off what happened so quickly.

"Psst." Rose stood in the hallway behind us. "Room for one more?"

At this, a rush of annoyance and a rush of heat. "If you'd like."

Outside, we sat on a low branch of the yew tree. Johanna was cross-legged in the grass, skirts tossed to one side. When had Sheila and I last sat here together? It felt like ages. I wished she were here now. I wondered if she ever would be again.

Rose positioned herself beside me, our hands braced against the branch, pinky fingers a hair's breadth apart. I stared at that gap, imagined how easy it would be to touch her. How impossible.

"Are you not worried about getting in trouble?" Rose asked. "You practically bumped Matron Sybil out of the way."

My hands moved to grip my stomach, a waterfall of adrenaline falling through me when I recalled the matron's astonished face. "It just seemed impossible to keep sitting there."

"We're rebels," Johanna said.

"Oh, yes," Rose said, "you two seem like a couple of true subversives."

I watched Johanna. Matron Sybil had wanted us to focus on the end of the video, the part where Johanna acted rash and unladylike. But my mind kept tugging back to the beginning. I'd never seen Johanna look so alive. In those ragged trousers. Inside the name Jo. It struck like a match in my mind. Not the pain. Not the shame and the scars on the back of her hand. The joy. The joy of being perfectly yourself.

"I'm sorry Matron Sybil showed that video," I said.

Johanna's mouth folded down. "Mama never—My daddy was the one who just let me *be*. There's been nobody who hasn't tried to change me since he died. Ma, the matrons—they've got me wrong. Or—I've got myself wrong."

Her chin shook. I watched her, the pain carved into her face, and felt the desire to pluck it out, to leave behind only what was good. Only Johanna. "There's not a thing wrong with you, you know," I said, testing the words in my mouth. "You're good, just as you are."

Johanna winced away from me. "You don't know how wrong you are," she said. "I sit in those lessons, *how to act like a fine young woman*, and—and every part of me strains away. I don't feel like a girl. Not the kind they want. But, not—not exactly a boy. Both, or—none." Johanna grimaced, every muscle bracing. Rose and I shared a concerned look. "This is what I hate. Telling it. It makes sense inside my head, but the moment I say it out loud—"

"It makes perfect sense to me," I said.

Johanna lifted her eyes to mine. I was seeing her, fair eyebrows and wobbling chin and eyes a fractured blue. Seeing this person, perfectly made. Who didn't fit only because the rules had been written that way.

"Do you want to be called something different?" Rose asked.

"My sisters called me Jo." She shook her head, face clouding. "But, what would be the point? To the algorithm, I will only ever be Johanna."

"Well, if you need name ideas," Rose said, "I'm rather partial to Sullivan."

Johanna smiled, unsure. "Why?"

"It was the name of my pet turtle," Rose said.

Johanna stuttered a laugh, and I watched it happen again, the pain cast off like water shaken from a dog's coat.

"I doubt Johanna wants to be named after a turtle," I said.

"Are you kidding?" Rose exclaimed. "He was a great turtle."

The air shifted. Rose had hauled us away from despair. Everything about her was exactly what the Meadows was designed to steal. So how did she seem so at ease? I looked back at our hands, resting on the branch, our fingers that could be touching with almost no effort. Just a decision. Rose turned her eyes there too. I felt heat build in me.

I jumped up, hiking a foot onto a higher branch. "Race you to the top."

I climbed higher than I had in a long time, near the spot where the branch had snapped and I'd fallen in my first year. I outpaced Rose, who was still scrabbling up the middle branches. My breaths came sharp. Why did I have the impulse to impress, to show Rose how capable I was?

"You ought to be careful," Rose called up. "Don't the matrons have rules about not showing off your underwear to new classmates?"

From where she stood on a bottom bough, Johanna laughed a scandalized snort.

"All of our underwear is the same," I said lightly. "If you've seen one you've seen them all."

I spotted Rose's smile, even from up high, a white crescent against the peachy brown of her skin. "I'm not so sure about that."

I felt my ears heat. Rose hauled herself up beside me, bracing a hand against the trunk. "Eleanor, can I ask you something?"

"Okay."

"Why do I have the feeling you don't like me very much?" she asked.

I glanced away. "Do you need everyone to like you?"

"Most people do," she said.

I squinted at her. "How do you *do* that?"

"Do what?"

"How do you . . ." I trailed off. "Like yourself so much?"

She breathed a laugh. "It's not hard."

"If you say so."

Our bodies were inches apart, suspended inside the green dome of branches, inside this pocket of silence. I could feel her eyes leaving fingerprints all over my skin. "They've gotten to you," she whispered. "The matrons."

I glanced around. There was no way to explain that I inhabited a no-man's-land within myself. My paper dolls, the different parts of me, at war, unable to decide—about Matron Maureen, and the future she offered. About the Meadows, and the parts of me it wanted to cut away, what I wanted gone and what I wanted to guard. About Rose, most of all.

"You can't know that," I told her.

"But I'm right," she insisted.

I felt myself still. Inside me, shutters closing. "And now I suppose you're about to give me more advice? *Don't change for anyone.* What else? Start dressing for myself? Live in the wastelands? Be with whoever I want?"

Rose lifted her chin, mouth pulled into an infuriating smile. "Why not?"

I looked for a branch, ready to climb down.

"What's stopping you?" she asked. "Obviously it's *them.* But I wonder, if they didn't exist, whether you'd still find a way to deny yourself the things you love."

Bright white electricity poured into my veins. "Stop—*pretending* to know me," I said. "Do I need to remind you that we met not even a month ago? Have you read my file or something?"

For the briefest moment, Rose blanched, her gaze shrinking.

"*Have* you?"

I leaned toward her, but instead of firm ground, my foot stepped into open air. My vision had funneled black on all sides, with Rose at the very center, and I'd somehow forgotten we were high in a tree. Just as I felt my weight shift, slotted into the crevasse between branches, just as my stomach flew into my throat, Rose's hands grabbed me. Clutched my rib cage.

"Got you," she breathed.

I gulped air in, my lungs bucking. I couldn't look at her, at her mouth, at the realness of her skin. An electromagnetic warmth seemed to roll from her like waves.

I turned away, finding solid footing on a branch. And then I saw it.

The wound where the branch had broken, years ago, a gash in the trunk the size of a spread hand. I looked closer, puzzled. The trunk was covered in gnarled brown bark, a spatter of green lichen. But the wound—where it should have been the tawny color of raw wood—it was—astonishingly—white. Solid white, shining like bone.

I unspooled myself from Rose's arms and touched the pale surface, rough from where the branch had broken. "The inside of the tree is . . ."

"Yes." I studied her expression. It contained no surprise. "I assumed all of you would've figured it out by now."

I felt my vision blur, a sick feeling clawing up my throat. "Figured what out?"

"This place. It isn't what you think."

I cast around. The perfect fields. Perfect sky. Perfect roundness of the buildings atop their perfect blanket of green grass. The question had always been not what this place wasn't but what it *was*.

"You seem to know a lot about the Meadows for someone who's only been here a month."

"I haven't been *alive* for a month."

"Then where are we?" I demanded, to Rose, to the air, to the algorithm. "Where are we that there's no weather? That the trees are—are made of plasticore?"

Rose's forehead knit. "That's the question."

My mother's voice: *Learn where you are, first thing you do.* I'd thought she was paranoid, coloring something wonderful with her dark slant. But this tree—another lie. Such an ugly word, Matron Sybil had said once. They preferred the polite sidestepping of the truth like they preferred to smooth over snags in conversation.

I pivoted away. I wouldn't let Rose see my face, like a thumb under a hammer, stunned. Briefly, I peered up at the sun, making its clockwork rotation of the sky. I watched the cloud, shaped like a crown, appear and shift across the blue the same way it had every day. The same way it would forever.

CHAPTER 33

"Eleanor! Always a pleasure." The young man at the door smiles as though he's greeting an old friend. He goes by Ed now, though when we met in the Meadows, he was Edward from the Pines. Since that day at the garden party, his face has turned angular, jaw shadowed with stubble.

"Ed," I say, teeth slightly gritted. Most boyfriends stay away when I arrive for adjudications. "How's your work? Made any of those lavender apples yet?"

"And more besides. My department manages the periscope tech too. Really quite remarkable what the engineers can do. If I told you the half of it, you'd never recover." As Sheila enters the room, he pulls her into him. A grimace flashes on her face, but she smooths it away. I feel enraged for her—Ed lied for months about the possibility of her joining his department.

Sheila keeps her eyes directed at the ground. There's a tense spot somewhere behind my rib cage. It's been there since last week. I'm aching to leave, to see how Sheila really is, to ask if she's looked up Rose's residence number, but we must go through the motions of the adjudication and stand here politely wasting time with Ed.

"Oh, show her your prototype," Sheila says. "He's very impressive, Eleanor. I showed you his Taste of Paris, but this is even better."

Ed smiles so wide, his cheeks ball up. "If you insist." He sits on the arm of the sofa and pulls something from his briefcase, the recognizable white frame of a periscope. It's expandable, and he pulls on it idly with his fingers, shrinking and enlarging the frame.

"Everyone has a periscope in their pockets these days. But they probably never stop to consider the technology involved. We've been able to print for a long time, but printing doesn't do much good when you don't have the space to print. That's where these come in." He holds the periscope up, resembling a salesman showing off his wares. "Scientists have debated about other spaces for centuries. It was just theoretical until someone discovered how to cut through space."

I feel myself bristle as Ed launches into his explanation, listening to this boy who only knows things because the world has handed him that knowledge. I'm struck with the desire to pop his bubble, to remind him who he is. Who we all are. Some of the male reformeds I've met have Ed's confidence, in their fine suits, advancing within their departments, a pretty girlfriend on their arm. The flash of accomplishment can hide many truths. For a while.

"With enough energy," Ed continues, "we can sort of . . . open a doorway into another space. Like finding a door in your house that opens onto a completely different house that nobody knew existed." I watch Sheila, absorbing Ed's words carefully, but there's a twinge of longing hidden far beneath the muscles of her face. Sheila can make twenty different kinds of stitches, but she can't give a speech like Ed's giving.

"What was his name?" I ask. "The scientist who discovered this?"

"*Her* name, actually," Ed says, clearing his throat. "Adele Martinique. She died around the Turn, and what a shame. She made it all possible."

"A woman," Sheila says, a wrinkle between her brows. What is she thinking, I wonder. Is it how, if that woman were alive today, they likely wouldn't allow her to work on the technology she invented? They'd have her cutting meat in a deli?

"So far, we've got it programmed for a desert island, or an arctic glacier," Ed says. "I can turn up the temperature for you if you choose that one. My department is even working to replicate some of the cities we lost before the Turn. We think historical tourism is going to be a big market."

I glance at Sheila. "Have you ever been inside?"

She's about to speak, when Ed says, "She's not very interested in this kind of thing, are you, Sheila?"

Sheila pauses, mouth still open, then looks at him. "No, it's all a bit over my head."

I stare at her. I want to shake her by the shoulders, tell her she shouldn't be letting Ed suck all the air from the room.

Ed holds up the frame again. "Want to try, Eleanor?"

An idea comes to me. "What about space?" I ask. "Like, the empty space that the scientist first found—what it looks like before you've printed any scenery. Can I go there?"

"There'd be nothing to see," Ed says.

"But it's possible?"

Ed's eyes shift to the side. "I suppose. I'd just have to remove most of the code." He taps on his screen and with a faint hum, the periscope flickers to life. Inside, a square of black. The same infinite black as the periscope in the Meadows' kitchen. Ed expands the frame to a shape slightly wider than my shoulders.

"Here we go," he says, holding the frame above my head. "When you want out, just lift it off the ground and you'll be right back here."

I take one last glimpse at Sheila before Ed slides the frame over my head, then my shoulders, and my torso, until the frame sits around my feet, only a square of gray flooring visible. I can feel my heartbeat in my throat. I stand inside emptiness. My eyes try to focus on something, anything, but there's only unending darkness, depthless and without texture. I take a breath, but even the air feels insubstantial, like it's only allowing me oxygen as a favor. I close my eyes and attempt to see with my ears: It's as if the air vibrates, a barely detectable *wub wub wub* like the shaking of sheet metal. Though perhaps it's only the sound of the tiny bones and cavities inside my head. Inside Sheila's apartment, I'm sure it looks like I've disappeared.

"Hello!" I call, expecting an echo, but the space absorbs my voice as though I hadn't spoken at all.

I crouch, like I've done a million times before on a dock, gazing into the depths of the ocean. I spread my fingers and test the space next to me. Empty, like Ed said, and I wonder what would happen if I stepped off this square of vinyl and allowed my body to drop. Would I fall, or would the air hold me like it held the frog in the kitchen periscope in the Meadows? Would it disassemble me? I stare down, deeper than any sea.

Light suddenly splashes my eyes. I cover my face with a hand, grimacing. When I crack my eyelids, I'm back in Sheila's apartment. Ed holds the frame in his hands.

"You were in there for ten minutes," he says. "What were you doing?"

"Nothing," I say. "There was nothing there."

Ed nods. "That's what I told you." He collapses the frame to the size of a small book and pushes it back into his satchel. "Well, I'd better be off," he says, swinging a suit jacket on. "You ladies have fun."

He pauses in the doorway. "It really is a pleasure to see you, Eleanor. I hope it's all right to say, but when you've retired from your position, I'd so like us to be friends. You'll be matched, and we could all have dinner. One day, the children could even play together."

Acid pools in my stomach. "Have a good day, Ed."

The children could even play together. To me, Ed remains as he was a couple of years ago, a round-faced boy, trying his best to impress Patron Gilbert. Sometimes, it takes seeing someone from before, like Ed, to remind me that we are all not so much older than we were.

Sheila and I walk through streets decked in evergreen wreaths and bright-colored ribbon, past an enormous pink tree in the square that people are hanging with silver baubles. The Quorum relaxed restrictions on the old holidays, scrubbing them of religious meaning, and people in the city have embraced the season.

Sheila and I have entered a new phase: It's customary to hold real-world adjudications when a reformed is nearly exited, observing them beyond the confines of their home.

"Sheila, how are you?" I ask.

She doesn't look at me, and only offers a short "Fine, Eleanor, thanks."

We can't speak openly on the street anyway, not with this many people around, so we walk in strange silence. It worries me that we seem to have no conversation. I don't know where we stand. We pass a glowing toy store where children congregate around a window display of a tiny silver family, each no larger than my thumb, moving on their own outside their miniature house. The children laugh as a tiny dog lifts its leg on a silver tree.

Everywhere we go, I glance around for June. There's a chance, however slight, that I'll catch a glimpse of her shopping, or heading to a compulsory tea party. To know she's okay, to tide me over until next week when I'll see her again.

Like a tongue searching out a sore tooth, my mind touches on June often, each time sending a lemon-sharp bolt through my body. I think of her out of order: The wind whipping her curls when we explored tide pools. Her missing-toothed six-year-old smile laughing wildly when I put her dog in a dress. Her empty gaze when talking about her fiancé Charlie, like the flat eye of a washed-up seal I found on the beach once, not yet milky but obviously dead.

With Rose, my feelings are simple. I miss her. I want her. I can't bear that I hurt her. But June is a puzzle I can't solve. I know my feelings for

June from before—the day at the market in the Cove, the slow mingling of our breath—are behind a door that can never open again.

"Looking for someone?" Sheila asks.

"Uh—no," I say. I'm distracted, I know. I should be trying to draw Sheila out. "What would you think of visiting that bridge I showed you last week?"

"I thought today was about observing me in the real world," Sheila says. "I have shopping to do. Between the Young Wives Club, and prepping for a dinner party with Ed's work friends, I don't have many spare minutes these days."

"Of course," I say, not trying to keep the worry from my voice. "Afterward, then?"

Sheila doesn't respond, leading us toward a quaint house, sandwiched between high-rises, framed with a dainty fence and square of artificially green lawn. Incongruous in the bustle of the city. "What is this place?" I ask.

"A grocery installation," Sheila says. "They're basically real-life advertisements. Whatever you see in the house, you can buy and take with you."

Sheila flashes a glance at an eye by the entrance and the doors hiss open. We enter into a spacious living room of plush orange carpet, inside a sunken area with a couch and a screen. I take in the brightly lit space, rich wives bustling nearby, who don't need food vouchers but have unlimited credit by virtue of who they've married.

An itch begins in the back of my mind, following Sheila from the living room into an expansive kitchen, the floor checkered and cabinets the color of pistachio. She looks like any of these wives, opening the refrigerator where there's a stack of shrink-wrapped packages of re-engineered meat. *Printed from the cells of authentic pre-Turn cows!* the label shouts. On the counter, there's a pyramid of shining apples the color of bubble gum. I lift one, shaped like a heart.

"One of Ed's designs," she says, smiling, and drops one into her bag.

I clear my throat. "How is everything with Ed?"

"He's been very thoughtful lately," she says. "We even tried kissing last week, and I have to tell you, I didn't hate it. Only took us a year. Makes me less nervous for . . . you know." She moves toward the kitchen pantry.

I grapple with what to say, impatience rising in my chest, wondering if, once we're done here, there will be any time left. To talk. To allow her to drop this act, this pretense. To ask about Rose's residence number. The idea of waiting another month to see her sends a spike of panic through me.

A gray-haired woman enters the kitchen and picks up a box from a display on the counter. Through the cellophane, I make out rows of what appear to be pea-sized candies.

"Those are all the rage, apparently," Sheila says, showing me a box. "You swallow one and it expands inside your stomach. Something like cotton fluff, and afterward you feel full."

I shake my head. "All this food, and people fill their stomach with cotton."

A shadow crosses Sheila's face, and I realize too late that she was planning to toss the package into her bag. "You get nutrients from it too." When I don't respond, she sighs. "I don't expect you to understand, Eleanor."

My stomach twists. I sense the gray-haired woman, examining a tin of sardines, darting a glance at us. "Understand?" I mutter.

Sheila frowns. "It's just different when you're matched." Sheila puts the box back on the counter.

"Why—Sheila? Is that you?" a voice calls from across the kitchen.

For the first time today, a real smile breaks over Sheila's face. "Betty!"

Betty is only a year older than when I saw her last, but she seems to have grown both more sophisticated and bouncier, in her emerald satin dress, her copper hair in a long bob.

"Eleanor, this is my friend Betty," Sheila says. "We met at the Young Wives Club."

I attempt a smile, but the whole farce feels embarrassing. Reformeds are not allowed to acknowledge the facilities in public. Betty extends a hand. "Lovely to meet you, Eleanor. I hope I'm not interrupting."

"Not at all," Sheila says, looping her arm in Betty's.

I try to hide the bright, hot flash of jealousy that cuts through me. "So, Sheila," I say, trying to return to the interview. "What have been the highlights of your month?"

"Well, I tried to make a pie," Sheila says, smiling. "For the Young Wives Club."

Betty bursts out in dainty laughter. "Oh, good, tell that story!" A place in my jaw tightens.

"It's all pre-married girls or newlyweds," Sheila explains. "I honestly thought they'd be the worst bores, but they're quite funny. My pie was a disaster, but they all lied and said they liked it, except for Betty."

"I said I hadn't tasted such a good pie since I was little," Betty says.

"And when I asked her what kind of pie, she replied, 'Mud!'"

Their laughter flings around the fake kitchen like birds. A feeling of cold creeps over my skin. I feel as though I'm watching a play. Sheila's put on an entire character. Only weeks ago, she would have shown me her feelings freely. I wonder if she shows Betty now. Or if it's just that they can pretend together, playing paper dolls.

Betty shakes her head, still grinning. "Well, it was lovely to see you both," she says. "I need to get home. Tad's boss from the Department of Prisons is coming for dinner. I promised a pot roast." She holds up her shopping bag, where the rounded weight of packaged meat rests heavily. I'm struck by the desire to smack it out of her hands.

Betty gives Sheila a squeeze around the shoulders.

"I'm done too," Sheila says, turning to me. "Shall we?"

I nod, a cascade of relief unloosing inside me. Finally.

Outside, I turn to her. "Let's go to the bridge."

Sheila pulls away. "I really need to get back."

"Don't tell me you have a pot roast to cook too."

"So what if I do?"

My brow furrows. "Just a few minutes, Sheila. Please."

She sighs.

Inside the quiet stone room under the pedestrian bridge, I turn to her.

"Just—tell me how you really are," I say.

"Would you believe me if I said I'm fine?" she asks. "Good even?"

"No," I say. "Ed lied to you. Your dream—"

"Was just a dream," she says with perfect neutrality. As though it doesn't bother her. As though she's moved on.

"Sheila, don't pretend with me," I say. "Maybe with everyone else, but not with me."

Sheila frowns. "I'm not pretending."

"You don't seriously like all of that Young Wives Club garbage?" I ask. "Baking pies? That's the sort of thing you always hated."

"People change."

I shake my head, the worry and frustration I'd managed to keep tucked away spilling out. "Is this another ruse—like in the Meadows? Tricking the matrons into believing you're reformed? So what if Ed lied—there must be another way. You were right—what I do, it's not enough. We need to do more. *I'm* trying to do more."

"There is no other way for me, Eleanor," she says, weary. "Believe me. I've thought it through."

"So the solution is to what?" I demand. "Become Betty?"

She huffs out a laugh. "You're never satisfied, are you? In the Meadows, you wanted me to go along, to keep safe. And *now* you think I should fight back? Eleanor, I've grown tired of being miserable. Spending the past year rewatching the Meadows again and again in my mind. Wondering if I'd played the matrons' stupid game earlier, if I'd be in the Department of Engineering now. All that . . . *wanting*—it's exhausting. I've accepted my place in the world, and I feel—relief. It's not happiness, but it could become something close. If I let it."

I stare at her in disbelief.

"One day you'll see, Eleanor. Not now, in your two years of suspended animation. But soon you'll be in my exact spot, and then you'll see."

Something shifts between us then. It feels like watching the white sail of a ship grow smaller and smaller as it steers out to sea. Here is my best friend's face, indecipherable to me now, and I search there too long for the girl who once believed in her own goodness so much, not even the matrons could snatch it away.

I know the answer before I ask the question. "Did you look up Rose's place of residence?"

Sheila keeps her eyes pointed firmly away. "No."

"What about Ed's screen?"

Sheila's forehead wrinkles. "Eleanor, what I told you about that—I've stopped. It won't do any good now. And snooping through my fiancé's screen isn't who I want to be."

"Fiancé?" I ask. "He's asked you, has he?"

She shrugs. "We were nearly at the end of the courtship period anyway. It wasn't exactly a surprise."

"Congratulations," I say, a pit opening in my stomach.

Sheila adjusts her collar, flattens the front of her dress. Performs the precise motions of becoming the girl the world expects her to be. "I can't endanger Ed's position. You must know that."

She reaches for my hand then, and I let her take it. She gives a faint squeeze before letting go. As she leaves, I remember our hands all those nights, reaching through the pale violet air, bridging the space between our beds, to touch fingertips. Holding each other up.

CHAPTER 34

"The girls are saying you've lost your mind." Rose stood beside me, several strides into the meadow fields. I was bent at the waist, plucking flowers from the dry earth, examining their frayed root systems, splayed like strange thin fingers.

"If it's Betty, she's been saying that since we arrived here," I said, rolling dirt between my fingers, testing the fine grain of it.

"Are you going to tell me what you're up to?" Rose asked.

I straightened. "The yew tree is . . . engineered, I guess. Like a prop in a theater production. I just wondered—what else here isn't real?"

"What've you found?"

"Nothing," I said, tossing the flower stalk to the ground. I squinted into the distance, thinking of the archway where, somewhere beyond the gently rolling fields, Marina disappeared. "I don't know where we are. I don't even know if we can leave. I don't know—*anything*."

All at once, the not-knowing grew too heavy. A whale, when it's beached, dies under the weight of its own body, air slowly crushed from its lungs. Could that happen to a human? Crushed beneath questions, asphyxiated by doubts.

I turned to Rose, eyes level. "Where are we?" I whispered. "Do you know?"

Rose regarded me for a long moment. "I can't say."

Can't or *won't?*

"But it's safe to assume that everything in this place, *everything*, is for a reason," she said. "The matrons don't do anything by accident."

I needed Sheila. I'd gone looking for her that morning to tell her about the yew tree, and found her in the Comportment classroom with Betty, practicing walking, straight-backed, with books on their heads. *Laughing*, like real friends. "What do you want, Eleanor?" Betty had asked when she saw me.

"I—I have something to tell Sheila," I'd said. "Something urgent."

"What is it?" Betty demanded.

I looked firmly at Sheila, silently trying to reel her toward me. "I'm not telling you."

Betty smiled indulgently. "Well, then it must not be so very urgent," she said in a simpering voice. "We're busy, but I'm sure Sheila can find you some other time." Sheila passed me an apologetic, close-mouthed smile. I chewed my lip. Betty speaking for Sheila, as if she wasn't even there. I had the impulse to check Sheila's pulse, to search for signs of life. Was she still in there, my friend?

Rose caught my eye. "You were kind to Johanna the other day."

"Anybody would be."

She took a step closer, voice low. "There are places, you know. Enclaves."

Rose told me, then, about the one she'd lived in, clusters of shacks, and dusty streets stretching across the desert. The sun burning so hot, they say a human will boil alive if unsheltered too long, all our fluids and jellies turned to steam and only a dried husk left over. Too difficult to maintain a peacekeeper post. At night, when it cooled, women could walk together with hands clasped, men could lean against each other, precisely placing a kiss on the other's neck. Not quite safe, but not hunted. There, Rose had kissed many girls.

Heat prickled painfully up my neck. "You could do that?"

"In the enclave, you can do whatever you want."

"Then maybe Johanna should go there," I said. "Maybe we all should."

Rose nodded. "If we can find a way out." Her tone had shifted. Now she looked as serious as I'd ever seen her.

I cleared my throat. "You must feel pretty confident the matrons can't hear us right now."

"Look around," she said, gesturing at the open fields. "I don't think anyone's listening."

"How do you plan this escape?" I asked. "The fields go on forever."

Rose bent close. "There's rumors of a door. A door in every facility that leads to the outside. They disguise them, make them look insignificant. Know of anything like that?"

My mouth opened, on my tongue was what I'd seen—the shuttle, that brick archway, the other place it opened to. Supply shuttles came every month, and when they did, they must've used the archway. Rose's plan solidified in my mind: If someone timed it just right—walked through at that precise second the archway changed—

I looked at Rose. She'd go back to her enclave. Back to the girls she'd kissed, perhaps to one in particular. I'd never see her again. I hardly knew her, and I wasn't entirely sure if I even liked her. But the idea of watching her walk away—

"I don't know of any door like that." My mind reverberated with the lie, a hammer striking a steel pan. But Rose was hiding things too. "Yesterday, when I asked if you'd read my file, you didn't say no."

Rose's mouth shifted to the side. "I don't need to read your file to read you."

I let out a noise of frustration. Why did it always feel like Rose had the upper hand? "And what can you read? About me?"

She paused, sliding the dark circles of her eyes across my face. "Just one thing," she said. I followed the movement of her mouth. "You look really good in denim."

Despite myself, I laughed. And in the next moment, the air shifted. The magnetic poles of us, bouncing off each other, seemed to flip. Seemed to draw us together. As I watched Rose, the laughter drew from my face, my focus absorbed by her eyes, by her mouth.

I heard the crunch of footsteps, just before a small, uncertain voice called from the lawn. "Eleanor?" I turned to see Sheila, hands wringing. "Come with me?"

By the time Sheila and I arrived in the common room, several other girls had already come and gone, trimmings of their hair mounded in a corner. I leaned in close, the knowledge I'd held inside bursting out of me like a geyser. "The Meadows," I whispered to her hurriedly. "It's not what we thought. The yew tree—"

Sheila held up a hand. "I don't want to know." Her voice was solid.

I blinked. "Then why did you come get me?"

Just then, Matron Calliope appeared in the doorway, followed by a middle-aged woman, her deep brown skin glowing with careful makeup. "Who is that?" I whispered. Sheila seemed unsurprised at this woman's presence.

"I'm Mrs. Charles," the woman said, setting down a leather bag and holding out a hand to shake Sheila's. "You must be the lucky girl. I'll be helping with your hair today." Mrs. Charles's own hair hung to her shoulders in a smooth, mahogany drape.

My eyes traveled from Mrs. Charles to the strange materials she was pulling from the leather bag. A screen, and wires. "What's going on?" I asked.

"This procedure is popular with ladies in the cities," Matron Calliope explained. "I'm glad you decided to try it, Sheila. No heat or chemicals. Practically painless."

"You're a very fortunate young lady," Mrs. Charles called cheerfully, her fingers sorting through an explosion of colorful wires. I followed them with my eyes, where they joined together at a central point, a metal disc the size of a coin. The surface was dotted with tiny, sharp nubs. Needles.

"How does it work?" Sheila asked. Her jaw was tight.

Mrs. Charles carefully grasped the metal disc between her fingers. "Do you know what DNA is?"

"Sort of," Sheila replied.

"It's rather remarkable," Mrs. Charles said. "Inside a single strand, there's contained all the information needed to replicate an individual. For enough money, you can print new eyes or a strong heart from a young healthy person. Today, we're printing hair."

Sheila's fingers gripped the chair. She stared at herself in the mirror, focused.

A knot tied in my belly. "But you love your hair," I whispered.

"It's only hair," she said lightly.

"Is that true?" I asked.

She turned to me, her expression decisive. "It's fine," she said, "as long as the choice is mine."

I nodded. Giving in to what the matrons wanted for her, changing her hair— This seemed too far for Sheila. Was she still only pretending? Or had the matrons finally managed to change her? "I—I'm sure it will look beautiful," I told her.

Her smile filled with trepidation. "Hold my hand?" she asked. I slipped mine into hers. Friendship is really just a decision. One you make again and again.

"This will make a lovely color for you," Mrs. Charles said, holding open a folder where loops of hair in every shade were fastened. She pointed at one, golden brown.

"Whose DNA is it?" I asked.

"A donor," Mrs. Charles said. "We can only guess."

Sheila bowed her head as Mrs. Charles applied the metal disc at the base of her neck. When the needles sunk into Sheila's skin, she winced, gripping my hand. "Almost there," Mrs. Charles said, chipper. "After, be careful not to comb your hair too aggressively around the device. If it's removed, your new hair will disengage. Something of a shock when that happens. Ready?"

Sheila regarded herself in the mirror. She had combed out her twists, and her hair bloomed from her scalp in a halo of dark curls. This, the girl her father had known. The girl he said was good just as she was. Quiet tears coated Sheila's face.

Practically painless, Matron Calliope had said.

Finally, Sheila gave a nod. With a quick, efficient motion, Mrs. Charles slid two fingers across her screen, as though turning a dial.

Sheila gasped, her body unloosing a shiver. The hair she'd had all her life, coils of ebony, corkscrew-tight, drifted suddenly to the floor, pushed free from follicles. Replaced by shining straight locks the color of honey.

For a moment, we all froze, transfixed.

Sheila's fingers grazed the glossy golden hair, hanging rod-straight to her shoulders. She watched herself, a hint of steel in her gaze. That faraway look telescoped and I saw what lay way back, burrowed deep inside her. I didn't need to take her pulse. I could hear her heartbeats patterning the air, reverberating across the common room, beyond these white walls, pounding past the meadow fields, and out into the world. To the matrons, this would look like reform. Defeat. But I could see it for what it was: defiance.

"How long would you like it?" Mrs. Charles asked, fingers hovering above the screen.

Sheila's jaw tightened. "Longer."

Mrs. Charles moved the dial. Hair grew past Sheila's shoulder blades. "How's that?"

The tears had dried on Sheila's face. She stared at her reflection. "Longer," she said. "Long enough to braid."

CHAPTER 35

"Have you heard of a door? A secret door?" Rose took to murmuring this in the shuffle between classes, in the quiet moments just before bed. Each girl shook her head. Nobody knew of a door. But they knew why Rose was asking.

A quiet question threaded through their minds. I could see it their faces, in the doubt between their eyes. If Rose found a way out, would they go?

"You know something about this door, don't you?" Sheila whispered from her bed after lights out.

Despite Rose's assurances, despite never finding an ear anywhere, I didn't trust that the matrons couldn't hear us, so I just nodded.

I could make out the shine of Sheila's eyes in the dim light. It felt like the beginning, in our new soft nightgowns, passing whispers to each other in the pale darkness. "Why won't you tell her?" she asked.

I paused. "It might not even be safe."

"Is that the only reason?"

"I barely know her."

"You didn't answer my question."

All the hushed, nighttime whisperings from the other rooms had ceased. There was nothing in all the world, it seemed, but silence and Sheila's question. "I'd never see her again," I whispered.

Maybe Sheila suspected the matrons could hear us too, because she didn't speak the question that was obviously on her lips. *Then why not go with her?*

"I—don't know who I'd be on the outside," I whispered.

"Maybe you'll surprise yourself."

Somehow, I doubted that. "What about you?" *Will you go if Rose finds a way out?*

She shook her head like I knew she would. "The boys from the Pines are coming back for a formal dance, did you hear?" she asked. "I'd never dream of missing that."

"Sure," I said. "Maybe you'll find your future husband."

She snorted a laugh.

I turned over, looking at her, golden hair fanned out on her pillowcase. "How do you make a choice?" I whispered. "About which direction your life is supposed to go?"

Sheila stared up at the ceiling. "You just do, I think," she said. "And wait to find out if you made the right one."

"What are you painting?" I asked.

Rose had her easel turned away. For once, she painted without complaint, dabbing her brush on her palate unrestrainedly. "Top secret," she whispered.

On one side of the room, Matron Sybil lectured on modesty as we worked. "It is every woman's responsibility to guard nature's greatest gift." On the other side, Matron Maureen was chatting with a cluster of girls about the upcoming dance with the boys from the Pines. It was all so . . . normal. So, why was my spine prickling with dread? Why did the clock on the wall seem to be counting down the seconds before something terrible happened?

Rose. Rose was the reason. Her furtive whisperings. Her hands running down walls as we walked to class, searching for a seam, a hidden door. In the air, the unspoken implication: *escape*.

"Eleanor." I could sense Matron Maureen, a splash of red in my periphery. It had been weeks since she'd given me the orange. I knew she'd expected me to seek her out, to tell her I'd accepted her offering of peace, but I never had.

"Matron Maureen," I said, swallowing nervously.

"The Meadows?" she asked, regarding my canvas, thick with tiny lilac brushstrokes. "I always hoped you'd try another self-portrait."

"Never did figure out the face," I said.

She smiled. "Those are important."

I smiled. She smiled. We smiled at each other. A careful, polite game of Pass the Smile. A prickling tension filled the air between us. I wondered if she'd come out and ask, *Don't you like me anymore, Eleanor?* And what would I say?

"I feel we got onto the wrong foot somehow," Matron Maureen said. "And I'm certain it's my fault. Being a matron—well, it's not without complications. I hope you know that everything we do, it's for a reason."

It felt eerily like what Rose had said about the matrons, but the way Matron Maureen phrased it, it sounded more caring, less sinister. "I understand, matron."

"You do?" Her brows were pushed toward the middle. "That makes me so happy. I was beginning to feel we'd lost touch. I know! How would you like to take a walk with me? Later this week perhaps, after Matron Sybil's next seminar?"

Unexpectedly, I found myself smiling. "Okay."

"Wonderful," she said. "It'll be like old times."

I thought she'd leave then, but she stood looking at me, as though debating something.

"Is there something else, matron?"

"I meant what I said, Eleanor, back in your first year. About you being special. About a homestay, if you still want it. I wanted you to know," she said, voice low. "Regardless of—of anything, you are always welcome in Teagarden. You only need to get there."

I felt unable to speak. A deep well of warmth opened in my throat, that old feeling, that old idea—of family. Matron Maureen promised it. And out of everything on earth, what could be more enticing? Even now, I was still that bundled-up baby, waiting on a doorstep.

"Almost done," Rose said as Matron Maureen walked away. She didn't appear to have caught any of our conversation.

"Can I see?" I asked, leaning toward her.

"Ah, ah!" she exclaimed. "All will be revealed."

Matron Sybil moved to the center of the room. From the deep pockets of her dress, she pulled a purple bud and held it up so every girl could see. We paused to watch her. "You each carry inside of you a perfect flower," she said. "See how beautiful? But, handled too much, touched by too many, the flower fades. Wilts. A flower is polluted when it's touched. Touched by others. Touched by yourself."

From beside me, Rose snickered.

"What?" I asked.

"Consider me wilted," Rose muttered.

My cheeks burned.

I hurried to the sink, swirled my paintbrush with shaking hands in the water and turpentine, the smell sharp in my sinuses. If I ever needed it to be true that I could change, it was now. Now that what the matrons taught was no longer theoretical, now that Rose had taken up space in my peripheral vision, sneaking glances, assembling a patchwork knowledge of her. The tendon running up her forearm. Her squared, oblong fingernails. Rose, who, like the sun, I knew I shouldn't look directly at, but like a fool, my eyes drew to anyway.

We were never to be undressed near other girls. A hard rule, enforced especially as we grew older. A single piece of skin enough to flip a switch, to turn us into animals, ravenous, to push us right back into the place we'd come from—thinking of girls the way we ought to be thinking of boys. They weren't wrong.

Still, impossible to keep ourselves covered all the time. The joy of glimpsing a piece of hidden skin was a careful secret, one I squirreled away. A blue-veined wrist. V-shaped muscle at the back of a neck. Even as I was steeped in the matrons' words, even as I wished these parts of me scrubbed away. Because the next day, a thigh showed unexpectedly beneath piles of ruffles. Breath-catching. Enough to carry like a pearl for hours, and into the shower room that night, where my fingers would find my own thigh, my own soft places, where I'd let the explosion be what it was.

Matron Maureen smiled at me from across the room. I smiled back, swallowing a rise of hope and dread. *You are always welcome in Teagarden. You only need to get there.* Her meaning had been clear. *You only need to choose the right path.*

"My goodness, Rose," I heard Matron Sybil say, regarding Rose's painting. "I don't think I've seen anything quite like this."

Some of the girls stood to see. On their faces, raised eyebrows and swift glances in my direction. Sheila was there, looking my way with concern. My cheeks prickled with heat.

I dried my hands and edged around the group. On her canvas, Rose had painted a girl, lying on a carpet of purple flowers, hair fanning around her head. I was startled at the perfection of it, at Rose's talent. Until my eyes rested on the girl's face.

The girl in the painting was me. My cheeks were rosy, lips slightly parted. And her eyes. Twin circles of blue paint, flecks of white, staring ahead in a way I was certain I never had, almost daring. I recalled the woman in the poster above the market back home, gaze oriented demurely to the side, to her husband, her children. The whole effect of Rose's painting—of lips, of eyes—was the opposite.

Nearby, Matron Maureen watched. Her typical smile had transformed to a flat, emotionless line. Her eyes turned from my face to the one in the painting.

Blood pooled hotly in my cheeks. A place deep inside my ears pulsed with a sound like the ocean. Rose looked up at me, smiling, satisfied. "What do you think?"

"Wh—why?" The only word I could conjure.

"We were supposed to paint what we wanted," Rose said. With that smile. With that gleam in her eye. Around the room, a rivulet of stunned laughter.

So, this is what Rose thought. I was a joke to her. She, with her lips that had kissed countless girls. She, who had roamed the wastelands and survived.

I didn't plan it, but as I watched the slow trajectory of my hand, I also didn't stop myself. My fingers splayed, I slashed across the wet paint. The group gasped. The careful bow of my mouth, the daring twin pools of my eyes—gone.

"It's better this way," Betty said, snorting.

And I thought, *Yes, it is. It looks more like me.*

CHAPTER 36

I ran from the classroom to the dormitory and the white-tiled bathroom, turned on the tap. When the water turned scalding, I let it fall over my hand, paint shedding like a layer of skin, my painted face sliding down the drain.

I could sense her footsteps before I heard them. She leaned against the open bathroom doorway. "Room for one more?"

"Leave me alone, Rose."

"I won't try to convince you to talk to me," she said loftily. "There are plenty of people here I could have a great time with."

Well, do it, then, my eyes tried to tell her. I could outwait her forever. And if doing so would cut tiny wounds into me until I was just bloodied, crosshatched meat, so be it. "Why did you do that? That—painting."

"Some of my finest work. Too bad somebody vandalized it."

"I'd do it again."

"I can paint it again." She was the tiniest bit shorter than me, but her body seemed to angle itself tall.

"I meant," I pronounced, "why you chose to humiliate me in front of everyone."

"*Humiliate* you?"

I huffed, frustrated. "You made me look like someone bold, and brazen and," I said, grasping, "and—and forward."

"Oh, my," Rose said, hand to her chest. "Not . . . *forward*."

I crossed my arms. "Painting a picture like that—you'll be on the matrons' radar now."

She smiled. "I think I already was."

"Well, I wasn't," I yelled, tears springing to my eyes. "There are things I could lose, you know. And everyone thought I looked ridiculous. You made me look like something I'm not."

Something in Rose's gaze shifted, then, a kind of confused tweak between her brows. Her mouth opened carefully. "I only painted what I see."

If Rose saw that, did the others? Did the matrons? Everything depended on nobody knowing what lay beneath the surface of me. On nobody noticing when my eyes traced the pronged tendon in Rose's neck, followed the triangle of skin visible where her top button was loose, wondered what would happen if I reached out and unfastened the next one. And the next. "That is *not* me," I insisted.

Rose only shrugged. "If you say so."

The silence that followed seemed to drum. I wondered when the others would return.

"Where'd you really learn to paint like that?" I asked.

I expected another non-answer, but Rose let out a long sigh. "My mamá," she said. "Along with dance and piano. Everything a Gutiérrez girl should know. I mean, *Walters*." She frowned deeply. "Until I understood that she'd never be happy with me. I was never going to be the pretty girl in a fluffy dress at my Fifteen party."

"I thought you grew up in an enclave."

"I had to go there," she said. "After they got rid of me."

"Got rid of you?"

She studied me, frowning. "Do you remember that jacket, from my first day here? It's why I thought you should've taken it. You can't give up parts of yourself, not for them. I learned that a long time ago. Not even when they offer you oranges. Or a homestay."

So she had been listening. My cheeks burned. "I don't even know if I'll do the homestay."

"But you think about it," she said.

I glowered at her. Rose would never comprehend the many versions of me folded up behind the neat exterior, the parts of myself that wanted so badly to simply be what I was. But the other parts were louder. And the matrons, loudest of all.

"What do you think you'll accomplish, fighting the matrons?" I asked. "Even Sheila figured out that was a losing game."

Rose drew her eyes down my face. "Have you ever wondered why they teach the boys mathematics and engineering, but here you learn needlepoint and cooking and how to speak a dead language? It doesn't matter if Matron Calliope likes your stitches, Eleanor, or Matron Maureen says you comport yourself well. All that approval is worth nothing. Haven't you figured that out yet?"

I swallowed, an idea scratching at the back of my mind. "When did you know?" I asked her, my voice a whisper. "That we're wrong."

"We are not wrong," she said.

"Then when did you know that *they* think we're wrong?"

Rose shook her head. "Is it possible I was born knowing?"

I searched my mind, rifled for a single moment when someone, anyone, had spoken it in words. But we'd learned it like we learned colors, with our suggestible baby brains. The posters always a father and a mother. Anyone who lived differently did so on the Outskirts. Unmarried women. Elderly bachelors. June's father, remarried too quickly to mourn. My own mother, it occurred to me, in a dawning rush. Both of them: The one who raised me and the one who gave me away. Stella took me in knowing it would make her an outcast. And my birth mother, who must have given me up knowing it was the only way for her to live a normal life.

"When no one like you exists," I said, "it's not hard to figure out that you're wrong."

"But we do exist," she whispered.

"Look at us," I said. "We do exist."

Joy, this bright thing, this sharp beam of light, cut through my middle. I gasped from the suddenness. Pain and joy. Enmeshed in the same moment, breathing the same air. How can so many different truths exist at once?

How, when I look back, was the Meadows both a black hole and a bright spot? How do I shudder recalling the claustrophobia of the place, and how do my eyes blur when I miss the feeling of never being far from the sound of laughter?

Many things can be true at the same time.

How I wanted to change who I was so badly it burned,

and

Next moment, longing to glimpse the skin of a girl beneath her skirts, a bloom of want between my legs,

and

Hating myself for it,

and

Body-tired at the chore of hating,

and

For a moment, just a moment, imagining maybe I was okay, maybe I was even good,

and

Look around, Eleanor, for god's sake, look at where you are, look at who you are, face the truth,

and

Sheila whispering, *There's not a thing wrong with you,*

and

Loathing the matrons,

and

The crackle of pride beneath my ribs when: *Good job, Eleanor, I'm proud of you, Eleanor, what a good girl you are,*

and

Thinking maybe I could love a boy, if I really tried,

and

My stomach writhing at the idea,

and

Well, I haven't got much choice, do I?

and

Wondering if maybe I could make a life for myself, a future, beyond the walls of what I could imagine,

and

Being astonished by Rose,

and

Being angry at Rose, wanting nothing to do with Rose,

and

Wanting to be so close to Rose, we'd collapse together, same body, same soul,

and

Turns out, falling in love can look like something different every minute. Can look like chest banging, blood effervescent, air-floating love, never-will-I-not-want-her love,

and

Can look like a gut punch, like my heart is a skinned knee and Rose the pavement, like watching myself slow-motion smash to the ground, each piece flinging away till I wonder, *Will I ever get those pieces of myself back?*

In that moment, these truths, contradictory though they were, seemed in perfect balance. I hardly knew Rose. I didn't know if what I felt for her could be called love, or if it was just the effect of the smell of her skin, a chemical reaction set hopscotching between blood cells. Whatever this was, Rose was something to me, maybe something important. I owed her the truth.

I turned to Rose. "Meet me outside, after lights out," I told her. "I have something to show you."

I led her down the road, through the twilit meadows. The flowers made jagged outlines against the darkening sky. We seemed to hold ourselves in suspension, the air tense with a kind of resistance, lit up electric between us.

When we arrived at the archway, Rose stood in its shadow, regarding me.

"The night you arrived, another girl left," I said slowly. "I went to the roof and saw—saw this archway change. Her shuttle ran right through it and disappeared." Even if Rose was certain the matrons couldn't hear us out here, a nervous fist still gripped my stomach, speaking dangerous knowledge so openly.

Rose ran her hands over the brick surface. "This is it."

"I should have told you before."

"Why didn't you?"

Because I didn't want you to leave. I still didn't, though for snatches of moments, I imagined going with her, setting off beside her on that black asphalt road.

I cleared my throat. "I wasn't sure of you yet."

"And you're sure of me now?" she asked.

I smiled. "Definitely not."

She let out a laugh. "Good."

It was as though my senses were finely tuned, but only to Rose. The slow heat radiating from her body. The warm, smoky smell of her. The shiver it sent through my middle.

"Will you try to get out?" I asked.

Rose cast her eyes around. "Eventually."

"The next supply shuttle isn't due for a month," I said. "Though the boys from the Pines are coming for the dance sooner than that."

"If I had my way, we'd take off right now," she whispered.

"Where would you go?"

Her eyes ranged the air, imagining. "A—a cabin in the woods. You and me."

I squinted, dubious. "You think they wouldn't find us there?"

"I've got it all planned out," she said. "Satellites can't see through trees, right? We'll be hidden."

It felt important, then, to play along. I leaned toward Rose. "Can there be a lake?"

"Of *course* there can be a lake." She grinned.

I walked ahead of her, cutting through flowers in no particular direction, watching the horizon where the fog unloosed its hushing over the fields. Each bud seemed to hold its breath. Every time I glimpsed Rose just behind me, my heart found my throat, a tremor beginning within me. A warm hand slipped around my waist then. I flinched, then softened into her. Her arms wrapped around my middle from behind, held me to her. She pressed the sharpness of her pelvis into me. A shuddering breath escaped my mouth. I wanted. I wanted and wanted and wanted.

Her mouth found my neck, testing the skin there with her teeth, breath breaking warm on my collarbone. I slipped my hand behind me, searched until I grazed her waistband. Slipped my hand beneath it.

The sound of her breath caught in my ear. That I could evoke that kind of sound in Rose. I turned around and pulled her into the flowers, tumbling down on top of her, and kissed her, hard, then soft, then all ways. Trying everything, moving every way.

When the fog washed over us, powder-white, I heard Rose gasp. We couldn't see each other. Only fingertips and breath and muscle. My hands found the smooth warm plane of her middle, her pliant belly, found her waistband again, slipped fingers beneath again, made her breath catch again. This time, farther, brushing the soft places of her. All my other senses paled. I was only touch now.

"Yes?" I asked.

"Yes."

CHAPTER 37

"Eleanor." June sighs when she meets me on the street.

We stand feet apart on the sidewalk, unable to embrace, and a tiny creature wriggles in my heart. I knead my sternum with my fingertips. I'd forgotten this feeling. Intrusive now. Like a foreign body. My own body wants to reject it, the idea—the hint—of hope.

She's just stepped out of a huge brick building that houses the Department of Medicine, our adjudication scheduled for her lunch break.

I want to ask about her bruises, my mind in the past week fixated on whether there are new ones. "June," I say. "How are you?"

She looks pained, her smile falling away. "Please don't."

I nod, furious at how powerless I feel to help her. In my report, I requested more sessions, *to aid in her rehabilitation*. Mrs. Collier miraculously permitted three more visits, after which a decision will be made about June's reformed status. Though Mrs. Collier made no reply to the whole passage about Charlie's conduct.

Above, the light is deadened, though it's midday. Clouds so dark, the sky appears stuffed with steel wool. My mind rests on Rose, a particular moment. *If I had my way, we'd take off right now*, she'd whispered. *For—a cabin in the woods. You and me.*

Rose spoke with such earnestness, I couldn't tell if she believed in this plan, or if it was simply a salve to take the sting out of the Meadows.

I look at June now. "Come with me," I say. "There's someplace you need to see."

June runs her hands over the black-painted door. "You saw people come out of here?"

"A whole restaurant too. Or a bar? There was music. I thought I might've dreamed it, but last week, a woman walked through that door. And I swear she was from that band that visited the Cove." June's expression morphs, as though the world's opened up like a map before her. "And I had this feeling that—I just want to get *in*." I jiggle the handle. "I tried the retina scanner and picking the lock, but I couldn't get it open."

June's already pulling two pins from her hair and kneeling in front of the doorknob.

"It's an old lock," she says. The bridge's underbelly fills with the sound of faint metallic scritching as June digs into the lock again and again.

"It's pretty rusted. I'm not sure if I can—" As June speaks, there's a soft clunk.

She turns to me and an unconscious giggle falls from her mouth, an I-can't-believe-that-worked laugh. She steps backward, the door still closed. I take a breath, grasping the handle and for the briefest second, allow myself to consider what I'll see. A groundskeeper's work room? Or that place, full of people and music and life? *You'll find her behind a door.* Perhaps—perhaps Rose will be there. The air inflates with sweet-tasting possibility.

I pull the door open. And draw in a breath. Before me, a stone wall. The same stone the entire bridge is made of. My hands spread over it in disbelief, searching. Maybe, my mind says weakly, it's only a partition. But my fingernails dig into mortar. The stone is solid. There's no one on the other side.

My body turns cold. "I—I swear I saw it," I say weakly.

"I believe you," June says.

Why should she, though? I hardly believe myself. My arms fall limp to my sides. I was on the ground when I saw those people. Panicked. The entire thing could be just another delightful manifestation of my disordered mind. But—the woman in the yellow dress. The woman who walked into the same building where Mrs. Collier works. How to explain her?

"Something odd about all this," June says, peering at the door, head cocked sideways. "Why would anyone set an empty doorframe into the side of a bridge? And put a retina scanner on it?"

I shake my head. More questions. More and more and more. Why can't I be like those people I pass every day, the men in sharp suits and women in neat dresses whose faces are calm without trying? I know the answer: Because, when the world is made for you, you need never question it.

"I think I really hoped it was real," I say, head falling into my hands.

June stands beside me. "I'm still glad you brought me here."

I turn my head sideways to look at her. She smiles, and our eyes linger on each other. The air between us grows hot, the way eyes can draw heat when there are too many words unspoken. The heat crests, and I wonder how much longer I can stay inside her gaze without burning up.

June clears her throat and suddenly speaks. "Can I tell you something that happened at my Young Wives meeting last week?"

I smile, both grateful and disappointed she's broken the silence. "Tell me."

"Did you know they offer a special instructional seminar on . . ." She pauses for effect. "Tongue kissing?"

"What?" I ask, laughing.

"'Because you have to be ready to satisfy your soon-to-be-husband's every desire,'" she quotes. "They actually call it, 'kissing with your whole heart,' but I can't stomach that."

I snicker. "I think a lot of girls probably learned how to kiss with their whole hearts inside their facilities."

June lets out a loud guffaw. "I know I did."

I smile, remembering the girl from the Canyonlands. "Tasha."

June nods, her smile slipping. "And Rose?"

Maybe it should feel strange, but these girls we loved sit alongside us without awkwardness. They are part of who we've been these past years. Except, it's not past for me, is it? There is still Rose, I remind myself. I'm going to find her.

"Did your friend find out where Rose is?" June asks.

I shake my head. "She couldn't take the risk."

Maybe it's the cold, but June's freckled cheeks seem to flush, the color arcing down her neck. "How long did you know Rose?"

"Only a few months."

"You've been apart much longer than you were together," she observes, not entirely neutral.

"How long did you know Tasha?"

"Three years," she says, her eyes trailing the river behind me. "It felt like defiance, growing this spark in a place that only wanted to snuff it out. And sometimes I can't stand not knowing what happened to her. But—" June looks at me then. "But she'd want me to move forward. And I want that for her."

Rose and I never had an agreement that we'd be together forever. I rarely peered into the future beyond our time in the Meadows. I don't owe her loyalty, and if she's out there somewhere, she doesn't owe it to me. But I have something that June doesn't. What came after. The endless nights picturing a bullet tearing through her temple. Knowing it was my fault.

I can't tell June this. If she knew what I did, she'd never speak to me again.

"June, I can help you," I say. "I can write my reports so you look reformed. But—you've got to play along. Start looking after your place. Maybe . . . comb your hair."

She chuckles. "Eleanor Arbuck, giving me personal grooming advice?" she asks. "The girl who had to be pinned down before she'd consent to a bath."

I smile. "Just tell me you'll try."

June shakes her head. "I'm not going to live my whole life pretending."

"Girls do it all the time." With a pang, I think of Sheila. Not pretending to pretend anymore. "Where would you go if you left the city?"

"Home," she says. "But Charlie would never agree."

"He wants to stay in the city?"

She shakes her head. "He hates it here. Hates that all he can afford is an apartment a stone's throw from the city wall. He wants to request relocation to the outer suburbs, where he grew up. After we're married." She sighs. "What about you? Would you find your mother again?"

Once reformeds spend two years in their placements in the city, they can request to be transferred to their home districts, either with a partner or to find a match. I picture the Cove, my mother, but shake my head. "I don't think she'd welcome seeing me."

June's eyes become detached, as though viewing something far away. "The day you left, Stella visited my house. She was distraught. Not crying, but almost . . . frozen."

I frown, disbelieving. "My mother hardly said a word to me at the train station. And—in the Meadows, I earned a call with her, but she refused to take it."

June looks at me, thoughtful. "She really was upset, Eleanor. More than I'd ever seen. I remember thinking it was like—like her mask had cracked. My dad sent me to my room, but I overheard your mother saying, 'She would've found a way to stop this.'"

My heart thuds painfully. "*She?*" I ask. "Who did she mean?"

June shook her head. "My dad wouldn't tell me."

I cast my eyes around the bridge, at the river, at the tall buildings, the great gleaming slab of the city wall—desperate, just then, to understand anything. I've thought about what June told me last time. *You find her, Eleanor.* I wanted to have an answer for her, to proclaim, *I found her! The girl I once was!* The way you'd hold up a coin discovered in a coat not worn for years. But the girl I was seems lost to me now. I don't know what pocket to scrounge through to find me.

"I wonder what she suspected about me," I say. "All the times I'd run to the water to meet your boat when it came in."

"My parents knew." At once, her brow lowers. "We had a neighbor— remember Mrs. Johns?"

I nod, recalling the woman who refused to buy vegetables from my mother.

"She'd ask me things," June says. "'What do you girls get up to? Nothing that would carry shame into your home, I hope.' She—she saw us kissing in the market." June's eyes dip for a fraction of a second, and I long to pause time, freeze-frame her face, analyze the emotion that ripples through her muscles. Is it regret? Or something like I feel—a fire brewing low in my belly.

June clears her throat. "A week later, I got my letter."

"What?"

"I wondered if she ever realized what she'd done to me." June clamps her bottom lip between her teeth. Her eyes lose focus, her gaze drawing back in time. She seems unconscious of the fact that her eyes have filled with tears. "From any window, I could see the canyons, miles and miles of red rock. That place—the most beautiful I've ever seen. That was the worst—the worst thing they did to me." Now she's choking on her tears, gulping. Hurting, getting these words out. "I'll never trust something that beautiful again."

Looking at her face, I feel a calamity in my chest. My heart thrashing. Without thinking, I take her hand in mine. Grasp her warm skin. There are no cameras here, but it still feels reckless. Because there's still Rose, still the unending desire to find her, to know that she's safe. For a moment, June and I don't look at each other, only at our clasped hands. Hers, warm brown. Mine, milk pale.

"At work, I can search for anyone on my screen," June says. "I found my dad and stepmom. And I saw a new record, a baby boy. They called him John. He's a year now." Her lips tighten around her mouth. "I always look at one thing first. Their death date. Because if they died, I wouldn't even know."

My eyes trace the dense freckles spanning her face. "When you're reformed, you can visit."

She casts me a dubious look. "Why do you keep pretending that I'm going to reform?"

The sadness on June's face hardens into fury. It's a good thing we're not in view of an eye. There's feeling inside of June, so much that it almost pours out of her, and I have the impulse to stopper it, find the cracks and seal them. "How do I make sense of it, Eleanor?"

I shrug, silent. You ignore it. You swallow it. You pretend it away until you spit up gobfuls of bile and blood. And then what? I know it doesn't work, but what does?

June watches me closely. I try not to be too aware of the moment her eyes drop to my mouth. "Don't you ever get angry, Eleanor?"

I blink at her. "Angry?"

"I have daydreams about finding them," June says. "The matrons. The Quorum. The messengers on the goddamn dispatches. Every one of them. I imagine hurting them, squeezing their necks until they stop breathing. Some kind of justice. Eleanor, don't you ever just want to break this whole place down? I worry if I don't get out soon, it'll be me who's squeezed until I can't breathe."

I remember now, how little June keeps hidden. No June-shaped paper dolls relegated to the bottom of a pile. Unseemly, Matron Sybil would have called it, to tell the world you're hurting. To say it aloud, like pulling an organ from your body.

What should anyone do with someone else's hurt?

"Even if you could track them down, they're protected," I point out.

Around June's eyes, her skin tenses in confusion. "Don't you want to pay them back, for any of it?"

I shift beneath her gaze. "I didn't like it, and it was miserable sometimes, but I never blamed anyone."

"Never *blamed* anyone?" she demands.

"How can you be angry at something so big? Like being angry at the sky."

"Eleanor," she says, her voice low, almost pleading. "When someone hurts you, you *have* to get angry at them. If you don't, who *do* you get angry at?"

"Nobody," I whisper. "I told you."

But June is shaking her head. "It has to go somewhere." Her eyes grapple across my face. "You get angry at yourself."

I feel something in me stagger away from her. I don't want to think about this. I want the familiar numbness of looking the other way. *Cat face, smile face.*

Just then, a chime from my briefcase. I reach for my screen and read the details. "I have to go," I say. "Another adjudication across town."

June's looking at me, and I'm looking at her. We feel sort of outside of time here, away from real life, and the moment I leave this space, it will all come rushing back.

"According to my calculations, we have five minutes left," June says. "You owe me my full session."

I smile. "I don't have a choice."

"But I need your help," she says, cocking her head. "How else am I going to reform?"

We've already done this a few times, sidestepped the dreadful reality. A joke slipped in alongside despair. That's what June's doing now, inviting me into a place where we can pretend.

I shake my head dramatically. "There's not much I can do for you."

"I'm a lost cause, am I?"

"Afraid so," I say, shrugging. "Seems you'll be relegated to a life of smashing men on rocks and stealing their treasure."

She laughs. "Well, you can't go anywhere without this," she says, slipping the screen from my briefcase.

"June," I say, with mock seriousness. "That's government property you're waving around."

"It's mine now," she says, lifting the screen out of my reach.

I turn toward her, my eyebrows rising. "Give it to me."

"Come and get it," she says, her smile dimpling her cheeks.

She holds out an arm and shoves me lightly. I reach for the screen, but she pulls it out of my grasp. I fall forward and clutch her around the waist. Suspended animation. Like two carved statues in a glossy-paged book at Mrs. Arkwright's, the marble so perfectly chiseled, you could see where the fingers of one pressed into the thigh of the other.

It's always been physical with June and me. Running and shoving and rolling down hills so fast and hard, our clothes would rip, my homespun trousers, her rag-bag dresses. More than once, she'd shove a dusty, bald knee into my kidney during a race. And, at eleven, when we had a real fight, fists and words flying, we both fell from the lip of a tide pool into the frigid ocean. We grasped together, letting the sea roll us around, laughing and sputtering so hard, we forgot to be upset.

June blinks up at me, breath coming quick, brown eyes reeling me in. She smells warm and sweet. So close, I can see the faint outline of her heartbeat beneath the skin of her neck.

I reach and slip the screen out of her hands. "You might be quick," I say. "But I'm taller."

"You win," she says. We step apart.

I clear my throat. "Let that be the last time you hassle an officer of the government."

"I've been warned," she says, chuckling. Her cheeks are rosy.

And then I stand for a long moment, smiling at her. The sun has parted the bulkhead of gray clouds, and golden light slants in through the curve of the bridge behind her, reminding me of another day, in the alley at home, air salt-smelling, the girl I loved backlit by sun.

"I can't believe it's you," I say.

"Can't believe it's you." June's eyes turn down with sadness. The tug of *what if*. What if we'd never been apart? What if, all our lives, we'd been allowed to be exactly who we were?

"I thought we'd have forever," I say.

"I thought we'd have a million years."

CHAPTER 38

The videos came often now. Some banal, some excruciating, all sparking the same pulse of shame. This one showed a large farm, enclosed on all sides by a pristine grid of white fences. Farmhands led cows, and every so often, a small red-haired child ran through the yard, several others trailing after.

"Go on," a girl's voice said. "Talk to him."

The camera zoomed in on two girls standing near a line of cows at a feed bunk. Betty looked remarkably like herself, though a little younger, perfectly put together in a simple green dress, even on what looked like a sweltering, dusty day. Beside her was a girl about her age, beautiful, with a wide pale face and dark hair.

"*Clara*," Betty said. "He's working."

"He doesn't look very busy to me," Clara said, watching a young, slightly gawky farmhand wiping his brow beside a water spigot.

Betty ignored him, going down the line of cows, giving each one a stroke before moving to the next. "Did you forget I'm leaving in the morning?"

In the Fine Arts classroom, the floor had once again been cleared for a large screen. Betty watched herself with a mild smile. I didn't care about Betty's video, not with Rose beside me, sneaking a glance every minute or so, and I had to tuck my head to hide my smile, the air between us filled with a warm, excruciating tension.

"You won't be in the Meadows forever," the girl, Clara, said onscreen.

"I know," Betty said. "I have to come back for Diamond." She had arrived at the last cow in the row. She sat on the edge of the feed bunk and placed her palm over the cow's brown cheek. The cow paused eating and watched Betty with its glassy eyes, fringed in long lashes.

Every so often, Betty glanced toward the eye recording her, passing it a brief smile. It made me shiver. What a well-worn habit this was. What a strange one.

"I thought your father had a rule not to name them," Clara said. "They're not pets. We don't get attached."

"I'm not attached," Betty said, still running her palm over the cow's downy cheek. I thought of the frog I'd found. This Betty was a girl who could sense the heartbeat of another creature. Why hadn't that girl made it to the Meadows? I glanced to where Betty sat, Sheila beside her, her golden hair braided into a crown.

Onscreen, Betty looked up at Clara. "Anyway, my father promised not to complete Diamond. I raised her from a calf, when she was so sick she'd already been recorded in the books as dead."

Clara wasn't listening. "Look, he's done with his break," she said, pointing her chin at the farmhand. "Go on, Betty! It's obvious he likes you."

Betty chewed her lip. "I don't know."

Clara huffed. "You've been this way all the time I've known you. Don't you like them? Boys?"

Betty's brow hunched in a familiar way. Angry. But seeing her from above, I could sense her body tighten with fear too. "What a question, Clara! Honestly, scrub out your mind."

"Then why do you seem to prefer the company of cows to boys?" Clara asked.

"I prefer the company of cows to *everyone*." Betty's fingernails dug into the right sleeve of her dress. "I just haven't found the right boy yet."

"There's one standing right there," Clara said.

I glanced again to Betty, across the room. She sat poised in her chair, chin pushed forward, watching the screen with studious attention. This was the moment in the video, I was sure, when she'd slip. When she'd reveal that it was the beautiful friend she loved.

But, onscreen, Betty trailed her eyes across her friend with the same impassive expression she'd had for the farmhand.

"Keeping out of trouble, girls?" A man strode across the yard, a slash of deep red hair visible beneath a short-brimmed hat.

"Yes, Father," Betty said, shoulders falling back, spine straightening. There was something procedural about this new scene. A well-worn tension between Betty and her father.

"Chores done?" he asked.

"Yes, Father, before breakfast."

"Even the stables?"

Betty nodded. "Even the stables."

He peered through his low-perched glasses as though Betty was a specimen to be examined. "Your dress looks wrinkled," he said. "When did you last iron it?"

Betty glanced down at her dress. Smooth and immaculate. "Just this morning."

"And your fingernails need scrubbing," he said.

She fanned her hands, perfectly clean. For a fraction of a second, fire flashed in her eyes. "Yes, Father." Her fingers found her forearm again, gripping.

"Why are you always holding your arm like that?" he snapped.

Like a marionette with its strings cut, Betty let her hands fall quickly to her sides. "I didn't realize."

Betty's father regarded her with skepticism. There was something about his remarks that didn't land, something searching.

"Mr. Albertson," Clara piped up. "Will you tell Betty she ought to be friendlier? I've been trying to make her say hello to Peter and she refuses."

Betty shot Clara a venom-filled glare. Clara flashed a smile and skipped away across the yard. Betty's father squinted again, that suspicious, puzzled expression, as if Betty were a bigger tangle than he knew how to sort out. "Peter might take over one day," he said. "Unless you still imagine you'd like to run the operation?"

Betty's eyes flared. "Of course not. I want to be just like Mother."

Her father crouched to look Betty in the face. "The eyes of the algorithm are always watching, Betty. His ears always listening."

I'd known a few people like this in the Cove. The saints and symbols of Before had been erased, but the need to believe found ways—worship of the algorithm, of the Quorum. The pursuit of a life that adds up clean as numbers.

Her father pointed a finger directly at the camera. I felt chilled by his stare. "I wonder what He sees when He looks at you," he told Betty. "I wonder what your life footage will reveal." I saw then—it wasn't Betty's fingernails or her dress that he found lacking. Something deeper. Something perhaps even he couldn't put a finger on.

"Father, you've asked me that every day of my entire life," Betty said. "There is nothing."

He peered at her. "Would you have me believe that when He shows us the footage at the end of your life, there won't be a single clip in which you violated nature?" her father asked. "He hears all, Betty. He sees when we break the natural order of things. He listens to our lies—"

"I never lie!" Betty exclaimed, the dam holding back her anger finally bursting. "I've never once told a lie—"

"Do not interrupt me—"

"I never disobey," she said, breathless, words surging forward, face a livid red, glasses slouching down her nose. "I never swear or raise my voice. Never *touch* anyone. I never even *think* in a way you don't want me to. I never do anything wrong. Ever. There's nothing for the algorithm to see. *Nothing*."

Her father regarded her, unswayed. "There is a perfection in nature," he said. "A perfection in numbers and science. In this magnificent place"—he swept his hands toward rolling hills encircling the farm. "But perfection has a way of making the *im*perfect stand out."

The room froze at this speech. My eyes flitted over their faces, slack-jawed and silent. Rose's smile had fallen away and she watched with rapt attention.

When Betty's father walked away, he called behind him, "And stay out of the yard when the tractors come through. You'll get hurt."

Onscreen, Betty didn't tremble. There was something in her face that seemed to step backward, to pull deeper inside of herself. And then she recalled the eye her father had pointed at. She turned to it and flashed another smile, as though posing for a picture.

Beside me, Rose's entire body had drawn taut as a bowstring, her fingers shaking in her lap. "Rose?" I whispered. "Are you okay?" But she didn't seem to hear me. Her features had compressed, a flat mouth and hooded eyes pulled toward the screen.

"Hello, Peter." Betty's voice called through the classroom speakers.

"Hello, Betty." Onscreen, the boy trotted over to the feed bunk. He took off his short-billed cap and gestured at the sky. "Fine day."

"Very fine."

"Your father told me you were chosen for a facility," he said. "I knew you were destined for something great. You'll come back to see us one day, won't you?"

Betty smiled demurely, looked through lowered lashes. "Of course I will," she said. "I couldn't—couldn't stay away from you."

The boy's cheeks pinked. "I'm sure you won't miss these sacks of meat, though," he said, gesturing toward the row of cows.

"Oh, I'll miss her," Betty said, turning to the cow she'd been caressing. "She's my favorite. Aren't you, Diamond?"

Peter frowned as Betty's fingers fanned out along the jagged plane of Diamond's cheekbone, twining into the tuft of dark hair atop her head. "I've never understood why we do this when the engineers can just print food," she said.

"People in the city pay a lot for authentic meat," Peter said.

"And that's enough?" Betty asked.

"That's enough," he said. Peter wrenched at his hat in his hands. "Betty . . . I thought you knew. This entire row is scheduled for completion tomorrow."

Betty's brow drew down. "After I leave?"

He nodded.

"Not Diamond, though."

Peter hesitated. "The entire row. Your father's orders."

A tremor ran across Betty's features. She opened her mouth as though to object, but closed it again. There was no objecting. Betty had no more say than Diamond. In this matter. In any matter.

"I never understood why we call it completion," she muttered. "Though Father's explained it a dozen times."

Peter turned. "Well, these animals were born for one purpose. And when that purpose is served, its job is complete," he said, awkward. "I'd better get back to work. Nice talking to you, Betty."

Betty's eyes stretched again, across the scrub surrounding her farm. Reaching, they seemed to be. Reaching for the farthest point on the horizon. Absently, she still stroked Diamond's cheek. Something happened on her face then, like a person receding into a house. Closing doors and shutters. Locking up for a long departure. After some time, without a word, she turned from Diamond and walked to the house.

In the classroom, Betty batted her eyelashes as the lights came on. Beside her, Sheila's eyes were focused on the floor.

Matron Sybil stood before us for a long moment, silence falling heavy as snow. "Betty, I have to say, it was difficult finding any footage of you transgressing," Matron Sybil said. "You have comported yourself most excellently, all your life."

The smile Betty made could have powered the whole electrical grid.

"Was your father referencing something when he asked if you'd like to run the farm one day?" Matron Sybil asked.

Betty nodded. "I'd asked him once. I was the oldest. I thought—I could do a good job. I had an idea to end completion on the farm."

"Rather defeats the purpose of a meat farm, does it not?" Matron Sybil asked.

Betty smiled. "I was young and silly. Even the cows sensed what was expected of them. They walked into the completion room bravely. They never ran away."

Beside me, Rose had begun to tremble. Muscles coiled, a gathering of electricity like a generator, the air around it tart-tasting and alive. It might have been Betty's lack of outrage on her own behalf. It might have been her father caring enough to warn her about tractors, but not enough to see how his words carved her up. It might have been the quiet way the rest of us took in this video, long accustomed to the taste of poison.

Matron Sybil nodded. "And what your friend said was correct. You had no interest in Peter. Nor any boy, for that matter?"

Betty shook her head. "But I don't need to feel it. I can make myself do many things."

At this, Rose spoke. "And that's a good thing? Forcing yourself to do things you don't want to do?"

Betty blinked. "I think that's called being an adult."

Matron Sybil smiled. "Very wise, Betty."

Rose, silent, resembled a bomb in the slow process of exploding. I should have contained her somehow. Should have scooped her outrage from the air and stuffed it back inside.

Rose's hand went up. "Matron Sybil, I have a question."

"I'm sure you do," Matron Sybil replied patiently.

"Why couldn't Betty have run the farm one day?"

Matron Sybil chuckled as though Rose had made a delightful joke. "That would be quite impossible. One of the first articles of the New Constitution speaks clearly to the roles of women and men."

"The New Constitution," Rose repeated. "Can you show us?"

"I don't have a copy on hand."

"Have any of you read it?" Rose asked, turning to the room. She was greeted with quiet stares. Rose took a breath. *"We hold that everything has a perfect order, and in that order, a perfect place for each citizen,"* she recited. Rose had the New Constitution memorized? *"We hold that ambiguity of gender shall be expunged. A civil society builds a border around the genders."*

Across the room, Johanna held my gaze. The air felt stiff. Someone coughed, and someone sniffed, and most averted their eyes from Rose, intensity rolling from her like something molten.

"Each citizen shall clearly inhabit the region they were born into," Rose continued. *"Every man shall employ logic and control in his devotion to his country, his domestic realm, and himself. Every woman shall perform the vital work of supporting the endeavors of men and producing future generations. No deviation from this order shall be permitted."*

As Rose finished, Matron Sybil tucked away a mildly irritated expression and smiled. "Praise family," she said. "And how much easier life is, knowing what we are here to do."

"And if we don't agree?" Rose demanded. The planes of her cheeks had gone a deep red. "If we'd like to do something other than supporting men? Than reproducing?"

Silence. Before, Rose had been a welcome diversion. Entertainingly contrary. But now, the tide seemed to turn. She was going against all our programming. To smooth away wrinkles in conversation. To keep silent and small. To imprison our difficult thoughts inside our minds.

Matron Sybil strode to the center of the room. "Rose, it truly isn't your fault," she said, her voice compassionate. "You have missed vital years of learning. What you don't know—what these girls do—is that women are capable of tremendous flexibility. What we once wanted, we can learn to unwant. What we once ran from, we can embrace with whole hearts."

My eyes turned to my wrist. *Cat face, smile face, holiday tree*—

"That is *not* my purpose," Rose said. "I thought I knew what this place was. I pictured shackles and—torture. But you—you are so much worse."

I had never heard a louder silence. The breath of every girl, held tight. The breath of the Meadows itself.

"Rose, that is *enough*," Matron Sybil whispered, the slightest quiver in her cheeks.

"Matron Sybil, I thought questions were welcome," Rose said.

"I will not allow you to denigrate the work we do here. Nor will I permit you to dismiss the duties of women. They are sacred." Matron Sybil straightened. "As your own mother would have hoped you'd understand by now."

Rose's face went blank, her intensity gone.

Matron Sybil clucked sympathetically. "Your mother did her best with you, Rose. She tried everything, I think, to guide you to the correct path."

Rose drew in a slow breath. "Don't—don't—" She held up a hand.

"I suspect, Rose," Matron Sybil pronounced, clipped, "that there is a place inside you that knows the truth. That this rebellious streak will be your end. Stop fighting and come into the fold. You can even see your mother again."

I'd assumed the last thing Rose would want was to see her mother again, but judging by her anguished face, I had that wrong. "None of it is true. *None* of what you teach here is true. Families have looked all different ways forever. The world didn't collapse because of divorce, or wickedness, or because women married women."

But Matron Sybil only shook her head.

Rose stood then. Her voice, for the first time, was small and terrifying. "I will never embrace your path." She turned toward the girls, all of us staring, stunned. Never had the calm of the Meadows been so shattered. Sheila's face was half horror, half grin, her breath coming fast. "If any of you has any sense," Rose said, "you'll plug your ears and hum for the next six months. And drown out their lies."

CHAPTER 39

There's no reason to believe I can break into Mrs. Collier's office. None. But once the idea burrows into my mind, I can't pull it out. I sit in the white box of my bedroom, sealed inside, and by the time the sunrise paints pale tangerine on my wall, desperation has coalesced into decision. The door under the bridge goes nowhere. June is trapped with a boy who will hurt her for the rest of her life. The reformeds I thought I was helping are like Sheila, lost inside a life that will crush them. And Rose. She's somewhere I'll never find.

Unless, that is, I can access a state computer. I can't do anything for June, or Sheila, and the door is a dead end. But I might—*might* be able to find Rose. And somehow, by saving Rose, I have the unfounded sense that I might save them all.

"You look nice," Clark says. I enter the living room wearing something close to my normal uniform, a white buttoned shirt and straight blue skirt.

"I thought the blue was . . . something," I say, glancing down at myself.

Clark nods seriously, just as he does everything. "It is," he says. "Something."

"I don't want to go."

Clark adjusts his tie in the mirror, his suit a meticulous black. "Nobody wants to go."

Any young person can attend mixers: reformeds and naturals, pre-married couples and uncoupled people like Clark and me. For us, the mixers aren't just about having fun and socializing. They are designed for finding a match.

"Leaving already?" Clark asks as I make my way to the door.

"Just a quick errand to run first," I say, glancing away so he can't spot my lie. "See you there."

Mrs. Collier's office is situated at the top of a slim white building that juts high above the skyline. The elevator opens to a reception area, the desk occupied by a red-haired secretary with lips drawn in sharp-looking pink. I nod at her, clamping my shaking fingers together. "Good day, Mrs. Lee," I say, forcing my voice steady. "I have a meeting with Mrs. Collier."

Mrs. Lee frowns at her records. "Mrs. Collier is out this afternoon."

"Right," I say. "She said she might be. She told me to wait in her office if I arrived before her."

Mrs. Lee has seen me at least a dozen times over the last year. She knows my face. But for a long moment, she considers me, pursing her pink lips. Can she see my heart beating? Can she make out the stipples of sweat on my forehead?

"It should be unlocked," Mrs. Lee says finally.

I turn toward a nondescript hallway lined with closed office doors, and let out a long breath. Outside Mrs. Collier's office, I turn the handle and close the door softly behind me. Inside, I drop every ounce of calm and sprint to her screen. It's awake—no password required. I barely register the strangeness of this because my fingers are flying, hunting for a database or search function. Her screen has hundreds more features than mine, folders inside of folders, programs I've never seen before. I let out a frustrated grunt.

And then I spot it. The state directory. My fingers shake as I punch in Rose's number, my senses honed on the glowing glass. 341.43.980—

"Eleanor, what a pleasant surprise." I lift my eyes to where Mrs. Collier stands, framed in the doorway, and for a brief moment see myself through her eyes: frazzled hair in my face, sweating, hunched over her screen.

"Mrs. Collier, I—I—"

"Please," she says, gesturing at the chair opposite her desk. "Take a seat." She closes the door behind her.

Slowly, I make my way from behind her desk and perch on the edge of the chair, spring-loaded and prepared to jump away at any moment.

"I'm willing to unsee what I just saw," she says.

"Mrs. Collier, I can explain—"

"How have you been this week?" she asks. So she's going to toy with me. She sits behind her desk in her typical neat suit, straight hair draped over her shoulders. Beyond her window, a strangely pale afternoon darkness has fallen over the city.

I cast my eyes around, my stomach fumbling. "My work is . . . satisfying."

"Beyond your work." She looks at me meaningfully. "You are a whole person." This idea sits uncomfortably in my chest. "Have you had anything on your mind?"

"Nothing."

"Not Rose?" she ventures. She doesn't even glance at her screen.

In my lap, one hand pulls together into a fist, fingernails pressing into skin. I place my fear there, all of it in those screaming sickles slicing my palm, so it won't show on my face.

"I'm going to ask something of you, Eleanor. Because you're one of my best adjudicators, and it would be a pity to throw your life away. Stop looking for Rose."

My face doesn't budge, but I feel as though I may disintegrate. "What harm is it doing?"

She regards me with surprise. "There are things the Quorum needs to remain buried."

I squint at her, my mind teeming. "I'm only trying to find my friend."

"Even so," she says. "I wanted to make you aware, so you might choose a different path." *A different path. The right path.* The phrase strikes like a bell.

"You told me Rose died," I say. "I suppose that was a lie?"

"Officially, it's the truth," Mrs. Collier says. "But the truth is . . . complicated."

"Why does the Quorum care about Rose?" I press. It's reckless. I can't stop.

"They care about order. And Rose is the opposite of that. Not that the Quorum is afraid of her. They've already got the Circle on the run. You've heard of them, I expect?"

I nod, remembering what the adjudicator on the train had told me. "A subversive organization."

"A ragtag group of misfits who want society to run backward." She leans back in her chair. "Eleanor, if it's any consolation, Rose is somewhere you could never reach. The wise choice—the responsible choice—is to give up the search. It won't end well for you."

The air fills with Mrs. Collier's threat. I take a steadying breath. "And if I don't?"

Mrs. Collier touches the pad of one finger to a button on her desk. The recording device, clicked off. I gape at her. Whatever she's about to do, it'll be off the record. Pain spears my gut, icy and sharp.

"Sorry about this," she says. "I have to give them something. They're listening to me too." Mrs. Collier laces her fingers together. "Eleanor, what do you think happens to adjudicators who fabricate reports?"

A cold dread falls over me. I thought I was being so secretive. But Mrs. Collier is like the matrons. Allowing us to keep secrets only until they're ready to use them against us. I cast my eyes around her neat office, at the white sky stuffed with snow. Helpless, that's what this feeling is.

"How long have you known?"

"Some time," she says. "You gave yourself away. You're so thorough in other ways. It seemed unlikely you were leaving out details simply because you'd failed to notice. You notice everything, I think."

A twisting inside of me. A glass jar, pressed over my head. And me, always the mouse.

But, I register with surprise, something new in this moment too. The feeling of a muscle inside my chest, encircling my rib cage in a slick band, and now it tightens stubbornly, urging me to defy her. To tell her I will never give up on Rose.

"A question occurs to me," she says. "When you were in the Meadows together, did you consider going with Rose, when she escaped?"

"No."

She nods, her thin mouth downturned. "What did you think about Rose's escape idea?"

I clench every muscle, hold myself steady. "Some of my peers had goals that didn't align with those of the Meadows," I say. "Rose was one of them."

"But not you," she says.

I shake my head. "I—I was a follower."

She leans forward, the energy in the room shifting in a way I can't comprehend. "How much do you remember of your time there?" Her voice is tinged with urgency.

"I remember all of it."

"But do you?" she asks. "I was reading your records earlier. In one interview, you told a matron—Matron Maureen, it was—that you thought you were bad, deep down. Rotten, like an apple."

I remember that day. "And?"

"I wondered, *were* you such a rule follower? Or did your body know exactly what was going on, and fought it, every step?"

I stare at her, my breath shallow.

"I was a psychologist, before. Not that the state lets me advertise that fact," she says. "I asked because your comment reminded me of something. When we experience a traumatic event, the body keeps us safe by fighting or fleeing. But what if we can't fight or flee? The trauma doesn't have anywhere to go. It's stored, in the mind, in the body. I think a wound, long ignored, could start to look like what you described. Rotten."

I squint at her. "What wound?"

She straightens. "Maybe none. It was only a question."

My mind swims. Trauma, she called it. A wound. I recall that some animals play with their food before devouring it.

On impulse, my hand goes to my coat pocket. And touches paper. Paper that wasn't there as I was walking here. Without meaning to, my eyes widen. I shift my face back to neutral, but Mrs. Collier has noticed.

Her eyes draw a line from my face to the hand in my pocket. "What have you got there?"

"Nothing." Terror pulses through me. I drag in my breath slowly, to keep from gasping.

Her mouth cocks sideways. She doesn't extend her palm. Doesn't need to. Her eyes are made of metal. She knows I'll give it to her.

My heart beats deeply, a thousand pounds of blood in there. Anything could be written on this paper. What would happen if I refused to show her? I'd be done. Certainly as an adjudicator. Maybe in every way. Prison. Dead. Forget finding Rose, or seeing June again. They'd wrestle it from me, those jumpsuited men. Either way, they'd see what's written there.

I place the folded piece of green paper on the shining surface of her desk. It springs open, and I can make out the words written inside.

You have the key.

Fear surges acidic up my throat. I glance at Mrs. Collier's patient face. "S-someone's been leaving me notes. I don't know who."

"Someone's been leaving you notes, and you didn't report it," she says. "I wonder what that means. Did you simply not think it worth mentioning? Or have you been misrepresenting yourself as reformed?" Mrs. Collier considers me, unwavering. "Are you reformed, Eleanor?"

"O-of course."

"Nothing we say can be heard by any ears but our own," she says. "Are you reformed?"

I can only gape at her, terror working into my muscles.

She slides that grin on again and quickly stands. "I want you to come with me."

I back away. "I'm not going anywhere with you."

"Eleanor, please," Mrs. Collier says, as though to a petulant child.

When I think about this later, maybe I'll notice the frown she wore, two crescent moons framing her mouth. Or remember the recording device, still switched off. Or note how she never opened the piece of paper, because she didn't need to.

But now, all I can sense is the drumbeat of fear in my ears. An acid taste at the back of my throat. My body shaking, but at such a low frequency, I think it could rumble me apart into pieces.

I slam into Mrs. Collier's office door and fly down the hallway, past Mrs. Lee, who utters a faint cry of surprise. On the street, I run. Fog has drowned the city, and streetlamps illuminate circles of pavement like pools of spilled milk. By now Mrs. Collier has alerted the peacekeepers, my face loaded to every one of their screens. How can I get out of the city? The commuter trains don't travel beyond the wall, and intra-border trains require advance booking and official approval.

I slow myself to a walk, though every part of me wants to run. Something Mrs. Collier said, about trauma. Where will all this fear be stored?

Is there even any space left inside me, or have the shelves of my mind been stuffed to capacity?

For the first time, I take in where I am. I've made it ten blocks from Mrs. Collier's office. A crowd of young people mill about the street in flouncing dresses and bulky suits. The high windows in the building behind them glow with warm pinkish light. The mixer.

The dance hall is warm and smells faintly of perfume and bodies. Groups of young people cluster along the edge, and couples drift to the piped-in music that suits the style of dancing where the partners hardly touch.

I spot Clark standing alone at the edge of the dance floor. At mixers, they serve a bubbly, slightly alcoholic beverage called a sparkler, and by the look of his flushed cheeks, he's already had a few.

"You made it," Clark says in surprise. "Were you running?"

"Just cold out there," I say, my lungs still burning from my sprint.

The doors of the dance hall burst open, and I flinch, certain it's peace-keepers charging in to grab me. But it's only a loud group of young men jostling into the room.

Couples drift past, girls in billowing dresses, pleats of pastel. Their dates wear oversized suits, shoulder seams frowning on their boy bodies. I recognize some of the girls from adjudications, but plenty of the couples drifting past know nothing of a facility like the Meadows—not the truth of it.

"Do you think I'll ever fall in love with one of them?" Clark asks, eyeing a girl wafting past in a mustard-colored dress. "Is it even possible?"

I set aside my worry for just a moment to focus on Clark's face, for once showing the tiniest scribble of frustration between his brows. He's always so contained. "Many have."

He leans his back on the wall. "Or say they have."

"Clark," I say. "How many sparklers have you had?"

"Unimportant," he says, taking a swig from his fluted glass.

I smile at him. "You're supposed to invite one to dance, you know."

"What about him?" Clark asks, his head rolling against the wall toward a rosy-cheeked boy with bouncy brown curls standing with a group of girls laughing uproariously at something he's said. "He looks fun."

Oh, Clark, I want to say. What I would give to strip back the cover of the world, rewrite the code underneath, make it possible for him to approach that boy and extend his hand. In Clark's fine, stoic face, I see his entire life, a denial of want. "He looks fun," I agree.

Clark gives his head a little shake, pulls his eyes from the boy. "No, you tell me. Who should I ask? I can't tell."

"How about her?" I gesture toward an uncertain-looking girl in a pink dress with straps too large that keep slipping down her shoulders. She doesn't look like a reformed girl. Not poised enough, not controlled enough. "Nobody's asked her. You'd make her night."

Clark looses a sigh, pours back the remains of his sparkler, and approaches the girl. When he extends his hand, she smiles broadly and does a clumsy curtsy.

Clark cuts a fine figure in that black suit, his tall dancer body, square shoulders. I glance over at the curly-haired boy, still surrounded by giggling girls. He can't keep his eyes off of Clark either.

I've thought about marrying Clark. Easier that way, if he agreed to it. At least I know he's not going to hurt me, like June's boyfriend. But I wonder if a stranger would be better. After the wedding, we'd be required to consummate. An inquiry launched if I didn't become pregnant within the first year.

My eyes flick to the doors again and again. The fear has emptied me out, and now my most overwhelming feeling is a muffled sort of exhaustion. I listen in on a nearby group of boys and girls, talking of their work assignments and potential matches, feeling a million miles away. I think of the periscopes—a space between spaces. Others my age have gone off toward their futures. But I've chosen to stay frozen between worlds.

I will have to marry one day. Maybe if I'd stayed in the Cove, I could've pushed it off, but even there, the algorithm watches. I'll have to make children with him, and take classes on wifely duties, attend meetings of the Young Wives Club with other women more polished and dutiful than I could ever be.

"Eleanor!" I startle, fear flooding me. The peacekeepers. I turn, and my body recognizes her before my brain does. Instinctively, my stomach tightens.

Marina's hair is in a long black drape, and she wears an elaborate turquoise gown that brushes the floor. "It's Eleanor, isn't it?" she asks. "We met at the mixer last month."

"Right," I say. "Nice to see you again, Marina."

She grins, the faintest wink in the corner of one eye. "Can I offer you something to drink?" she asks, leading me toward a punch bowl beside a large freestanding speaker. Music plays loud enough that we won't be overheard.

"I can't believe I'm seeing you, Eleanor," Marina says. "Remember how intent you were on ignoring me in year two?"

I smile, remembering like looking backward at a point on the horizon almost too small to see. We talk about the other Meadows girls we've seen in the city. She ran into Penelope, who works now in the Department of Communications, still hoping to be selected as a messenger of the state, and Alice, matched with a governmental aide.

"I've seen Betty," I tell her. "She's married now. Living the life she always wanted."

Marina shakes her head. "I was so sure one day she'd crack, and her true self would come spilling out."

I nod. "I assumed you'd be married by now too."

"I didn't get the highest recommendations from the matrons, if you can believe it. My dad found me a job at the Department of the Family, filing paperwork. That's where I know Mabel," she says, gesturing to a blond girl across the hall who keeps glancing our way. "Eleanor, this is a strange time to say this, but I don't know when I'll get another chance. I wasn't at my best in the Meadows. It's taken me a long time to figure some things out."

I blink at her, surprised. "What things?"

Her eyes scan around us, careful nobody can overhear, though the music, now a staid symphony piece, continues to bellow from the speakers. "I watch the dispatches now and cry. Those children. Sent away to kill that thing inside of them. I think the Meadows ended up working backward on me. Every word the matrons said made me surer I was good after all."

"Is that why they sent you away?" I ask.

"That," she says. "And that I finally told Matron Sybil I wouldn't reform and I thought she was full of shit."

I gape at her. Marina, who wanted to hide her secret more than anyone. A tiny fist of jealousy sinks into me. I ache to ask her how she's done it, this unlearning. Instead, I say, "I always wondered why you got sent away from the Bay."

She cocks an eyebrow. "You can't guess?"

"A girl?"

A little smile climbs up her mouth. "There is always a girl," she says. "Even now." She casts her eyes at the blond girl. "But she's scheduled to be married."

My heart stutters for her. "I wish there was somewhere for us," I say. And because I can't stop myself from asking, I say, "Rose—did you hear about her? The girl who came after you?"

Marina nods. "Penelope told me. And I saw her that night, in the corridor, just for a moment."

"She talked about a place in the wilderness, a cabin on a lake," I say. "Somewhere just for us, somewhere we could disappear."

Marina smiles. "From what I heard, Rose wasn't the kind to be content whiling away her days in the woods."

The accuracy strikes a sore spot in my chest. It was always a daydream. The cabin, her, me—Rose would grow bored in a month. "So you know?" I ask. "About the escape in the Meadows?"

Marina nods again.

"You haven't heard where they are, have you, the ones who tried to get out?" I ask. "My supervisor told me Johanna was rehabilitated."

Marina shakes her head, mouth set in a grim line. "There is no record of Johanna after the escape. No prison record. No reformed record. Nowhere."

My head spins. Mrs. Collier lied about that too? Was everything she ever told me a lie?

"You don't—you don't know where Rose is, do you?" I ask.

"No, but—" A crinkle forms between Marina's eyes. "That girl isn't who you think she is."

I feel everything in me orient to Marina. "What do you mean?"

"Something I heard at work," she whispers. "I shouldn't be talking about this."

"Tell me."

When she speaks, Marina's mouth hardly moves. "Rose wasn't there for the same reason as us. She wasn't there to reform."

No, I think. Rose may have resisted reforming, but she was still one of us.

My eyes pull to the doors, but not out of fear this time. A couple enters the room. They're beautiful, and more than one person stops to

315

trace their path across the gleaming floor: A stocky, muscular boy, thick dark hair bisected by the pale line of a severe part. And a girl in a blue dress, billowing from her waist in rivulets of tulle. *June.*

"Good luck, Eleanor." Marina smiles knowingly and moves smoothly into the crowd.

June's eyes flare wide when she sees me. It takes her a moment to recover. The last time I saw her, our bodies were pressed together, her hand holding my screen out of reach.

June hustles her boyfriend over by the arm. "Charlie," she says. "This is my friend Eleanor. We grew up together."

Charlie takes my hand in his and shakes it hard. "Great to meet you, Eleanor. Any friend of my June's is a friend of mine."

My June. I swallow down a swell of bile.

"Well," Charlie says, looking around. "We should dance."

"I want to talk to my friend for a moment," June says.

But Charlie takes June's hand and tugs her onto the dance floor. "We're here to dance, aren't we?" June looks back at me, apologetic.

I watch Charlie turn June around, moving her body in his hands. He's slightly shorter than her, but he pushes her around in a way that suggests solidity. In my chest, something brewing. My throat, tight. *The blue blush of bruise wrapped around June's ribs. The haggard look in her eyes.* The feeling in me to rip Charlie apart.

"Ahem." A boy stands near me. Pale eyes in a wide face. Dust-colored hair. "My name's Bryce. Would you like to dance?"

I give him a considering glance and take his hand. On the dance floor, Bryce places his hands around my waist, and I want to collapse away from him. Instead, I grind my teeth, holding every muscle tight.

"You're a fine dancer," he says, smiling. His teeth are scummy, like he forgot to brush them for a few days.

I wrestle a stiff smile onto my face. "How is your work, Bryce?"

"Great," he says. "I'm the youngest intern in my department. We're working on the government's mainframes. Important stuff. We keep the lights running, so to speak."

He glows a little, saying this, and an unexpected pit of fury opens up within me, at this room, at this world, at this boy who has probably never had any reason to doubt his place in the world, even for a minute. "Your family must be very proud."

"Oh, they are," he says. "My test scores were the highest in my class."

I nod distractedly, craning my neck to spot June and Charlie, across the dance floor.

"Did you hear me?" Bryce asks.

"Yes," I say, eyes meeting his again. "Bryce. That's an interesting name."

"My parents named me after a beautiful canyon place they visited before I was born. They said, when I was born, I was so beautiful that I reminded them of that place." I can picture it, little baby Bryce on his parents' lap. Surrounded by so much love, he doesn't go through the world flinching at shadows or throwing up acid.

"That's a reform facility," I say. "They send kids there now. The Canyonlands."

His face hunches in surprise. "You know about that?"

"I'm an adjudicator."

He ducks his head, whispering. "I work in the department that makes them. Codes the entire world."

I nod, forcing my face into amazement. What does he mean—*codes?* "That must be fascinating work."

Bryce darts a glance around. "I know we're not supposed to talk about them," he says. "Top secret and all. But seeing as we both already know." He lowers his head and speaks close to my ear. "I'm working on one called the Marshes. The engineers get to put in little clues. Tricks for the inhabitants."

"Tricks?"

"Nothing too obvious," he says. "I heard a coder got in trouble a few years back for opening a periscope in front of an inhabitant for a fraction of a second, just to spook her. But, at that exact moment, a frog jumped through, right into her lap."

A blanketing numbness washes over me. The entire world seems to stop turning and all I see is Bryce, his lips, slightly chapped. His mouth, smiling. "A—a frog?"

He shrugs. "Feels like an office legend to me. But now they make us keep our tricks small. I'm debating between a single gold button under a floorboard, or a snakeskin, just to throw them off a bit. Nothing so noticeable that they'll figure out where they are. Or, where they *aren't.*" He huffs a laugh.

The noise of the mixer dims to the throb of my own heartbeat. My mind tunnels with memory. A thimble. A single blue feather. Words etched under my bed. *She lied.* Words that disappeared when I tried to show Sheila. Every secret that was just ours. Every spark of joy.

An ember of rage burns in my chest.

A cloud that repeated in the sky. The clockwork fog—

All of it—the work of some indolent boy behind a screen.

The shuttles with blacked-out windows. The road dead-ending into flowers. How you could walk forever without getting anywhere.

The archway to nowhere.

To everywhere.

Each beautiful piece of that place.

Every fine thing.

None of it, not a bit of it, real.

CHAPTER 40

Rose's outline scribbled bold against the bright blue sky. "Where are you going?" I'd lost my breath trying to keep up. "Rose, what are you doing?"

"Getting the hell out of here," she called back, cutting through the flowers with quick, muscular strides.

"Out of where?" I called.

She gestured around with both arms. *This place*, the gesture said. *This whole goddamn place.* Rose turned on me, expression ferocious. "Eleanor, how have you lived here for *years*?"

I came to a halt. "You're mad at *me*?"

"How have you not wrung the life out of every one of those matrons with your bare hands? Have you not fought back *at all*?"

Shame fell over me. "I've fought back. In—in my own way."

"Bending your head and drawing pictures on your wrist?" she demanded. "Dreaming of living in one of their houses, after everything they've done? Who is that helping?"

A burst of humiliation flashed behind my eyes. "Point your blame where it belongs, Rose. It wasn't right for Matron Sybil to talk about your mother, but don't take it out on me. I—I got here when I was too young to know better."

Her mouth screwed into a knot. "*I* knew better."

I stepped back at the venom in her voice. She'd been the same age as me when she'd run away from home.

Rose considered me for a long moment. "Do you know who brought me here?"

I shook my head, confused by her sudden change of subject.

"Do you know who visited me every week after I was taken from the enclave? Who picked me up from the city and rode with me in the shuttle?" she asked. When I didn't respond, she leaned forward. "Matron Maureen."

A quick trip to the city, she'd said. *Meadows business.*

I stare at Rose. "But—Matron Maureen had no idea a new girl was coming."

Rose shook her head, pityingly. "Eleanor, I wonder if a part of you wants to be lied to. If a part of you enjoys being told how wrong you are. Eats it up. And so you let yourself marinate in their hateful words, and you swallow your anger, and you make yourself so small nobody even sees you, let alone expects anything from you."

I felt her words sink into me, touching on nerves, forking like lightning. "I don't get to be angry," I said. "I *have* to sit there quietly and take it."

"Why?" she insisted. "Why don't you fight back when you know it's wrong?"

I felt myself squirm away from the intensity of her gaze. I had no answer. I grappled around my mind for something, anything, to explain.

"Why, Eleanor?" she repeated.

At once I felt lit up by rage. "Stop talking."

"Why don't you fight them?" Rose demanded again. "Why?"

"Because!" I burst out. "Because—I'm scared."

"Of what?"

I cast my eyes to the sky. What had I been scared of, this entire time? Not just here but in the Cove. As far back as I could remember. "Of—of being alone." The words came loose, like a tooth pulled by a pair of pliers.

The quiet that followed was almost painful. "What do you mean?"

"When your birth parents don't want you, and your mother doesn't want you, and the country doesn't want you, and the world doesn't want you, it's obvious that it's *you* who's wrong. It's *you* who has to change." I shook my head, tears falling hotly down my face, no way to contain them. "I—I don't want to be alone forever. To be like my mother. Living in the Outskirts. I don't want a husband, but what's the alternative that won't kill me with loneliness?"

The heat in Rose's face faded. Her eyebrows unstitched from each other, and her expression became gentle, worse to confront than her fury. "You believe them?"

I turned away. It seemed impossible to explain how I felt, the paper dolls, the parts of me that pulled toward the matrons and the parts that wrenched away.

"You believe them." Her voice was low.

"I don't know!" I shouted into the strange blue air, into the fields waving their purple fists. "I don't know, I don't know! This is what you don't understand," I said. "What Sheila never will. If you grow up so wrong you'll never be loved, and you come here, and they say you can be good, you can fix what's wrong—wouldn't you take it? Wouldn't you think about taking it?"

Rose regarded me, her face intense in a way I couldn't make sense of. "Even if Matron Maureen's not deceiving you about the homestay," she said, "why would you ever want to live with her? The promise of oranges and not being alone?"

Suddenly, I felt exhausted. My limbs hung from me. And something Matron Maureen had said in our first year slid into my thoughts like a bright red ribbon: *When you're raising your own child one day, Eleanor, and you come upon the edge of a cliff, should you give them a choice between the cliff edge or life?*

"There's a cliff edge inside of me," I told Rose. "Or so Matron Maureen says. Everything she's done has been trying to pull me back from that cliff. She cares about me. More than my own mother did. How do you—how do you just walk away from that?"

There was a long, strained silence. When I looked up, Rose's eyes were unfocused.

"My parents didn't really throw me out," she said. "I left."

I studied her face. "Why?"

Her gaze shifted out to the fields, tracing the shapes of flowers against the sky. "My mamá cared so much about protecting me. When I listened to a game too loudly, she'd say 'Rosario, your eardrums won't make it to thirty.' 'Rosario, don't look so close at your screen, your retina will be ruined permanently.' She could grasp the ways my *body* might be damaged. But when I told her I couldn't survive as the person she wanted me to be, she said I had no choice. I wonder about all those parents who protect their child's body. And all the children who will die with perfectly intact eardrums. And perfect retinas. And bodies that shouldn't be dead but are, because the damage was inside them."

I observed her. The mass of black curls. The brown of her skin gleaming against the stark blue sky. "So, you left."

She nodded. "I always knew how much she loved me. But someone can hurt you with their love." She lifted her eyes to mine. "The night of the dance, the archway will turn on. Eleanor, I'm getting out." Her voice was a period at the end of a sentence. "Will you come?"

My mind buzzed so loudly, I couldn't hear my own thoughts. Escape was only an idea before, but now, it had become something solid and real. Like she really believed she could do it. "It just . . . feels sudden. And— what good will escaping do? We won't beat them by running. We won't beat them by storming the steps of the Quorum."

"And how do you propose beating them?"

I was surprised to find I had an answer. "Maybe—talking."

"You want to have a conversation with the Quorum?" she asked, incredulous.

"Most *people* aren't the Quorum." I thought of the Cove, the villagers. "That's how we beat them. By talking. By seeing each other."

"If you say so."

I took a steadying breath. "There are other ways, Rose. If—if you pretend to reform, they'll give you a job. Maybe in a government department. Think of what you could do, from the inside."

Rose's face clouded. "Do you think I can just step out of who I am, like changing clothes? Is that your plan? Leave here, and get married to whatever man the state hands you, and pretend that this life is the one you want, and 'change things from the inside'?"

"Rose, don't you see?" A hot, bulky feeling materialized in my chest. "That's the only way."

Rose stepped backward. "You can stay here, Eleanor," she said. "You can live out your days in this place, and in your file, have nothing but glowing words from the matrons, and get assigned to the nation's top husband, and do such a good job for other people at the cost of your own happiness." She took another step back. "But I'm getting free. And I'm taking as many people as I can with me."

"Eleanor!"

Matron Maureen stood in the doorway of the matrons' quarters, waving. "Ready?"

I let out a shuddering breath and glanced behind me, Rose already far away, engulfed in flowers. I turned toward Matron Maureen.

She studied my face, which felt warm and tight with dried tears. "You seem unsteadied, Eleanor." Her lips pursed. "Anything to tell me?"

I shook my head quickly, my mind becoming a vault—holding in the fight that still stamped the air, holding in Rose's plan to escape, holding in what happened last night, the two of us inside the fog. "Nothing," I said.

She nodded. "I've been so busy, I almost forgot our plan to walk together," she said. "Making preparations for the final test."

I watched her. "Is that so?"

The final test had again become a frantic topic among the girls. Betty had been trawling for clues, asking Matron Mary, "Will this be on the final test?" with every new Latin conjugation we learned. Matron Mary finally exclaimed, "For goodness' sake! The final test is set by Matron Sybil, and she alone knows its contents." We didn't know when the test would be administered, waking each day half expecting to find the Fine Arts room cleared of easels, and thick test booklets waiting on tables.

Matron Maureen leaned toward me now. "I'd like to give you a hint."

"You don't have to do that. I'm hardly destined for Best Girl."

"You know no such thing," Matron Maureen said. "It's not much of a hint anyway. More of some general guidance." She faced me, her pale green eyes sweeping over my face. "Do you know who sits on the Quorum?"

I shook my head.

"Their names aren't public knowledge, but we know they are men of technology, and engineering, and science. It's said that the Quorum imagines the solution to any problem in the context of numbers and mechanics and unbreakable laws of nature. It's from this perspective that the Quorum sees this part of us—this defect. It is something that can be removed. Like a bad line of code. Or a broken microchip. Lifted out, and the rest of the machine keeps running."

"Why are you telling me this?" I asked.

"The girl who understands this best," she said. "The girl who takes this into her heart, that girl will master the final test."

"But, what if . . ."

"Yes?" she asked.

I thought of the wild running of my childhood, the calluses on my heels, and the denim jacket, and Rose in the meadow fields the other night. "They think they can lift it out," I said, "and the rest of us stays. But what if it's not just a part? What if it's—braided into who we are? And it can't be killed without killing the rest of us?"

As I said the words, they grew firmer in my mind. This—*this* I believed.

Matron Maureen stilled. "Eleanor," she said. In this light, her eyes were pale as celery. "It's not about whether it's possible, but whether you *want* it to be." She studied me. "It's what I wonder about you sometimes."

"I do," I said quickly. "I do want it to be."

Matron Maureen shook her head. "I wonder if there's something inside you, pulling you toward defiance, that perhaps you don't see." Her eyes held me in place. "I think you want to choose the right path. You don't want to end up like your mother, destitute in some grubby cottage. Or your birth parents, for that matter."

The world seemed to tilt. "You—you know about my birth parents?"

Matron Maureen's mouth fell open, as though surprised she'd let that slip. "Well, yes."

"You do?" I demanded.

The corners of her mouth turned upward. "There's very little that we don't know."

"Who are they?" I asked.

Her brows flattened. "The matrons have a plan for that, and I'll leave it in their hands."

I gaped at her, muscles vibrating. "But—*you're* a matron."

Matron Maureen cocked her head. "I wonder why you'd want to know anything about them, Eleanor. They abandoned you."

"I don't know that," I said. "Maybe they planned to come back." I felt my cheeks heat. Aloud, it sounded like the dream of a child.

Matron Maureen leaned in, speaking softly. "Do you imagine they'll return for you one day?"

I shook my head, tears threatening to well. "A part of me maybe—a small part . . ."

"Hopes?"

I nodded. Though it wasn't so much hope. It was . . . like breath on an ember. If I stopped giving it air, it would blink out. We all had our dreams. Sheila hoped for the Department of Engineering. Penelope, a place on the dispatches. Johanna, to decide for herself who she was. Rose—to escape.

"It's my fault," Matron Maureen said. "I was in the office this morning, reading your file, so it was at the front of my mind." I followed her gaze to the matrons' quarters, at the edge of the lawn. "You'll forget about it, won't you, Eleanor?"

"Yes," I replied, pulling my eyes away from the building, and smiling.

CHAPTER 41

"So what do you think?" Bryce asks over the noise of the mixer. "The gold button or the snakeskin?"

Tricks for the inhabitants. I look into his face, recalling how the frog departicalized inside the periscope. Briefly, I wonder if the state erases people this way. If they shunt a criminal inside, press a button, and watch their cells lift away until their soul comes loose. A dark clarity descends over me. And for a moment, I picture it. Bryce, flung apart by his own machine. Dismantled piece by piece. Like they did to us.

"The gold button," I say, smiling.

Bryce nods. "Yeah," he says. "I bet that'll keep the girls occupied for a long time."

"I take it you didn't attend a facility?"

"Oh, no," he says, nose wrinkling. "Can you believe we thought those places were for the best and brightest? I was crushed when I didn't get in." He chuckles.

"Why do you think they lied to us about them?"

Bryce cocks his head. "They had to tell us something. So those people would go willingly."

Those people. We've stopped dancing. Shouts ring out from across the hall. My heart stutters, but it's not peacekeepers. My eyes draw to where

June's been dancing. A boy with a shiny, heavy-browed face roars at Charlie. Their voices echo through the hall.

I drop Bryce's hand and move for a closer look. Charlie is red-faced, shouting back. The other boy's date, a girl in a poufy tangerine dress, pulls on the boy's arm, trying to haul him away. Charlie takes a step closer and pushes the boy in the chest. The boy stumbles back, his date almost losing her balance. His expression gnarls with fury, brows bunching until his face resembles a fist. He hauls his body forward and shoves Charlie back. June puts an arm around Charlie's waist, dragging him away, but he lashes out with his arm and connects with June's cheekbone. She bounds backward, clutching her face.

I run to her. "Are you okay?"

June blinks through stunned tears. "He's going to get himself arrested. That boy made some comment and set him off."

Red has begun to bloom over June's cheek. I remember the bruises beneath her dress. *It's not enough. It's not enough.* Sheila's words beat alongside my heart. I hid the facts of June's unhappiness from the state. And now what? She's free to marry this person?

The boys yell open-mouthed at each other like junkyard dogs, and there's a hint in the air of where this might go, with just a nudge—the world watching Charlie explode.

"Will you really let him talk to you like that?" I say quickly into Charlie's ear. I tell him what a real man would do. What a strong man would do.

Charlie squints at me, my words cutting through his kinetic cloud of anger. And then with his compact body, with his surprising muscle, he cannonballs himself into the boy's stomach. The boy's mouth funnels as the air leaves him. Charlie doesn't let him catch his breath before his fist connects with the boy's jaw, head snapping to the side. And connects again, and again.

The boy's date screams. June looks on, arms limp. When a clutch of boys hauls Charlie off, he makes wild swings until they give him a wide berth. He drags his blood-stained sleeve over his mouth. "Don't anybody touch me!"

When the peacekeepers arrive in their white jumpsuits and black belts swinging with tactical supplies, I hide behind the crowd, heart thudding. But they're not here for me. They grab Charlie by the wrists. His body writhes like a fish on hot sand, but he knows better than to throw fists now.

On the dance hall floor, a smear of blood. Someone finds a mop. The music begins again. A waltz. Girls in bountiful folds of fabric swish across the floor. And through it all, June stands still.

I take her hand, limp but burning hot, and wave to Clark as we leave. He's standing near the curly-haired boy from earlier. He shoots me a quizzical look, but nods silently.

June and I plow through the doors, into the street where mist has fallen like an avalanche, filling every cranny in every road. The air cracks with cold and wet, and I breathe it in, whole lungfuls of it, to steady myself.

"Are you okay?" I ask June.

The skin under her eyes looks tired, bruised. On the hem of her dress, a smudge of blood. "I think so." My body is freckled with gooseflesh, but beneath the straps of her dress, June's arms and neck are pink-tinged, glowing, like she's got a furnace inside.

I scan the street, the dark shapes of people shuffling within the fog. "Let's get you home," I say. *And get me out of sight*, I think.

But as I'm saying it, a voice flings up the street. "Eleanor!"

The figure is only a dark oblong inside the mist, but my whole body recognizes it.

"June," I say. "We have to run."

CHAPTER 42

We have the key.

Light slid across my pupil. I clenched my eyes shut, vision reduced to a pulse of red. While everyone had marched to dinner, I'd skimmed off and walked to the frosted glass door of the matrons' quarters.

My parents had lived my whole life behind a door in my mind. I'd only ever opened it a crack, to peek. But now, Matron Maureen had flung the door wide.

I heard a faint hydraulic gasp. When I opened my eyes, blotchy with the afterburn of the retina scanner, the door to the matrons' quarters stood slightly ajar.

The door glided open on silent hinges, revealing a large kitchen, bright and gleaming. I padded inside, through the kitchen, and down a hallway lined with a row of identical doors that could only lead to the matrons' bedrooms. At the end of the long corridor was another door, made of opaque glass. Here, I sensed in some bone-deep part of me, were answers.

I opened the door to a kind of office. Expansive, with a large desk and a tall arched window facing the twilit fields.

Spanning one of the walls, an enormous screen glowed with a warm white light. Icons shaped like white boxes made a grid there, each labeled: Sheila Evans, Johanna Thornburg, Rose Walters. All our names, plus rows more. Previous cohorts, going back years.

Eleanor Arbuck. My file was right there, but for a moment, I hesitated, finger crooked over the throb of light. Every part of breaking in had been strangely easy. Why did they make it so easy? *Give us the rope to hang ourselves.* That's what that boy Danny from the Pines had told Edward, right before they sent him away.

I swallowed, and opened my file.

Inside, more icons. Dozens and dozens, all unlabeled. There was no way to know which I needed, so I hopped around, opening windows haphazardly. In one, I found notes dated the first day we'd arrived. *Willingness to conform. Relationship with Sheila to be monitored.* Text in different colors, different matrons. My eyes flitted, wanting to devour every word—*seeks approval from matrons and peers, adept at self-control, a very promising pupil, expected to reform—*

My fingertips pulsed with my heartbeat. Not much time. I touched an icon at random. On the screen, the arc and plummet of soundwaves—an audio file. A hushed voice emerged, slightly garbled. I held my ear close to the screen, straining to hear.

"I wish—" A child's voice, whispering. "I wish for a new bow for my violin—mine has lost five horse hairs this week."

My heart stilled. It had been years, but I knew that voice, speaking my most ardent wishes into the Wanting Hat. They had recorded even that. Of course they had.

"I want to keep my extra coin from darning socks," my voice whispered, "and to buy sugared plums when they arrive at the market." I lifted a hand to my mouth, fighting the convulsion of a sob. Had I ever been so small? "I wish that the fishergirl will hold my hand," I said, quieter. "I wish that she would kiss me—"

I slashed my hand across the screen, closing the file. I stood frozen for a long moment, taking slow breaths, sipping the air like you do water when you might be sick.

With shaking fingers, I opened the next file, and found my mother staring at me. *Stella Arbuck*, the caption read. Her governmental identification photo captured the face I remembered, grizzled and frowning. *Adoptive mother*, it said. *Around the Turn, Arbuck was coded as a "potentially subversive person." However, she has exhibited little deviant behavior since. She has lived without incident on the Outskirts of Coastal Region 43.*

I didn't know how much time had passed. Perhaps dinner was over and the matrons were now crossing the lawn. But my parents were here. I couldn't leave till I found them.

I closed Stella's file and opened the next. A man's face this time, round and smiling, a fan of creases at the edge of each eye. Something familiar in them. Brown and small. Like mine.

Michael Williamson. Occupation: school teacher. Unmarried.

Father, I thought. The idea broke over me like dawn. I'd never given specific thought to a father. Maybe people who grow up without snow never know to miss it.

In his file, one thing stood out: His death date. The day after I was born.

I knew what I'd find in the next file. A woman's photo appeared on the screen. My vision tunneled, all my thoughts drawing to a point, like moths and she was the only light for miles. My eyes flitted across her file, searching for the one piece of information I needed.

A date of death. The same day my father died.

"Her name was Cora St. James."

I spun around. Matron Maureen had her shoulder braced casually against the door frame. On her face, an expression of nothingness. I'd been so absorbed, she might've been watching me for minutes or hours. Acid pulled into my stomach.

"Matron Maureen, I—"

"She was forty when she died," Matron Maureen continued. "Lived a few villages over from where you grew up. Unmarried."

I stood still while inside me something crashed. All of the half-hopes, almost-dreams, all the things I only ever allowed myself to picture with eyes partly closed.

"Why, Eleanor," Matron Maureen said. "You look upset."

"Am I in trouble?"

She moved across the room. Everything seemed to go too slowly, like some giant was holding down the hands of a clock: the billowing of her dress, the delayed booming in my chest, the creep of the night sun across the lavender sky. She rested on the edge of the desk. "Of course not, Eleanor," she said. "Everybody should know who made them."

Not a day ago, she forbade it. The knowledge of this rang in my mind. "Who was she?"

"She was a lawyer," Matron Maureen said. "When the world changed, she gave up her job. But, not entirely. She became a subversive agent."

"A subversive?"

"Oh, they had little protests back then," she said. "Men who refused to work, women without husbands. Yelling at buildings a hundred stories high, thinking their voices would carry up to the people at the top."

"Did it work?" I asked.

Matron Maureen lifted an eyebrow. "We're here, aren't we?"

I gazed at the woman on the screen. Her face, unsmiling and rigid. Her long hair hanging in a chestnut drape. Pin-straight, like mine. A flat bottom lip, like mine. Eyes slightly wide-set, like mine. My mother.

"This woman didn't protect you," Matron Maureen said. "She put her own desires above motherhood. When you were born, she abandoned you to a stranger, Stella Arbuck. A woman who didn't love you and never would."

Examining her sparse eyebrows—same as mine—and the tapered tip of her nose—same as mine—I wondered why a woman a day beyond giving birth would place her baby on the doorstep of a stranger.

"They both died the day after I was born," I said.

"Shot at a protest. Most subversives were, in the end."

My face wanted to fall apart, another Eleanor to emerge, the one I kept hidden like an ugly bruise, because nobody's supposed to lay eyes on how sad you are, deep down. Too sad, maybe, to keep going. Now the sadness knit like black thread across my eyes, through my muscles, my bones, pinning me to the ground.

"Eleanor." Matron Maureen's voice was sweet like Meadows flowers. Sweet, the way a mother's should be. "You can look at this like you were unwanted, almost the moment you arrived in the world. Or you can look at this as the greatest opportunity for change."

I peered at her, the fall of her auburn hair, her gentle pink smile. The way she seemed to always be present at black moments like this, tugging me after her. "Matron Maureen," I said, "why are you really here? In the Meadows."

She was silent for a long time, carefully arranging the folds of her dress, a precise white waterfall. "Because once, not long ago, I was just like you. I made a choice. And afterward, everything got so much easier. I want that for you. For every girl."

"What choice?" I asked. "To change yourself?"

"Not only that," she said. She paused, seemed to make a decision. "You were right, what you said about it being impossible to remove just that single piece of us. To kill it, we must kill the rest." Her eyes took on a sharp glint. "The girls who succeed are the most skilled killers."

I squinted at her, cold filling my gut. "Drinking the turpentine."

"There are other ways." There was an unpracticed way to her words, like she'd perhaps not spoken them aloud before.

"It wasn't easy," Matron Maureen said. "She fought. But I won. Squeezed the life from her. Held a funeral, even. The other girls thought I'd gone screwy, digging a giant hole only to cover it up with nothing inside. But I knew. And now, when I think of her, it's with some sadness, the way you think of a dead relative, but also with relief, knowing that she is never—not ever—coming back."

I pressed the back of my fingers to my mouth. From the screen, the photograph of my mother peered at me. Dark eyes. Flat mouth. Shot dead. For fighting the way Sheila once fought, the way Rose did and thought I ought to. And Matron Maureen, her spirit sloughed off and buried among redwoods.

Outside the window, the meadow fields breathed their breath, violet blooms asking, *Who will you become, Eleanor? Which death will you choose?*

CHAPTER 43

Terror has a taste. A metallic tinge. Inside my body, a gland throws open its doors, ejecting chemicals to help me survive. If it's fight or flight, I'm choosing both.

"Who is that woman?" June asks as we run, holding yards of tulle in her fists. Already, we're a few blocks from the dance hall. I dare a look behind me, but the street has vanished inside fog.

"My supervisor," I say, breath fast. My vision pulses at the edges, an encroaching blackness. Fear has worked into my muscles. But still we run, feet slapping the wet pavement. "She found out about me."

"Eleanor!" Mrs. Collier's voice echoes down the street. I turn and see her again, striding toward us, a large black umbrella open over her head. Close. Too close.

I sprint faster. June stumbles and falls heavily into the street. "Damn this dress!" She gathers armfuls of blue fabric before setting off running again.

"June, she's only after me. If you're caught—" I break off. "I need you to run the other way. Go home."

"Very funny," June breathes. "Come on, let's get off the main road."

We sprint into a side street, bracketed on both sides by the gleaming bulk of skyscrapers. And finally, the river, shining through mist and painted over with the fluorescent reflections of buildings.

All at once, an idea strikes me. A ridiculous idea, an absurd idea, one that surely won't work. But—what if it does?

We run down the river walkway, and I skitter down the embankment beside the pedestrian bridge. June scrambles after.

"She must be right behind us," June says, panting. "Why are we stopping?"

"I have an idea," I tell her.

You have the key. That's what the note I received earlier said. What if it's like in the Meadows? The way into the matrons' quarters was easy as the retina scanner.

It didn't work last time, but what if they've given me the key? What if I *am* the key?

I approach the black-painted door and hold my eye near the scanner. Its red light crosses my vision and I hold its stare. It won't work. Mrs. Collier will find us, peacekeepers right behind, and I'll be inside a prison complex by nightfall. I'll never see June again, and Sheila, and Rose and—and I make out a growing hum. The sound of a lock releasing. I look down. The door appears the same as it ever has, but when I try the handle, it turns.

This time, the door doesn't open to a blank stone wall. It doesn't open to a restaurant, either. Inside the door frame, another door, made of polished wood. I grip the doorknob and push.

June gasps. On the other side, there's a street where no street should be. This street is as misty and dark as the ones we just ran through, but the buildings that frame it are only a couple stories high. They look old-fashioned, with wrought iron balconies and slate roofs. Windows cast warm squares of light across the damp pavement.

"What is this place?" June asks.

"I don't know," I say, and there's no time to wonder. I step through the doorway. June follows, and I slam the door behind us.

We fill the empty street with the sound of our panting breath. On this side, the door is set into the front of a brick building, each window capped with a dome-shaped awning. I take it in with dawning comprehension: We're inside an invented place. An engineered place. Like that infinite crack of space I stood inside of in Sheila's apartment. Like—like the Meadows.

All at once, the truth comes to rest in my mind like a feather on my palm. The Meadows felt unnatural and wrong—because it was. The archway was a periscope, camouflaged as a ruin so we wouldn't suspect its purpose. When it switched on, Marina's shuttle jettisoned back into reality. Everything inside—every flower, every building, even the yew tree—coded by a team of programmers in the city.

I lean against the door and take several gulping breaths. I don't know where we are exactly, but we're safe. *Safe.* Mrs. Collier won't find us here. I feel a cool wash of relief.

When I open my eyes, June is smiling. In our shared glance, there's an understanding that we've escaped from danger, and now the danger seems absurd. I let out a hushed laugh. Her smile stretches wider, and soon we're both shaking from quiet laughter.

Except.

Except, something sharp claws at my throat. Pinches the muscles in my neck. Might be the cold. Might be nothing. Then, a tremor inside my chest. Someone knocking at the walls of my body. The abrupt tightening of my airway. The drawing of blood away from my arms and legs so I am struck suddenly, dumbly, cold.

Panic. The feeling of safety, gone. The fear was only drawing away like a wave, and now it's slamming back down. My face must change, because June's smile falls off. *Breathe*, I think. *Cat face. Smile face—*

Doesn't work. None of it ever works. The fear is too great, the fear— of what's going to happen if the panic runs through me, the fear—like bulls down a street Mrs. Arkwright told us about once, in some country far away, and people were smashed to bits, their bodies flung like a child flings a rag doll. It will happen to me. I push against it. Push with all my might.

"Eleanor, what is it?"

I shake my head, tears blurring my sight. "Something's wrong," I choke out.

"Nothing's wrong," June says. "We're safe."

"Go," I say. "Go home."

"I'm not going," she says, and her words break like starlight across my vision, diamond white.

I must fall, because when I notice my body next, it's spilled on the ground. I curl into a nautilus on the damp sidewalk, grip every muscle to guard against this. But how do you guard against your own veins, your muscles, your mind?

June seems to understand. She's kneeling beside me, her face very close, her mouth shushing softly. "It'll be okay," she whispers. "You'll be okay."

But I shake my head. Tears squirm from the crook of my eye. "It won't." I feel convinced of that. Nothing will be okay. "I can't—"

"You can," June says; a slow tear tracks down the bridge of her nose, falls to the pavement.

"Eleanor." A shadow crosses the street. Mrs. Collier, standing beneath the golden glow of a streetlight. Somehow, I have the energy to sit and skitter away, kicking backward against the pavement until I connect with a brick wall of a building. Try to stand. Fall again, palms scraped, breath gasping.

"Stay back!" shouts June. "Leave us alone."

"Eleanor, you're not okay," Mrs. Collier says, glancing at June, then kneeling beside me. She sets down that large black umbrella, folded now, and places a cool hand to my forehead. The delicacy of it, the suddenness, the strangeness of being touched after not being touched for such a long time. I look into her face.

"You called the peacekeepers," I choke out.

"I didn't call anyone," she says. "Because you haven't done anything wrong."

"I had the paper."

"I wanted to tell you in person," she says. "But you ran."

I shake my head, understanding nothing. Nothing.

From her pocket, she pulls a small notepad, fans it with her fingers. Inside, slips of blank green paper.

"You," I whisper. I rest inside this new reality, the world quiet and white and packed in cotton wool. "But—you're Mrs. Collier."

She smiles. "I wanted to help you," she says. "And you can stop calling me *Mrs.* Most people who know me call me Sam, or Dr. Collier. I told you—I was a psychologist, Before."

"What?" I say. And then my muscles shake again. I clench my eyes, push against the panic with every muscle.

"Don't fight it. You won't get anywhere fighting it," Dr. Collier says. "Let it in."

I can only shake my head.

"What do you think will happen if you let it run through you? If you feel it?" she asks.

"I'll die," I whimper, recalling the musicians, and the peacekeepers slamming their bodies to the ground. That's what the panic is. A deadly force. To give in is to let my body be smashed to ribbons. "I'll die."

"You won't," she says. "It only wants to be felt. It's been ignored for too long."

My eyes dart from her, to June, standing in her creased and blood-flecked dress.

I feel the weight of it, the weight of everything I've pushed back. Instincts swallowed, truth denied, whole versions of myself locked away, all of it fighting inside the purse of my stomach. Pain I packed away, coated in pearl, bursting now inside my cells, rattling the membranes like prisoners. Demanding to be felt. Finally.

At last, I look at it. An enormous wave, cresting over my head. All this pain, untouched for years and years. The matrons taught me pain, but I taught myself to keep it. Letting it go would mean looking at it. Seeing it for what it is.

"I don't want it to be true," I say.

"I know," Dr. Collier is saying. "But it is true."

It really happened. They hurt me. All of them. The matrons, who should have taught me, but instead educated me in shame. My mother, who should have shown me love, but couldn't. My parents, who should have kept me, but who let me go.

I unclench. For a moment, the panic watches, uncertain. And then, like a logjam cleared, tears. Not a torrent. Not a bone-breaking wave. A slow, warm wash. An acknowledgment. That things aren't okay, that things haven't been for a long time.

CHAPTER 44

"Where are we?" June asks, turning a full circle, taking everything in.

"I think—a periscope," I say. "Inside one."

Dr. Collier glances behind her. "We tend to call them doorways. And we call this place the Village."

We? June mouths to me, forehead wrinkled.

June and I follow a few steps behind Dr. Collier as she guides us through misty streets. The buildings are smaller than in the city, made of limestone and brick, but these streets hang with the same cold fog as the ones we just ran through. "We try to replicate the outside weather, to create some authenticity," Dr. Collier says.

"I saw a place before, through the doorway—a restaurant," I say.

"The Black Cat," Dr. Collier says. "When I added your retina, I programmed the doorway to open here. Most people need a moment, their first time, to gather themselves."

I try to make room in my mind for this knowledge—that, here, a door isn't just a door, it can open to anywhere. I feel both utterly emptied and crammed with vivid energy. This place—not just a restaurant, but an entire town. Occasionally, someone's shadow crosses the slick pavement from apartments above. An electric thrill passes through me. There are others. Others like us.

June whispers to me, "Do you trust her?"

I press my lips together. Dr. Collier knows enough to ruin me. She knows I've been fabricating reports, and searching for Rose. She knows I'm not reformed. But she's been leaving me messages. Helping me. "We'll see," I tell June.

We arrive at a tall building with an illuminated marquee proclaiming *The Black Cat*. Inside, muffled sounds of music strain through brick walls. I glance at June, her eyes stretched in trepidation or excitement or both. We follow Dr. Collier inside.

Music falls over us in a curtain of sound, drums vibrating the air, horns blaring, the marrow-deep hum of an upright bass. Hanging lanterns fringed in glass beads douse tables and booths with pools of golden light, and everywhere groups of people talk and drink and touch, shouts of laughter carving through the music. My eyes can't decide what to focus on. Maybe the women in suits. Or the couples dancing. Or a gold earring, a sparkling skirt, a waxed mustache—all existing on the same person. One whole side of the club opens to an inner courtyard filled with tables. At one, two women in secretarial uniforms kiss deeply, fingers entwined. I look away, my heart a molten ball.

And calling from the back of my mind, the note: *You'll find her behind a door*. Maybe the door we walked through. Maybe Rose is here, in this room. I scan every face, strain for her voice.

I find the source of the music, a band in black suits, the shining noise of brass and breath punching the air. I track the pulsating beat of the upright bass to the stage, and the woman who plays it—a woman I recognize. Today, she's in a slim-legged tuxedo, but when I saw her before, she wore a yellow dress, and before that, in the Cove, the tattered clothes of a traveling musician.

Before the stage, there's a wooden dance floor, but nobody dances like at the mixers. Here, partners are glued together. Every age and gender, every color, glittering and joyful and alive.

Look at us. We do exist.

I turn to June. Her face is slack with amazement. "Is this real?"

"Very real," Dr. Collier says, smiling. I try to fix my face into a neutral gaze, like I've learned to do, but I find I've lost the desire. I let my face be what it wants. Melting like my heart, like my whole body, into something deeper than surprise. Something like wonder.

"Who are all these people?" I ask, but Dr. Collier doesn't hear, bouncing on her toes to scan the crowd. "Ah, there she is."

A woman approaches. A woman whose head is shaved, who wears an oversized shirt, buttoned to her neck, who dresses like I've never seen a woman dress. Before I know what's happening, the two of them are kissing.

"This is Adele, my wife." Dr. Collier beams.

The two laugh at my expression of shock. "What about your husband?" I ask.

"Harvey? He's over there, with his boyfriend." Dr. Collier nods toward the dance floor where a middle-aged couple leans against each other, dancing, or melting together.

Dr. Collier leads us toward a table, and I watch her transform, slackening the strings of herself, every ligament loosening. She slips an arm around Adele's lower back.

My eyes scan the room, what Adele calls a speakeasy, a hidden place, invitation only, and listen to her explain that people like us have always had places like this, have always found each other, hopscotching history, no matter the difficulty. *People like us.* Adele's words find me through a gauzy veil of awe. I watch two women who look like young wives dance with arms linked together, every once in a while breaking apart to laugh, big-toothed laughs, grasping each other, arms flung over shoulders and necks like old comrades. Like June and I once were with each other. I sense her beside me, glowing in my periphery like a prairie fire on the horizon. All these bodies, together. I have the sudden, hot impulse to take her hand. And, it occurs to me, there's no reason not to.

On the booth beside me, I slip my hand over June's. She grasps it under the table, the corner of her mouth lifting.

"How—how are all these people here?" I ask. "Did they all come through the door under the bridge?"

Dr. Collier shakes her head. "Only a few are assigned that doorway. Some have doorways in their homes, and some use doorways in other dead zones. We make sure only certain people can access this place. Hence the retina scan. Adele can explain it better than me. She's a genius with technology."

Adele smiles, a sunburst of lines radiating from her eyes. "Had to hide that fact, when they took over. Bad things happen to women with knowledge," she says. "We're installing doorways all across the country. Hoping to get them into as many places as possible."

"What for?" June asks.

"A safe space, primarily," Adele says, glancing around the room. "But beyond that, travel. We can connect any periscope in the world to the Village. Someone in the Outskirts could walk through a door and into this space, and then out another door and into the city. It'll help with mobilization, when the time comes."

Mobilization. June and I exchange a glance. It occurs to me that a word as common as "village," even spoken outside, wouldn't snag the attention of the algorithm. "Isn't it risky?" June asks. "Using state technology this way?"

"It might be," Adele says. "If it actually was their technology."

A memory prickles at the back of my mind. What Ed said, about the inventor of periscopes being a woman—Dr. Adele Martinique.

"*Yours.*" I feel my eyes widen. "I thought you died."

Adele nods. "Officially, I have. Haven't been outside in years."

"So, do all of these people live here?" I ask.

"Some do," Adele says. "But we need people on the outside. And some find these spaces claustrophobic. You have to get used to breathing computer-generated air. Maybe you know the feeling?"

I nod. How I'd felt at the Meadows. Unsettled. The unnatural quiet.

"Even with the best coders, we can't fully replicate the real world. Real sunlight. Real birdsong."

"Are you two really married?" I ask.

"Not in the eyes of the state," Dr. Collier says. "But we held a ceremony, here, on the roof."

A smile passes between the two women, a history and a love that's had time to grow. I think of the facilities, Margot and Penelope broken up, June and Tasha, Ed and his friend Danny, Rose and me. The false-starts, the early flames of love snuffed out before they could grow into something sturdy and deep like theirs. "I live here," Adele says. "I couldn't exist out there as the woman they want me to be."

Adele's gaze shifts to beyond my shoulder. I turn, half expecting to see Rose walk in. But two older women step through the doorway, behind them a tidy living room just visible. They look like respectable widows, but the moment they step through the doorway, their arms link in a way that puts a lump in my throat. "Technology is the Quorum's smoke and mirrors," Adele says. "With it, they appear much larger than they are. The moment we learn to hack their doorways, it's over."

"The Circle?" I ask. "*We* is the Circle?"

Adele glances at Dr. Collier, and nods. "People like us, and anyone who doesn't look like those propaganda posters. Eventually, we'll surround them—the Quorum, the state, the people who run the facilities. We're always looking for recruits."

And of course, I think of Rose again, because if she were here, she'd join them in an instant. Probably be leading them before long. I smile at the idea. But in the next instant, I recall Marina's words. *That girl isn't who you think she is.*

"Mrs.—Dr. Collier," I say. "Is—is Rose here?"

The time it takes her to speak is interminable. The ocean sound of my heartbeat in my ears nearly drowns out the music. Dr. Collier sets her lips together thoughtfully. "No. I'm afraid not, Eleanor."

"I thought—your note said, *You'll find her behind a door.*"

"She is," Dr. Collier says, regarding me seriously. "Officially, Rose Walters is dead. But there was something about her record that never sat right with me. Her location was listed as 'secure.' It nagged at me. If she were dead, why would she have a location at all? I started scanning through records for other reformeds, and discovered that there are a handful of others like Rose. Dead, but with a location listed as secure."

My scalp prickles. "A computer error?"

"Perhaps," she says. "But I had a suspicion something else was going on. Something larger than Rose, something the state wants to keep quiet. Obviously, we couldn't ask Rose where she was, but it occurred to me that we could ask the algorithm's *version* of Rose."

My mouth opens. "So you sent me to the Registrar's Office."

"I had a hunch you'd be able to get something useful out of her."

And I did. I got Rose's place of residence. Something snaps together in my mind. *Technology is the Quorum's smoke and mirrors. "You'll find her behind a door,"* I say. "You meant inside a doorway—inside a periscope."

Dr. Collier nods. "Every doorway has a serial number. That number you found at the Registrar's Office—"

"Then you do know where I can find her," I interrupt.

Dr. Collier shifts her eyes toward Adele. "Not exactly," Adele says, frowning. "When we ran a search on the number, the location came back classified. That usually only means one thing."

"A prison," Dr. Collier says.

At least she's alive and not in a cemetery vault, like Sheila suggested. In prison, but alive.

"Prisons are places like this too?" June asks. Her mouth is in a tight line, and I only now realize that she's taken back her hand.

Dr. Collier nods, her expression sour. "They make places out of code, and trap people there."

My heartbeat quickens. "How do I get to her?"

Dr. Collier sighs. "First, you'd have to learn the physical location of Rose's door. Any door can be programmed to open into the Village. Prison cells are different. They're only accessible by an official doorway located at a specific, permanent address."

Adele sighs. "But, even if we knew where the door was, we'd also need a state employee's retina scan. Nobody high up in the Department of Prisons or Engineering has yet come to our side. Believe me, we've tried to hack the prisons."

I slump back in my seat. Behind my eyes, images play out—the place where Rose must be. They can make it look like anything.

"Your final note," I say, looking up at Dr. Collier. *You have the key.* "You wanted me to come here, didn't you?"

Dr. Collier nods, smiling. "I knew early on that you were fabricating reports. I wanted to tell you the truth of who I was, but we have to be careful. The Village is precarious, and it's protected only to the degree that all of us guard its secret. When we invite someone new, we must be certain about them. Absolutely certain."

"How did you decide you could trust me?"

"I could see you growing more and more desperate. Waiting outside that door under the bridge. Even taking reformeds there." Dr. Collier glances at June. "You seemed determined to get yourself into real trouble before long. That, and you had a couple of people in here vouching for you."

Dr. Collier glances behind me where someone new steps through the doorway. I have to blink, uncertain whether I'm seeing correctly. Clark, and beside him the curly-haired boy from the mixer. The moment they enter the restaurant, their hands clasp.

"So, they finally let you in," Clark says, grinning as he steps up to our table. He's still wearing his suit from the mixer, but everything else about him has changed, as though someone turned on a light behind his face.

"What are you doing here?" I gasp.

"Trevor has a doorway," he says, glancing at the boy beside him. "This is my—my boyfriend." Clark's entire slim face erupts in a smile.

"You vouched for me, I take it?" I ask, glancing between him and Dr. Collier.

Clark nods. "I might have placed a couple of notes in your pocket too."

"Why don't you explore?" Dr. Collier says, gesturing at the room and beyond. "Find us later, when you're ready to leave."

I don't know if I'll ever be ready to leave. June and I follow Clark to a table, and Trevor returns from the bar with glasses of something fizzy and tasting of ginger.

"How did you meet?" I ask them.

"Trevor's a reformed of mine. The worst one I've ever had," Clark says, laughing.

Trevor raises his hands in a shrug. "Hiding doesn't come naturally to me."

"We might move here," Clark says. "They'll give us our own apartments."

I shake my head, everything aswirl. "I was never sure about you," I tell Clark. "You were so convincing."

"So were you," he says. "When Dr. Collier first asked me if I suspected anything about you, I told her I was certain you were really reformed."

"Nobody's really reformed," Trevor says. "And if they are, I'd challenge them to come here for an hour and not drop the whole act."

I smile, picturing Betty here. What would she do? What would any of us do if we knew it was safe to be who we are?

The music shifts to a loud song, and Trevor's eyes go wide. "Shall we?" he asks. Clark takes his hand, and the two of them wheel onto the dance floor.

"Dance with me," June says, pulling me after her, me in my stodgy work clothes and she in her flouncing dress speckled in Charlie's blood.

I grasp June's hand nervously—everyone here must be able to tell that I'm an adjudicator. But we're surrounded by people, young and old, wearing the clothes of shopgirls and office workers and state officials. It seems understood that, regardless of who we were outside, in here, we're the same.

The air is painted with sound. I feel it work inside my body, filling my lungs, vibrating tendon, muscle, bone, playing me like an instrument. I don't know what I'm doing, but I do it anyway. June's face is shining, and she keeps laughing at nothing, at the joy of this moment. Now I understand why the state took away music. We dance until the air grows a tang of sweat and flushed palm prints form across June's cheeks. Her dark hair has come loose from her hairpins and she looks more like the girl I knew in the Cove.

That's when I see them. The man in a leather coat and high heels. His hair dyed a vibrant shade of pink stark against his deep brown skin. And the person beside him, with short blond hair and a narrow pale face and blue eyes that again seem so familiar. They remind me of someone I haven't seen in a long time.

"Johanna," I say, realization striking me, and though the word should be absorbed by the music, Johanna turns around and bounds toward me. We embrace for a long moment. "Is it really you?"

"Yes. But it's just Jo now.'

I nod, finding myself grinning. "I'm sorry—Jo. I saw you. Under the bridge."

"Later, I regretted not pulling you inside with me, Eleanor. But we have to be careful about who we bring here. You remember Ezekiel?"

I regard the man beside Jo. "You've been officially dead for three years."

Ezekiel chuckles. "Guilty. Jo's been begging Dr. Collier to let you in. They can't shut up about you, actually."

I beam at Jo, their hair and clothes changed, but something else too. Like a bird that's lived all its life in a cage finally stretching its wings. "But—what happened to you after the night of the escape?"

"The Circle intercepted the prison transport I was on. And they brought me here."

I nod, the entire astonishing reality breaking over me. "And you're—you're happy?"

Jo smiles. "I'm helping. It's not like this all the time. During the day, this place is for business. The business of changing things. It's all happening, Eleanor."

When I look at them, I feel it. Something like hope.

June and I escape the sweaty heat of the dance floor for the quiet of the roof. We sit on the edge opposite a sky draped in a pink swath of cloud. The roof looks out over the small city, limestone and brick buildings with wrought iron terraces and patches of gardens. I can still hear the music, vibrating the roof beneath me.

Beside me, June smells warm and sweet. A shiver runs through me.

"I can't get it out of my head, what happened earlier," June says. "Charlie and that boy."

"What set him off?" I ask.

"He said something under his breath about Charlie," June says. "How he *moved*. Maybe he suspected something. Did I tell you? Charlie went to the Cliffs."

I turn to her, stunned. "Charlie's like us?"

June's mouth draws into a frown. "He never talked about it. But all that manly stuff, all that walk tall and don't take shit from anyone, I think he picked it up there." She draws in a shuddering breath. "Charlie had to hide who he was. I think—I think a person can only do that for so long." She doesn't say *We're hiding too*. She doesn't say *I wonder how long until it comes out in us*.

What happened to us—we can swallow it, until our stomachs rot. We can numb it, until one day we can't feel anything. We can pretend it didn't happen, until our minds become mazes that we can't trust. There is no way to pack it into a suitcase and slide it under the bed.

Maybe for the ones who get good at pretending, it won't come out for years and years. They'll be forty or fifty, and their heart will explode. Or they'll barehandedly squeeze the life out of someone else's body. Or they'll, quite without warning, walk into the ocean until their life disappears. And everyone will be stunned. And everyone will blink in perplexed anger. *She was so happy. Always so happy.*

I think about the city, the real one. Sky shot through with buildings, each pockmarked with tiny squares of light, each light a human being. How many people, in their beds, are falling apart right now?

June glances at me. "You egged Charlie on, didn't you?"

I nod. A spike of guilt cuts through me. "I feel bad for that boy," I say. "I do. But, I remembered what you said—the only way Charlie would face a consequence is if he did it to someone else."

A kind of relief pushes onto June's face. "Those peacekeepers arrested him," she says. "If they find him guilty, he won't be eligible to marry. They'll move me back into a dormitory for single women. I'll have to be matched again—six months. But I can put in a request to relocate. To leave the city." She sends me a hesitant smile. And though I know I should be glad for her, grateful she's not going to turn herself in, I can feel my heart slowly shattering.

"Leaving?" I whisper.

"Well, if my adjudicator declares me reformed," she says.

"Your adjudicator would have to be pretty nice," I point out.

"Oh, she is," June says. "She's the best."

We look at each other, the air turning warm and distorted, breath coming short. The half-moon curves bracketing June's mouth, an almost smile, fall slowly away. The moment turns dangerous, eye contact sustained too long. My heart beats deep inside me, not in my chest it seems, but lower, an aching thud.

"Eleanor, you must know, all this time . . ." she says. "How—how I've felt about you."

"June," I say. "You're leaving."

"Even more reason to tell you," she says.

But I shake my head, because what's the point of another shred of happiness that won't last?

June frowns. "It's Rose, isn't it?"

I open my hands. "For a year, I thought she was dead."

She looks at me, her mouth trembling.

"June—"

She sniffs, looking away. "It's all right, Eleanor. I have no right feeling hurt. You never promised me anything. I think I just hoped—just hoped—"

"June, you have it wrong."

"Then—why?"

I shake my head. My feelings for Rose are muddled now. They feel . . . fragile viewed through the time passed. I rake my hands through my hair. "I thought Rose was dead," I say. "For a year, I thought she was dead—because of me."

June frowns. "But they said she was killed by peacekeepers, trying to escape. How could that be your fault?"

I go cold. This—what I never wanted June to know. This—what I fear she won't be able to understand, or forget. I open my mouth but the words stay lodged, fighting to get free.

"The—the peacekeepers," I say. "They were there because they knew about the escape. Someone betrayed her."

It takes a moment for my words to fall through the air and settle over June. "You?" she breathes.

"So, you see," I say. "I have to get her out. She's trapped where she is because of me."

CHAPTER 45

Water drummed the white tile of the shower room, steam gathering in nimbus clouds along the ceiling. I clicked the lock and turned to face Sheila.

"Rose has a plan," I said, the shushing of the water drowning out my voice. I half expected Sheila to tell me to stop, that she couldn't risk getting involved, but she only nodded, face solemn. This night, the night of the dance, I told her, the boys from the Pines would arrive in shuttles. The archway would open, and we'd walk through. While the others danced, we'd be on a black asphalt road, hurtling toward a new life.

Sheila's brow drew down. "What if you miss the window? And it closes before you can go through."

"Then we walk back to the dance," I said. *Or we get transferred, or worse.* The implication rang in the steaming air. I could see it in the crease between Sheila's eyebrows.

"It's usually *you* who worries about *me*," she said.

I smiled. "I wouldn't be alone. Rose is telling some others. Only the ones she can trust."

Steam had gathered in tiny stippled droplets on Sheila's face. "I can't come with you."

I nodded.

"Matron Sybil told me I've *made great strides*. And Matron Gloria said she'd never eaten a more delicious pineapple upside-down cake."

"But how's your hollandaise?" I asked.

We broke into quiet laughter. I didn't want to leave this room. I wanted to stay with Sheila forever. But the dance was only hours away.

"I found my parents," I say.

Her eyes widened.

"They're dead," I told her. "They have been, my whole life."

Sheila closed her eyes and let out a breath. "I'm sorry. What were their names?"

The question surprised me. Only Sheila would think to ask. "Cora and Michael," I said, my throat in a knot. "But it's—it's not the same as—" Not the same as losing a real parent, I wanted to say. I didn't even have memories of them.

"Shhh," she said, pulling me close. The air was humid and warm, the same temperature as tears, and they slid from me noiselessly.

Sheila leaned back. "Eleanor, you sure about this? You don't know where you'd end up. You could be stuck in the middle of nowhere."

"Rose will pack supplies."

"But—where will you go, after?"

I swallowed. "I've been avoiding thinking that far."

Sheila considered me. "What would happen if you thought that far?"

I might not want to do it, I thought, but didn't say. She could read it on my face.

The next hours clipped by and with every smiling glance from Rose, a hot dread fell over me. In the clothes closet, I debated pants, but instead chose a drop-waist blue satin dress. Rose had found a full tuxedo. The common room overflowed with taffeta and lace. Once, we'd scoured the

Meadows for any sign of the previous cohort, for thimbles and feathers, and doubted we'd ever be like them. Now, here we were.

Since everyone had dressed up, it was impossible to tell who would go with Rose.

How many? And how many would stay?

At dinnertime, the girls departed for the dining room, chatting excitedly about the dance, unaware others weren't joining them.

"It's time," Rose said to the remaining girls, a handful crowding around her, faces stretched with excitement and fear. Penelope among them, and Johanna.

Doubt ballooned in my chest.

Rose crossed to where I stood, a step inside my room. "Coming?" she whispered.

I knew better than to speak aloud all my fears—that the archway wouldn't open, that we had no plan for afterward. "What if we waited?"

"We're ready now."

"What if the matrons know?"

Rose shook her head. "I was careful." She gazed at me, eyes pleading. "We could have a life, Eleanor."

Sudden tears tracked, hot, down my face. There was no right choice. "There are other ways," I whispered. "Stay with me."

"I have to go," she said. "Unless you think up a way to stop me."

Desperation burned. In that moment, I didn't care if the matrons heard. "Rose, you're not good to anyone inside a prison cell. You—you're not good to anyone dead."

She shook her head, dismissing my fears like dust shaken from a rug. She'd do what she wanted, exactly what she wanted. That wasn't new. What was new: how her eyes had seemed to lose dimension, becoming a determined, flat plane.

"Maybe we'll find each other," she said. "One day. The cabin on the lake." She angled toward me and our lips found each other, almost instinctively. The others faded away, their small gasps little gossamer things that floated in the air around us.

Rose pulled back and, without a word, led the group from the room.

Unbearable, the silence left behind. The white honeycomb we'd lived in since we were children, empty now. A frantic fluttering in my chest, something banging against my rib cage. My legs moved. I was almost out the door when Sheila cut through the silence.

"Where are you going?"

I hadn't even registered her there. "I have to stop her."

"You can't stop someone from wanting what they want."

"Then what can I do?" I felt hot tears again.

"Let her go," Sheila said softly.

I heard Rose's voice. *I have to go. Unless you think up a way to stop me.* And once the thought was in my head, there was no digging it out.

In the dining hall, I looked around the room. All the matrons were there. No—nearly all. "Eleanor, don't you look lovely." Matron Maureen approached.

"Where's Matron Sybil?" I asked.

"In the office, I'd imagine," Matron Maureen said. "What's the matter?"

But I was already running down the corridor, out the main entrance. Outside, Rose's group had made it some distance down the road, close enough to still call out to.

At once, I wished for rain. For something to fall from the sky and extinguish this heat, this terror in me, this singular thought in my mind. *Rose—dead.* And if not dead, gone from me forever. Unless I did something.

My breath coursed through me like an ocean current. Muscular, steady.

I walked to the matrons' quarters. The red light of the retina scanner splashed over my eye. Through the doorway. Footsteps soft on a white floor. Down a long, white corridor, glowing with its own light.

I gripped the handle. And turned it.

CHAPTER 46

Maybe everything, all along, was leading to this.

That crisp, white envelope. These clean, lit halls. Best and brightest. Before that, even—the bundled parcel on a doorstep shadowed by a maple tree that never should have lived.

Maybe everything, even what had yet to come, funneled me toward this: fingers clasped around the door handle.

The future hulked nearby: a face and backbone I could control, the pale petals that fall on a wedding day, the wide knuckles of some man, and in my mouth, the word *husband*. The daily, determined effort it would take to tell myself this was the life I desired.

Maybe it wasn't ever about changing things for Rose, or keeping her with me just a little longer. Maybe it was a turning away from what I couldn't tolerate seeing. A pain I couldn't coat in pearl no matter how hard I tried.

How do you make a choice? What does it take to push through a moment you can never undo? The flexing of muscles, the turning of a wrist, the slipping of a metal bolt from its socket.

I pushed open the door.

"You have done a brave thing," Matron Sybil said to me, after, in the quiet hollow of the matrons' office. Her hand rested lightly on my shoulder.

"You look exhausted, Eleanor. Why don't you skip the formal? Head back to the dormitory and get some sleep?"

I gaped at her. The idea of sleep felt impossible. "They'll be near the archway by now."

"I expect they are."

"Well—aren't you going after them?"

Matron Sybil smiled. "It's already taken care of, dear."

I blinked at her. "Taken care of?"

The truth was visible inside her easy smile. Matron Sybil hadn't needed me to tell her about Rose's plan. She already knew. But it wasn't the matrons who would fetch them.

Matron Sybil's grip on my shoulder turned hard. "Eleanor, you need your rest—" she began, but I twisted away and slipped from her grasp. I careened out of her office. Past the white tents set up for the dance, onto the dusty road. The muscles in my legs burned. As badly as I'd ever needed the girl from the Cove back, I needed her most now. *Just run. Run like you remember running. Run like you're on a cliff above the ocean, and you're twelve, and you haven't yet learned how hard the world is.*

My breath came ragged. A stitch slipped like a razor between my ribs. I kept running. Had to get to them before they made it to the archway.

The brick arch stood stark on the horizon. Near it, the black silhouettes of the group, approaching it. Faint, high notes burst on the dusky air, excited squeals and laughter. I could make out the short crown of curls on Rose's head, craning her neck with the others to stare, awed, at the door. I recognized the pale outline of Johanna bouncing on the balls of her feet.

"Don't—" I gasped. "Don't go through!" They couldn't hear me, the air suffused with a nervous thrill.

And then I heard it. Buzzing, like the drone of a faraway hive. It throbbed, pulsating even to where I stood, vibrating my teeth.

I was still too far away. I waved at them, frantic. "Don't!" My voice came out ragged.

Then in the span of the next second, several events:

The archway switched on with a palpitation of electricity. For a moment, I thought my eyes had been tricked. There was no road on the other side. No slick black asphalt, but a large gray room. The concrete that made up the ceiling and walls looked freshly poured and sterile. Johanna had her back to the archway. She saw me, her face breaking into a grin. She thought I'd decided to come after all.

Several peacekeepers stepped forward then, in their white suits, batons and prods crackling with blue light.

My breath felt wrenched from me. "Run!" I screamed. This time, I was close enough for them to hear.

The girls facing the archway saw, their limbs rigid, faces suddenly hunched in fear. Rose sprang back. She'd really thought they'd get out.

The peacekeepers reached forward. Johanna still faced me, our arms nearly touching. She was smiling when one of them grabbed her, twisting an arm behind her back. She cried out.

I lurched to the doorway and grasped Johanna's free arm. "Got you," I breathed.

Around us, the others screamed and scattered, zigzagging from the archway into the fields. Three peacekeepers stalked after them, disappearing into the flowers, prods stuttering to life. I'd lost sight of Rose.

The other officer strained against Johanna's arm, and we performed a momentary tug-of-war in the way of children fighting over a doll. Johanna's blue eyes were wide, glassy. I braced a foot against the brick of the archway, pulling backward with all the muscle I had.

Johanna's fingers were tight around my arm. Her hand grew slippery. I gripped harder. I could feel the bones in my fingers bowing. Johanna glanced behind her and kicked, striking the officer's throat with a sickening thud. A flicker of relief crossed her face.

The officer dropped to the ground, clutching his throat, as another ran into the concrete room. He grabbed the back of Johanna's dress and hauled her into the air. For a moment, she was suspended inside the archway, halfway between worlds.

Johanna looked at me with huge, panicked eyes. "Let me go," she whispered.

"No. I've got you."

"Eleanor, run," she said.

She relaxed her hand, muscles slack, and slipped from my grasp, her fingers splayed in the air for a moment before she collapsed in a heap inside the concrete room.

I toppled backward, spraying gravel as I crashed to the road. In the next second, the buzzing sound whined to a climax, cramming static into my brain. And without warning, the archway switched off.

Silence.

A silence that stunned with its suddenness. A silence that felt wrong. The unnatural silence of the Meadows.

I sat in the middle of the road, legs splayed, panting deep. I cast my eyes around, frantic. But there was no one. Only the empty eye of sky above me. Only the flowers who looked on with faces that said nothing.

CHAPTER 47

Rain.

What I remember most about leaving the Meadows is rain. Years inside blooming purple fields. Years without a single drop. A snowflake. A gust of wind.

How did it take us so long to see what the Meadows really was? Should've been obvious, in the perfection of pale sky and white buildings and girls wound up like ballerinas in a music box, ready to dance on command, to play the part they'd written for us.

All those years, and they sent me away, just like that. Passed me the words *Best Girl*. The rumble of the shuttle, and its stopping. Stepping outside, cranking my head to take in the city. Still smelling of purple flowers. Mouth still tasting of Rose.

The city opened up like a machine, buildings of metal, floor of slate. And from the sky, rain. Tiny missiles falling from a mile above. Connected with my temple.

And I cried. Because there were things I couldn't make sense of. And one of them was the shivering droplet pulling down my face. The feeling of my body recognizing it.

CHAPTER 48

June stands on the train platform, a small suitcase in her hand.

Once, people flew in airplanes, plumes of exhaust filling the sky in lines of angry white breath. What must that have been like, sensing the presence of a hundred strangers above your head? Nobody my age has been inside the sky.

"Don't look so tragic," June says. "We'll see each other again."

"I'm not so sure."

"You don't want me to go?"

I shake my head. "But I understand why you need to leave."

I wrote my report, recommending June for release from adjudication. Dr.—Mrs. Collier approved it, declaring June reformed. In the Cove, the algorithm will still monitor her, and she will need to match again within six months, but she's an unmarked citizen now, free to live where she likes.

"You could live in the Village," I say. "I could visit you."

June smiles sadly. "I don't want to hide. This world"—she glances around—"I'm beginning to think it doesn't have to be like this forever."

"You're only saying that because you're happy right now."

"I am happy," she says, then takes a deep breath. "My mother told me about past civilizations that have fallen. It's not all at once. They fall slow. It takes time. A million tiny mistakes. With people like us, they made a mistake. One day, everyone's going to wake up. And then it's fast. Suddenly, it's very fast."

I recall what Jo said the day before, about things changing. There is hope, but my mind guards against it. "Not in our lifetimes."

June sighs. "I know there's a very loud part of you that says things can't change. It's like a cawing bird in your ear. Shouting all the time about hope, how hoping is hurtful. It's trying to protect you, I think. But maybe one day that bird will see that hoping can lead to something good. Maybe it'll quiet down. Just a little."

I swallow a heaviness. "What if I make it quiet down and there's nothing else there?" Nothing inside me. Nothing but black rot.

June angles her head toward me, and with her eyes, it's like she pulls my chin up until I'm looking at her. "Maybe you'll find another little bird to talk to you," she says. "One that's been forced to be quiet for a very long time."

Behind her, the train's horn blares. June slides something out of her bag and places it in my hand. It's the photo of us at Mrs. Arkwright's house, me the sun and her a wildfire. On the back, in cramped writing, a letter. "Read it later."

She is about to step onto the train. About to be shuttled far away. And I think, *Why did I find her again only to lose her? Why did I give up the chance to kiss her when I could?*

If I had my way, I would put my hand behind her head, weave it into her hair. I would bend my face down to hers. I want to taste the heart of her again, the heat of her mouth, the softness of her body bending against my hipbones.

Rose, I think, at once. I can't leave her. If she's in prison, she's there because of me.

Maybe my face changes. Maybe I bend back, even just an inch. Because June frowns, and turns, and steps onto the train. She gives a little wave. And disappears inside.

Eleanor,

The algorithm knows unknowable things. My baby brother, John, has eleven new teeth, and his hair is thick and corn-colored, like his mother. Janna Nelson stole the Wanting Hat and isn't allowed in the sanctuary building anymore. When I searched for your mother, I found something I didn't expect.

She sought the help of the healer who lives by the waterfront, and then again the doctor, when he passed through several months ago. It seems your mother is sick. I don't know how bad it is, but it's something to do with her stomach. I'm sorry I don't have better news. I debated even telling you. But I thought it would be wrong not to share.

At work, I searched for Rose. I had to see the face of the girl who captured you. The photo was from her arrest, before the Meadows. She had a cut on her upper lip, and her eyes bored into the camera. And I thought, If Eleanor likes angry girls, maybe it's good news for me. Because I'm angry too. And Rose is gone.

I want you to have this photo. I've held on to it for all these years. Now it's your turn. Maybe in another five years, we'll meet again and you can return it.

I really do hope we'll meet again.

June

Angry girls. That's what June said. The only ones I've ever loved, Rose and June. Sheila. Even Marina. Brimming with a fire they could barely contain. Hurt flying from their mouths, screaming at the sky. There is something so good about rage. I never witnessed it growing up. My mother's fire burned low and constant. Never bursting forth. I think I always craved a little bursting forth. The clarity of it, the catharsis. To say, out in the open, *Here's what we're dealing with. Here is the truth.* With my mother, there was always something just below the surface, easy to pretend away, so I questioned whether her clenched jaw was normal, or her stony silence, or the way she held herself like she was keeping back a tidal wave.

If you're not angry at the people who deserve it, you get angry at yourself.

I wonder, for the first time, if my mother had someone to be angry at.

The bride and groom request the honor of your presence in celebrating their marriage.

My screen buzzes, and for a moment I imagine it's June. But it's only a wedding invitation. I've dismissed the same notification three times already this week. I receive these from reformeds occasionally. Maybe they know what I've done for them, or else inviting their adjudicator is expected. The date of the wedding is today. Clearly they don't expect me to show up.

In my room, I find it, the familiar brush of paper in my coat pocket. Green paper. Longer than any of the previous notes, the handwriting sloppy and hurried.

Director of my department is asking questions. An inquiry into your reformed status. They will come for you by tomorrow. The doorway is always open to you.

They're coming for me, those men in tactical suits, with their batons and guns. I feel the compulsion to run, to the bridge, to go through the doorway and disappear. But—

Rose.

They will come for you by tomorrow. So. I have a day.

I look at the photo that June gave me. I don't want to think about it being another five years before I see her. Who will we even be in five years? If it's anything like the difference between us five years ago and now, we'll be new versions of ourselves. I think—I want to be there to watch June transform into the person she'll become. I glance back at the photo. June, with her untamed hair and wild grin. Me, head tipped in mid-laugh, shoulders back, holding my violin beneath my arm. That scratched up thing that I loved anyway. The initials of some long-dead musician etched on it. CSJ. I always wondered about them, who they were—

I squint, staring at the carved initials for a long moment, holding back my mind before I allow it to go where it wants to.

My birth mother's name was Cora St. James.

CSJ.

Cora St. James was the first owner of my violin.

I glance out the window, struck by the urge to shake the walls of these buildings. Of this city. Of the world. My mother lied. She didn't get my violin from a scrap heap. My body is lit with clean, white anger. I want to find my mother and scream at her until she tells me the truth. The truth she hid from me all my life. I want to march into the Department of Prisons and demand to know where they're keeping Rose. I want to save every one of my reformeds from the life they're hurtling toward with disturbing efficiency.

Desperation pours through me.

No—this is not how I solve things. Not by marching, or running, or fighting. How did I tell Rose I'd fight? By talking. There's only one person I know who might be able to help me.

Betty's husband, Tad, works as an overseer in the Department of Prisons. I imagine showing up at her doorstep, how she'd delight in turning me down. Maybe Betty won't help me. But I'm desperate enough to try.

When I knock on the door of Betty's brownstone, I'm surprised to see it's not her who answers, but her husband.

"Tad?" I ask. There are deep bags beneath his eyes, and his hair, once perfectly pomaded, is ruffled. "I'm a friend of Betty's. We had dinner about a year ago."

"Of course." Tad nods distractedly. "You'll have to remind me of your name."

"Eleanor," I say, glancing into the dark room behind him. "I was in the neighborhood. I thought I'd drop by."

"That's—that's very kind of you," he says. "Come in."

Inside, the house is shadowy. Curtains drawn, the air somehow thick. There's a strangely empty feeling here. I don't know why, but my heart accelerates. Tad falls into a chair across from me. "Should I have offered you a drink? I'm not a very good host. Betty did all of that."

"I'm fine," I say. "Is Betty out?"

"Betty's . . . gone," he says.

"Gone," I repeat.

He shakes his head, as though lost. "A week ago. Officially, she contracted a respiratory illness."

I watch him, my body grown very still. "Officially," I repeat. I glance around the room. A week since anyone's tidied it. A week since Betty's been here.

"What happened to Betty?" I ask, but he seems not to hear me, his eyes staring, vacant.

"We didn't know each other long," he says. "Married less than a year. I didn't know her well. I was at work so much. But I—I can't imagine her not being here when I get home."

I lean forward. "Tad, what happened to Betty?"

"I kissed her cheek, and walked to the front door," he recounts. "She stopped me and said something about video footage."

"Life footage," I say, skin prickling with trepidation.

"That's it," he says, rubbing his eyes. "She said 'I'm certain you'll enjoy my life footage. I worked so hard on it.' I didn't understand. I put it down to female silliness. But maybe—maybe I ought to have listened."

Tad looks at me suddenly, intense. "You're her friend," he says. "Was there any clue? Any reason to suspect that she'd do this to herself?"

I swallow hard, struggling to breathe. At once, I'm falling. Spiraling through the air, like I've imagined, from my balcony. Ripped from my bedroom by peacekeepers. Turpentine coursing down my throat. I've tasted the idea of it. Pressed it to my skin like a blunt knife, watched pain bloom over my vision. Just an idea. Not yet more than an idea.

I watch Tad, his face fallen into his hands. "There was no clue," I tell him. "Nobody could've seen it coming."

CHAPTER 49

My limbs shake for a long time, on the train, up the elevator of my apartment block, onto the balcony to gulp down handfuls of frigid air. Betty, gone. My body rejects it. It feels like a mistake. A living girl, unbreathing. The urge to bury this thorny fact. To crush it. To draw images on my wrist. But—*no*. I will feel it all.

The cusp of the horizon glows red. In the Cove, this meant good luck. All it means here is that, far off, in the wastelands, a fire is burning. It will be quickly contained, the acid tang of artificial rain, but for now, the air glows as though the earth is bleeding.

We didn't do this—a defiant thought, rising to a point. We were not responsible for the world burning. Love cannot do that. Marina's words. Sheila's words. Now, mine. Tears coat my face, singed with cold.

There was nothing.

Not anything.

Wrong with me.

I have to believe it. Even when I don't. I trace the long fall to the pavement below, the path a body might take. The only possible conclusion of our time in the Meadows.

I decide, finally, I don't want it. I don't want this to be my end.

It's still not yet noon. I have all day to find Rose. But how? Breaking into a prison doorway is impossible even for Adele and the Circle. How will I manage it?

The bride and groom request the honor of your presence in celebrating their marriage.

My screen buzzes again, that same notification. I sigh and turn to flick it away, and for the first time catch the name of the bride.

Sheila Evans.

My heart slams shut. *Please. Please don't let it be true.*

The wedding is held in an old church in the middle of the city. All of the religious meaning has been stripped away, but couples still prefer them for the optics. This one is very old, hand-cut stone and a large plot of grass and ancient trees. Inside the odd cavern of the city, buildings jutting on every side, this spot has a strange silence.

I find a seat on a shining bench near the back. A little girl drops petals down the aisle. Groomsmen in suits and vests. Hard to tell who here is real family, and who is rented for the occasion. The groomsmen do a reasonably good job of acting jovial, elbowing each other when Sheila emerges. Golden hair falls down her back in a shining curtain.

I watch the entire ceremony, my insides wrestling. Part of me feels tectonic plates ripping up the earth beneath me. Sheila, *married.* To that boy who doesn't know her. But, a different part, just as strong, insists that this is the only way this story was ever going to end. More than that, this is the best option. Better an Ed than a Charlie.

After the ceremony, guests filter onto the lawn. I stand away from the rest. I recognize Sheila's mother, shifting in her shined shoes, her face drawn. Into my head, the image of a thirteen-year-old Sheila receiving her letter to the Meadows. Small, bright girl, so alive. Her parents tried to stop her from going. Tried to prevent a day like today.

The flower girl is twirling around in her sparkling dress, still throwing petals that she never seems to run out of. An actor, I decide. A cluster of pastel-dressed girls my age huddle together, whispering behind gloved hands, all apple-cheeked and blushing, cheering as the happy couple emerges. The Young Wives Club, I assume.

"Eleanor, you came." Sheila wraps me in a hug, skin hot and clammy. Her face surprises me. Beaming. Bright-eyed. Happier than I've seen her in a long time.

"Congratulations," I say, hesitant.

Sheila smiles, strangely shy. "Oh, Eleanor, I'm so happy. I never thought I could be so happy."

"I'm—I'm pleased for you," I say. "But—I'm surprised."

"I know," she says. "But, Eleanor, I told you, I made a decision. I could mourn the future that was never mine in the first place. Or I could embrace reality." She lets loose a held breath. "I've done it. I let it all go. I'm happy."

Something hot and impulsive fills my veins. The state is onto me, and I find I don't care about eyes anymore. I don't care about ears. I care about Sheila. "After all they did," I say to her. "What about *doing* something? Finding the people responsible?"

Her brow draws down. "Is this some kind of test? My adjudicator finding me on my wedding day to ask me subversive questions?"

"I'm not here as your adjudicator."

"Are you here as my friend?" she asks. "Because if you were, I have to think you'd understand the person you're talking to. You'd see that I'm doing what I know is right."

I open my mouth but can think of nothing to say. Misery pools in my stomach.

Sheila stares into the distance, eyes roving. "We never did figure out what the final test was, did we?" She lets out a breathy laugh. "Maybe it's life. Maybe it's just living, as a person in the world. The tests never end."

At her words, that desperation from earlier rips through me again. Looking at Sheila, I think, yes, this is how stories like ours end. Sheila will spend the rest of her life hiding. But I don't know if I can do it anymore.

"You were right all along, Eleanor," she says lightly. "Those of us who wanted more . . . Well, we learned."

Why is it that Sheila and I can never be in the same place at the same time?

"I wish you hadn't," I say. "I think I'm learning what you knew all along. There was never anything wrong with us." Spoken aloud, my words strengthen. "Sheila, they *lied*."

But Sheila leans backward, eyes cloudy with fear. "Don't say things like that."

She's right. It's not safe, speaking so openly. But I only have a day until the state knows the extent of my crimes—yes, crimes, I realize with a dull flash of terror. I should feel more afraid, but the only emotion I can find is relief. They already have enough evidence to hang me. For the first time since I arrived in the city, I can say what I really think, outside in the open air. "Did you hear about Betty?"

Sheila's eyes dart away, at the sky, at the grass. "She caught a bad cold. It happened fast."

"It wasn't a cold."

She's shaking her head. "You don't know that."

"That's what the Meadows was always leading to."

"Not me," Sheila says.

"There are other deaths." I recall what Matron Maureen said, about killing that part of herself. Holding a burial. Sheila's aware of the many ways a body breaks, under the weight of secrets.

Just then, someone calls for her. Ed is standing by the church, grinning. Sheila returns the smile, waving.

She turns to me, drawing in a shaky breath. Then she reaches into her white clutch. Into my hands, she places something small and metal. A key. Inked on the metal with black marker is a string of numbers and characters that resemble a passcode. "I hardly know why I'm doing this," she says. "The apartment will be empty for a few hours."

"But why—"

"The code should work. Maybe you'll find what you've been looking for," she says. "Ed never did learn to put his things away."

I nod, curling my fingers around the key.

For a moment, Sheila watches Ed over her shoulder, shaking hands in front of the church. She turns to me again, brown eyes warm. "How do you make a choice?" she asks. "About which direction your life is supposed to go?"

Reluctantly a smile crosses my face. There was a time when I asked her the same question. "I think you just do," I say. "And wait to find out if you made the right one."

"Then let me make it," Sheila says. She turns back to the church, in her hands, fistfuls of white.

CHAPTER 50

In Sheila's apartment, I find Ed's screen on the kitchen counter beneath some paperwork and crumpled food wrappers. I enter the passcode and the screen comes alive with a digital click, a door unlocking. I riffle through for only a moment before finding the periscope directory. Rose's place of residence returns an address, almost instantaneously. She's close, only on the other side of the city.

I leave Sheila's key on the counter after rubbing the passcode from the metal with my thumb. The ink transfers to my skin, and I stare at it for a moment, considering the risk Sheila took for me. The marks we've left on each other.

Before I can waver, I find a napkin, scribble the address to Dr. Collier's office, alongside a message.

If you find out you made the wrong one.

I leave it in the kitchen, where Sheila will find it before Ed.

My hand is on the doorknob when an idea rings through me. Ed's screen hasn't yet gone to sleep, still glowing faintly on the counter. Hesitatingly, I approach, tapping lightly on the universal individual directory. I type slow, weighing every letter. *Cora St. James.*

Her picture matches the one from my file, heavy chestnut bangs, serious mouth. I swallow a knot in my throat. Still alarming, how she resembles me. I scan the screen, but the information is identical to what I saw in my file. Her subversive past. Her death date, the day after I was born. Nothing new here.

I see a button labeled *Records*, and click on it. Links appear, to articles mentioning Cora. They used to record all kinds of things in newspapers. My fingers hover over the topmost article. An obituary. Only a few scant lines.

Cora St. James died in her home in the early hours of the morning on November 19. A devoted lawyer, she fought for justice for each of her clients. She is survived by close friend Stella Arbuck.

The sun is nearing the horizon, casting long shadows on the pavement, as the commuter train leads me away from the city. Out in the open, I feel wrapped in a blanket of dread, scanning endlessly for peacekeepers. Have they made it through my reports yet? Have they discovered the ways I've deceived? Are they, this moment, coming for me?

And what to make of this new knowledge? Cora and my mother— friends. *Close friends.*

I disembark on a quiet street lined with stone houses, each featuring several blooming rosebushes behind wrought iron fences.

The address I found leads to a stately white townhouse. Pillars flank a thick, oak slab of a front door. Behind it—Rose.

A woman in a crisp white uniform answers my knock. "How may I help you?"

"I have an appointment with the head of the house," I say.

"The lady of the house is out," the woman says, uncertain. "Perhaps you're mistaken."

A voice calls from inside. "Anna, close the door. Do I need to remind you that it's winter?"

At her voice, every muscle and sinew in me tenses. The air seems to shift around her as she approaches, and a lightning bolt of fear hits my heart. She wears a casual green dress, the first time I've seen her in anything other than white. Her auburn hair strikes my eyes like a spotlight.

"Matron Maureen?"

Her face registers no surprise. She smiles a true smile, astonished and delighted. "Just Maureen now," she says. "Eleanor, how lovely to see you. Come. Anna will show you to the solarium."

"Right this way, miss," Anna says, ushering me inside.

I follow her, though my mind pinwheels. This is Teagarden, where Matron Maureen lives. The address registered to Rose's prison. But how could a prison be here? The place feels soft—pinkish glow of lamps, plush pale carpet, smell of dried flowers. The house's back wall is a curved plane of glass overlooking a sprawling garden.

"Some tea, Anna," Matron Maureen says, and points me to a chair beneath the curved glass roof of the solarium. "Sit, Eleanor. You're a guest here." She reclines in her chair, gazing at me, eyes warm and crinkling. "So, you've finally made it to Teagarden."

"This is your house?" I ask, swallowing a clutch of nervousness.

"My mother's," she says. "I'm just here until I decide my next steps."

Anna returns with a tea set. While Matron Maureen prepares herself a cup, I look around the daintily appointed space. This is where I could have been living. I have visited hundreds of homes in the last year on adjudications, and I always had the upper hand. Not here.

"Is your father home?" I ask.

She sips her steaming cup. "He died when I was young," she says. "Not that I saw him much before. He was very important."

"Your mother wasn't required to re-match?"

"She was coming up on the age cut-off," she says. "And, those rules are a little flexible when you—well, when you live in Teagarden." She smiles. "Eleanor, I'm so pleased you're here. I'd love to catch up, but I assume you've arrived with a mission."

"Yes, I—I'm looking for answers."

"A noble quest," she says in that conspiratorial way she had in the Meadows. "But you were always filled with the most noble stuff, Eleanor."

There's a feeling in my body like shrinking, my bones telescoping until I'm dwarfed by her, the same feeling of shame clawing at my gut as when she showed me the video of me kissing June. *Eleanor, can you possibly know how disappointed I am?*

"I—I'm here for some information about Rose," I say.

"Oh, Rose," she says, smiling. "She certainly made life interesting, didn't she?"

I blink, rattled by her informality, her smile, how she leans across the table like we're old friends catching up.

"After Rose was captured," I say, voice hard, "she went to prison. A particular prison cell."

"Yes," Matron Maureen says, sipping her tea. "That was a very important element of this entire thing."

This entire thing? "I know the doorway is registered to this address," I say. "And I'd like your help getting inside."

She frowns. "I could do that," she says lightly. "But, I do wonder, Eleanor, if you've based your decision to come here today on the assumption that Rose *wants* to escape. I'd hate for you to be disappointed."

I squint at her. "Why wouldn't she want to escape?"

Matron Maureen twirls a teaspoon around her cup and looks to the back garden. Elsewhere in the city, the world is barren and bitter cold, but the back garden, covered, I realize, in a glass case, is blooming. Just as she'd described.

"The matrons were aware of everything that happened in the Meadows," Matron Maureen says. "Of an evening, we'd tell each other the most entertaining thing we'd heard that day. Silly stories, diversions. Matron Sybil told us once about a rumor that the final test would involve surviving in the meadow fields. Whoever made it longest with no food or water would become Best Girl. Oh, how we laughed."

Heat fills my cheeks. In my lap, my hands become fists. "Are you going to tell me about Rose now?"

"Oh, but, Eleanor," Matron Maureen says brightly. "I am." She presses me with her green eyes, mischief in them. I'm swept by a feeling of seasickness, disoriented being in her presence again.

Suddenly, she stands and strides toward the door to the garden. "I feel like a walk, don't you?"

"Please," I implore, standing. "Please, just tell me the truth."

She smiles sweetly. "I feel like a walk. If you don't wish to accompany me, Anna will escort you out." Her eyes twitch to the ceiling. I don't look, but sense, in the fuzzy aura of peripheral vision, a mesh ear there. Listening.

I follow her into the back garden, overgrown and filled with every kind of plant imaginable. Above, the glass ceiling hangs with dollops of condensation, and from vents, steaming air descends like slow rain. I drag in a breath, humid and warm.

Matron Maureen strides toward a huge tree, an umbrella of glossy leaves hung with orange orbs, the atmosphere around it sharp and citrus-smelling. She wrenches an orange from the tree, sending every bough shaking. "For you, Eleanor." I watch as my own hand reaches out and takes it.

I look from the orange back to her, recalling the first time I was alone with her. "The fog in the Meadows," I say. "You told me it was a natural phenomenon."

"One of the few, regrettable times I was forced to lie," she says. "The fog is medium, what's used in periscopes to print. Say a girl found a way to burn down the fields. Medium repairs any damage to the facilities. It's also a simple security measure. Don't want the sheep wandering too far. The fields really do go on forever."

"Why not just build a wall?" I ask.

"They did, in the beginning. The founders had a different methodology back then. A little more . . . direct. The children fought back. Mutinies, violence. My mother suggested a softer approach. Children obey so much better when they don't know they're being controlled. Ah, my favorites," she says, stopping to admire a tangle of tall flowers. The smell almost knocks me sideways, pale and vaguely sweet, and all at once I'm transported back to that place, every cell in me flinching.

"The flowers in the Meadows were an amalgamation of several of my mother's favorites. Carefully crafted," she says, fanning her hands over them. "I told her not to plant them outside. No one knows what may happen, plants made of ones and zeroes transplanted in the real world. Might infect the groundwater, kill all the native plants. Well, she did it anyway. 'I created those flowers myself,' she said. 'I want a few for my garden.'"

A slow prickling draws up my spine. "Your mother is—"

"Yes," she says. "You know her as Matron Sybil."

My body thrums. There was always something about Matron Sybil that seemed familiar. I can almost feel my skull expand to accommodate this idea.

My eyes are pulled toward something small. I step toward the orange tree and make out a jade green chrysalis clutching a branch. I smile. I haven't seen one since I was a child.

"'Butterflies have the most remarkable nature,' Matron Maureen says.
"'When it's time to become something new, they build a chrysalis and

allow their bodies to dissolve. They erase themselves in the pursuit of transformation.'"

I turn to her. "Matron Sybil told us that," I say. "The day after we learned the truth of the Meadows."

She lets out a small, breathy laugh.

"What?" I ask.

"The truth of the Meadows," she says. "Did you really think there was only one?"

I squint at her. "Your mother sent you to a facility," I say. "Her own daughter."

Matron Maureen arches an eyebrow. "Especially her own daughter."

"But how could you forgive her?" I ask. "How could you become a matron too?"

"I didn't always understand," she says. "But, she did it because she loved me." She regards me, her eyes still so kind and patient; a place inside of me wrestles. "It was the same with you, Eleanor. You needed someone to love you enough to help you change. You could have it still. You could transfer to a homestay here, any moment."

"What makes you think I'd ever want to live here?" I ask.

Her eyebrows raise in surprise. "I think it's the thing you want most in the world," she says. "Family. Someone, at last, to love you."

"You only want to change me."

She smiles. "I resisted too, at first. Granted, I gave up after year one, so forgive me if this seems infantile to me in someone of your age."

I wrench my eyes from hers and look again at the chrysalis.

"This one will be out soon," she says. "The monarchs think it's spring in here," she explains, "so, they emerge early. They're not viable. So we have to—" She mimes grinding her heel into the soil. "Poor crooked little things."

I can only stare at her.

"I've thought about you, Eleanor. If only you'd had a bit more time. Everything got . . . rushed at the end." She turns to me. "My mother told the butterfly story to every cohort. It really happens that way—they allow their bodies to liquify, and then are molded into something new. But if the process is interrupted . . ." She stares sympathetically at the chrysalis, and sighs.

When she looks at me again, it's with eyes that blaze. "It's simple, really, Eleanor. We wanted to change you because there was something in you that needed to change. I thought you might have managed to wrestle it free, but no, I can still see it. Like that painting that Rose made of you. She saw it too. What a shame. You could've been extraordinary."

Once, I would have wilted before such a speech. For so long, her voice has been the one inside of me. But now, for once, her voice sounds thin. The bud of an idea forms in my mind. Looking at Matron Maureen in all her ordinariness, I imagine: because they taught it to me, it must be possible to un-teach it.

"There was never anything wrong with us," I say. "We were good, just as we were."

I feel it behind my ribs, an incendiary feeling. The hot breath of it fills my lungs. I look down at my fingers, watch them bend as I ask them to, watch them shift the orange, so perfectly cultivated, from one hand to the other. In my mouth, I feel the slickness of my teeth. I'm aware of the muscles not just in my face but in my whole body, the fine-tuned mechanism of me.

"I came here to find Rose," I say. "And I think you'll help me. Because I believe a part of you knows what you did to us was wrong. I think you know there was nothing in us that needed to change, nothing at all."

Her face is composed, but her eyes haven't lost any of their fire. "You never did learn what the final test was, did you?"

I shake my head, annoyed at this deflection. "There was no final test."

"Oh, but there was." Her smile curves smugly, like someone holding a winning chess move. "How do you think you did?"

An uncomfortable itch shivers up my neck. "I assume I passed."

"Not only did you pass," she says. "You had our highest score. How do you think you got Best Girl?"

I've gone over this question many times. What could I have possibly been best at? "Comportment?"

"No."

"Certainly not Latin," I said.

She shakes her head. "No, not Latin. Or needlework, or fine arts."

"What, then?" I demand.

"Rose." She lays down the word, places it carefully. When her lips move again, it takes a long time before the sounds register. "Rose was the final test."

I close my eyes. My body goes silent, and for a long time, I hear nothing. Empty spaces—a shell, a cup, the rushing of blood inside the hollow places of my ears—all start to sound like the ocean, if you listen long enough.

When I open my eyes, I see that Matron Maureen's mouth moves, but all I can take in is the smell of purple flowers, their scent magnified. Sound too. Their little stamens and pistils knocking together in the breeze sound like a stampede.

"—wasn't sure you girls would believe her, but she was truly that convincing."

I blink a few times. The world rushes back. "What did you say?" The words fall from my mouth slowly, dribbled like saliva.

Matron Maureen turns to me. "Rose . . . before she came to the Meadows, she was arrested in a compound in the wastelands."

I nod.

"It was around then that we were searching for a candidate for the final test. My mother came up with the idea, originally," she says, a pluck of pride in her voice. "We insert an actor, a performer. To test the girls. To challenge you. To discern if what we've taught you has really stuck. I performed a couple of times myself before I aged out. The actor, whoever she is, will always culminate her time by attempting to orchestrate an escape."

The information falls down around me, the weight of it crushing. "She was acting?" I say, sounding far from myself. "All of it—a lie?"

"Oh, no," Matron Maureen says reassuringly. "You most certainly met the real Rose. We almost didn't select her. Feared she was too . . . erratic. In the end, she did an admirable job."

"But—*why*?" I ask. "Why would Rose do that?"

"She didn't do it because she wanted to," Matron Maureen says. "There's always a bargain with these types. First, we show them the general prisons, maybe lock them in the Brimstone for a week or two. After the squalor of that place, they'd agree to any terms. Say yes, and they get to design their own prison. Anything they can imagine. Whatever books they want, whatever food. And live out their days there. The choice was easy for Rose. Given everything, the choice would be easy for anyone."

Numbly, I recall what Marina told me at the mixer. *That girl isn't who you think she is. She wasn't there to reform.*

Matron Maureen claps her hands decisively. "So, you see, I'm not sure Rose would welcome seeing you, Eleanor. If you imagine you're going to—I don't know, rescue her?" Her mouth stretches in a smile. "The consequences for escaping now would be far worse. Her face uploaded to every satellite. The rest of her life, on the run. And when they catch her, she won't get a custom prison. Just as they can create prisons to benefit certain prisoners, they can create prisons specifically designed to torture. Maybe she'd watch her own mother killed every day. Or listen to terrified screaming until she went mad. Rose knows that she's living in her best-case scenario."

If I were Rose, would I want a visitor? I never imagined I'd be less a rescuer and more an interloper. I feel the old poison of Matron Maureen's words work into me. I gaze down at my hands, one still grasping the orange, at the spiderweb of veins at my wrists. I move a finger to draw there—*cat face, smile face*—feel myself pulled into nothingness, like the moment just before falling asleep.

Wake up. It's a voice from deep down, as though hidden under and under and under myself.

I draw my eyes up the length of me. I have legs. I have veins, blue with life. I have lungs, and I can fill them up.

The orange falls from my grasp.

"Take me to Rose," I tell Matron Maureen. "Take me to her now."

CHAPTER 51

Matron Maureen leads me into a small, cream-carpeted room, empty but for a doorframe of black metal set into the wall. She places her eye up to a red light, and with a hum, the doorway switches on. On the other side, a wide expanse of lawn dappled with golden sunlight, and the edge of a teal-colored lake. *Somewhere in here, Rose.*

"My mother matched my retina scan, in case of emergency," Matron Maureen says. "I've never gone in there, though. I honestly don't know what to expect."

I study her, the pale trajectory of her nose, her tidy auburn hair. There's a ripple of something in her face that I've never seen, a kind of quiet, befuddled defeat. "Why are you helping me?" I ask.

"The secret of the Meadows, and places like it," she says, "is that we never forced you to do anything. We knew of every bad thing you did, and we allowed it to happen. Control you too fiercely, and we'd never know who had truly reformed. It's the same now. Your freedom isn't a threat. It reveals exactly who you are."

No walls, no punishment, but the ones inside our minds.

"You really thought you were doing good."

"We were never anything but kind," she says. "What I told you, about a flower needing nurturing to grow, I meant it. It worked for me. I wanted it to work for you too, Eleanor."

"I'm not sure how well it worked for you," I say.

Matron Maureen ignores me. "When you're ready to leave, use this key." She places a flat square object, beveled with metal points, in my palm. "You'll exit from an unmarked door downtown."

"What will stop me from staying?" I ask, gazing through the doorway at the rolling grass, ruffled by a slight wind.

"Nothing." She shrugs. "Another suspected subversive agent in prison. The state might give me a medal."

"And what will stop me from taking Rose with me?"

"Nothing," she says again. "Only that she'd be detained before she reaches the city walls."

I swallow, nod. And step inside.

The lawn slants toward a small round lake, and I have to squint, eyes shot through with sunlight. The lake is so transparent that, even from here, I can make out fallen trees crossed like spilled toothpicks under the water, the eel-shaped bodies of seaweed reaching toward the surface. And behind me, I know without looking, a cabin, just visible between pines.

It's even more than I imagined. Chimney of round stones, smoke unwinding like skeins of gray silk. Log walls patched with moss, and the whole picture is somehow glowing, friendly. In the air, birdsong. Woodpecker, bluebird, meadowlark. Patterned on a one-minute rotation. On a branch, I glimpse a shy goldfinch, flashing like a coin falling through the air.

How many times has Rose heard these digitized snippets of sound? Were the bird voices ever real, or were they generated with code and keyboard and fingers of a programmer working in the Department of Prisons?

She lied to me, I remember. Maybe there was a good reason, but still.

She lied. All along, Rose was the final test, placed specifically to root out our badness, our deceptions. The idea of not finishing this settles in my mind. I don't need to do this merely because I told myself I would. The doorway stands just there, on the edge of the lawn. I can use the key and walk through a nondescript doorway into the city.

And then I hear a voice. Singing. And the angry part of me burns out, replaced by another that doesn't know what anger is, that just wants to see Rose's face again.

I knock on the rough wooden door, and the singing stops. Something falls inside the cabin, a surprised sound, pottery shattering. And Rose is at the door, looking like she's marched straight out of my mind.

Her entire body goes limp from shock. She looks like someone who hasn't seen another human being in a long time.

My muscles hum, a growing buzz, every cell pinging against the others, wary and angry and leaning toward her, and longing for her, and pulling in the opposite direction, wanting to run the other way.

Many things can be true at the same time.

"Eleanor," she whispers. And collapses against me. Leans into me with all her weight, and I lean into her, my fingers gripping her back. Something loosens in my throat.

"Rose."

"I have to cut my own hair now," Rose says. "And the food is rationed. But sometimes they send cookbooks, and I've learned to make basically anything I want. It's not so bad here. Really, not so bad."

We sit on the dock, toes making ripples on the water. I hear her, but not. More like, I observe her through all of my senses, like I can taste her words, hear the color of her eyes, see the pulsing heartbeats beneath the surface of her neck.

"Tell me how you're here," she says. "And are you real?" She lifts my arm, examines it as if searching for lines of code I might be made from.

"I'm real," I say, smiling.

"I know you are." She considers me. "They can't create a lifelike person. Not their eyes. Especially not yours."

"But you have a bird," I say, recalling the goldfinch.

"Not real," she says. "I tried to catch him hundreds of times, but I finally discovered that he's only a circle of light that appears every hour."

For a long time, we exchange no words, only looking, drawing our eyes over each other to spot what's new, what's the same. Her hair has grown a little, curling at the back where her shirt collar touches her neck.

"I feel like my heart is going to pull out of my chest," she says, smiling.

I laugh. "We're doing ourselves permanent damage." I turn to her, as though each cell in me is a flower, its face pulled toward the sun.

"How did you find me?" she asks.

"I've been looking for a long time." And I tell her about the last year. Believing she was dead. "Matron Maureen told me you were the final test."

Her eyebrows draw together. "I've thought about what I'd say if I saw you again, but I couldn't think of a single reason you'd forgive me."

"It doesn't sound like you had much of a choice," I say, and I find the bands of anger and mistrust loosening. "I have something to apologize for too."

"You told Matron Sybil."

I take a quick breath. "Rose—I'm sorry."

"Don't be," she says. "Telling didn't change anything."

"I should've kept your secret," I say. "Once I realized that she'd sent for peacekeepers, I ran for you. But it was too late."

"Part of me was glad you told," she says. "Best Girl. Set up for a good, safe life. Better than the ones who followed me."

"But it still hurt you, that I wouldn't go with you?"

She looks out over her lake, a perfect green marble. "I guess it did. I spent a long time missing you, and being angry at you, and feeling that, if you'd just come with me, we might've made it. A real escape."

I shake my head. "I thought I saw things so clearly. If you could just camouflage yourself, just play the role they wanted for you, at least you'd be safe. But that's—I know now, it was never a choice. And if it was"—I think of Sheila—"it wouldn't have led you anywhere good."

"I was always supposed to orchestrate an escape, Eleanor," she says. "That's what I was brought there for. The final test. Whoever followed me, failed. But at a certain point, I started to believe I could outsmart the matrons. I was so focused on getting out, I didn't really look at you. If I had, I would have seen that you didn't want it."

I frown, recalling how readily I'd gone along at first, just to keep her. I feel it again now, like I'm a planet whose gravity is oriented toward her. It's strange. Being in Rose's presence feels something like seeing Matron Maureen had. How easy, to slip back into the Eleanor I used to be.

I know, though, I am not the same. I have a gravity of my own.

That afternoon, I mill around the cottage as Rose makes lunch. One big room, walled with bark-coated logs, patches of lichen hanging lace-like, and a small sitting area with a shabby couch and chair before a fireplace. Rose shuffles around a tiny stove, and my eyes follow a set of rough-hewn stairs to a loft with a bed covered in a red-checkered blanket.

And a shelf of books. I thumb through some. Well-worn, each read a dozen times. In the corner, a clothesline, hanging with drying laundry.

"They give you pants?" I ask, touching a muslin pair, crinkled from drying.

"I have to make them," Rose says from the kitchen. "The only clothes they send me are dresses."

"Stupid," I say, "that certain things are for women and not others."

"Not here," she says. "Nobody to tell me what's for me and what's not."

My mind turns to my mother. She could've said something just like that. And all at once, a throbbing in my heart, a sudden frightening ache. "My mother," I say. "I learned she was friends with the woman who gave birth to me. All my life, she told me she never knew who my real parents were. I can't figure it out. Why she'd lie."

"She must have had a good reason."

"I don't want to know," I say. Because for once, I want the anger. I want to feel myself light up with it, burn with it. I don't want to understand someone's possible good intentions, not when the result is a darkness braided into me. Not when the matrons saw it, homed in on it, used it to their advantage. "I found out she's sick." I tell Rose about June, about her letter, the stomach issue my mother discussed with the doctor.

Rose considers me. "If I ever saw you again, I was going to tell you something," she says. "Your mother, the woman you grew up with, Stella. *She's* your mother."

I feel myself scowl. "What are you talking about?"

"Matron Sybil had me read every girl's file before I arrived. Information I could use to test you, to push buttons. That's what she wanted me to know about you—it's Stella who's your mother. They thought your parentage was your weak spot."

"But—but I look nothing like Stella."

Rose lifts her shoulders. I remember what June told me my mother said after I left for the Meadows. *She would've found a way to stop this.* I feel an itch, to understand.

A small mirror hangs on the wall, and I catch a glimpse of myself in it. My adjudicator hair, precise, meticulously maintained. I'm not an adjudicator anymore, I think, with a jolt. They're searching my records right now. They'll discover I'm not reformed.

What will I do now? For so long, I've been on the path they set for me. Now that I can, what will I choose? How will I stay safe doing it?

I look at Rose, recalling the day we met, on the auditorium stage with those racks of clothes. For the others, the future was only an idea, but I was already patterning myself on the girl I was expected to become. Choosing something for myself is an unpracticed muscle.

"Rose," I ask, eyes still fixed on the mirror. "Did you say you cut your own hair?"

After lunch, I unfurl my hair from its bun. Heavy, this uncaged thing, all its weight loosed. Rose combs her fingers through. Goosebumps bloom along my neck.

"Here?" she asks, touching my hair at my collarbone.

"Shorter," I say. She places the scissors near my chin, clips through the wall of chestnut with a crisp sound. How much of this hair grew in the Meadows? I watch it fall like ballast tossed away. My hand finds my neck, uncovered now.

"Nobody in the city has hair like this," Rose says. "You won't blend in."

She's right. The moment I step outside that doorway, I won't fit. But I already don't fit. I'm not an adjudicator anymore. Before long, I won't even be a real citizen.

"I don't intend to."

CHAPTER 52

Rose and I spend the afternoon strolling around her lake and into the forest, which extends only a few dozen paces before terminating in a white wall, like the fog in the Meadows made solid. I follow it with my eyes, where it disappears into the blue sky.

"I've tried to get through it," Rose says. "Chip away at it. Nothing is strong enough. And besides, I doubt there's even anything on the other side."

Nothing but empty space, I think, running a hand over the wall's surface, solid and slightly rough, the same material so much of the Meadows was made from—the round white buildings, the inside of the yew tree. It occurs to me how imprisoned Rose really is here. It takes only a minute to walk from the wall back to the dock.

"How do you make sense of it, what happened to us?" I ask, trailing my bare feet through the green water. In this quiet place, in this moment of calm, I am beginning to comprehend the scope of the pain. How much work will be involved just to understand it.

"I think you just feel it," she says. "You just have to feel it."

I grope around in my mind, fingers reaching in a dark room. What do I feel?

"They took our happiness," I say. "They took the pride we could've had in ourselves. They—they took away discovering this about myself. I was catalogued by the time I was thirteen." I breathe out. "The algorithm only tells the truth. But I wish it had let me find out for myself."

Rose's eyes rove across my face. "I always wondered whether you liked the matrons. If you believed them."

"They made sense to me," I say. "I'm scared that they'll always make a little bit of sense."

I close my eyes and breathe. Inside me, the desire to reject the matrons' words. Finally, my body working them loose like splinters.

"They were experts, Eleanor," she says. "They worked on each one of you, carefully. There was nothing in the Meadows that they didn't know about, and they used it all. If it worked, it's not your fault."

"Even Sheila couldn't beat them," I say. "She got married. She—she chose it."

Rose frowns. "I guess they were even right about her."

Behind my sternum flickers a point of heat. I begin to burn with something like rage. They were right about Sheila because they crafted a maze for her with only one exit. Same as Rose, I can see now. Same as all of us.

Not me. I will not walk through the exit they've made for me. I'll make my own.

"Remember when I told you I'd have a conversation instead of fighting?" I ask.

Rose smiles. "I thought you had a screw loose."

"I thought you did too," I say. I loved Rose, her intensity, her longing to be free and roam and be a thousand things at once. But it was those things that I also found the most terrifying. If I could have, I would have plucked out those parts, like lines of code. And she, I suspect, would've done the same to me. How did we make it through a place like the Meadows, knowing how painful it is to be asked to change integral parts of ourselves, and then turn around and do it to each other?

We loved each other. *But someone can hurt you with their love*, she'd told me once.

"You could stay, you know," Rose says, eyes averted. "Stay with me."

I could. Beyond this door, a world where I will be a criminal, where peacekeepers may be searching for me already. I cast my eyes around. This perfect snow globe. "I can't."

"But isn't this what you wanted?" she asks. "A place for us. Safe, forever."

"It is," I say. This is what I longed for. Safety, away from the world. No chance of hurt. I've seen the city now, sensed the grid of streets stretched around me like a great ocean and felt as trapped as I had in the Meadows. My own body has been a prison I've cowered inside of. "But I don't think I want that anymore."

Rose holds very still, absorbing my words. "What do you want?"

Something old and hard is being discarded, like the hollow shell of a baby tooth pushed free, the ivory nub beneath both new and strong. I don't have to be a stack of paper dolls, keeping parts of myself buried. I can be one Eleanor, one confusing, conflicted Eleanor.

"I want to play music again," I say. "To run again. I want to talk to people. I want to sit still and let my heart be peaceful. I want to see Sheila. And I think I want to find my mother." I don't say *I want to find June*. To see her again, even just once more.

"And the state will just let you do that?" she asks, eyebrows raised.

"No," I admit. "But—but maybe I'll find a way. They're not as big as we thought."

"Well," Rose says, looking away. "Good luck."

"You could come with me," I say.

Her eyes twitch to the side. "They could be listening," she says warningly.

"Matron Maureen already knows I'm on a rescue mission," I say. "She said there'd be nothing stopping you from leaving."

"Except I'd never make it outside the city," she says.

"Maybe you don't need to."

Before I can reconsider, I dip my finger into the green water of the lake and draw a map on the dock, shading it with my body. A map to a door underneath a bridge.

In the warm air, the map disappears. "Remember that?" I ask. "In case you change your mind."

Rose nods. Something plays out in her face, a push and a pull. Rose has inhabited my mind for the last year. When we knew each other before, I longed for a quiet, peaceful prison. If I could have stayed in the Meadows with her, I would have. But I no longer want to be trapped. Not by walls, or my own body. Or another person.

In the dusky dip of the sun behind trees, I stand before the doorway. A shade of doubt passes through me. Had Matron Maureen told the truth about this working? But when I place the key against the keypad, the doorway switches on with a familiar hum. The rectangle of grass is replaced by a darkened alley. How is it possible that only yesterday I left the Village? I feel as though I've lived a thousand years.

Rose and I stand opposite each other, the air filled with things we don't know how to say. Rose moves forward, the vaguest invitation, and we spring together. "Eleanor," she says into my hair.

I only nod and release a long breath. In my fist, I grip the key Matron Maureen gave me, the metal pins printing dots into my palm. I slip the key into the pocket of Rose's trousers without her noticing.

She pulls away suddenly, her eyes lit up. "I almost forgot." She darts back to the cabin and when she returns, she's holding a jacket. Made from denim.

"I wanted you to have it, when we got out," she says.

I hold the jacket in my hands, and all I can do is stare.

Then I take my raincoat off and swing the denim jacket over my head, let it fall onto my shoulders. Still a perfect fit. And though I put my raincoat back on, I know it's there.

"We'll see each other again," I say, certain that it's not just a wish.

"I'll hold you to that."

"Goodbye, Rose."

"Goodbye, Eleanor."

I pull the hood of my raincoat over my head, stride through the doorway. And that's all it takes to walk away from her.

CHAPTER 53

"They're still conducting the inquiry," Dr. Collier says.

The Black Cat is quiet tonight, the only other diners the permanent residents of the Village. I've filled Dr. Collier in on the events of the day.

"I'll do what I can, but it's not looking good," she says, considering me seriously. "Eleanor, I'm not sure you understand what you're up against. You'll be coded unreformed. Possibly even as a subversive subject. If the algorithm glimpses your face, anywhere in the country, you'll be flagged. They'll come after you. All your life, you'll be hiding."

There's a hollow in my chest, and in it, a black hole, a pull of fear. But, today, there's joy wrapped around the terror. Somehow, I find myself smiling. "Is it ridiculous that I don't care?" I ask, laughing. "I've been hiding for so long. I'll take this hiding over that one."

She smiles. "Well, if you get tired of hiding, you have a home here."

I pause. "Will you do one thing? Promise you'll watch over my reformeds."

Dr. Collier nods. "And speaking of that, there's someone you should see. Arrived a few hours before you. She's on the roof."

Sheila's golden hair still carries the loose curls from her wedding that morning. She sits with legs draped over the roof edge, regarding the small city and night sky dotted with constellations.

"The sky in the Meadows never had stars," I say.

Sheila turns, smiling. "Eleanor."

"I didn't think you'd come," I say, sitting beside her.

"I didn't think I would either," she says.

Sheila looks down at her left hand, bare of her wedding ring. "Parts of me really did feel happy to be marrying Ed," she says. "It was such a relief. After I found out that the Department of Engineering was a fantasy, I saw the other young wives living their lives, worrying about nothing but making dinner and keeping their husbands happy, and I thought, *I could do that.*" She swallows. "Even when they told me Betty died."

A sharp feeling pushes through my chest. "I wish I could've helped her."

"I was angry with you," Sheila says, "for saying how she died. I wanted to believe the lie. I knew if I started questioning one lie, I'd begin to see them all again."

"Is that how you ended up here?" I ask.

Sheila pauses, tucks a lock of hair behind her ear. "Tonight's our wedding night," she says. "We've shared a bed for a year, but we've never—never been together. After the wedding, I stood staring at the bed. I asked myself if I really wanted this. If I wanted *any* of this. It was like the parts of me that I'd buried finally said 'No more.' I left without saying goodbye."

"And you came here," I say.

"I never imagined a place like this could exist." Before us, the town is half-asleep, several strands of silver smoke reaching from chimneys, a scattering of windows illuminated with golden light. "Do you think you'll live here?" she asks.

"I might," I say. "But, first I'm going back to the Cove."

"To see June?" she asks, one eyebrow arched.

"Yes," I say. "And—to talk to my mother."

For a moment, I don't speak, only watch the city. The dark silhouette of a person leans on their balcony. The scraggly limbs of house plants draw tendrils in the air. Everyone living here must have a family. How many sent them to the facilities without a backward glance? And how many still watch the road each day, hoping for their return?

"She lied to me," I say. "About so many things."

Somewhere behind my sternum, the barest flicker of anger. Just an ember, but I sense I could make it grow, breathe it into something unquenchable and raging. To demand answers. To return to the cottage and shout until she tells me the truth. "And she didn't just lie," I say. "She failed at everything a mother is supposed to be."

Sheila studies me, curious. "You sound a little like the matrons."

"What?"

"You get to be hurt," she says. "Of course you do. But if you made room alongside, I wonder what other truths you might find."

I see the Cove, then, and the cottage, craggy skeletons of herbs drying in bundles from the ceiling beams. Bands of sunlight penetrating gaps in the walls. My mother, at her spinning wheel. My mother, icy presence in the corner. My mother, arms crossed. Cutting remark. Or no words at all. My mother, silent.

And also, my mother, working, every day. To protect us. To keep us safe.

My mother, a burning inside her eyes.

My mother, a bundle of contradictions.

What other truths could she have been concealing, all this time?

"I wish—I wish my dad could see this place," Sheila says. "Can you believe Adele Martinique designed it?"

"Did you meet her?"

She nods, her grin spreading slow, how the sun advances each morning, a degree of light at a time. She turns to me, excited. "Did you know she originally designed the periscope tech to cure scarcity? Water, food, energy—we can make it all without straining the planet. And—and she said she could teach me."

Warmth blooms in my chest. I think of the girl whose hand I clasped on the first day in the Meadows. Charging the air nearby with her aliveness, with the strength of her dreams. "I had a feeling you'd like it here."

Sheila nods, her smile slipping a little. "I wonder if Ed can ever forgive me. We didn't love each other, but I think I really hurt him."

"You don't owe anyone an apology," I say, "for living the life you want."

Sheila looks up at me, sheepish. "Actually, I do," she says. "Before I left, I took something." She reaches into her purse and pulls out a screen. Ed's screen.

"Do you think there's code for the facilities on there?" I ask.

She nods in a way that seems to say *Much more than that.*

I shake my head. "Didn't I say? You'll change the world one day, Sheila."

"So will you, Eleanor. I just have a feeling." She slings an arm over my back, and we pull each other close.

Friendship is really just a decision. One you make again and again.

"This is as close as we can get you," Adele says the next morning, standing before a doorway in The Black Cat that opens onto a sleepy rural street several miles from the Cove.

"I wouldn't stick around the Cove for longer than a couple days," Dr. Collier says. "From now on, if you're not in the Village, you'll have to move." She places a black umbrella in my hands. "A trick, to block the satellites from seeing you," she says. "This doorway is set to unlock with your retina. You're always welcome back."

When I stride through the doorway, it's to the salt-chalked air of the ocean, wind blowing hard enough to nearly knock me sideways—like a dog celebrating your return home. *Where were you? You were gone so long.*

I open the umbrella over my head. In every square inch of the city, there were ears and eyes, and though the Cove has fewer, I'm still careful. If I let the umbrella slip, satellites could pick up my face and post it a heartbeat later to every peacekeeper's screen within a thousand miles. Still, in my chest, there is a loosening, a feeling of having a little breathing room. The state might be looking for me, but they think I'm in the city. Under this umbrella, I feel as close to unseen as it's possible to feel.

As I walk the miles to the Cove, I think of what June said. *You find her, Eleanor.* The girl I used to be. At the time, I could hardly remember the girl I was in the Cove, but now, memories douse me like hard rain. One in particular. Not of me. My mother.

Besides when she was asleep in her straw-stuffed mattress, I don't know that I ever saw my mother stop moving. Sowing seeds of vegetables. Bartering with shepherds in the upper prairie. Scouring the woods for hair that deer had shed, stomping at her spinning wheel until she'd turned the tufts of nothing into threads of something.

I think of what Sheila said, about making room for more truths.

My mother's movement—so much like running.

This question beats in my mind, persistent. What was she afraid would happen if she allowed quiet in, even for a moment? What would she hear whispered in the dark? I never understood her. But now I have whispers of my own.

One of the only times she ever rested was on our occasional trips to the beach, a tiny spit of sand shrouded by black-rock cliffs taller than any building I'd yet seen.

We'd go down there on hot days, when the weather was calm. Squalls could march in quickly, and if that happened while you were at the beach, there was almost nothing to do but let your body go and watch it bash itself against rock. People always died down there. But we took the risk. Human beings need to do something other than strive toward survival. They need to feel alive. Even if it means dying is right over their shoulders.

My mother would step her thickly muscled body into the swimming costume she made herself, gauzy cream-colored cloth that covered her to her knees but left her shoulders exposed. Almost like something mechanical, her shoulders. The rotating parts of her visible beneath the surface, the knob of bone and fan of shoulder blade, the gnarl of muscles working under skin. I wondered whether I'd look like that, after decades of this kind of life.

On those journeys, I'd lie on my back in the water, let the waves push me around. Close my eyes and trust that the ocean, with its strong hands, would guide me back to shore.

"You look like sea trash," she'd say. "Why don't you try swimming?"

"I like this," I said. The feeling of being supported. Of not having to try.

"Why did I spend months when you were eight teaching you to swim?"

You taught me to swim so I could feel safe enough to do this, I thought but didn't say.

On these trips, my mother actually swam, cut through the current with her arms like oars. There was always a moment when her cream-colored back would disappear below the water, the engine of waves moving, moving, and my mother somewhere inside. What would happen if she got thrown out to sea? If a current slipped around her ankle and smashed her head against rock? I'd be alone. My mother was not warm, but she was all I had.

And then her head would pop back up, hair flattened to her skull in a dark helmet. She could never get far, even with her dense muscle, the ocean always stronger.

We sat on the beach, drying off, chewing on dried meat, the air so bright, I had to squint, and my head swam with the leftover undulations of water, and my body was wracked with cold chills and burning from the sun, confused. That must be why I asked her what I did.

"When will you tell me about where I came from?"

She shuddered, as though prodded with a sharp stick. Part of me drew back, fearful of what would happen next, but another part grew large. Emboldened. Once it was said out loud, I thought I deserved an answer.

"Ever?" I asked. "Will you ever tell me the truth? Everyone knows I'm not really yours."

Her eyes were focused on the water lapping the shore. "You're not mine, are you?"

"I only meant, it's not a secret. You could just tell me. It wouldn't be hard."

Her face was unreadable, but the knots of muscle in her shoulders coiled tighter.

"You'll not learn that story from my mouth, Eleanor," she said. "Don't ask me again."

And she stood from the sand and walked into the water. Her body convulsed, the first impact of cold, breath-catching. She strode out farther, until the water was to her waist, stretching like a midnight blue skirt around her body. Here, she'd normally join her hands together into a trowel shape and dive. But she kept walking, the water around her shoulders now, striding deliberately, as though it was a struggle. Up to her mouth now, and her nose. She wanted to out-muscle the ocean. Finally, her head vanished under.

I don't remember screaming but, afterward, my throat was raw and ripped apart. She didn't come back, not for a long while. And when she did, she bobbed up, and I saw in the arc of her arms, in the muscle of her, that she was not dead.

She was floating. Limbs spread. Star-like.

Giving in. Letting the current tow her back to shore.

———————————

For hours, I walk along the coast roads. They slough off in places, down the cliff, skittering into the water. It's most of the day before I find the Cove. By the time I arrive at the market square, shuttered and quiet, the sky is blushing with twilight, and coral-colored clouds stripe the air. The market square looks much as it did. Except, the cannery wall is blank. The poster of the man, woman, and children—gone.

The main street is quiet. Only a few fishermen returning from sea, docking their boats and unpeeling themselves from their overalls. June's father sees me, holds up two fingers in a greeting. June isn't with him. I wave back, swallowing disappointment, and make my way up the hill.

I arrive in the new darkness, sky slick and star-freckled, the old maple a craggy silhouette at the cliff's edge. She answers when I knock. A creep of movement washes over my mother's face, eyes widening, forehead pulled taut. "Eleanor," she whispers.

I nod, closing the umbrella. "Yes."

"Well," she mutters, glancing away. "Don't let the warm air out."

CHAPTER 54

My mother doesn't ask what I'm doing there. She sits in the same cold silence I grew up inside of. Almost impassive, as though she'd been expecting me. Her eyes don't leave the glow of the fireplace.

"Are you going to ask why I'm here?"

"I expect you'll tell me, if you so choose," she says. I notice how tightly she holds herself.

I think, *Fine. That's just fine. I'm not here to give her answers. I'm here to get them.* "I have some questions."

"I expected as much."

I clear my throat. "June told me you were sick."

Her eyes grow wide. "How would she know a thing like that?"

"She worked in a medical lab," I say. "She accessed your file."

"Of all the invasions," she huffs. "What about privacy? No, ask another question."

I feel myself ruffling at her stoicism. "Why didn't you take my call?"

My mother squints. "What call?"

"I earned a call with you," I say, a lump forming in my throat. "They told me you—you declined."

And when she says, "Nobody from that place ever contacted me," I think, *Of course they didn't. Of course.*

"Did you know why they sent me to the Meadows?" I ask.

"I—" She shakes her head. "We heard rumors. All different things. But they have schools for everything. They might've been telling the truth."

"But you suspected, about me."

She nods. "I suppose."

"When did you know?"

"After they took June," she says. "Her father found me. Said we should—I don't know, storm the gates of the facilities. As if these were places we could find on a map. I had to tell him that you and June were gone. He was angry, that I could just let you go like yesterday's rubbish, he said. Like I was the one who sent you two away."

A dull ache pulses through me, hearing how June's father fought for her. How my own mother didn't fight for me at all. "In the Meadows, I found my birth record," I say. "It said that my birth parents were named Cora St. James and Michael Williamson."

My mother's eyes flick away, toward the ceiling, toward the ground, into her lap where her hands are clasped, fingers locked together tightly. "That's right."

A stream of breath leaves me. "So, you're not my mother."

She turns to face me. "What makes a mother?" she demands. "Didn't I raise you?"

"Only because you had to. You didn't want me. You didn't act like a mother."

I feel my hurt grow too large for conversation, for anything but rage.

Her face is still completely neutral. "I don't know why you came here. It sounds like you have all the answers." She walks to the kitchen, aimlessly touches different objects—a clutch of rosemary, a wooden knife handle, the carving block—in search of some task to put her hands to.

"I found Cora's obituary," I tell her. "It mentioned you. It said you were her friend."

She speaks with her back to me, shoulders hunched inside a brown homespun sweater. "I knew I shouldn't have written that. Foolish."

I gape at her. "*You* wrote it?"

When she doesn't respond, I stand, speaking to her back. "I need you to tell me," I pronounce carefully, "where I came from."

She turns, and I can see something writhe beneath the surface of her face. Anguish. She never has told me, and I imagined she never would. Dragging the secret from her throat would be a painful thing, a kind of backward choking, a wrenching up.

But, like it's easy, like this whole time it's been easy, she speaks. "You weren't abandoned."

My eyes draw up to her face. My body goes cold.

"I didn't open my door one day to find you. Maybe I liked that story because it erased everything that came before. How wanted you were." She clears her throat. The whites of her eyes grow pink. "How you were mine, from the moment you were an idea in our heads."

She speaks slowly, with effort now. I lean forward, grasping at the words falling from her mouth, hastily sorting out what they mean.

"But you never—you never treated me like you were my mother," I say.

"I was never supposed to be doing it on my own," she says. "I didn't know the first thing about nurturing children. That was all Cora."

The remark stings, deeply. She didn't know about children, and I wasn't a good enough reason to learn. I look at her, fiddling with her thumbnail. "Who was Cora?"

"Cora was my wife." It comes out in a whispered sentence, an almost-not-there sentence. "We were your parents."

I take in this knowledge, a stone passed between our hands. It sits heavy with me, a truth I don't know what to do with. "And Michael?"

"Our friend. Michael helped us make you, but he wasn't your father, not in any real sense," she says. "He gave us what we needed, and we managed the rest. It seemed impossible that it should work, but . . ." She shrugs.

My eyes follow her face, rough-hewn cheeks and nose and chin, like something carved from wood. Once, she loved someone. Cora, who might have run her fingertips across that same face and thought it beautiful.

The information drops through my mind, each piece slotting into a space that had, for my entire life, been empty. "You were my parents."

"We were," she says. "For a short time."

And then, it's as though a storm cloud draws across her face. Her eyes go far away. I recall Cora's obituary. They weren't given much time to enjoy being parents.

"Is that—is that when Cora died?"

The muscles in her brow quiver, and for a moment, I think Stella will finally unfurl all the sorrow that she's held back. A note of terror fills me. As much as it's necessary, it's also impossible to imagine, my mother falling apart. Like seeing the earth crack in two.

But, quickly, she rearranges her face. Swallows down whatever she's feeling.

"I'm tired," she says. "And it's a market day tomorrow. I need rest."

She goes to make ready for bed.

"Can't we just—"

"To bed," she commands. I know it will do no good to push her now.

That night, I sleep in my childhood bed. My mother kept it all these years, though I hardly believe I once fit inside it. I stare at the thatch ceiling hanging with bushels of rosemary and thyme. How many hours did I spend in this spot, thinking of June? Here I am, doing the same. I wonder if she's in town, and if so, whether her father told her he saw me.

The last time I lay here, I was leaving for the Meadows. I could barely sleep from excitement. A twinge, a burrowing hurt, remembering it. The girl whose limbs were still short, whose stomach had not yet clawed itself apart, whose face had never been taught to shield who she was. I imagine pulling her through time, saving her from what lay ahead. I'd let her rest in the shallow waters as long as she liked, and run in the fields until every muscle burned. And if anyone asked me who she was, I'd say, "She's mine," and keep on walking.

CHAPTER 55

Light breaks on my face in tepid white. In the distance, a boat's bell clanks, a small bright sound. "Out of bed," I hear my mother say. "Market day."

Into baskets we pack potatoes, kohlrabi, parsnips, woven cowls and scarves, rush our fingers down stems of sage and lavender to collect in sachets of paper. My mother has a stall in the market now, all her own. "You have quite the inventory," I tell her, outside, under the umbrella. Her cart sits behind a chestnut pony she's dubbed Horse.

"June's father told me I have good wares and I ought to give them the credit they're due."

"I agree," I say, eyeing the cart and pony. "Life's gone on without me."

"It has," she says, securing a rope around Horse's chest. And then she frowns. "But not a market day goes by that someone doesn't ask about you. When June came back, everyone wanted to know whether you'd follow."

"So, June's back?" I ask, hoping my voice sounds casual enough.

"Oh, yes," she says. "Helping her father. Like before. Maybe she'll come by the market."

"Maybe," I say. She'll have to be matched again within six months. And I can't stay in the Cove longer than a couple of days. A black thread sews through my heart. We have no more future here than we had in the city.

When we arrive at the market, I fix my eye on the docks. The *Musketeer*, June's father's ship, is already out to sea. Something else catches my eye. The blank cannery wall. "Where's the poster that used to hang there?"

"Some villagers took it down," my mother says, arranging vegetables in piles inside her stall.

"Why?"

"They were tired, they said, of looking at people who are nothing like them."

I squint at her. "The peacekeepers let them?"

"They haven't been seen in months," she says. "Trouble in the bigger towns. The Cove isn't a priority."

I watch her, the careful set of her mouth, the deliberate business of her hands. Distracted, always. To pull focus from what she doesn't want to think about. *Cat face. Smile face. Holiday tree. Rainbow.*

"Did you have anything to do with that?" I ask her.

"Might have," she mutters. "Might have suggested we paint something different up there. Maybe a memorial, to the ones we lost. Even if they might only cover it with another poster."

I imagine Cora's picture. And their friend Michael. She still hasn't told me what happened to them. But I nod, and say, "I like that idea." If it's a kind of peace offering, it seems she accepts it.

She asks me to work the stall while she makes deliveries. I agree, but as soon as she's gone, I regret allowing her to leave me alone. Villagers congregate around the stall, less to buy items and more to pick me over for knowledge. Few ever venture outside the Cove.

"What's the city like?" a little girl wants to know. She wears overalls, and has pulled away from her mother's dairy stall.

"Big and noisy," I say. "And full of strange inventions like out of someone's imagination. Cherry-flavored celery. And lavender apples."

The girl's eyes sparkle. "I think I should like to get a letter one day. So I can go to the city too."

My heart stumbles. "Oh, you don't want to go there," I tell her. "The Cove is better by far."

And then someone approaches, her face just as wrinkled, her smile familiar. "Mrs. Arkwright."

"Oh, Eleanor, look at you." I let her wrap her spindly arms around me. "There are those who'd hoped you'd be married to a Quorum member by now, settled in some grand home. But I'm happy to see you're not."

I smile. "Me too."

She grips her woven shawl around her shoulders. "I insist that you come by and tell me all about your travels."

"All right," I say. "Though I must warn you, it's not all happy stories."

"Figured as much. But those are the stories that need to be told," she says. "Still playing your fiddle?"

"Haven't touched one in years, I'm sad to say."

"Well, you ought to pick it up again," she says. "Those musicians have been by the Cove again, you know."

My eyes widen. "They have?" I find that I'm whispering.

She nods. "Every few months. Just listen to the breeze. You'll hear them. They play almost as well as you. Almost as well as your mother."

I laugh in surprise. "Everything's different around here, it seems," I say. "Has my mother taken up the violin and not told me?"

"Not Stella," she says, eyes bright. "Cora."

I'm stunned. "You knew Cora?"

"Knew them both. Lovely couple. Couldn't be more different. A flower and a thorn. But, boy, did they love each other. They bought that cottage on the cliff, just before you were born. Cora thought it was the perfect spot for a family of blow-ins."

I catch my breath. "I only just found out."

"I would've told you, dear, ages ago," she says. "But it was too sad to speak of for a long time. And dangerous, not that I cared about that. The peacekeepers haven't taken me yet. But Stella would've had my head. I knew she'd tell you in her own time." She pats my arm. "You come see me. You and June."

"Between us," I say, leaning forward. "I'm not staying long."

"But you'll come back," she declares with such confidence, I laugh. Like she's read the roadmap of my life.

"I wouldn't be so sure," I say. "I'm not exactly made for this place."

She tips her head to the side.

"I—" I search for an explanation. "I've always felt—like that maple tree by my mother's cottage. A non-native species. Blown in from who knows where. This place was supposed to kill it, but somehow it survived."

"Now, where did you get an idea like that?"

I smile. "Read about it, in one of your books."

The skin around Mrs. Arkwright's eyes fans as she squints at me. "Sometimes you have to let the place change."

"What do you mean?"

"This area wasn't hospitable to that tree when those books were printed. But, for better or worse, the world changed. Wait long enough, and it always does." She pats my arm, says "Come see me" again, and shuffles off to the fishmonger's stall.

When my mother returns, she tells me to take a break. "Don't have to speak to every villager. They're just looking for a good story."

And yet, out of the dozens of villagers who spoke to me today, none of them was June. I shouldn't feel so miserable. What is it that I've felt for June, since childhood? Could you really call it love? Or was it that we were the only ones like us? Was it simply *You are here and so am I.*

"Are you sure you're okay?" I ask my mother.

"You're referring to my diminished health," she grumbles. "It's something with my stomach. The doctor saw me, gave me some powder that's supposed to staunch the acid."

"But you're okay?" I ask.

"I'm feeling better," she says. "Now go."

I open the umbrella and tell her, "See you at home." I wind through the village, up the alley where those musicians performed so many years ago.

"Eleanor!" a voice calls on the wind. I'm on the last street before the climb to the bluff, nowhere near June's house, but my heart hopes anyway. But when I turn, it's Margaret Johns, sweeping her front step. "I didn't know you were home!" she calls, walking over.

I take a wary step backward. "I was just helping my mother in the market."

She closes the distance. "And June. Both of you back. What good news."

A quick, bright fury erupts within me. Greeting me like the other villagers, when she's the reason for every bad thing that happened. "Are you going to report me to the peacekeepers? Like you did those musicians? Like you did June?"

Her face drops. "Of course not."

I hold a hand before me. "I don't know what you could possibly have to say to me. And I'd really rather not speak to you again."

I turn and stride away.

"They took Tilly." Her voice comes out strangled.

When I turn, her face sags, miserable. Tilly, her youngest daughter, pulling at her skirts, smiling up at me on market days.

"Sent her to the Glacier," she says, tremblingly. "Won't even tell us where that is."

She looks much the same as before, her immaculate skin, blond hair just so. But something has been let loose inside of her. "And I suppose you feel differently about the facilities now?"

"I don't know," she says. "I—I don't know what to think."

I feel a slow ticking in my body, my blood cooling. I recall what I told Rose. *That's how we beat them. By talking. By seeing each other.*

"I'm sorry about Tilly," I say.

"I—I wonder if it's me who should be sorry," she says. "I wonder if—if it's me who was wrong." She speaks tentatively, as though these ideas are not yet fully known to her. "Your mother invited me to a meeting. She and the others—Mrs. Arkwright, the Forsters—they're looking for ways to set things to rights. They took down that stupid poster."

"Will you go?"

She frowns. "Maybe."

"I hope you do," I say. And though I doubt I'll ever forget what she did, I decide she looks stronger than I've ever seen her. We pause for a moment. Her seeing me. Me seeing her.

Strong, I think, to decide you were wrong. Strong, I think, to do something about it.

I climb up to the bluff and stand above the ocean, waves crashing below in plumes of white foam. Around me, a whipping wind rustles the fields of heather. The *Musketeer* has returned to the dock. A thin blade twists in my heart. June must know I'm in town by now. Why hasn't she come to find me? For the same reason I haven't gone to find her?

A bark flies on the wind, from across the field, to where I stand on the cliff edge. My heart shifts at the sound. I turn to see Captain running up the bluff toward me, his white hair in salted ropes, tongue lolling. And trailing behind, in her old anorak, stiff with salt, hair a blustering halo: June.

"Captain!" she calls, and stops in her tracks. The two of us stand and stare, and for a moment, we are the only people in existence, the whole rotation and trajectory of the planet for only us. Until Captain barks impatiently, and I reach down to ruffle the fur on his back.

"He got away from me," June says, breathing fast. "Must've known you were up here."

"I looked for your father's boat," I say.

"I stayed in today," she says. "I heard you were back. I wanted to see you."

"Here I am."

Though no ears can hear us, the words don't come. Between us, there seems an expanse too large to traverse. I wonder if too much has happened for us to ever be easy with each other again.

"Expecting rain?" June asks, gesturing to my umbrella.

"To block the satellites," I say, pointing at the sky, churning with slate-colored clouds.

June's eyes widen. "They're looking for you?"

"If they're not now, then soon," I say. "I can't stay here longer than a few days."

June's face falls slightly. "You'll go back to the Village?"

"Or . . . somewhere," I say, gazing out over the ocean.

"Seems like one of us is always leaving," she says.

There's a feeling of distance, as though we're trying to have a conversation while standing on opposite sides of a bridge.

"June, how are you?" I ask.

She kicks at the dirt with her boot. "Getting re-used to life here. The Cove feels so slow compared to the city, it's easy to forget everything still waiting for me. I'm already in the directory at the district Registrar's Office. I got a notification today that some boy would like to meet me."

A jealous ember burns in my throat. "Do you think you will?"

She laughs. "I still have six months. And if anyone asks, I'm still in the grips of mourning over the loss of my dear fiancé."

I smile. I don't know if the world will be any different in six months, but at least June has that much time. "I saw they took the poster down in the market," I say. "I heard the peacekeepers have left the Cove."

She nods. "There're rumors swirling—that the Circle is up to something. Dispatches interrupted, the Estuary cut off from power and liberated. Things are changing, even here." She looks up at my umbrella. "What about Rose? Did you find her?"

"I did."

She brings her eyes level with mine. "But—she didn't come with you."

I shake my head.

June frowns. "You're okay?"

"It was her choice." June pauses, waiting for more, and I exhale a long breath. "I think, for a long time, I've been searching for someone to say it's all right. *I'm* all right. To—forgive me," I say. "For the matrons to forgive me for who I was. For Rose to forgive me for betraying her. For my mother for—I don't know, for being stuck with me. I was looking for someone to explain why I felt so wrong inside. And I decided, if it were up to me, I'd be done apologizing for who I am."

We look at each other again. I take her in, the pinch between her eyebrows, the frown on her lips. And I realize there's distance between us only because I'm making it. Because nothing is certain, and the world is broken, and what I feel for June might be too fragile to exist. But there's also the vaguest flicker of hope. Hope that could fill up the space between us if I let it. That could fill the entire world.

I take a step closer, so my umbrella covers us both. My hand finds the waxed canvas lapel of her coat, and I pull her near, so we make our own shelter against the wind. My fingers span, and find the softness of her cheek, slide into her hair.

"You should know," I say. "I'm probably coded as a subversive subject by now."

A smile breaks across her features, faint rays fanning at the corners of her eyes. "A subversive subject?"

"You may not want to be seen with me."

She shrugs, glancing around the bluff. "I don't see anyone watching."

June's lips part, a triangular window of teeth and tongue and breath. Slowly, I place my mouth there. Her nose is cold, but her breath warm. I pull back and look at her, gripped by something half-sad. And then I kiss her again, gently urging her lips open, tasting the warmth of her. She leans her body against mine. And we stay this way for a long time, in our shelter, in our pocket of warmth against the buffeting wind, Captain standing guard.

"That might be the first thing in a long time that I've done just for me," I say, my hand still twined in June's hair.

"Well," she says. "Maybe you should do more of that kind of thing."

"I agree," I say. "And I'll start by racing you home."

I sprint from the bluff and take off running through the field, awkward with the umbrella, toward the simple cottage and an old maple tree and the stony cliffside that I grew from.

"Not fair!" she calls after me.

We race side by side, Captain barking between us, my muscles remembering what it feels like to run.

CHAPTER 56

Wind whistles through the cracks in the cottage walls. The fire has died down, and my mother has nearly finished her tiny glass of brandy. It's just the two of us. From beneath my bed, I pull out my tattered violin case. Inside, the crimson velvet has rotted somewhat, but the fiddle looks just the same. I run my fingers over the letters carved on top. CSJ.

"She wanted to teach you," Stella says from her place by the fire. "After she died, I never thought you'd learn. But you picked it up, like it was in your blood."

Something confounds me, still. She and Cora planned for me. Got help from their friend Michael to make me. "You said you wanted me. So why did—why were you—" I find I can't ask the question. *Why were you the farthest thing from motherly?*

She shoots her eyes away, like casting a fishing pole, searching for something, a way to explain. "Cora was the nurturer. She wanted to build this home for you, to fill it with soft things. A fire every night, books to read to you. I was nervous about having a family, but I thought, *I'll be the provider.* I'd make things. Patch a roof. Keep us safe. But the provider doesn't mean much when the nurturer is gone."

I imagine how much would've been different if Cora had been in my life. It's a sorrow I can't consider right now. "What happened to her?"

"We thought we were being careful. We had the story all planned. We were sisters. They were just beginning the matching protocols, but we were old enough that it wasn't required. We'd say that someone abandoned you. That was the only way single women would be permitted to raise a baby, and people did that back then, leave their babies. It was an easy lie, one I kept even after Cora died. I knew if people found out how you'd really been born—two mothers—they'd take you away.

"Cora hid her pregnancy and gave birth at Michael's house, a few villages over. The next day, we'd return here and start our life. Outsmart the state. Cora worked so hard for you, Eleanor. She wanted you so deeply. But they stormed the house. Someone had reported a violation against family. Cora thrust you into my arms, only barely alive, and told me to run. I knew as soon as I left that they were dead," she says, voice low and wrung-out. "Even before I heard the shots."

She looks at me. "I've wished every day to trade places with her. Rather that than live with the punishment of knowing it was my fault she died. My fault you had to grow up without a real mother."

"Your fault?" I ask. "What could you have done?"

Her mouth opens. "Something," she says. "Anything."

All these years, I've polished this pain like a coin. Contemplated it from all angles, understanding just how she hurt me. How, in all that time, have I never looked at the other side? Now I observe the lines cutting across the planes of my mother's face. The pain hidden behind her eyes.

"I know I hurt you, Eleanor. I didn't love you in the right ways," she says. "But, I—I was under water. Every day, it was there in the room with us—the tragedy of you growing up without Cora. I don't know how to make you understand."

"I do understand," I say. And it's true. Impossible not to understand someone who carries around their own brand of poison, sips it throughout the day as though from a flask. I consider, for the first time, if she did the best she could.

I lift the violin from its case again. For the first time in years, I put bow to string. Unplayed so long, it takes some fidgeting with the pegs to make a solid sound. I play the song I made up, the Longing Song, filled with everything I wanted as a child, dreams placed inside it like prayers into the Wanting Hat. In the years I was gone, without my knowing, the song emptied. The notes ring out hollowly, echoing like a vacant trunk.

But, as I play, the song fills up again, with new wishes. New dreams. I was never able to paint a self-portrait in the Meadows, but I do now, with this music, seeing myself as I really am. I find myself wanting something. I find myself thinking I could find it.

"Whenever you played, my gut would twist, for how much you looked like her," my mother says. "And Michael." Tears slide across her face. Tonight, she has spoken more than I've ever heard. Out from under all that silence, I wonder what she will do now.

I consider her. My mother. "I look like you too," I tell her.

"You look like yourself."

EPILOGUE

I hear them again. The ones I've been waiting for.

Over the rolling hills, the sound of a string, plucked by a calloused fingertip. Vibrating across houses, winding down streets, into alleys. Past the docks and ice buckets packed with fish, recently alive. The high note of a song threads through the open window near a village woman straining cheese through a cloth, past cattlemen and their lowing cows. The rhythm begins to assemble into music. It starts like a whisper.

It grows.

I don't hesitate. I follow the sound. I'd follow it anywhere, even if it meant crossing chicken yards of strangers, and through craggy tide pools, and across the ocean itself.

I find them where they idle outside a field of high grasses, the ocean gasping behind, shoving its spray into the air. There they are, with their skin burnished by the sun, limbs crisscrossed by scars and blooming bruises and tattoos and body hair and loops of braided string.

I see another join me. Watch her crest the hill, the one I have never stopped thinking about. *June*. Put her hand in mine. Pull her under my umbrella. I find in her eyes the knowledge that whatever we've suffered, we are here now, alive.

With them, I start moving, and in this way I will never be caught. In this way, I feel what it feels like to be Eleanor. The me that I thought I'd killed. The pain kicking me in the stomach all those years—it was her, fighting to get out, to live. I've got so many bruised spots, places that will be prodded the rest of my life. Sometimes, I only flinch. Sometimes, I double over in pain. Sometimes, I wish to grow cautious again. Or quiet. Or hold myself small.

But I remember that pain only wants me to stand with it. To see it. To remember the place it was born:

My home, on the bursting oceanside, in a room that smelled like rosemary.

In the Meadows, in clean white spaces, in a blooming paradise, in the body of a girl.

In the city, inside the acid-tasting walls of my own despair.

On the road, I grow calluses and play new songs and remember what it feels like to exist inside music. I hear of others who decide to give up hiding too. I see them again. I hear their stories:

An artist I once knew who has been working on a project in secret. In the night, she hangs a series of paintings above the city. At first glance, it looks like the same old poster—man, woman, children—except it's people like her. Two women. Two men. With skin and cheeks and noses and lips like hers.

The workers of an office, who stand from their desks one day and walk out in rebellion, led by a girl singing a song that flows in the blood her ancestors gave her.

A boy who has grown up being called *girl*, a word that never felt right, who decides that he wants to be called something else, and it's time to start asking for it.

And another, who is neither boy nor girl, who is all and none, who lives now inside the name Jo, who helps others know that they can too. We meet most holidays, with as many from the Meadows as we can scrape together, Sheila and Penelope and eventually Marina, filling The Black

Cat with pineapple cake and spiraled ham and deviled eggs. Each year, they insist that I make the hollandaise. The place inside of me that longed for dinners and laughter and family sees—they were here all along.

At night, we step outside and gaze into the sky, at the glinting white sparks of satellites circling. Nobody speaks it, but we're all thinking of her, the one we lost. I look up at the sky and smile.

Eventually, the day will come when I'll see Rose again. Rose, who, when she's ready, will place a key in a lock. Will find the bridge, and the door, and there, with her fight and fire, will help the world to right itself. When we meet, it will be with an old familiarity. With a comfort in knowing we're two planets with gravity all our own.

And one day, through a doorway, a small woman will walk, her neat black hair shot through with gray. When they embrace, they'll stay that way for a long time. "Te amo," the mother will say, in the language that will never be taken from them again.

But before all of this, there is Sheila, who after learning to hide herself, decides to unhide. With her husband's screen and access codes, she sneaks with the Circle into his office at night. In the darkness, half-illuminated by the glow of screens, she stands before a bank of monitors with live feeds of dozens of facilities: round white buildings, the periwinkle blushing of twilight. Each monitor labeled. *The Glades. The Redwoods. The Meadows.* One by one, she shuts them down. *If someone started it, someone can end it.*

And far away, young people, alongside their matrons and patrons who trapped them inside, find themselves standing suddenly in a desert at night, their facilities switched off like screens. This dry, empty place is dotted with doorways, far from the nation's view. The air feels sudden and brisk, and the stars slowly wink at them from above.

It's then that Sheila touches the metal coin at the back of her head, lightly at first, grazing it with her fingertips, thinking *I get to choose.* When she pulls it free, skeins of gold fall abandoned to the ground. A forgotten knowledge, a seed thought dead, begins to bloom. *There is nothing—there has never been anything—wrong with me.*

And still others, who take back their names, their language, their music. They dig up the old words, the vocabulary of who we are, write it on signs, paint the air with their voices, move together in the streets, uncountable footsteps shaking the world. The words that tell us we are many. The words that make them afraid. The words that make us free.

AUTHOR'S NOTE

Dear Reader,

The characters in *The Meadows* have traveled alongside me for years, whispering of their struggles and dreams, their fears and longings. It's impossible for a novel to capture everyone's experience of life, especially one as complex and varied as the queer experience, but I hope I have done justice to Eleanor, Sheila, Rose, June, Jo, Betty, and every other character's story.

The seed for *The Meadows* took root after I learned about the reality of conversion therapy in the United States. Like many, I had believed the practice to be eradicated—the stuff of history. But conversion therapy still happens—and more often than many people realize. Yes, an increasing number of state laws have passed in recent years banning licensed mental health professionals from performing conversion therapy on minors, but enforcing these bans is difficult. And the practice remains rampant—and legal—in other settings, notably within religious organizations.

I don't know if books can change the world, but I know they can reflect the world back on itself. The events of *The Meadows*, though augmented and fictionalized, represent reality for countless LGBTQ+ people.

In many communities, even in states where the laws have changed,

LGBTQ+ youth are hardly more protected than before. Practitioners of conversion therapy have gotten sneakier, more covert. They're camouflaged within so-called "life coaching" facilities, in underground counseling centers that hide behind terms like "reparative therapy" and "spiritual warfare," and inside the offices of bishops, pastors, and priests where children sit for weekly counseling sessions.

Conversion therapy has been widely denounced by the medical and scientific communities, including by the American Medical Association and the American Psychological Association. While many parents and family members who push conversion therapy believe they're acting from a place of love, the practice inflicts extreme psychological distress, increases the likelihood of suicide, and has been proven to be ineffective. In contrast, LGBTQ+ youth with access to safe, affirming community spaces, homes, and schools have lower rates of suicide, anxiety, and depression.

One of the most effective ways to affirm queer youth is to respect their preferred names and pronouns. I was very aware of this while writing, particularly regarding the character Jo, who we know both before and after they've come into their true gender identity. While I knew how Jo would later identify, they would only claim that identity toward the end of the book. At every point in the story, I attempted to describe Jo as they defined themself at the time.

When I started writing *The Meadows*, I wondered if its themes would be as relevant by the time the book would go to print. In the years since, American culture has embraced the queer experience like never before, with many more books, shows, and films by queer creators, presenting an array of queer experiences. Unfortunately, during the same period, the political climate in parts of the United States has grown only more hostile toward LGBTQ+ people, with a barrage of recent bills condemning trans athletes, drag artists, LGBTQ+ books in school libraries, trans youth receiving gender-affirming care, and the mere mention of the existence of queer people in schools. I'm angered and heartbroken daily by what's happening in my country, but I've learned enough about queer perseverance throughout history to know we're not going anywhere.

If you have lived within an intolerant family or community or experienced the psychological violence of conversion therapy, I hope you know that you are not alone. Your gender identity and sexuality should not and cannot be changed. If you are in crisis or looking for support, below this note are resources that can help. You are worthy of a beautiful life, and your presence in this world matters.

Despite adversity, prejudice, and mistreatment, queer people have always been resilient and joyful. Throughout history, we have found each other—in bars and nightclubs and community spaces, inside of whose walls we get to be exactly ourselves. The name of the speakeasy in *The Meadows*, The Black Cat, is borrowed from perhaps the first-ever gay bar in the United States. I felt confident that, even in the hostile society Eleanor lives in, she would find community with other queer people.

At the core of my mission with this book, I aimed to explore the aftermath of trauma through the lives of the kids at the Meadows, and how an identical traumatic event can play out differently in different people. But trauma is only ever the beginning of the story. It's impossible to tell a story about trauma without discussing what comes after—the healing, the growing, the pain, the panic, the undoing and remaking of yourself, the painful, complicated, beautiful *after*.

With the help of therapists, a loving community, medication, and many other practices and strategies, it is possible to heal. The first step is often acknowledging the truth and being willing to feel the pain that comes with it. This really happened. This is a scar on our country and our world, and it's a scar within everyone who has ever lived within a homophobic or transphobic system.

Healing from trauma is possible. As Eleanor discovers, it starts by seeing and by being seen.

I see you. You are good, just as you are.

—Stephanie

RESOURCES

National Suicide Hotline: 988

Trans Lifeline: (877) 565-8860

Crisis Text Line: 741741

The Trevor Project: trevorproject.com/resources

PFLAG for parents and families: pflag.org

ACKNOWLEDGMENTS

I'd like to start by thanking my editor, Jessica Dandino Garrison, whose brilliant ideas, unwavering support, and generous guidance shaped this book into what it is. I can't begin to express my gratitude for the influence you've had on this book and on me as a writer. And to my agent, Jennifer Laughran, a wonderful advocate for her authors and a true font of wisdom and support. I appreciate you more than I can say.

I've been beyond lucky to have the team at Dial and Penguin Young Readers on my side. Thank you to Jen Klonsky and Nancy Mercado for your support of writers and creatives. To Elaine Demasco and Kristin Boyle for the beautiful cover art and design and Jenny Kelly for the beautiful interiors. To Jenn Ridgway and Coleen Conway for your enthusiasm and advocacy. To Felicity Vallence and Shannon Spann for your awesome digital marketing and promotion. Special thanks to Squish Pruitt for your keen insights and helpful feedback, to Regina Castillo and Kenny Young for the thoughtful copyediting, and to Sharifa Love-Shnur for your wisdom and guidance.

To my writing group friends, Aileen Keown-Vaux, Leyna Krow, Alexis Smith, Anne Kilfoyle, and everyone who has joined us. The Spokane writing community is full of smart, supportive, brilliant creative minds and I'm grateful to be in your company. To the wonderful students and staff at the many schools I've worked as a school librarian: I've been so lucky to share my days with you.

Infinite gratitude to the librarians, booksellers, and bloggers who have read and championed my books. To all school librarians who do the vital and often unseen work of showing children that they are not alone. And to the many teachers and school librarians who shaped me. As educators, the seeds you plant often don't bloom until years later. I hope you know what a difference you made in my life.

Thank you to my entire family for your support and love, especially my mom, John and Kate, Matthew, Linda and Andrew Corbett, and the Harris/Jennings clan. And to Adair, Mere, and Fletcher, for being the brilliant, thoughtful, amazing people you are. May you never question how worthy and wonderful you are.

To Jerilynn, my best friend, my love, my National Treasure. You've been on this adventure with me from the beginning, holding my hand when the world felt dark. Thank you for being you.

Finally, to every queer kid. You have wonder inside of you, and I hope you show the world.

STEPHANIE OAKES is the author of *The Sacred Lies of Minnow Bly*, which was a Morris Award finalist and a Golden Kite Honor book, and *The Arsonist*, which won the Washington State Book Award and was an ALA/YALSA Best Fiction for Young Adults pick. Stephanie lives in Spokane, Washington with her wife and family.